WEIGHT EXPECTATIONS

CIPHER OFFICE BOOK #1

M.E. CARTER

WWW.SMARTYPANTSROMANCE.COM

COPYRIGHT

DEDICATION

*To the Ladies of the SmartyPants Romance Universe first launch:
Y'all… this has been a total trip! I have enjoyed every single moment
with all of you! Here's to new friendships and cementing established
ones. I couldn't put together a better group of people to go on this
adventure with! Let's do it again!*

CHAPTER ONE

RIAN

There it is. The death machine.

Otherwise known as a treadmill by people who think walking but never getting anywhere is fun. But for someone like me, who hasn't stepped on a piece of exercise equipment since… well, ever, it's known as Killer.

The Grim Reaper.

The Angel of Death.

I know it's already taunting me. Just like my doctor did when she said I needed to go on a diet or death was imminent.

No, really. She said that. I swear.

Alright fine. I'm lying. She didn't actually use the words "imminent death". It was more like, "Rian, you're thirty-seven years old, and you're morbidly obese. I'm not asking you to become a skinny minnie. I'm asking you to be proactive with your health."

Health, schmealth. It's a family trait. We're all big-boned, no matter how much rabbit food we eat.

Fine, those are more lies. My little sister likes to run marathons— outdoors. With a destination. And a finish line.— And while she's not skinny per se, she doesn't fall into the overweight category anymore. Now she's considered curvy.

Voluptuous.

Luscious.

Every time her fiancé says it during family dinner on Sundays, I want to puke. My mother, on the other hand, smiles and clutches her heart like it's the most romantic thing she's ever heard. My dad just ignores it all.

I would never tell my doctor this information, though. She doesn't need more evidence to use against me. My cholesterol level has done enough.

Which is why I'm here staring at the daisy pusher-upper.

Taking a deep breath, I build up the courage to try. Gingerly, I step onto the machine, clinging to the handrails for dear life. As if they would collapse under the weight of me if I fell while it was in motion. And yes, that's a very real fear. I have several of them right now.

1. The treadmill collapses under my weight before I even turn it on.
2. I trip and fall over the side, face-planting in front of a gym full of people.
3. I can't slow it down while gasping for air, thereby flying right off the end and landing on my amply padded ass, again, in front of a gym full of people.

All are very realistic fears considering these flimsy handrails couldn't withstand the weight of one of my thighs. Why are they even here? Moral support?

Standing up straight, I want to give myself a pat on the back for not falling off so far. Granted, I haven't really done anything yet, but still. Baby steps. Now to figure out what all the buttons mean...

My brain gets very close to overload as I try to figure out which "on" button actually means go. For some unknown reason, there are more than one. Maybe it's this one...

Pressing a pink button, the monitor in front of me comes to life, but it's not the television. I couldn't get so lucky. Nope. Now I have touch-screen options, too. Seriously? This is why people don't go to the gym.

You need to be a freaking tech genius just to get the damn equipment to work.

"Do you need help?" A voice next to me comes out of nowhere and I startle, clutching my hand to my heart. He smiles while I take a second to assess whether or not that was my first official heart attack or if I've just had too much exercise for the day.

I'm sure my doctor would say neither was the case, but she's not here, so I'm going for the dramatic.

"Sorry," I finally spit out. "It's my first time here, and I guess I'm a little jumpy."

And that's when I look at him. Like, *really* look at him. And oh. My. Why have I never come to the gym before? If this fine specimen is any indication, I have been missing out. No one says I have to come here and participate. I saw plenty of people sitting at the smoothie bar when I walked in. You can't convince me they're all here for their health.

Well, I mean, it is a smoothie bar so they're at least partially here for that reason.

But still! With his dirty blond hair cropped close to his head and the perfect amount of scruff, I could stare at him all day. And that's before I notice his biceps. Holy smokes, has he got guns. His shirt clings to him in such a way that I know there are some rock-hard abs under there. And those thighs. Don't get me started on those thighs that are peeking out from under his athletic shorts as he props his leg up on the machine or I may just combust right here on this death machine.

Then I notice the staff t-shirt.

Ah. Now his inquiry makes more sense.

"No problem. I'm Abel."

"Hi, Abel. I'm Rian."

His eyes widen in surprise. "Ryan, huh? That's an unusual name for a woman."

I wave my hand around reciting the same explanation I have for the last three plus decades. "No, not Ryan with a 'y'. Rian with an "i". My dad's name is Brian and my mom's name is Riann, and they decided to combine the two to come up with Rian."

And I'm rambling. Because why wouldn't I when a hot guy is talking to me? To his credit, Abel doesn't run away screaming. His smile actually widens. Color me surprised.

"That's a really cool story. When my wife and I were having our daughter, we couldn't decide on her name. I'm Abel. She's May. So our first is Mabel."

Of course, he's happily married with kids.

"That's cute."

"Thanks. We like it. So." He claps his hands together, startling me again. "Enough procrastination. You're here for a reason. Are you determined to use the treadmill, or are you interested in something a little more intense?"

I narrow my eyes at him, knowing this sales game well. I'm a master at it myself. "Do you get kick-backs from how many people you train, Abel?"

Now it's his turn to look startled. "What?"

"How much to take the class you're pimping?"

His eyebrows shoot up, and I know he's surprised by my candor. "I —I don't know. I don't have the prices on me."

"So, the only reason you came over here was to sell me something?"

His face pales and I start to feel bad. He doesn't know me from Adam. He doesn't know I don't really have a bitch mode. I just like messing with people sometimes. Maybe I've taken it too far.

Patting his arm, I decide the charade isn't worth it today. Not with this guy. If he's this visibly concerned, chances are he's genuinely nice. "I'm just kidding with you, Abel. I work in sales, too."

"Wait." He takes a step back and crosses his arms. "Was that a procrastination tactic?"

I cringe. "Did it work?" I ask sheepishly.

He nods, a look of appreciation on his face. "Almost. If you would have kept it up for just a few seconds longer, I probably would've cut my losses and walked away. Now you really need to sign up for a class. You owe me."

My jaw drops. I didn't give him enough credit. He's as much of a smart ass as I am. I bet he contributes more to the commission pool than anyone else in this place, just by flashing that fake embarrassed look.

"I can't believe you just turned that around on me," I say to myself, shaking my head in disbelief.

"Work here long enough, and you learn how to keep up with the shady ones." He leans over and presses a yellow button on my machine. Sure enough, it comes to life.

"How did you do that?" I say louder than I intend. Looking around, it doesn't appear that anyone noticed, but I still make a concerted effort to lower my volume. No need to draw unnecessary attention to myself in case this venture goes terribly wrong. "Seriously. Teach me all the things."

Abel laughs a deep rumble from deep in his chest. Damn. Add that sound to the list of reasons his wife is a lucky woman.

And yes, I'm objectifying here, which I know is wrong. But when you are thirty-seven, have never been married, have no prospects, and haven't had any for years, it's tough to hold the boundary on appropriate thoughts.

Not that I'm worried about being an old maid or anything.

I think.

Maybe.

I don't know. It seems to change depending on my mood. Some days I'm happy as a clam being single and ready to mingle. Others, I could emotionally eat my way through a Dairy Queen.

Huh. Maybe I fall on the anxious side of love more than I realized. That's what landed me here, right?

Unexpectedly, the ground beneath me begins to move.

Abel must notice the fear on my face because he immediately uses that smooth, deep voice to calm me. "Relax. We're starting slow. Just look straight ahead and walk."

Okay. I can do that. Just walk. I'll be fine as long as we don't go any faster.

"Why are we going faster?" I screech, as Abel presses more buttons. "And why is it going up?"

Abel laughs again, only this time it's not a deep timbre. This time it's an annoying ruckus, ruining my carefully laid plans to start slow.

"Relax, Rian. I bumped it up to Level One. In truth, that's closer to the same level as walking directly on the ground."

Oh.

"Oh." Well, now I feel stupid and dramatic.

"We're going to put you on an interval. We'll go in five-minute cycles. Three minutes at your slowest pace, one minute at your medium pace, and one minute at your fast pace. Repeat the cycle for thirty minutes."

I look at Abel like he's lost his damn mind.

Sucking in breath, I propose a compromise. "I was thinking of starting more with a stroll."

"A stroll?" Clearly amused, Abel doesn't bother stopping the machine until we have a solid plan. Nope. He keeps pressing buttons that do God-knows-what and smiles. He. Smiles. A smile I no longer consider attractive, but smarmy and conniving. His poor, poor wife.

"Fine. I'll settle for a meander." Pointing my finger at him for dramatic effect, I add, "But that's my final offer."

He shakes his head and finally stops pressing buttons. *Finally.* And yet... I'm still moving. This isn't good.

"Nope. Thirty minutes of intervals and then I'll come back here to work on some stretches with you."

My eyes widen, both in disbelief and possible terror at what "stretching" might entail. I ate a bean burrito for lunch. Does he not understand the kind of danger "stretching" might put everyone in?

"I don't think I like this plan. And I'm not paying for this training session, Abel, since it's unauthorized." I try to cross my arms like an obstinate child but end up grabbing the handrails when I lose my balance. Clearly, I can't walk and be defiant at the same time. "Come to think of it, when you walk away, I'll just leave."

"No, you won't. You don't know how to turn off the machine."

"Dammit," I grumble and turn my head away dramatically. He's right. I am totally and completely at his mercy until he comes back to get me, or the power goes out. I'm all for a man taking control and getting me sweaty, but this is not how I imagined it would go. "Fine. I give up. I will do these intervals for thirty minutes. But if the video of me falling and my shirt being ripped off goes viral, I'm telling the ladies of *The View* and all their watchers that you are my trainer. I will ruin you!"

He chuckles again and it makes me want to take his wife to a support group for wives of hot, chuckling, unable to be manipulated husbands. The poor woman.

"Are you always this dramatic?"

"Always," I say without hesitation.

"Good. I like it. See you in thirty."

"It's twenty-eight minutes now!" I call after him as he walks away. "Don't you be a second late!"

He waves at me over my shoulder, never looking back.

I will never admit it to Abel, but the stretches weren't as bad as I thought they would be. There was one time I had to clench a little, but for the most part, my muscles feel really relaxed now.

Plus, I enjoyed the conversation with Abel. He gets my humor and throws it right back at me. He even convinced me to try out his strength training class.

Yeah, he's got jokes of his own all right, manipulating me like that.

Besides figuring out how to get the electronics to work, the biggest obstacle was showering. Whoever designed these box shower stalls in this place didn't take into account that people come to the gym to get skinny—they don't start out that way. So, there I was, my "morbidly obese" self, trying to figure out how to shave my legs without my rear sticking out of the curtain into the hall while getting sprayed in the face with the water.

Pretty sure I had to break down and position myself in one of Abel's stretches for it to work. And I'm still not sure I didn't moon a passerby.

But no matter. Once I finally contorted myself around and got my clothes on, I was pretty proud for acting like a real gym rat. Of course, this was after dropping my pants inside a puddle in the stall. Thank goodness they provide blow dryers. Otherwise it would have looked like I had an accident before I even left the building.

All that extra effort to clean up made me thirsty, so I've decided to reward myself with a drink.

Sidling up to the smoothie bar, I decide to try my hand at an organic, GMO-free treat. Because nothing says heart health like drinking plants. Or so I've heard. Besides, I don't see vodka on the menu. Bummer.

Wiping her hands on a towel, the clearly frazzled and overworked bartender, or should I call her a smoothie-tender approaches.

"What can I get you?"

I purse my lips and give her a deer-in-the-headlights look. "Uhhhh, I have no idea."

She leans against the counter. Suddenly, she doesn't look over-whelmed. She looks... interested. "Ah. Newbie, huh?"

"Is it that obvious?"

"Considering I know just about everyone who walks through those doors," she gestures to the front of the room, "and I've never seen you before, it's an educated guess." She pops back up off the counter like she didn't just get comfortable. "I'm Tabitha, by the way. And here is a list of some of our best sellers. Most of these are creations I came up with on my own."

Taking the list from her hands, I peruse the different items. I'm shocked to admit, some of them look pretty good. My mouth starts watering at the thought of having a Dreamcicle smoothie. Then, I see one that catches my eye.

"Ooooooh. What is this chocolate bar shake?" I'm sure my face has lit up from the prospect of gooey caramel and rich milk chocolate in my mouth. I might like this gym after all.

"That is one of our best sellers. Made with chocolate protein, almond butter, a little almond milk, banana—"

Very quickly, Tabitha recognizes the glaze of disappointment that is replacing the stars in my eyes, especially when she gets to something called vanilla greens, which makes no sense whatsoever. "I lost you, didn't I?"

I nod blankly.

"Well, then, you'll just have to trust me. It's good."

"Can you add a Snickers bar to it?"

She laughs, and I can't help but wonder if she's a former smoker. Something about the rumble in her chest reminds me of my late grandma who smoked two packs a day for twenty years.

I remember when Nanny quit. We avoided her house for weeks until she finally didn't want to throw her flip-flops at everyone for eyeing her wrong. Nanny never did pick up a cigarette again. But she never lost that smoker's voice either. Just like Tabitha.

I shrug at her and then give her the go-ahead because, what the hell? I've already tried walking on the death trap and played contortionist in the shower. Why not add drinking pureed rabbit food to the list?

Tabitha raps her knuckles on the counter once and turns away from me to a different counter cluttered with blenders, containers of fruit, and jars of strange concoctions that are no doubt intended to increase my digestive health. The way she mixed things at such a rapid pace, like it comes second nature and she doesn't really need to think about it, is impressive. Almost like watching Tom Cruise flip bottles around in *Cocktail*. Except without the flying alcohol. Or the happy side effects to making me forget my near-death experience earlier.

Of course, I catch Abel's eye at the same moment I'm remembering how glorious I looked covered in sweat. He smiles at me and gives me a thumbs-up. I really, really need to send his wife my condolences for marrying that guy.

He's going to be so fun to verbally spar with when I'm here. Especially if I don't have to physically spar with him. I shudder at the thought of dancing around with boxing gloves on.

Mere seconds later, Tabitha hands me a clear plastic cup filled with brown liquid and a straw.

I flick my gaze up to my new friend, and she raises her eyebrows. "Go ahead. Let's see what you think."

Slowly, I reach for the straw and pull the paper off. Inserting it in my drink, never taking my eyes off hers, I bring it to my lips and take a quick pull. I make note of the flavors as they cross my tongue:

Chocolate

There's that almond butter she mentioned. Not bad.

Ew. EW! That must be the greens she mentioned.

Wait... there's more chocolate.

Oh, some banana! That's a nice surprise.

"Well?" she finally asks, like my opinion is that important to her.

I nod a few times in appreciation as I take another drink. "Not bad. Surprisingly, it's pretty good."

She raises her fists in victory, which seems a little over the top for a successful smoothie, but who am I to judge? I was just mentally patting myself on the back for showering without flashing the entire locker room.

"I have yet to have someone tell me they hate it. And I have a wager going with the boss man. If fifty out of fifty customers tell me they like it, I win a hundred bucks."

"How does he know you're telling the truth?" I ask around my straw. I might get another one of these things if I finish this one too quickly.

She shrugs. "He doesn't. We use the honor system."

Tabitha turns to help another customer and her answer rolls around in my head. *But how does the boss know she's honorable? What if she's lying through her teeth? Will she still take the money? And how long does it take to convince fifty customers to try a chocolate smoothie?*

Still contemplating the logistics of the bet, I glance up and my whole body freezes when I come face-to-face with the most beautiful man I've ever seen in my life.

"Hey, Carlos," Tabitha says nonchalantly to the god in front of me.

Carlos. I think to myself. *Carrrrrrlos.* Hmm. Even in my head, I can't roll my r's.

Seriously, though. That is one good looking man. I'm almost positive a ray of light from heaven is shining on *Carlos's* head and the heavenly hosts are singing.

Probably no older than forty, his chiseled jaw could have been carved out of marble. The taut muscles of his upper body move and flex as he orders his drink. Crystal blue eyes twinkle when the most gorgeous smile crosses his face. And then... and then he runs his long fingers through thick dark hair.

His eyes flick over to mine and I lick my lips in anticipation of what's to come. The feeling is short lived because it turns out, he wasn't looking at me but through me, obviously not even registering that he was just staring my direction as he turns away.

Yeah, those heavenly hosts come to a screeching stop in my head. I roll my eyes at myself for even thinking a guy like him would ever look at a girl like me. I've got almost four decades under my belt, so I know how this works. Pretty guys stick with pretty girls. It's always been that way and it always will be that way.

And as if I couldn't be even more ready to ditch this joint and cut my losses, suddenly Abel sidles up next to me, lacing his fingers together and resting them on the counter.

"I see you're having a healthy dinner. Your doctor would be proud."

Licking my lips of the chocolate mustache I'm sure I'm sporting, I retort, "If I was four inches taller, my doctor would leave me in my carb-induced peace."

"Doubtful. Skinny-fat is a real thing. You'd be surprised."

I raise a single eyebrow at him, mostly because I have no idea what he's talking about, but I'll be damned if he's going to win this round. I'm already dehydrated from all the sweating he made me do. It's making me grouchy.

Taking in my reaction, he chuckles softly. "Okay, okay. I'll lay off. But I really do think you'd like the strength training class I teach tomorrow night. I have a group of really fun ladies in there you'd get along with. We work hard, but we have a good time doing it. And just so you know, this isn't just about getting a sale. The first class is complimentary, simply so you can check it out and meet some people."

Narrowing my eyes, I make a show of taking the last long slurp of my smoothie before answering him. "And if I don't like it, you won't pressure me to try again?"

He hangs his head in defeat, or maybe it's to regroup. I need to keep my guard up with this guy. If I'm not careful, he'll have me back down to a size eight, and who wants to exercise that hard?

"I can't say I won't pressure you at all. But if you don't like it, we'll stick to the treadmill for a while. Deal?"

He puts out his hand to shake mine. I hesitate for just a moment but realize I don't have much to lose. Except maybe my pride. And my ability to walk up and down stairs after leg day. But this chocolate bar smoothie might be worth it.

Finally, I reciprocate and give him a firm handshake, so he knows I'm no pansy. "Deal."

"Great." Patting out a short rhythm on the counter, he stands to leave. "Six o'clock sharp. Don't be late and bring a water bottle."

"You really should provide one for me since you suckered me into it," I call after him.

He doesn't respond, mission clearly accomplished, but Tabitha does. "Are you doing Abel's strength training class tomorrow night?" My guard immediately goes up.

"Yeeees?" I squeak out. "Why?"

Tabitha throws her head back and laughs. "Oh, you poor, poor dear. I'll have some extra ice packs on hand. I've only done it once, and I thought I'd lost my ability to use my arms permanently."

I cringe. "Oh, god. That sounds horrible. What have I done?"

"They're vultures around here," she continues which does not make me feel better at all. "And once you get sucked in, you're stuck for life."

I gasp and throw my hands over my mouth. "Ohmygod. I've stumbled into the *Hotel California*."

"Worse. Welcome to Weight Expectations, Where Great Things Happen." Tabitha gestures toward the big sign hanging behind her. Then she leans forward on the counter and whispers conspiratorially. "Also known as workout hell."

CHAPTER TWO

CARLOS

"Ten," I announce to myself through clenched teeth and continue blowing the air out through my lips. Deep breath in as I lower the thirty-five-pound weight, then begin the process of bending my arm and bringing it back up again. "Eleven." More blowing air out. Just four more to go before I can rest for sixty seconds.

The sweat is more than just beading on my brow at this point. Everyone has an area of their body that is weaker than the others. Mine just happens to be my arms. That also happens to be why I do arm day at least twice a week. It's been hard work building up these guns over the last few years.

Just as I get to fifteen, a brand-new gym rat walks by. The smoldering look she gives me in the mirror proves that all the sacrifice I've made to turn my body into a lean machine has been worth it.

I didn't always look this way. I was your average guy with an average body when I met Quinn Sullivan and started working for him. Quickly, I realized "average" was not the norm at Cipher Systems. If I wanted to keep up professionally and personally, I needed to be better than normal. I was already a head above the rest with my intellect. I just needed the body to match.

Not gonna lie… turning heads on the regular now isn't a hardship.

Carefully placing my weight on the floor and picking up my water bottle, I keep my eyes on the woman as she struts over to the adjacent room and grabs the suspension bands that are hanging from the ceiling. I haven't seen her before and I'm here almost every day. But it's clear she's no stranger to the gym. She's wearing spandex shorts that cup her tight rear and a fancy sports bra over her ample breasts, her defined abs on display for everyone to see. No doubt she's trying to intimidate the other hardcore gym rats. I've seen those power plays happen more than once over the years. Usually it's over the attention of the men in the room.

Or in particular—me.

I make no apologies for "befriending" some of the women here. It's only natural for attractions to occur when you're wearing next to nothing and showing off your flexibility. More than once I've thanked the gods of Yoga for bringing that exercise back into fashion.

Cocking my head, I watch as the woman places her feet in the bands and stretches herself out on the floor in a plank position, body hovering, her long blond ponytail hanging down around her cheek. Slowly, she moves her legs this way and that, stretching and contorting in ways that make sure every muscle in her body is flexed simultaneously. She glances up once, just once, to make sure I'm watching.

This is the dance I do often at my home away from home. The quick glances. The flirty smirks. The way body language becomes an invitation for something more. The moves are always the same. Only the players change.

This is the way I like it. There are no expectations, no deep emotions. Just surface level, short-term hookups that include mutual appreciation for the physical part of life and all that it entails. And I'm good at it.

Some might say that's an exaggeration or that I'm overcompensating for my insecurities. But I'm much more of a realist than that. I know I have flaws. Like having to do twice as many arm days. Sex, however, is something I just have a natural ability at. Giving women pleasure, and I always give them pleasure, is a gift I'm happy to give.

Glancing down at my smart watch, I have thirteen more seconds to rest my arms and stretch my imagination. I watch as the woman leans forward so her shoulders are holding the brunt of her weight. Slowly, teasing me, she begins to spread her legs, wider and wider giving me a glimpse of—

"Hey, man!"

I try not to startle, or snarl, at my gym buddy, despite his impeccable timing.

Shooting him a half-hearted glare, I lean down to pick up my weights. These biceps won't grow themselves. See? Humble.

"You love sneaking up on me, don't you?"

Slow breath out, lift, deep breath in.

"I didn't sneak up on you. Never do," Nick argues as he peruses the weight rack, looking for the right set. There are multiple pairs in the weight he needs, but for whatever reason, he prefers the one set that has a random orange smudge on it. "You just lose awareness of your surroundings whenever a pair of short shorts and nice *rack* walk by." He forcefully grabs the weights, making the entire weight rack shake. I'm sure it's his way of trying to be ironic. It doesn't work, but I give him credit for trying.

"Do you blame me?" I grunt, continuing my motion. Nick may be fun to hang out with, but he's not the best workout buddy I've ever had.

One would think with his being an internist, he'd be more organized and meticulous. He's not. At least not in this environment. Sure, he lifts hard and he's a good spotter, but he also never shows up on time and doesn't stay focused on his training. That's probably why he always finds me. I have a very specific workout regimen to adhere to:

Protein shake and various vitamins and probiotics thirty minutes before my workout.

One hour of weight training.

Thirty minutes of cardio.

Thirty minutes of intense stretching.

Shower, shit, and shave.

Protein and vegetables thirty minutes post workout.

Six days a week, every week, regardless of vacation, holidays, or weather.

If Nick wants to join me for it, that's fine with me. He keeps me company and has proven to be a decent wingman on the few times we've gone out. I've never been able to figure out why he doesn't take the lead when it comes to the ladies, but it doesn't hurt my feelings.

My supposed workout partner watches the hottie in the mirror for a few seconds before responding with a low-tone whistle. "Nope. No judgement from me. Just an observation." His head cocks to the side and I find myself focusing my gaze back on her to see what has him so interested. She's slowly maneuvering herself into a handstand position, legs still spread. "No judgement from me at all," he says quietly, eyes never moving off the scene behind us.

Finishing my set, I drop the weights and grab my towel to mop my face. "Are you planning to work out today or just stare at the eye candy?"

"Why can't I do both?" he grunts, finally getting up to speed, although his form leaves something to be desired.

"Exactly my point." One more set down. One more to go. "Why are you so late today, anyway?"

"Fifteen," he breathes and drops the weights. No way in hell was that fifteen reps on each side, but with definition like his, it doesn't really matter. Turns out yanking on people's appendages all day long gives its own kind of workout. "I had a last-minute patient. Emergency tibia fracture. From the way his leg was bruised I needed to make sure his blood disorder wasn't going to cause extra problems."

Just hearing about it gives me the willies. I don't necessarily have a weak stomach, just some very vivid memories of a friend snapping his arm in half in high school. No matter how many times I've tried to scrub the images from my brain, they're more than happy to torture me at times like these. "Please tell me it was a lesser injury than you thought."

"Oh, yeah." He waves me off like bone sticking through skin is no big deal. I guess in his world it's an everyday occurrence.. Yet another reason why I prefer managing the administrative side of the office at my job. Shredding my muscles with weights is about as much injury as I like. "Just a regular break. No surgery necessary and everything clotted like it was supposed to. How many more sets you got?"

"Just one. But then I'm heading into the cycle class that starts in five. You coming with me?"

He looks at me like I've lost my mind. "Hell no. I'm not trying to fit my ass on that tiny little bike."

Rolling my eyes, I grab my weights for the last time today. "You're missing out. The heavier the resistance, the better it is for your quads."

"Don't give me that bullshit. You only go because that new instructor wears tops that fall forward so you can see straight down into her bra."

A short laugh pops out of my mouth. He's not wrong. "It's not a bad way to spend an hour, that's for sure," I say with a groan, trying to talk, count, and breathe correctly at the same time. "But really, the cardio is killer."

"Eh. I'll pass. I think I'm going to concentrate on my stretching today."

Furrowing my brow, I watch in the mirror as he re-racks his weights. "Since when do you work on your flexibility?"

"Since you refuse to give yourself any time off from working out, which means I have a shot to impress the new hottie before you do." He whacks me with his towel and calls out, "Later," as he struts away.

Son of a bitch. I should have known he was going to swoop in when he had the chance. I watch as he approaches the woman who smiles when he greets her. Nick is nowhere near hard on the eyes, a fact she seems to appreciate. It takes just a few seconds before he's shaking her hand and their body language changes.

A lesser man would be annoyed after this turn of events, but I'm not a lesser man. Nick may be a doctor, but nothing says success like a focused mind and trim body. There will be other women. And they know where to find me.

CHAPTER THREE

RIAN

I glare at my single-serving Tupperware container, silently saying every prayer, chant, and children's poem I can think of that might possibly turn this salad into a large cheese pizza with mushrooms, black olives, and hamburger meat. Surely there was some magic to Jack Sprat and his wife, right?

Slowly pulling back the top, I peek inside. "Drat." I chuckle to myself because I'm a poet and didn't know it. Still, there's no magic inside this container. It's just romaine lettuce, cherry tomatoes, cucumbers, and some sort of oil and vinegar dressing I found on Pinterest that sounded decent. But my rhyming skills are on point today which has to count for something.

It's day two of following my doctor's instructions and the food already sucks.

To make matters worse, the overwhelming scent of Axe body spray floods my sinuses before I even hear the man of my nightmares approach.

Don't get me wrong—I like the smell of Axe when used in small doses. But Nolan Schmidt doesn't use it in small doses. I'm almost positive he buys it by the keg and bathes in it. Which might not be so bad if he didn't irritate me daily with his passive-aggressive comments.

I've never figured out if he knows he's doing it or if he genuinely thinks he's being helpful.

Leaning over me to grab a disposable cup off the shelf, he makes sure to see what I'm looking at. "Rabbit food for lunch today, Rian?"

I close my eyes and take a quick deep breath, trying not to choke, merely so I don't turn around and stab him with my spork. It's the only one I have with me and I'd hate to throw it away due to blood contamination. After a moment, I feel centered enough to paste a fake smile on my face and say, "Yep. It's never too late to get healthy. Not even at my age. Am I right?" Not the funniest self-deprecating joke I've ever come up with, but maybe it'll throw him off my scent. If he even smells anything besides himself. Come to think of it…

I discreetly bring the bowl to my nose and take a quick whiff. Nothing. Even the smell of my salad dressing is masked by his massive quantities of cologne. I just hope it still tastes like a vinaigrette and not "Musk of Man" by the time I eat it. You never know how much those scent molecules are going to infiltrate my taste buds. Kind of like when someone farts at the dinner table and you just know you're eating someone's poop particles. Or something very scientific theory like that.

This is why I work in sales at a cable company and not in a lab somewhere. Pretty sure coming up with my own theories on how science works would be frowned upon.

"I applaud your desire to get healthy." And so it begins. I know by the condescending tone in his voice, I'm about to be in for a real treat also known as a patronizing rant. Actually, that's sarcasm. I'm not looking forward to whatever he's about to say at all. "But there's more to losing weight than eating salad."

"I said I'm getting healthy. Who says I'm trying to lose weight?"

We all know I am. How else can I justify being morbidly obese and eating vegetables? Because I like the taste? Pffft. Even I won't pretend to enjoy the healthiness that's about to invade my body. But if I can put Nolan on the spot and make him as uncomfortable as he's trying to make me, it's at least worth presenting the question.

Unfortunately, by the way he looks me up and down, it didn't work.

"Rian, your health is at risk." I narrow my eyes at him, now just plainly pissed off at his wild assumptions and nerve. Sure, his presumptions are correct, but that doesn't mean he has a right to call me out on it. "But you've got to understand that just eating a salad now and again isn't going to help. It takes years of correctly balanced meals and exercise to get your body on track after so many years of damage."

His words don't just stun me, his gall does as well. Yes, I'm over-weight. I see it every day when I look in the mirror. It's a fact of life. But it's no different than me having brown hair or him having a receding hairline, but you don't see me handing him a pamphlet for that fancy bottle that sprays hair on your head, although I need to make a mental note to do just that. My body is what it is and having extra pounds doesn't mean I'm any less important than Jill in accounting, who has probably never had to diet in her life, and it certainly doesn't give him or anyone else the right to talk about it.

Just as I open my mouth to speak, a woman's voice pipes up from across the room.

"Hey, Nolan, are you going to the Connecting with your Customers conference next week?"

Francesca. My co-worker. She sits in the cubicle behind mine and is probably the chattiest person I know. With her petite features and even more petite frame, she complains about getting carded on a regular basis. I'm sure when she's my age she'll feel differently on that topic. Don't get me wrong, everyone wants to be taken seriously. But I'm pushing forty and I have yet for that to happen. I wouldn't mind a few teeny-bopper jokes if the trade-off was porcelain skin like hers.

Turning his attention away from me, Nolan smiles wide at Francesca. Now that he has an audience, he's turning on the charm. I might just go blind from this amount of wattage.

"I am, and I'm looking forward to it. Are you going?"

Francesca makes a face like she smells something bad, although I doubt it's from the cologne. "Heck, no. Why would anyone subject themselves to that?"

Nolan sputters like he's shocked she would say such a thing. Frankly, I'm a little confused myself. Just last week she was disappointed that it had filled up before she could sign up. "It's always good to improve your skills. You can never be too good at the job, Fran."

"Francesca," she corrects and licks the ketchup from her giant-sized cheeseburger off her thumb. What I wouldn't give to be sharing that burger with her... "I just don't see what the point is. It takes years of conferences and webinars to combat bad habits we all settle into. Especially as technology and policies change. If change can't come immediately, why bother even trying?"

Nolan continues looking confused, but I'm trying not to laugh. I picked up on that sugary-sweet voice the second she started talking and he has no idea she just threw his words back in his face. I suppose that's one of the benefits of being self-absorbed. You never know when the joke is really on you.

"I heartily disagree with you, Fran."

"Francesca."

"Self-improvement is vital to maintaining a healthy workplace. Every little bit helps."

Francesca says nothing, but her eyebrows raise just slightly like she is waiting, probably for his lightbulb moment to come. I, myself, am waiting with bated breath in anticipation, abnormally excited by this exchange. But I also work in a cubicle. This is literally the most drama I'll ever see outside of a *Real Housewives* marathon.

When it becomes clear the analogy is completely lost in translation, Francesca gives a quick nod and, "I suppose you're right," before going back to her juicy burger that smells so good.

Nolan goes back to babbling about clean eating while I leave him to fill his coffee cup. Fortunately, the powers that be refuse to spring for the sixteen ounce size so it doesn't take him long to finish up and leave.

Lowering myself in the chair across from Francesca's, I give her an incredulous look.

Glancing back and forth for a few seconds, she finally caves. "What?"

"What was that?"

"What was what?"

Propping my elbows on the table, I quirk a single eyebrow her direction. She knows I'm not going to let this go. If there's one thing I'm good at, it's holding the line until I get the answer I want. It's how I ended up in the Top Twenty-Five Sales Employees last year. Not because I'm great at selling cable packages to the folks of the Greater Chicago area. I'm just stubborn.

Finally, she rolls her eyes and caves. "Fine. I hate that guy."

My jaw drops. "You don't hate anyone."

"Truth be told, I hate a lot of people. I just keep it to myself. But that guy," she points out the door, "that guy is the worst of the worst, and I was tired of hearing him talk."

I can't help when a laugh pops right out of my mouth. "This is a side of you I've never seen before."

She shrugs and takes a big bite, talking around it as she chews. "I don't believe in recruiting others to hate certain people along with you. I can silently stew in my own hatred. Well, unless I'm drinking. If we ever go to a bar, remember not to ask me about our co-workers."

Finally feeling as if the air has cleared enough for my food to be in the safe zone once again, I peel the lid off my salad and spear some lettuce with my fork. "You're making me a little nervous, Francesca. How do I know you don't hate me?"

"Because you're not an asshole."

"Well, that's comforting to know."

She drops her burger on her plate, grabbing a tiny packet of ketchup and peeling it open. Sitting next to her was a mistake. I've never wanted to burn a plate of vegetables before, but right now, they look so terrible next to her lunch, all I can think about it setting them on fire and putting us all out of our misery.

"I just hate when people are holier than thou, ya know? It makes me feel all ragey inside."

I try hard not to giggle at the image of this tiny woman raging. Would her punches hurt or feel like a kitten playing with a ball of yarn? My money is on the kitten.

"People assuming they can remark on other people's bodies is a huge pet peeve of mine, in case you didn't notice," she continues. "And it's about to get worse so I'm bracing myself, I guess."

My stomach takes this moment to let out a loud, embarrassing growl. I guess there will be no food burning today. Instead, I sigh and take my first bite of my first salad on my first official day of eating healthy. Yesterday didn't count. I didn't want to go to the gym and then overdo it on vegetables. That just sounded like a disaster waiting to happen. Someone should remind that trainer Abel that baby steps are a good thing before he gets me on that treadmill again.

"What do you mean it's going to get worse?"

Francesca lets out a giant sigh before dipping a fry in ketchup and popping it in her mouth. "Remember the company physicals we're required to take to keep our insurance premiums down?"

I nod in response as I chew, making a mental note to mix this salad dressing again. It makes the leaves palatable, even with the small Axe aftertaste to it. "How could I forget? I'm eating the results of mine right now."

"My blood work came back. My cholesterol is so high, HR is threatening to increase my rates because I'm a health risk. Can you believe that?"

I shake my head no, but really, I can believe it. I was threatened with the same thing until all my blood work came back normal. I thought they were going to lay me off, but apparently, they found a new victim in my bite sized co-worker. "Can they even do that? Legally?"

Francesca gives me an incredulous look. "It's the Sandekes. You think they care?"

"They will if someone blows the whistle."

"And who would do that? I don't know anyone that wants to sleep with the fishes."

She's got a point. The Sandeke family aren't known for taking criticism well. It's best to stay out of their way sometimes and just do as you're told.

"I understand that heart disease, diabetes, and strokes run in my family," she continues as if the legalities are of no consequence.

Although now I'm watching her more closely, half afraid she's going to drop dead in front of me because of her jacked-up genetics. "But I'm just at risk at this point. Not even *high* risk. But do they care? No. So unless I want my monthly rates to go up, I don't have a choice but to get my cholesterol down."

"That sucks."

"I know. I hate rabbit food."

"Seems like they'd be more afraid of you losing too much weight."

She pauses briefly, mouth open and French fry halfway to its final destination. I can't tell for sure, but I think she just gave me the evil eye. Slowly taking her bite, she chews briefly before clearing her throat. "That's what I'll hear from everyone for the next six to eight weeks before my next test comes in. *Oh, Francesca, you're so skinny. You need to eat something. Oh, Francesca, why are you trying to lose weight? Oh, Francesca, men don't like a woman who is just skin and bones.*" She rolls her eyes dramatically and I have the suspicion this isn't the first time her doctor has put her on some sort of regimen. "Yes, thank you, Mother. I know all these things." Mother? Ouch. "But men also don't like women who are *dead*. Well, I mean there was that one guy on the news, but I wouldn't even bone him if I was six feet under."

Her comment makes me laugh. She's not wrong. That guy's lazy eye combined with his disheveled appearance made him look super crazy. That and the fact that he was having sex with dead people.

"You're not the only one." I stab a piece of lettuce with my fork and then sneer at it. Like threatening it will make it turn into a French fry. "Ever since my sister got engaged, all I hear about is how if I would just lose a hundred pounds, I could find a date. Who says I even want to date? If putting in that much effort to attract someone is what it takes, I'm not sure I have it in me to try to keep them."

"Preach, sister. I'd rather be single."

Not that I don't want to date. I do. But it feels like it's necessary to fit into some sort of mold for a man to even look at me. And why not? It's like everyone is trained to believe skinny is best. I can't tell you how many commercials are on for weight loss supplements and programs during primetime TV watching. I tried counting one night during my favorite emergency room/fire department/detective shows. I lost count when I had to take a potty break. And none of those shows have a fat actress in a leading role. Sure, she makes a great sidekick, but there is never any love interest for her.

Even social media has filters to thin out your face before posting a selfie. I have yet to find one that makes your face fuller, unless it's distorting you in other ways as well.

Healthy or not, fat has a negative connotation to it. The more of it you have on your body, the more negative that association becomes, and the less people consider you for dating prospects. And when you carry it around for most of your life—well, eventually you absorb the negative comments as directly about you. Even when logically you know they're not.

Aaaaaand now I've just gone on an internal tirade about the social implications of being a "big girl." I really need some of that hamburger Francesca is eating. Caring this much about what others think of me can only mean my brain cells are dying from the lack of nutrition already.

"I just hate eating healthy," she whines, bringing me back to the conversation at hand. "And as you can see," she gestures to her plate," I have almost zero self-control. So, when people start assuming I'm giving myself an eating disorder, they start shoving food in my face. It makes things a thousand times harder."

I find it oddly comforting that I have an ally in this dieting business. She may resemble a tiny little elf that I want to put in my pocket, but she understands the struggle. Go figure. "I have the opposite problem. It doesn't matter what I eat or how little. Someone is always going to comment that maybe I shouldn't eat as much."

Francesca clenches her fists and shakes her head. "I hate when people say that shit." She's not kidding when she says diets make her cranky. Even hearing about mine is making her agitated. "How is it the twenty-first century and people still haven't realized that the word 'pound' is not synonymous with 'illness' and 'skinny' is not the same as 'healthy'? My insides are practically shriveling up, and yours are probably pretty and pink and healthy. And you have boobs!" She bangs her fist on the table and I make a mental note not to turn my back on her for the next six to eight weeks.

"Here," I say gently, handing her another fry. "I think you need this."

"Thanks," she responds quietly and sighs contently as she chews. "But you really do have nice boobs."

She's not wrong. "I know."

Her lips quirk up in a slight smile. "This is going to be a long couple of months, isn't it?"

"I don't think I'll be searching for you in any dark allies, no." She chuckles in response. "And I might take your stapler for safe keeping just in case."

"Only if you give it back when you smell Nolan coming."

"Deal."

We sit in silence—her enjoying her burger, me not enjoying my salad— and I consider her words. I don't remember the last time someone complimented me on any part of my body, with the exception of my hair (Thank you, Pantene). Nor has anyone just assumed I'm healthy when the topic of my weight has come up. Not that it comes up often, but people who aren't obese don't realize how much it's talked about in a general fashion. It can get really irritating.

"Hey, I have an idea."

I glance up at Francesca. If it has anything to do with Nolan and that stapler, I might just go for it.

"I'm going to assume you brought that salad because it's hard to cook for one without having a ton of leftovers that go bad. Am I right?"

I nod because she is right. "I spent an hour on Pinterest last night and while there were a few things that made two servings, anything that looked decent was family-sized. Not only would it go to waste before I could eat it, I get bored with my food."

She nods in understanding. "Me, too. So, what do you think about the idea of trading off?"

Giving up on my lunch, I toss the Tupperware on the table and lean in. "Trading off, how?"

"Well, tonight make one of those family of four recipes. Eat your dinner, pack what's left as lunch for tomorrow and bring me some, too. Then tomorrow night, I'll make dinner and bring the leftovers for both of us the next day. That way we're only cooking every other day. Plus, I usually like other people's cooking better than my own."

I quirk my eyebrow at her. "Are you that bad of a cook?"

"Nope. I'm damn good at it. For whatever reason, even a PB and J tastes better if someone else makes it. Probably because it's made with love." She can't even say it with a straight face.

But she's also got a point. Half the cooking. Double the food. And someone to motivate my eating habits on this journey. If I knew I wouldn't have a gag reflex from the odor, I could kiss Nolan for tipping Francesca off to my plight.

"I'm convinced," I finally say, swiping a fry off her plate. "Now you tell me what you want me to make—cauliflower pizza or cauliflower enchiladas?"

We both grimace at the thought. "Aren't there any gluten-full options?"

"Not in my kitchen. Well, I mean, there won't be once I start cooking. It's so much better for you and right now there are too many options."

"I honestly don't know what I'll be in the mood for tomorrow," she says around the fries in her mouth. "But pizza is harder to re-heat. So, let's try the enchiladas. But please, not with cauliflower."

"Agreed. I'll make it with love instead, just for you."

She waggles her eyebrows. "Now you're talking. A little love is all we need."

"And low carb recipes."

Her face falls. "Don't remind me."

I nod in understanding as she pushes her plate toward me so I can eat more fries. We'll try again on Day Three.

CHAPTER FOUR

CARLOS

"Hey, Dad," I answer when he catches me on my cell as I walk the last block to work. It's an early morning phone call, which is odd for him. Something must be up.

"Hey, son. How's the job treating ya?" Always the same question.

"Business is good. Can't complain." Always the same answer. "You're calling awfully early, aren't you? Sorry," I murmur and wave to a passerby as we accidentally graze each other. It's definitely early enough that not everyone has their balance yet.

"I wanted to catch you before work. See what you might be up to tonight?"

Oh, geez. I have a bad feeling I know where this is going, and I really don't want to do it again. Quickly, I flip through my mental calendar, praying for an out.

"Not sure. I need to get to work and check my calendar. Why, what's up?" I already know, but maybe I bought myself some time.

"Oh, I was hoping to introduce you to my new girlfriend."

Nailed it. Dammit.

My dad is a great guy. He's always been an involved father and always makes sure I know he loves me. For that reason alone, I want him to always be happy, which is why I hate trying to avoid him. I've just been through this more times than I can count and don't want anything to do with his love life.

Inevitably, he'll claim some woman is the love of his life. She'll have stars in her eyes and begin planning the wedding. Then, suddenly, he'll realize he's not the settling down type and leave her heartbroken. Nine times out of ten, he'll also leave her my phone number, under the guise of "in case of emergency," and I'll field drunken calls from those he left behind. It's the reason I no longer answer calls from numbers I don't recognize.

It's also why I'm damn sure anyone I date knows where I stand on relationships.

I don't have them. Ever.

Don't get me wrong, I inherited my love of women from my father. I love the way they smell, the way they taste, the way they feel. I love the sounds they make when they laugh. And I definitely love the way they moan underneath me.

But what I got from my mom, besides my blue eyes, is to recognize people's feelings and he hurts lots of them. No, I don't think my dad yanks his dates around on purpose. I think he's just too self-absorbed to realize the destruction he leaves in his wake. I have no interest in breaking hearts like that. I have too much respect for other people.

"Oh? How long have you been dating?" I ask with as much enthusiasm as I can muster.

"What's it been, sweetie? About a month now?"

Just as I suspected, she's there. It was probably her idea to meet me. I can practically see him sitting at his kitchen table, his latest girlfriend with her arms wrapped around his shoulders as he makes plans for us to have an early dinner at some fancy restaurant. It's a scene I've been privy to before.

Someone murmurs in the background and then I swear I hear kissing noises. So, I do the only think I can think—I quickly cut them off. "So not long, huh?"

"Not long at all," my dad says, his voice sounding more growly than normal which gives me a visual image I really don't appreciate. "But when you know, you know."

"Sure, sure." More kissy noises, which makes me wildly uncomfortable, but also may give me the out I need. "Hey, listen, I'm at the office so I'll give you a call once I get settled, okay?"

"Sounds good, son. I love you."

"Love you, too."

I hang up as quickly as possible and shake my head to rid myself of the images. I have a busy day today and it starts with trying to catch the eye of the woman who works downstairs. She's one of the many reasons I make sure to look my best every day. Her, and because it makes me feel good to know I can rock a suit with the best of them.

It helps that I spare no expense when it comes to my threads. Sure, at the gym or at home, I'm fine with dressing down and relaxing. Hell, the suit I met Quinn in was on the clearance rack at the outlet mall. There's no shame in that. But I've come up from those days of penny pinching with my amazing single mother. And putting on a finely tailored Armani jacket with pants that hug my butt in places women dream of—now that's a seriously good feeling.

I make no apologies for loving how I look. I work hard on my body so I can play hard with it later. Working out isn't enough. I'm also sure that all my hair everywhere is groomed to perfection. My clothes are always properly stitched, no buttons missing. And dental hygiene never, ever goes on the wayside.

Catching the woman who works downstairs eyeing my backside just proves what I already know.

I'm a catch.

I'm handsome. I'm fit. I'm wealthy enough to have a nice apartment in Hyde Park. You can't do much better than that.

Adjusting my cuffs, I finally catch her eye in the reflection of the elevator doors. A small blush covers the apples of her cheeks. Interesting. I've noticed her a few times before. Her cropped blond hair always hangs loose, barely brushing her shoulders. Short, flowy skirts with black pantyhose and stilettos are her go-to. I bet there's a garter under there. And red lips seem to be her trademark. I can think of a few things I could do with those red lips. I think it's time I finally introduced myself.

As soon as all the other worker bees exit our ride, she and I step in and turn to face front. Her, holding some files in her arms. Me, putting my hands in my pockets to fiddle with the keys stashed in there, while disguising my need to fidget. My mother always called it ADHD. My doctor called it anxiety. I call it my brain moving faster than almost everyone else around me and channeling it appropriately.

"Six, please," she requests politely. I press my thumb to the correct number and just for show, make sure she sees that I press the eighth floor for myself.

Her eyes widen momentarily, and I know she's impressed. Who can blame her? Everyone knows Cipher Systems. We're the best in the security business.

I return to my spot, but not even my fidgeting distracts me from the woman. I watch as she bites the corner of her lip, the sexual tension palpable in the lift. I turn my body ever so slightly toward her. With only a few floors to travel, I'll only have a short amount of time to introduce myself and have a conversation.

Just as the doors are about to close, a beefy hand appears, and the doors fly back open revealing Stan Willis. I sigh deeply knowing my window of opportunity has officially closed.

Stan is one of the lieutenants in our office. He's not currently in the military, but that's what my boss Quinn calls the massive men he hires to run the security operations side of Cipher Systems.

All of them are gigantic. All of them are beyond intelligent. All of them are lethal if they catch you trying to harm one of their clients. Worst of all, for whatever reason, they're all handsome, in a meathead kind of way, if you ask me. I'm pretty sure one of our marketing directors tried to convince Quinn to create a "Security Men" calendar at one point. Thank God, that was nixed. The last thing I need is a bunch of horny women having to be escorted from the building on the regular.

Not that I'm jealous. My co-workers are also the best group of guys you could ever know. Kind and loyal, they make everyone feel at ease. But working in an office that's run with military precision by a bunch of guys that could be mistaken for Navy Seals or professional athletes in both physique and brains isn't exactly the biggest confidence booster for a guy like me. I barely pass for six feet. That makes me a solid half a foot shorter than Stan. And judging by how the downstairs woman's eyes are no longer looking my direction, but his, she notices the difference as well.

I love my job. I really do. But no matter how attractive I may be everywhere else, working here can be a blow to my ego.

Standing on the opposite side of the woman, Stan looks over her head toward me and eyes me up and down. "Nice threads. New suit?"

I don't need to look in the reflection to notice the woman's reaction to his deep voice. She practically melts on the spot. So much for those after dinner plans I was hoping she'd be interested in.

"New tie," I answer more confidently than I feel.

He gives a manly nod of approval. "That pattern is cool. And the purple makes your eyes pop."

I freeze, one eyebrow shooting up to my hairline.

He shrugs his massive shoulders and turns to face front again. "What? I just call it like I see it."

"He's not wrong," the woman adds as the elevator slows to a stop. "You should wear ties like that more often." Then she steps out the door and turns the corner, leaving me confused as to what just happened.

Stan chuckles and claps me on the back. "Dude, she's into you. Have you asked her out? She's cute."

"I was about to when you stuck your hands in our elevator and got on with us."

He looks slightly apologetic, although I don't believe it for a second. That's another thing all the lieutenants are—bullshitters. "Sorry, man."

"No, you're not."

"No. I'm really not," he responds with a smile and shake of his head. "But I am glad I caught you. You're in charge of the new benefits package, right?"

And back to business as normal. As the Chief Operations Officer and man in charge of the entire administrative side of Cipher Systems, the coordination of the big Human Resources jobs falls on my shoulders. Yes, I have a benefits coordinator, but it's a big undertaking that must go through a new approval process every year. Mostly, it's making sure the company isn't getting screwed out of any money and the employees aren't getting screwed out of good healthcare. This year's plan was pretty much the same as last year's, so it was a no-brainer. But starting the day off with this question still puts me on edge.

"Not directly in charge, but the team reports to me. Why? What's up?"

The elevator doors open again, and we stroll through the lobby of Cipher Systems, nodding our heads at the receptionist in greeting as we talk. I make a mental note that we need to hire a second person for the front as our workload continues to increase.

"It's not a huge deal, I guess." I'm trying to keep pace with Stan, but his steps are slightly longer than mine. Suddenly, I'm glad I've taken so many spin classes lately to keep my cardio abilities up. "I tried to make an appointment with my regular dentist, but they said our insurance dropped them as a provider with no explanation."

I furrow my brow. That's odd. "It must be a glitch in the paper-work. I'll make a call and see what's up."

"Thanks, man." He claps me on my shoulder again. If he does it too many more times, I might lose some feeling in my arm. "And don't take so long to ask the cutie out next time."

He turns tail and heads back the way we came, no doubt going to check in with the security team and what new project we're working on now. I stay away from that side of things as much as possible. It's interesting, sure. But half the time they're talking about things that go way over my head. I'm not dumb by any stretch. I earned my MBA like everyone else. But the inner workings of their technology is not my forte. Add onto it that I feel like a shrimp around them and no thanks. I don't need that kind of negativity.

No, I prefer to hang out and be the big fish on this side of the pond. I have great staff who enjoy working together. I have a nice corner office with big windows. And I keep bankers' hours so my entire life doesn't revolve around my job. It's exactly the way I like it.

The only real stressor is my boss. Ever since Quinn Sullivan's wife, Janie, got pregnant, he's been difficult to deal with. I get that she's the love of his life and all that romantic crap I stay far away from, but he's rocketed himself from being a heavily involved boss into an abrasive, unfiltered micromanaging boss. He's been working from home a lot lately to take care of Janie after she had a health scare and was put on mandatory bed rest, but every once in a while, he still pops in. These days, it's best to be out of his line of sight when he shows up.

"Morning, Teresa." I smile at my assistant as she hands me a stack of papers. That's the way we start every morning— with her handing me all the pre-sorted items I need to deal with, in a neat little stack— the top priority always front and center for me to see and prepare for. "How's everything going so far?"

This is where a couple of odd things happen simultaneously. First, I see Steven, another lieutenant, coming my direction. The lieutenants never come on this side of the office unless something's wrong.

Second, Teresa's reaction to my question is different. She's not smiling. As I look closer, I realize she looks stressed.

"What's wrong?"

"Nothing's wrong. Sir." She stands up quickly and runs her hands down her pencil skirt, like she's nervous and not quite sure what to do with her hands. I know she's new here, but not new enough for me to realize this overly anxious reaction seems odd. "It's just, um, Mr. Sullivan is waiting for you in your office."

Before I can do more than freeze and look at her in question, Steven swivels and goes back the way he came. Looks like I'm not the only one who prefers hiding from Quinn these days. "I thought he was at home with Janie today."

Teresa licks her lips nervously. "He was. Mr. Sullivan said something about their medical coverage being denied."

My head drops to my chest. Another one? Shit. "That probably explains why Steven was headed this direction."

"Just so you know, Mr. Sullivan was very angry. Said something about benefits being the last thing on his list of things to worry when his wife needs Vicuna yarn that can only be made by sheering wild

Vicuna found native to the Andes Mountains every three years, and the only Vicuna yarn distributor is out of stock."

I pinch the bridge of my nose and shake my head because "I don't even know what that means," I whisper to myself. With Quinn, there is no telling. "Okay. I'll deal with it." I suck in a breath and reach for the doorknob, not sure what to expect when I walk in. Turning back to my assistant I add, "And, Teresa, if I don't make it out alive, let my mother know I love her."

Teresa gives me what is probably supposed to be a reassuring smile, but we both know it's a lie. When Quinn is on a rampage, you never know what is going to happen behind closed doors.

CHAPTER FIVE

RIAN

Rushing into the bridal shop, I wave off the sales associate that tries to greet me and race straight to my sister who is pacing in front of a group of mirrors.

"I'm here!" Dropping my bag on the red velvet couch, I barely notice the strap whacks one of the bridesmaids sitting there. She doesn't even look up from her phone when it hits her arm. "I'm sorry I'm late, Laney. The El was running behind schedule for some reason."

"You could've planned ahead, Rian. I'm only getting married once in my lifetime. This dress fitting is important."

I'm tempted to spout off the rising divorce statistics but knowing it will either fall on deaf ears or create unnecessary stress, I bite my tongue. Besides, my sister has been my best friend since we were little. It's only been since she started planning her nuptials that she's become extremely difficult to be around.

"I know," I acquiesce, but only partially. "It's so important you forgot to tell me about it until this morning."

My playful poke is completely ignored. Instead, she claps her hands together to get everyone's attention. Slowly, they all look up from their smart phones.

"Everybody, this is my sister Rian. Rian this is Kara, Lara, Tara, and Jade." Huh. Not only are they all named alike, except for Jade, they all look alike. Same petite build with muscular legs. Same glossy straight hair. Same blank look in their eyes. I bet it's the same look they have on their faces after running twenty-six-point-one miles—like they need carbs before they lose the will to live.

"Now that we're all here..." Laney gives me a pointed look which I ignore. Seriously. More than eight hours-notice would have been nice. "It's time to try on our dresses."

Everyone except me claps with excitement, and once again, I'm struck by how Stepford this all feels.

As the weird outburst dies down, a sales associate begins guiding us to various dressing rooms to dry on our dresses. Since we only had about six months to plan this wedding, Laney didn't have time to schedule a day to look for dresses. Instead, she had us send over our measurements to the sales associate she is working with for them to order a dress none of us have even seen. Laney promised she was picking styles that are flattering to our body types, but I have a hard time believing it. There is no way what flatters me is going to flatter the Stepford runners.

"Hey, where's Bendy?" Tara asks. Or maybe it's Lara. Kara? I don't know. Nor do I know who this Bendy person is.

Her thumbs flying as she sends a rapid text, Laney doesn't look up when she answers. "She can't make it. She got held up at work."

I'm curious to understand why this Bendy person isn't in trouble for not showing up when I got reamed for being two minutes late. "Who is Bendy?"

"My best friend." Laney locks her screen and throws her phone in her purse.

"Since when?" Seriously, I've known my sister her entire life and I've never heard her talk about this presumably flexible friend.

She shrugs and follows the associate who waves her to a chair where she can relax and drink some champagne while we model for her. "Since forever."

I give up. As long as Bendy is in charge of all the extra parties and celebrations, that's good enough for me. I have no desire to go purchase party supplies from the Triple X store at the edge of town anyway. And I don't trust any on-line erotica stores to be as discreet as they claim. I made that mistake once after a Ladies Only Party. My next-door neighbor still won't let me live it down after his dog got ahold of my package and mistook my treasure for a squeaky toy.

Trudging my way to the last dressing room, I close the curtain and begin the process of trying on my dress. The color is a beautiful shade of red, not quite as deep as a burgundy, but with a purpleish hue which I think goes well with my dark hair. The fabric is flowy which covers a multitude of sins and it's cinched tight underneath my breasts, giving me a nice boost.

I admit, I'm impressed with my sister's choice in dresses.

Sliding the curtain open, I strut my way over to Laney where I make a few exaggerated poses showing off how nice I look. She looks as delighted as I feel.

"You look so great!" she exclaims, clapping her hands. That seems to be the normal reaction with this group. "Go stand next to the others. I want to see how everyone will look next to each other at the front of the church."

I turn and begin walking onto the stage, but my heart plummets. Laney was right. She picked a dress that flatters all our bodies. Standing in a row, all the "ara's" look long and lean, tanned and tone. And I... I suddenly look like a beach ball.

This wedding is not going to be fun at all.

I always get nervous when I go out with new friends for the first time. It's stupid, I know, but you don't really *know* someone until you've met them for dinner and drinks. Talking to them in the office or online just isn't the same. Tabitha is no exception.

She's fun to talk to and she doesn't seem irritated at all by my sourpuss attitude toward all things exercise. But she's still the smoothie lady. She's basically the gym therapist behind a bar, except instead of alcohol there's flax seed. Whatever that is. I'm still not totally sure, or even why I need to ingest it. But so far, it hasn't killed me.

I was pleasantly surprised when Tabitha invited me to dinner with her and a few gym friends. I didn't know she enjoyed me as much as I enjoy her, and everyone likes to be liked, right? Granted, I almost cancelled on her twice, after trying on every potential outfit I own. I mean, what does one wear to dinner with gym people? Sports bras are out, not that I would be caught dead in one anyway. Or two. With the size of these knockers, it's necessary to layer up. It's a trick another big busted woman on a treadmill taught me when she caught me huffing and puffing and trying to be stealthy while holding the girls in place with my arm. I choose to believe no one else noticed.

After many a thrown pant and top, I finally landed on a plum colored wrap dress. Sort of. It looks like a wrap dress because of the side tie, but it doesn't really do any wrapping. Honestly, I don't know how women wear those things. I feel like it's just asking for disaster. All it takes is one car door shutting and a valet driver stepping on the gas at the exact right moment to be unwrapped like a Christmas present. No thank you. I prefer my clothes not to be torn right off my body. Well, at least in public.

Come to think of it, I don't think I'd like it in private either. Do you know how much a good quality garment costs these days? Unless Christian Grey comes knocking on my door and hands me his credit card, I prefer to be peeled gently out of my clothing, thank you very much. Not that I have anyone to give those instructions to, which actually works to my benefit. I need to get through my sister's wedding first before I introduce anyone into that crazy mess.

But after a compliment or two at work, I felt better about coming here tonight. I feel, dare I say it, pretty. Or at least I did, until my sister called to discuss yesterday's dress fitting.

"I know how hard it is for you to stand up in front of everyone, but it's my wedding, Rian. I want you up there with me."

"And I'm going to be, Laney. I've already bought the dress, so I'm not sure why you're bringing it up again."

"I saw the look on your face at the bridal shop. I just don't want you to feel inadequate because my other bridesmaids are from my running club."

Here we go again....

I love my sister. Laney and I are only a couple of years apart and growing up, we were the best of friends. We loved riding our bikes around the neighborhood, usually to a small pond at the end of the street. In hindsight, it was really a drainage ditch, but we didn't care. We called it turtle pond because there were always red-eared sliders to find and feed. They loved when we brought vegetables but weren't fond of bananas. A couple of times we found a turtle with an injury or who was small enough to become hawk food. We'd take them home and put them in a cage until they were big enough to go back to turtle pond.

Once we hit high school, turtle pond became a memory, but we had various activities that meant we didn't spend every minute together. We still stayed close—going to movies with friends that overlapped both our social circles and binge watching *One Tree Hill*, or whatever we thought was the best show on TV at the time.

But ever since she took up marathons, dropped a ton of weight, and found the man of her dreams, she's become, well... somewhat unbearable. I know she's not trying to be mean. She wants me to feel the same joy and contentment she's found. It's nice and all, but running without being chased by a bear, holds no interest to me whatsoever. Okay, let's be real. Running *while* being chased by a bear holds no interest to me either.

She hasn't quite figured out yet that we don't have the same goals. Hers might be to stay a voluptuous size twelve. Mine is to get to the enchiladas inside the restaurant as soon as possible because *what is that wonderful aroma*??

"Seriously, Rian. I remember what it was like to be overweight."

Knowing she can't see me, I give into my immediate reaction and roll my eyes. I would never do that if she could see me, although I've come really close a time or two. It just creates a fight these days.

"I remember always feeling so dumpy next to everyone else no matter what I wore, and I don't want you to feel like that."

I stop in my tracks and look down at the dress I painstakingly picked out. Suddenly, I don't feel as pretty as I did when I put it on. For the third time, I have to physically stop myself from hanging up on Laney and texting Tabitha to cancel.

"I'm not sure what to say to that, Laney," I say with all the calm I can muster. "I wasn't feeling bad about myself until this conversation started and now, I'm questioning whether or not I ever want to go out into public again."

"Oh, Rian, stop." I can practically hear her dismissing my feelings with a wave of her hand. That's the other thing about Laney that's changed. With her newfound confidence is the lost ability to be sensitive to anyone else's feelings. Or maybe just mine. "That's not what I meant, and you know it. I just want to make sure—"

"I don't flake out at the last minute or you'll have no choice but to fire a groomsman at the last minute to ensure the pictures balance and it's all Bradley's friends and family, so it'll cause a rift. Yeah. I know. With as many times as we've had this conversation, I can't forget."

She breathes out what sounds like a sigh of relief. "Okay, good. I just wanted to check. It's just so stressful, I know I'm a bit of a bridezilla right now…"

Ya think?

"So please just humor me if I ask you a dozen more times, okay?"

Oh, goodie. I always look forward to my family berating me because of the genetic gift of heft. It does wonders for my confidence levels.

"Yeah, well. If I stop answering your calls, you know why."

She titters her laugh, as if she thinks I'm not serious. If I was a bitter woman, I'd already be planning my cancellation the day before the ceremony just to piss her off. Too bad I'm a nice person. Mostly.

"Oh, Rian, you know you wouldn't do that to me. It's one of the things I love about you. You accept me no matter how wedding crazy I get."

Uh huh. Or so she thinks. I haven't bought my wedding gift yet.

"Yeah, I know. But listen, I'm out with some friends right now so I need to let you go."

She gasps. "Oh! Is it a guy friend?"

"No idea. I was invited to go with this group. I'm sure men will be there." I don't tell her where I met this new friendship circle. In fact, I haven't told anyone in my family at all about my new hobby, although the hobby part is more about bantering with Abel. I just put up with the rest. But if I let my family in on it, I know what would happen.

Nothing good. My sister would start making plans for me to join her at the half marathon, her fiancé would then make a gross remark about watching her boobs when she runs, my mother would get all emotional that her "baby is getting healthy," and my dad would grunt and ignore us all.

As much as it pains me to say it, I'd rather listen to wedding plans.

"Well, don't forget to fluff your hair, bat your eyelashes, and stick to salad! It's the safest, easiest thing to eat when trying to impress a man. But no onions!"

I pull my phone away to make sure this is still my sister I'm talking to. Since when does she put in so much effort to attract the opposite sex? This is a side of her I haven't seen before. It's kind of disturbing.

"Thanks for the advice. Gotta go."

I hang up quickly and drop my phone into my clutch, pulling the door open and enjoying the fragrance as I step inside. It smells like chips and salsa and hot tortillas warming in the back. I have arrived in my heaven.

The bar off to the right only has a few customers, Tabitha being one of them.

"Rian!" She waves me over while she takes a sip of her very fruity looking margarita. I'm so glad I live in Chicago. Tonight is the perfect night to take advantage of the designated drivers, also known as public transportation.

When I join her at the bar, she gives me a quick hug. The bartender, who is looking almost relieved that another patron showed up, drops a napkin and a quick, "What can I get you?" before I even sit down.

"Whatever she's having would be great."

"Strawberry margarita, coming up."

"So where is everyone?" I ask with a smile, noticing Tabitha is sitting by herself. So much for meeting some people from the gym.

She's not discouraged, though. "Almost everyone cancelled, so there's just going to be four of us."

Oddly, I'm not disappointed. I enjoy get togethers, but it's always hard to really talk to people if there are more than a handful. Just a few means I have a much better chance of remembering their names and faces next time I'm walking through the facility, avoiding people.

"Anyone I know?"

She takes another sip just as mine is placed in front of me. I join her in drinking and am pleasantly surprised when the flavor hits my tongue. Strawberry, sugar, and just enough tequila to make it worth my while. Not to mention, it's served in a giant beer mug with sugar on the rim. This is going to go perfectly with my carb-loaded, cheese-filled dinner. Francesca is going to kill me for this on Monday. But really, if I don't have one cheat day a week, how am I expected to stay on track?

"Do you know Carlos?" I shake my head, even though the name sounds familiar. I just can't place him. "You'll probably recognize him. He's there all the time. Never misses a day. He was supposed to have dinner with his dad, but something happened. Like he broke up with his girlfriend or something."

"Oh, no! And he's up for going out?"

She scoffs. "Oh, no, honey. Carlos isn't into relationships. His dad broke up with his girlfriend." She snaps her fingers like she just remembered something. "Oh, and Frank is coming," she adds. "He's the old man with white hair. Totally reminds me of the Rat Pack era. He's a hoot."

This is going to be an interesting blend of people. The smoothie bartender, the gym rat, the Sammy Davis wannabe and me—I feel like there's a joke in there somewhere.

Putting her mug down on the counter, Tabitha swallows quickly, eyes widening in delight. "Speak of the devil."

She leans over and gives the man who I assume is Carlos a hug. She's right. I do recognize him. He's the god who looked right through me on my first day at the gym. And yes, I know how pathetic it is that I remember. But how could I forget? Thick, dark hair with some gray on the sides that just makes him look more distinguished. Huge, blue eyes framed with long, thick lashes. With light brown skin, he's just under six feet, but seems much taller when you add in all that swagger. He exudes the kind of confidence I've never possessed.

"Hey, beautiful." He kisses Tabitha's cheek and immediately turns to the bartender, ordering just a bottle of water. Odd. I expected something fancier than that.

Tabitha groans. "Please tell me you aren't detoxing again. You're not fun to be with when you do that. Especially at a bar."

He flashes her what can only be described as a mega-watt smile and leans against the bar. "Not detoxing. Just making up for some unnecessary calories I ate the other night. I'm feeling kind of bloated."

I try really, really hard not to snicker, but I fail. I can tell through his gray t-shirt and jeans that he's got muscles in places I don't even know exist, and he's worried about bloating? Bloating is what I'm going to be after eating tonight's meal and it's nowhere near what his version is.

Fortunately, he doesn't seem to hear my reaction. Tabitha does, although she may already be three sheets to the wind as it seems more like she was just reminded I'm here.

"Carlos! You know my friend Rian, right? From the gym?"

He narrows his eyes and cocks his head at me, trying to place me. "No. I don't think I do. Carlos Davies." He reaches out his hand to shake mine, and I can't help but note that I've seen him several times, yet I don't ring a bell to him. Figures.

"Rian Thompson." I also can't help but notice that his hand is strong and warm. It dwarfs mine, which makes me feel oddly petite and gives me the urge to giggle. I may not need a second margarita. Clearly, it's gone to my head already. "Nice to meet you."

We pull away aaaaaannnnnnddddddd cue the awkward pause. You know what I'm talking about. When everyone is trying to be friendly, but no one knows what to say because we literally have nothing in common. Fortunately for us, we're called to our table.

Following behind both of them is a strategic move on my part. I have no interest for this Apollo to have a birds eye view of my backside.

We're seated at a table for four, still waiting on the final member of our party. I look through my menu while halfway listening to Tabitha and Carlos chat about some of the gym employees, a new protein mix Carlos might be interested in, and some woman named Alison who was a friend of theirs but apparently flaked on them. Something about a millionaire she met and suddenly her number changed. Sounds like she wasn't that good of a friend to begin with if you ask me, but I suppose I don't have room to talk. My sister keeps not-so-subtly trying to shove me out of her wedding.

I know deep down that's not her actual motivation for constantly bringing up my obviously inferior looks to her friends. But the more it happens, the less I believe her when she says it's just her bridezilla coming out.

"Well, hello gorgeous." I look up to see a man kissing Tabitha on the cheek and her giving an overly flirty response to his greeting. This must be Frank.

With a head full of white hair and a leisure suit on, I could see him breaking out a stogie right here in the restaurant and regaling us of casino lounge stories from the 50's. Tabitha was spot on. He could have stepped straight out of a time machine. I like him immediately. Especially when he turns to me, his eyes full of mischief and takes my hand in his, kissing the top of it.

"Well, well, well. I didn't realize I would be dining with not one, but two gorgeous women."

And that flirty giggle I stifled before pops right on out of my mouth. I'm sure my face is bright red as he sits. He doesn't seem to notice when Tabitha nods at me, eyes wide, mouthing, "Right?" and fans herself.

"If I was only forty years older," Tabitha says, eyeing him over the rim of her drink. Her flirt game is strong with this one. Although I don't sense it's remotely sexual at all. Just the banter of two good friends who enjoy each other's company.

"And if I was only forty years younger," he flirts back.

Suddenly, my insecurities fade away. This might be a fun night after all.

CHAPTER SIX

CARLOS

I've always liked Frank. He's been a staple at Weight Expectations since long before I started going regularly, and I don't think he ever misses a day. I don't think he really works out, but he's always around—chatting with members who are taking a break from their reps, hanging out at the smoothie bar regaling stories of times gone by, flirting with the staff in a way that doesn't come across as creepy or weird, just friendly.

He is one cool cat and basically my idol. He is who I hope to be when I'm pushing eighty. Hell, he still rides a motorcycle some days. Others, he brings his 1962 Chevy Corvette. It's in mint condition and when he throws on his shades, it fits his personality to a T.

Having dinner with him last night was a blast. He's just easy to be with and doesn't judge anyone. Ever. He's much too interested in having a variety of personalities in his life. Plus, he's always up for trying new things. Just last night he convinced the ladies to sip shots of tequila. Rian crinkled her cute nose up when he suggested it and argued that the scent association of tossing her cookies after a wild night in college is still strong, but Frank wouldn't let it go. This wasn't Jose Cuervo. No, he sprung for some top-shelf expensive stuff that went down smooth. I didn't drink it myself, but the surprise on Rian's face when she finally caved, left no room for doubt.

Speaking of Rian... I can't get her off my mind and I can't for the life of me figure out why. She's not my type in any way, shape, or form. Not just in her body type, which is larger than I typically go for, although she has a nice rack, that's for sure. But she's also too intelligent for my tastes. And witty. And funny. And charming.

Because who wouldn't want a woman like that? Me. That's who. All those personality traits lead to a life in commitment-ville and all the drama that comes with it. That's one place I have no interest in moving.

Still, I can't get her out of my head. Is it lust? I don't think so. But she's captivated me in a way I haven't felt in a long time. Maybe it was the enchiladas. Lord knows I almost caved and asked her for a taste. I haven't had creamy sauce like that in so long. Next to my bland chicken, they looked like heaven on a plate.

The moan Rian let out when she took her first bite didn't help either. Nothing makes your own dinner lose all its flavor than when the woman next to you makes sex noises while eating.

And I'm back to the lust issue I can't figure out. Not that I should be thinking about it anyway. I have work to do, and clearly, it's not going well.

Giving up on reading the latest memo from Karen about the insurance issues we're still dealing with, my fingers hover over my keyboard. I'm so tempted to google Rian's name and see what it comes up with. That's not weird, right? I'm the Chief Operations Officer at the fastest growing security firm in Chicago. Knowing everything about people is part of my job, isn't it?

Continuing the debate in my head, images of last night keep flashing through my mind.

"All I want is a baked chicken breast and some steamed vegetables on the side, but I don't see it on the menu," I tell the waitress who is listening way too intently to me. I'm used to it, though. She's not the first one to lean into me making sure I have a nice view of her cleav-

age. And I'm certainly not complaining about it. "Is it possible for the chef to make it?"

"Sure," she purrs. And yes, her words are definitely a purr. Down pussycat. I'm dining with friends. *"What kind of vegetables do you want, and do you want them seasoned or cheese on top?"*

Handing her the menu to give us a bit of distance, I smile kindly at her. "I'd love some broccoli and cauliflower if you have it. And no need for seasoning or cheese. I'll just salt and pepper when it gets here."

Pussycat moves over to Rian who orders the three cheese enchiladas dinner. I remember when I used to eat enchiladas. They were my favorite. But losing them is a small price to pay to keep this body in shape.

As the waitress makes her way around the table, I take the opportunity to get to know Rian a little better. She seems nice and if Tabitha likes her, that speaks volumes. It's not that Tabitha dislikes anyone. She just keeps her circle small. I'm not completely sure how I even got in it.

"So, Rian." I lean in on the table so we can hear each other better. "When you're not at the gym or dining out with friends, what do you do?"

For a brief second, she looks almost surprised that I'm talking to her. Strange.

"I'm a customer service rep at Sandeke Telecom."

Not at all what I was expecting her to say, but also piques my interest. The Sandekes own a whole lot of this town, some legitimately. Some not so much. And while the Telecom business is on the up-and-up, I can't help wondering what kind of environment it is to work in. Like the saying goes, it all starts at the top. Quinn's ability to drive everyone in our office crazy is proof of that.

"Yeah?" I say noncommittally, not wanting to ask the questions I really want answers for like, "Is it as misogynistic in your company as I hear it is in their other businesses?" Instead, I stick with "What all does that entail?"

She shrugs, still looking a bit confused as to why I'm speaking to her. But why wouldn't I? We're having dinner. She may not be my type, but I'm not a total asshole.

"Technically, it's customer service, but really it's a lot of up sales." *She takes a quick sip of her margarita before continuing.* "When people call in about their package or wanting to cancel, they're transferred to me so I can find out what's really going on. Then I present them with several options that might be better suited to their needs."

For the second time, she's caught my attention. Only this time, it's not as her dinner mate. It's as an operations manager who is always on the look-out for people with particular skill sets.

"Sounds like you're more of an account manager than customer service rep."

She shrugs and I can't help but notice she didn't realize I was giving her a compliment. "I suppose. Except I don't follow up with anyone, so I don't really manage anything."

"Maybe not, but don't sell yourself short. Up sales are hard. Especially if customers are already calling to cancel."

"You're telling me," *she half says, half grumbles.*

We glance over at Tabitha and Frank who are leaning so close to each other, they're practically sitting on each other's laps. Not unusual for them, especially when Tabitha is drinking. I don't think they've ever hooked up; at least she's never told me they have. But if this goes on for much longer, tonight might just be the night.

After watching them for a few seconds without them noticing, I realize whatever they're discussing is going to stay between them, so I might as well not interrupt. Rian seems to figure that out at the same time I do, if the slight blush on her cheeks is any indication.

"So," *she says, turning back to me,* "what do you do when you aren't at the gym or dining out with friends?"

I smile at her tossing the same words at me that I just gave her. "I'm the Chief Operations Officer at Cipher Security Systems."

Her eyebrows shoot up in surprise. "Wow. That's a fancy title."

"Fancy title. Not so fancy job."

"You sure?" *she jokes playfully.* "I bet you have a fancy office with *a fancy chair and a fancy desk. I bet even your assistant is fancy. Am I right?"*

"I don't know anymore. You've said the word fancy so many times, it's lost all meaning."

Rian laughs and I'm shocked by my own reaction to the sound. It's deep and throaty and makes my nerve endings feel like she's touching all over my whole body. It feels an awful lot like lust. What in the world is happening to me? I shouldn't be attracted to this woman for any reason except some interesting conversation while our other friends ignore us. Except, that's not what's happening. For whatever reason, this woman has caught my eye and I don't understand it. At all.

"I hate when that happens." I don't remember what she's talking about at this point, but I let it go. "I just mean it sounds like you have a really important job. Definitely important enough that I wouldn't expect to see you at a place like Jose Jose."

Now it's my turn to laugh. "What's wrong with Jose Jose?"

She shrugs playfully taking another sip of her drink. If she keeps this up, she'll need another one soon. "I suppose it doesn't seem fancy *enough for a guy like you."*

"There's that word again," I groan.

She just laughs, and that same sensation runs over my skin. Maybe I'm getting a fever. Surely that's a more logical explanation that lust, right?

"I just mean it sounds like you have a lot of responsibility and clout. Seems like it would be hard to make time for dinner out just for fun."

I take a breath as I decide how to answer. She's not wrong. The title does sound that way. Pretentious, almost. But that's not the way Cipher Systems operates. "From a business model standpoint, it seems like I'd be at the office all the time." She nods in understanding. "But from an operational standpoint, that's not how we work. The bulk of our company is round the clock, yes. But mostly that's out in the field. The part that I do is more in support of all that. And I'm really good at being proactive in that sense. Well, when my boss is keeping me in the loop." Her eyebrows raise in question and I wave her off. "He's just having a rough few weeks. Normally, there are no issues. But for the most part, my day is pretty much scheduled from the time I walk in until the time I leave. Once it's over for the day, it's truly over and I'm free."

"That's good." Rian drains her drink and pushes her mug to the center of the table. I gesture to it, but she shakes her head indicating she doesn't want another. *"I know the chief anything officer typically doesn't have a life outside of work. At least not at my company. I'm sure it makes it hard to have a relationship of any kind, so that's good that you have that kind of freedom."*

"Oh. Well, I have no interest in a relationship of any kind anyway, so it doesn't really matter. I just like that I'm not chained to a desk."

She cocks her head slightly like she can't believe what she's hearing. *"No interest whatsoever? Not even if she just falls into your lap?"*

I sit up straight and shake my head back and forth slowly. *"No way. Relationships are messy and pointless. It's much easier to just be single and enjoy life as a bachelor."*

This time, her brow furrows. I'm not sure why the voluntary single life is such a hard concept for people to understand. Why does everyone have to pursue a dating relationship?

"Sorry." She shakes her head and the expression off her face. *"I'm not trying to be judgmental. I just don't know anyone this age who wouldn't be interested in finding someone to share their life with."*

She's not wrong. Most people I know are all about finding "the one". *"Nope. I've never wanted to be tied down. Not in my twenties. Not in my thirties. Not now. Single life is the way I like it."* I don't know why I feel the need to justify myself to her, but now that this can of worms has opened up, I can't seem to stop the words from crawling out of my mouth, no matter how inappropriate they may seem. *"I don't mind having a physical relationship with someone, but only short-term."*

"So, you're all about the sex," she deadpans. Not that I should be surprised. I've had conversations like this before.

"Yes, but not like you think."

"Really?"

I catch the disbelief in her tone, but I ignore it. I'm oddly used to it by now. "Really. You know how when people fall in love, they say they've finally found their purpose for being here? Like being with that other person is their reason for being?"

She shrugs. "I guess. That's a weird way of saying it, but I suppose I understand the sentiment."

I nod. Maybe she will understand. "I feel like my purpose in being here is to give women pleasure. It's not about getting my rocks off, ya know? It's about letting a woman feel beautiful in that most intimate moment. It's about showing her that she's worth taking my time with. She's worth the effort of giving her that kind of pleasure. And I'm good at it. I know that sounds cocky and arrogant, but it's important to me that when I'm with someone, she knows in that moment, she's worth it."

Done with my rant, I wait for Rian to respond. When she doesn't, I look up at her, but can't decipher what she's thinking. She's not moving and it's like her entire body has frozen. I open my mouth to ask what's wrong, but I'm cut off by a baked chicken breast and broccoli dropping down in front of me.

Once everything is placed in front of us, our pussycat waitress asks if we need anything else. Rian immediately responds with, "I'm gonna need another drink."

I smile at her with confusion because she just told me a few minutes ago she didn't want another. Maybe she changed her mind because the food is here.

"Mr. Davies?"

My name being called through my intercom breaks me away from my thoughts of last night. Thank goodness. I was about to fall down the rabbit hole of how a really fun and insightful conversation suddenly turned awkward. I'm still not sure what Rian's change in demeanor was about. And she eventually warmed up again, but I don't like the thought that maybe my honesty changed her opinion of me.

Not that it matters. She's not my type. Right?

"Nancy wants to know if you have time to meet about those two open positions," Teresa, my assistant, says.

"Shit," I grumble and run my hand down my face. If Nancy, who is our hiring manager amongst a myriad of other things, wants to meet, that means she's having a hard time finding what we need through our regular channels. "Yeah. When is she free?"

"She was hoping you'd have time in the next ten minutes or so."

A quick glance at my desk calendar doesn't show anything that's not already accounted for. "That works."

"Okay. I'll let her know. Do you need anything before she gets here?"

Some focus maybe. But I don't think Teresa can help me with that. "No thanks. I'm good."

"Alright. Just let me know if that changes."

She clicks off, and I turn back to my computer. Despite my current predicament, Rian comes to mind again. Something she said last night about her job makes me curious about her. Well, that and everything else.

But one little Google search wouldn't hurt, right?

Before I can second-guess myself, I type her name into the search bar and wait to see what happens. It takes only a few seconds for her name on the same line as Sandeke Telecom to come up.

Clicking the link, it takes me to their website page where all the employee awards are listed.

"What is this?" I whisper to myself, leaning closer to my screen. Not only is Rian listed as being one of the top twenty customer service agents company wide, she's been given that honor multiple times.

As I keep scrolling, I find myself more and more impressed. She downplayed herself when talking about her job last night. She's not just good at her job; she's one of the best. I can feel my eyes widen the more I scroll.

"Holy shit."

I need her resume on file, and I need it stat.

CHAPTER SEVEN

RIAN

Cocking my head, I just watch as she runs. It's oddly fascinating. Like watching a baby deer galloping through the forest. Running on tiptoes, back stiff and straight, knees coming all the way to her chest, looking like she's going to step right off the front edge.

Then she stops, placing her feet on either side of the treadmill as it continues to spin. Turns the treadmill up faster, redoes her ponytail, messes with her music, gets back on and runs more. A little faster. Like she's loping through the forest now.

Then she stops. Does her ponytail again. Messes with her music again. Turns up the treadmill again.

Now she's running. Like a bear is chasing her. But would the bear catch her when she—

Stops again. More ponytail doing. More music messing. And I'm thoroughly confused now.

"Having a good time watching Bambi?"

"You guys call her that? That's so rude."

Abel snorts through his nose. "Actually, it's her real name. Her running style has nothing to do with it. Although I do enjoy the coincidence."

"Is that what it takes to have a body like that? To run like, like…"

"Like a deer?"

"Yeah."

"No. What she's doing has zero health benefit at all."

"Really?" I try to glance at him, but still can't take my eyes off… whatever it is she's doing.

"She runs for ten seconds and stops. I run further than that from my couch to the fridge. If your heart doesn't get a good solid pounding going, it's just a waste of energy."

"But she's so skinny. With such big boobs," I add to myself.

"Body type, babe. Some of the unhealthiest people I know are rail thin. That's why we work on health, not size."

I shrug to myself, remembering Francesca's words and her own struggles with cholesterol. It's better than focusing on the fact that Abel just called me babe. I know he means nothing of it, but I'm a full-blooded American woman. I recognize a hot guy when I see one, and Abel is definitely a hot guy.

"Speaking of health…"

I groan, knowing he's about to try to get me on that treadmill again. He'll call it "encouragement." I'll call it "harassment." Tomato, tomahto. Either way he'll end up convincing me to get back on Satan's belt of death.

"Don't groan. You haven't even heard what I have to say yet."

"If you want me to stand on the treadmill next to Bambi, the answer is no."

Abel lets out a low chuckle. I'm glad one of us thinks this is funny. "I wouldn't be so cruel."

Crossing my arms, I give him an evil glare. "Because you know people will be doing a size comparison if I'm standing next to her?"

"No. Because I know you'll get distracted when she starts galloping and face-plant. I hate cleaning blood out of tread."

I open my mouth to say something witty, but I got nothing. He's right. She's so fascinating to watch, I'd fall long before I got up to a meandering speed.

"I have a different proposition for you," he says, an evil gleam in his eye. I roll my eyes because I've already fallen for his trap once. I don't want to do it again. "Don't make that face at me. I only want to know if you've given any thought to doing my introductory weightlifting class. Free of charge," he tacks on quickly.

"You mean free the first time, right?"

He shrugs right back at me. "What can I say? I'm trying to make a living here. Besides, you may really like it."

I look up at the ceiling and let out a dramatic sigh. I'm going to do it. There's no doubt about that. But I can't just jump into the class without making Abel squirm at least a little bit. I'm already trying to lose part of myself in a very literal sense. All I have left is my manipulation techniques and melodramatics to win people over.

"You're so full of shit," he says before I can respond. "I can already tell you've decided to give it a go."

My jaw drops, mimicking my hands falling to my sides. "I've already lost my manipulation techniques? I've worked out twice. I shouldn't be a better person already!"

"You aren't."

"Aw, thanks. I think."

"You just remind me of my sister."

Batting my eyelashes, I continue to banter. "She's beautiful and voluptuous, too, huh?"

"No. She's a bullshitter like you." He puts his arm around my shoulder and guides me away from the death machines, toward a room filled with—oh, shit. Those aren't just death machines. I think those came straight out of a torture chamber and are complete with buckles and straps and other things I have no idea what to do with. "Welcome to Weightlifting for Beginners."

Abel walks away to greet some other women who appear to be as apprehensive as I am. No, that's not right. They look like they've resolved themselves to their fate. While they chat, I look around the room, eyes wide.

The room is a giant square with ceilings that are at least forty feet high. The second floor isn't closed in. Instead there is a track going around the perimeter of the room. Awesome. So there will be witnesses. Oh, please don't let Carlos see this.

Not that it matters.

Because he's weird and I don't like him.

No. No, I don't.

Anyway, on one side of the wall, someone is holding a very heavy looking bar, squatting low to the floor. Nope. Not gonna do that.

On the other side of the room, people are dangling from some sort of contraption with their hands on the floor, pulling their knees to their chest. HA! Joke's on Abel. I can't even dangle.

In yet another area, there are people on row machines. Those I recognize. What I don't see is the beautiful outdoors and a placid lake to row on. Seriously, why would you row in a gym when you could be having a picnic on the water? People are weird.

Then I look to my right and have to force myself not to run away. I'm not sure what those things are called, but last time I went to Cirque du Soleil, some skinny girl in a fancy leotard was showing off her flexibility while hanging from one of those contraptions.

"There's no way you can get bored in here, right?" Of course, Abel is smiling. He's in his element and thinks this is "fun".

I point to the dangling contraptions. "I am not putting on sequins and hanging from that rope."

Abel throws his head back and lets out a belly laugh. "Don't worry, Rian. We're starting you out slow. We won't use the suspension bands today."

"Or ever."

"Or for a few weeks."

"I will strangle myself so fast and then where will you be, huh? Sitting in a courtroom, tremendous biceps restricted by a suit coat, with me suing your ass off."

He gives me that look I tend to get when I'm being ridiculous. Which I know I'm being but seriously. Who wants to twist themselves up in that thing only to fall and slam their head into the floor? Not me.

"You can't sue me if you're dead, so I'm not worried." He ignores me when I scoff. "Besides, you stay on the floor when you use them. But we don't have time for explanations. Let me introduce you to the others."

There are others? Just what I need. More people watching while I work out. *I wonder if Bambi still needs a treadmill partner...*

"Ladies, I want to introduce you to Rian. She's going to be joining us for the first time today." Drat. He's faster than me. Now that they know my name, I'm stuck here for the next hour. "Rian this is Dee and Morgan. They're my regulars."

"Nice to meet you," I say politely, despite feeling a tremendous amount of dread. Neither of them responds, just give me sort of a nod hello. I'm not sure if they've already decided they don't like me or if they're out of breath. The panting should be a giveaway, but frankly, there is a literal Bambi galloping on a treadmill right now. Anything is possible in this place.

"Have you already done your cardio warm up?" They both nod at Abel, still not saying anything but confirming my more logical suspicion. "Okay. Then let's do one set of front lunges down and back followed by side lunges. Each side, for a totally of six laps."

That doesn't seem too hard. Lunges are just bending your knees a little more than normal when you walk, right?

Wrong.

So wrong.

So, so wrong.

I've taken one step and I'm already having a hard time getting back up. My new workout partners are already halfway across the room and I'm stuck one step in. Literally stuck. It's like my muscles have thrown themselves down imitating my childhood dog, Barry, when he was done on his walk. He would just plop himself down wherever we were and refused to get up. We had to carry him home every time. German Shepherds are heavy when they're dead weight.

That's what my legs are doing right now. They've called it quits and are refusing to move like my dead weight dog. Except there's no picking myself up and carrying me the rest of the way. Nope. I'm just going to fall over and lie on this floor, pretending I passed out while I wait for my humiliation subside.

Suddenly, a warm, strong hand grips my arm. Damn that Abel for being hot and married.

"Don't lunge so low. We're just trying to get your muscles warmed up, not workout yet."

"I'm not sure six laps *is* realistic for me."

He shoots me a smile as he watches my not-quite-as-lungy walk, just in case I try to fall over again. "I believe in you. Even if those six laps take you all hour."

I stick my tongue out at him because I know he's telling the truth. Damn his sister for making him immune to my half-hearted attempts at quitting before I begin.

Surprisingly, six laps don't take as long as I anticipate. It's amazing how much faster you can go when you're not stuck in the downward position. But it also gave me time to look around and observe the other patrons. It kind of surprises me that no one is smiling. Well, unless they're resting. I'm pretty sure I'll be happy, too, when I'm in the stop position. But maybe I'm not the only one here because I have to be, not because I want to be.

Except for Bambi, of course. I'm not sure I'll ever understand what her motivation is if she's not accomplishing something. But then again, I've got no room to judge.

Finishing my laps, I watch the other ladies in my class. I'm far enough behind them that they've already started with the workout portion of the program. Not that anyone else can tell. Sweat is sweat whether it comes from the warm-up or the actual hard part, so at least I fit in.

"You feel warm? Ready to work?" Once again, Abel has a giant smile on his face.

"Are you always this smiley when you torture people?"

"Always. It makes me happy to see others in pain."

Crossing my arms over my sweaty chest, I give him my best glare. It's not easy with sweat in your eyes. Nor while forcing my hands not to lift up each boob and wipe the sweat from underneath, but I give myself an A for effort. "You're a bit of a masochist."

"And you're a bit of a procrastinator. Enough talking. Let's do this." I need to up my game around him. He's too good at bullshitting.

Pointing to the white board attached to the wall, he starts explaining what all the scribble means.

"We're going to do some circuits today. Nothing fancy. Just some exercises to get your muscles moving. I've written everything down so you can refer back to it, but I'll explain it all. Follow me over here." I obey, which is so unlike me, but I admit he has me curious. I've always been stronger than I look so maybe weights will end up being my thing. A girl can hope anyway.

We stop next to one of the walls. There are several medicine balls sitting on the floor. They look almost identical to the ones we used to use in elementary school P.E. I'll chalk that up as ego boost number two... I was the master of medicine balls. They were fun to play with.

Abel scoops one of the balls up like it weighs next to nothing. "This is a really easy exercise once you've got the coordination down. But it's really great for your glutes, your quads, your shoulders, and your core."

Impressive. No wonder ten-year-old me was stronger than I looked.

Positioning himself facing the wall, Abel squats down and bends his arms. "Keep your legs apart, squat low, and as you come up," he shoots up and throws the ball against the wall, catching it as it falls, "toss the ball on the wall. Do fifteen reps. This is not a speed exercise so don't focus on going fast. Just complete them all. Sound good?"

I nod because really. How hard can that be?

"Good. Follow me over here."

I do as commanded and we walk to a different area. The only thing here is a really ugly stool. Immediately, I lean against it. A sitting exercise sounds right up my alley. Sit and Be Fit is popular for a reason, right? Abel, of course, laughs.

"Nice try. That stool isn't for sitting."

"All stools are for sitting."

"Not this one. Watch."

I move aside and to my horror, he jumps from the floor to the top of the stool.

"Uhh..." I stutter. "There is no way I'm getting this body off this floor and onto that stool unless we go back to its original purpose, which is sitting."

He just shakes his head, clearly still amused by me. I'm beginning to think he wasn't kidding when he said he enjoys people's pain. "I know. That's why I have a shorter one for you." He leans down and pulls over one of those plastic step aerobics benches with a bunch of risers underneath. "The goal is to eventually be able to jump on that stool. It's there for your motivational purposes."

I snort a laugh. He has no idea how lack-of-motivated I can be.

"You are going to use this one so we can get your muscles used to the movement. It's a lot lower but will still have the same effect."

"But if I miss, the whole thing will fall apart."

"And then you'll put it back together."

"But it'll be loud, and everyone will know."

"Then don't miss."

I cross my arms again, trying to ignore the boob sweat again. "You're not very nice."

"Then I've done my job."

"You sound like my mother when I was a teenager."

"I have a seven-year-old daughter. I've been perfecting my dad lines."

Sighing, I decide giving up and exercising is less effort than this conversation. "Fine. What's next?"

His eyes light up. Sadist. "Two more." He leads me to a couple of yoga mats on the floor. "Crunches. See how Dee is doing them?"

My new workout partner, who I have yet to genuinely work out with, is lying on the mat with a small weight bar above her head. As she brings her upper body to a sitting position, the bar stays over her head.

"I hate to be a buzzkill—" I begin.

"No, you don't," he replies.

"You got me. But I don't know that I can do a crunch without the bar, let alone with one."

He picks one up off the floor and hands it to me. "That's the beauty of these. They're made specifically for this kind of exercise. Use it to help you balance. If you move it just the right way, your core muscles will be working hard, but the bar will help pull you up."

Sounds hard and potentially disastrous, but I admit I'm curious to try.

"Last but not least—"

Oh, god. There's still more. There are only three of us. How is there more?

"Battle ropes."

I look at the long black ropes attached to some weird contraption that appears portable. That makes me a little nervous, but there are so many weights on top of it, it probably won't go anywhere. I don't think I have *that* much strength.

Abel picks up the ropes to demonstrate. "When you grab them, I want you to keep your legs apart and bend your knees. You're going to be using a lot of back muscles and we don't want to pull any of them."

I shrug, not seeing what the big deal is. It's a rope. How hard can it be?

"I want fluid motions when you lift the rope to eye level," Abel demonstrates while talking me through the motion, "and then slam it down on the floor." He goes through the motion several times, making it look easy. And loud. Very, very loud.

As he drops the ropes, he adds, "Got any questions?"

"Yes. Why did you pick an exercise that would draw the most attention to me, in noise alone?"

Without skipping a beat, he says, "If you know people are looking, you'll hold your form better."

"Seriously?"

"No. it's a total coincidence. But I was ready for some sort of complaint, so I'm really on my one-liner game today."

"Pffft..." I strut toward the ropes, confident in my rope-slamming abilities. "Joke's on you, mister. I'm gonna hold this form so good, you won't even know how to make it a real exercise for me."

I see the look on his face. He doesn't believe me. "I'm gonna time you. Keep a consistent speed for thirty seconds."

"Just say when."

He looks at his watch and presses a button. "Aaaaand….. when."

Lifting the rope and slamming it down, the first thing I notice is this is not the same kind of rope we used to climb in gym class. It's much heavier than it looks. I also notice that it doesn't matter if Abel is timing me—I'm still counting how many times this rope hits the floor.

Six, Seven, Eight...

The numbers continue in my head when Abel yells, "Ten seconds!"

"Left or finished?" My breathing has turned into panting now.

"You have twenty seconds left. Well, fifteen now."

Internally, I groan. I change my mind. I don't want to do this one anymore.

I feel the boob sweat sliding down my stomach into places there shouldn't be liquid. I have decided I pegged Abel correctly. He is well and truly a sociopath. There is no other explanation for this.

"Am I done yet?" I yell, using my last remaining breath.

"Ten more seconds."

"You need…" pant, "…to get…" pant, "…your watch checked…"

Abel laughs. Laughs! The jerk. But just as I think I'm going to fall over, he yells, "Time!"

I immediately drop the rope and find a wall to lean on, trying desperately to suck in some air.

"See?" Abel says cheerfully. "That wasn't so bad, was it?"

I. Am going. To die.

CHAPTER EIGHT

CARLOS

For years, people asked me if I was sad that I was the last single man among my family and friends. When I told them no, they would get odd looks on their faces. It happened every time. It was a cross between disbelief that I truly felt this way and pity that I would be so torn up about it that I would feel compelled to lie and pretend I was okay.

Not one of them ever cared to understand that I really was fine being the last man standing. My bachelorhood isn't something I resigned myself to the closer I got to forty because I never found "the one". No, my relationship status was the result of my own selfless desire to never trick a woman into thinking I'm something I'm not. I'm a gentleman that way.

What I am not, however, is a one-woman man. I have no desire for marriage. No desire to ever have kids. No desire to compromise my vacation plans, stop star-fishing when I sleep, or cook for two.

None.

I like my lifestyle but I also don't want to disrespect anyone by pretending I can give them what they want. And I don't want to waste their time on me when who they're looking for is out there somewhere.

Judging by how many of those friends and family who gave me

looks of disbelief and/or pity are now in divorce court and saddled with years of alimony, I'd say I'm not on the only one who feels this way. I'm just the only one who was honest with myself and everyone else years ago. I knew what I wanted way back then and never tried to convince myself otherwise in the name of "everyone is doing it". Now, it seems, they wanted the same things, too. They just never had the guts to admit it to anyone, including themselves.

My lack of baggage comes in handy for many reasons. Not the least of which is the edge I have in the dating world. I am a fantastic companion, and I know it. Especially compared to guys like that poor schmuck sitting at the end of the bar. He's obviously waiting for his rendezvous to begin, probably with someone he met online and hasn't seen before. The glances around the room and frequent checks of his phone are a dead giveaway.

Unfortunately, whoever he is waiting for is going to have some heavy suitcases to help this poor guy carry. He's drinking straight tequila, which tells me he's after self-medication and not enjoying the finer pleasures in life. The bags under his eyes indicate he hasn't caught up on his sleep after weekend visitation with his kids. And the redness in his eyes tell me those kids aren't the only reason he has sleepless nights. He probably lies in bed, wide-awake, wondering how he's going to be able to provide for his children and maintain his shithole apartment.

This is what happens when men lie to themselves about what they really want in life.

On the contrary, I'm sipping on an Old Fashioned because I have no reason to dilute the world around me. My eyes are bright and clear from getting enough rest, exercising regularly, and eating right. My bank account is solidly in the black and growing at a steady rate.

All because I never disillusioned myself into thinking I'm something I'm not. Or that I want things I don't just because they're culturally popular. Millennials caught onto the same benefits faster than Gen X ever did. I predict they have much happier futures in store than people I grew up with.

The door to the outside opens and a stunning redhead walks into the restaurant. She's wearing a tight green dress that shows off her ample cleavage. The dress is scrunched on the side showing off her hourglass shape and stops mid-thigh to reveal long, tone legs topped off with black strappy stilettos.

She's no Rian, but those heels will still look fabulous wrapped around my waist tonight. Although I'm not sure why Rian just popped into my head. I've only met the woman once, and while I enjoyed talking to her, she's not my type at all.

Focus, Carlos. Your date is here and she's a knockout.

Out of the corner of my eye, I see the wanker on the other side of the bar straighten up, hoping this is who he's waiting for. Fortunately for me, I know she's my date for the evening. Nick showed me her picture when he set me up.

Marley moved into Nick's building a few months ago. She's apparently been to his apartment a few times to hang out, whatever that means, and he says she's exactly the kind of woman I need in my life. So far, he's right.

She looks around the room for a few seconds until she spots me, and then a wide grin crosses her perfect face. She is quite possibly the woman of my dreams. My very shallow, very vain dreams.

I stand as she steps gracefully down the stairs and crosses the room to where I'm waiting. It doesn't go unnoticed that my single buddy, whom I've never met, visibly deflates when he realizes he's not the man she's looking for.

It's better this way for them both. He could never keep a woman like her happy, and she... well, I have a hard time believing she's ready to sacrifice her obviously impeccable taste to make sure his kids can continue in gymnastics lessons.

"Carlos?" she asks, her voice as stunning as the rest of her, as she approaches.

"You must be Marley."

If it's possible, her smile grows even bigger. The things I could do with that mouth...

"I'm sorry I'm a little late." I gesture to the stool next to mine and we sit. "I got caught up at work, and that of course made me miss my train."

"Those trains always have a way of closing their doors right as you come running up to the platform."

She laughs deeply and the sound makes my cock twitch. "That's exactly what happened. I swear it does it to me on purpose. But the silver lining is I'm getting really good at running in heels."

"You definitely have the calves to prove it," I add seductively, glancing down at her legs.

She doesn't react with a giggle or a wink like I'm expecting based on Nick's recommendation. Instead she grabs a drink menu and glances over it muttering, "What should I drink?"

Hmm. Interesting. I expected a little more flirting to start the evening, but it's only been a few seconds since she got here. I must be reading her wrong. Despite his very busy schedule recently, Nick's been my wingman regularly for a few years now, so he knows the kind of woman I'm after.

Beautiful.

Ready to scratch an itch and that's it.

Ditzy is not a deal breaker.

I flag down the bartender so Marley can order a drink. She chooses rum and Coke, which tells me she likes a good spirit as much as I do. Another interesting tidbit. Usually women like her order something like a cosmo or strawberry daiquiri. That tells me she's not like the usual women I date. I can't help but wonder if Nick pegged her all wrong or if I'm missing something.

While we wait for our reservation, which I scheduled for a short time after we arrived, we chat about the chances of a World Series bid for the Cubs and a funny article about a series of pranks pulled on the artist who designed the Bean. I had no idea he despises the nickname for his artwork, but after hearing about what an egomaniac he supposedly is, I'm not sure I care what he thinks of it.

The conversation puts me at ease and confirms that Marley is, in fact, everything I go for in a short-term relationship. And by short-term, I mean one night. Maybe two on a long weekend. But never more than that. What would be the point? If we're both here for mutual pleasure and a bit of companionship, there's no reason to ruin that.

"So, Carlos, Nick tells me you work in security." She takes another sip of her drink, then licks her red lips suggestively.

I watch the movement closely before answering. "He's partially right. I work at a security company, but I'm the Chief Operations Officer, so I'm over the back end of the business."

"So, you're the boss. Sounds like a lot of work."

"It is. But I love what I do. I get to make sure all parts of the company are working like a well-oiled machine. From HR to training, accounting and payroll, it all falls under me. I've got my hand in a lot of pots, but I like it that way."

"Doesn't sound like that leaves a lot of room for the people in your life."

I barely catch myself before furrowing my brow. Why is she worried about how much time I have for other people? Usually my dates are impressed by the fact that I'm the boss and probably make lots of money. Quickly, I brush off my initial reaction. I'm sure this is just her way of having small talk. I'll just need to be careful that she's not the overly sensitive type. If so, she only gets one night. Two would cause her too much heartache.

"It just takes some balance," I finally reply. "But isn't that what life is all about? Balancing work with pleasure?" I know I'm being suggestive, but from the way her cheeks redden ever so slightly and her breathing hitches, I think she's got the same ideas as I do. Still, there's no reason to rush. We haven't even made it to our table yet.

"And what, pray tell, does Carlos Davies do for pleasure? Besides eating at authentic French restaurants." She looks around the room as she speaks. "Speaking of which, thanks for suggesting this place. I love the feel in here."

"I'm glad you like it. And we haven't even gotten to the best part yet. Just wait until they call us to the back. It's been one of my favorite hidden gems for a while."

"Do you eat out a lot?"

"Not a lot. I'm a health nut, so I usually stick to clean eating. But being a single, childless man, I don't have a lot of responsibility outside the office. That affords me the opportunity to indulge myself every once in a while." Leaning in, I add, "Especially if I'm entertaining a beautiful woman."

She blushes again but doesn't make any other moves. No hands on the chest. No twirling of the hair. Nothing. Another odd reaction.

When Nick suggested I go out with Marley, he said she was new to the area and exactly the kind of woman I needed. I have no idea if that meant he wasn't interested himself or any relationship they had had already run its course. But I wasn't about to ask. The information would have been irrelevant anyway. He knows I like slim build, large breasts, tone legs, and no commitment. And I don't stray from my type. Why mess with a tried-and-true standard?

Before she has a chance to respond to my flirtation, the host, who presents himself more like a maitrê d', approaches.

"Pardon me, sir, ma'am." He nods politely at both of us. "Your table is ready if you would like to follow me this way."

We finish our drinks and I leave a generous tip on the counter before following him to a back room that is the restaurant portion of the building. If you didn't know this was both a restaurant and a bar, you would assume the front room is the only part, but it's not. Through a single door in the back is a narrow hallway that leads to an entirely separate room. It's reserved for the more high-end customers, and if you don't make a reservation, you aren't getting in. But I've lived here long enough and know the right people to be privy to this kind of intel.

As we tuck into our chairs and the host leaves us, Marley's excitement seems to build. "I guess tourists won't find this on any 'must visit' list or a Big Bus Tour, will they?"

"No, this place is known only to locals and only by word of mouth."

"I can see why. You wouldn't want to ruin the ambiance by having a rush of travelers in here."

Our waiter approaches and we put in drink orders—another Old Fashioned for me, a glass of lemon water for her. It takes him just a few more seconds to hand us menus, recite the specials for the day, and leave us to decide on our meal.

"Everything looks so good here," Marley remarks after a few seconds of silence. "I'm not sure I'll be able to decide. I'm already torn between the *Bœuf bourguignon* or the *Jambon persillé*."

The words roll off her tongue like she's a native French speaker. "You must have taken some French in school to be able to pronounce things so fluidly."

Her eyes glance up at me from over her menu and she smiles. "I majored in French actually, and studied abroad for two semesters before getting a job at the French consulate office in Houston. I've always wanted to live in Chicago, though, so when the opportunity came up, I jumped on it."

Suddenly, I have a sinking feeling Marley isn't the kind of woman I date. Intellectual typically means expectations, which would explain her lack of reaction at certain suggestive conversations. What is Nick up to?

"So, you're bilingual?"

"Trilingual. I minored in Spanish. It's practically a national language in the US, so I know I'll use it at some point."

I have a bad feeling I'm not getting laid tonight. This is not how my evening was supposed to go. Yes, Marley is built like a Barbie doll, but she has goals and aspirations. She has drive and motivation. She speaks three languages for Christ's sake. That means she likely has higher standards than just a one-night stand.

"But you use your French regularly? Are you a translator?"

Please say yes. Please say yes. Please say yes....

Marley's eyes light up as she lowers her menu, and I know she's about to gush about her job. This isn't good at all. The women I date hate their jobs and have daddy issues. Self-confidence and morally sound are not conducive for a little extra kink in my night.

"I'm an economics officer. I help identify economic opportunities for the US, specifically to the regions in and around France. And I help a little with bilateral trade negotiations."

"I'm guessing you have a business degree as well."

She smiles again. "Economics. It was my second major."

And there goes my opportunity to get laid. I have no interest in dating smart, motivated women. There is nothing wrong with any of those things. Hell, I'm friends with plenty of dynamic women. But friendship is where this must stay.

Dammit. I've been friend-zoned by my own convictions.

Which is why I don't know what angle Nick is playing at. All I know is he and I are going to have words about this on the next leg day. Maybe I'll add a few more reps just to be a dick. Lord knows he deserves it.

CHAPTER NINE

RIAN

"Ow."

Step.

"Ow."

Step.

"Ow."

Step.

Every time my foot touches the floor it feels like my entire body catches fire. I should have known when I threw the medicine ball so hard it bounced behind me and knocked Dee over like a bowling pin, it was time to stop. But did I? No. No, I did not. Stubborn Rian came out to play and decided weightlifting is her niche.

Stubborn Rian will now be going by the name Idiotic Rian.

Ignoring Francesca, who is staring at me, I try to gently lower myself into the chair at her table in the break room. Unfortunately, my arms are having nothing to do with this and they give out, so I end up plopping down instead, which doesn't do my glutes any favors. I have no idea how I'm going to get back up later.

"What's the matter with you?"

"My new trainer was the headmaster of a torture chamber in a previous life."

"What?"

"Nothing. I just worked out too hard yesterday. What's for lunch?"

She opens the lid of the Tupperware and lets me peek inside. "Taco soup. Lots of shredded chicken and beans and vegetables. Low on carbs."

It smells so good and it's not even warmed up yet. I think I've officially hit starvation mode after this much exercise. "Good. I read somewhere that protein is supposed to help your muscles recover."

"Have you tried yoga?"

I give her an incredulous look. "You mean bending myself into a pretzel? No. No one wants to see that."

I try to push myself to a standing position so I can satisfy my growling stomach, but suddenly starving sounds like a better option than moving. Next time, I'm making someone roll me around on my office chair.

Better yet, next time I'll throw the medicine ball at Abel's smug little happy face.

"Give me that." Francesca snatches the bowl I had the foresight to bring with me out of my hands. "I'll heat it up for you."

I sigh in relief. "You're an angel. A beautiful, food-bringing angel."

She looks at me like I've lost my marbles. Which I may have. Suspicious behavior number one is that I keep going back to the gym. "Seriously, though. Yoga will help you stretch out your muscles, so you aren't as sore."

"I'm not sticking my ass in the air in a roomful of people. Especially with all the Mexican food we've been eating lately."

She rolls her eyes. "So, find some bland recipes. I'm sure baked chicken and broccoli is on the list."

I gasp at the suggestion. Now she's just being mean for fun.

"Oh, don't look at me like that."

"The whole point of sharing cooking duties is so we don't always eat bland poultry and... and little trees."

The microwave beeps and she pulls the bowl out, stirring it before putting it back in. I don't know what it is about someone else making your lunch, but even the way she stirs makes it look more appetizing than anything I could make.

And I've officially sunk to a new low.

Turning to lean against the counter, she crosses her arms over her chest. "So then look up some clean eating recipes. There are a ton out there that don't take much effort. I'm going to try this crock pot beef and broccoli I found on my next cook day."

"Ohmygod, I love Chinese food." I lick my lips, praying I don't drool on the table. "I'll even suffer through eating more little trees if you bring me that beef."

"That's all it takes to get you to eat veggies? Some beef?"

"I'm not ashamed!"

She holds her hands up defensively. "Down, girl. I know you're hungry, but we only have," she turns to look at the clock on the microwave, "thirty-four more seconds until lunch is ready."

I sigh and try to lay my forehead on the table. The shooting pain in my shoulders tells me I can't stretch that way today. Really, I can't stretch any which way. Or sit. Or stand. Or walk. Basically, anything beyond being in a coma is painful at this point.

"I'm sorry for being snappy. But you don't need to worry. I can't stand up anyway so you're safe from my wrath."

"That's because you don't do yoga," she singsongs.

"Ugh, you aren't going to let that go, are you?"

"It's literally the only exercise I'll do."

The microwave dings and she turns to pull out our soup. The smell wafts my direction making my mouth water again. For as much as I want that beef, today's lunch is going to hit the spot. I already know it.

Francesca brings over the Tupperware and uses a random ladle she found in the drawer, probably left over from the last office potluck, to dish out servings for each of us. I know I'm staring way too intently at the food, but I can't help it. There's chicken and corn and beans in it. And chopped tomatoes! And when she sprinkles shredded cheese on top, I want to cry for joy. This is a taco lover's dream meal in a bowl.

"You know how creepy it is that you're staring at our lunch like you want to kiss it, right?"

"Yep. I am fully aware of that."

"Ok, just checking."

She places a bowl of steaming soup in front of me, a little bit spilling over the side. Quickly licking her thumb, she makes her own bowl before continuing our conversation. It doesn't go unnoticed that she took care of me first before taking care of herself. I have a newfound love for my friend and her understanding of how hangry I can get.

"So anyway, yoga."

I groan in response, and then immediately moan in appreciation when the taco goodness hits my tongue. This might be the best meal I've ever had in my entire life. Except for National Donut Day when I had a chocolate-covered, custard-filled donut for lunch. That was probably better. But this is damn good.

"This is really good, Francesca."

"Stop avoiding the topic."

I roll my eyes. I don't know why she's pushing this. "Not everyone is bendy, Fran."

"Francesca."

"I know. But if you're going to annoy me, I'm going to annoy you."

She sticks her tongue out at me playfully before taking another bite. "You don't have to go if you don't want. I just know the stretching helps your muscles recover faster and you get to lie down during part of it. I always fall asleep."

This is news to me. "You get nap time during yoga?" Maybe she's onto something. Napping is my kind of workout.

"That's not what it's called. It has a different name, but I don't remember what." She wipes her hands on her napkin and chews for a second. "I'm sure there's some actual benefit, too, but all I know is I doze off, which definitely centers me."

Taking another big bite, I take a moment to enjoy the spicy goodness in my mouth. For someone who says she hates to cook, Francesca really does have a knack for it. I'm going to need to step up my cooking game if she's going to make me a real cuisine several times a week.

I bet I can find a few recipes this afternoon. The phones have been relatively quiet today and I'm caught up on all my paperwork. I probably shouldn't even be thinking that. The universe seems to be able to hear my thoughts and I have jinxed myself into having terrible afternoons more than once. But if she's too busy wreaking havoc on other people today, maybe I can find something interesting to make.

Crap. That means I have to stop to get the ingredients tonight. Hobbling around the grocery store, even if I'm leaning against the cart doesn't sound like fun. I wonder how many people would stare or make ugly comments to me if I used one of those motorized carts.

Probably not a good idea. My luck, I'd accidentally drive it into a display, knock everything over, and still end up walking to get help, which completely defeats the purpose. It's best to stick to hobbling.

Sadly, the idea of going to the grocery store, plus the promise of a nap during exercise, is the only reason I have a teeny, tiny inkling of curiosity about this yoga thing. So tiny I'm not sure if it's that or pending heartburn from eating too fast.

"Fine," I finally say with a sigh. "I'll talk to my trainer about yoga."

Her eyes light up as she looks at me. "You were serious? You're working with a trainer?"

I'm not sure how to answer this question. Her friendship indicates she's just curious. Her facial expression, however, is more like a woman on the prowl. I'm sure Abel doesn't need another stalker. I've seen the way some of the women at the gym look at him. He's probably got plenty. "Yeeeeees...." I say slowly and cautiously.

"Is he cute?"

I nod and her face shows even more delight. I need to stop this before it goes any further. "And he's married."

She immediately deflates. "I knew it. All the good ones are taken."

"All the good what?"

Francesca and I both bristle at the sound of his voice. Although, I'm honestly surprised we didn't smell Nolan before he came in the room. He must have run out of Axe while bathing in it this morning. He'll never smell as good as Carlos, though. Not that I care, or anything. I don't even really like Carlos, but his fresh, manly scent hasn't been forgotten. I could get used to a man like that. Without the ego and narcissism, of course.

Catching Francesca's eyes, I blow an over-exaggerated, centering breath out, hoping she'll do the same before she loses the cool she tries very hard to hold onto whenever Nolan is in the room. She doesn't catch my cues, though, so I quietly say, "Namaste."

"Bless you."

I glance over at Nolan. "I'm sorry?"

He finishes making his coffee and turns to lean against the counter. Oh, good. He's planning to stay a while.

"You sneezed."

"No, I didn't."

"Hmm," he says as he takes a sip from his cup. It's clear he doesn't really care whether I sneezed or not. Which means he has some sort of motivation for being here. Immediately that puts me on high alert right along with Francesca.

The longer we sit in silence, the more curious I become, which I kind of hate about myself. I don't want to be curious about anything Nolan has to say. I've made that mistake in the past and one of two things is generally the outcome—I genuinely don't care, and it's wasted my time; or it makes me mad.

Apparently, I'm a glutton for punishment though, because I'm the first to cave.

"So, what's up, Nolan?" The question elicits a kick under the table from my so-called friend.

"Fred Paterson turned in his retirement notice today."

Welp, it appears the universe does, in fact, read my thoughts. My day has just gone downhill so fast, it will be a miracle if I don't burst into flames from the impact.

Fred Paterson is the department manager. He's been here longer than anyone else in the building and he's a fantastic boss—the kind of man who knows every employee's name and takes time to ask about their kids. His wife even makes Hanukkah/Christmas/Kwanzaa cookies every year and takes the time to individually wrap each one for hygiene purposes. And yes, she makes sure she equally represents all three holidays, so no one feels left out.

The cookies and his demeanor almost make up for the fact that Fred is slightly sexist. Not in an infuriating "women should be barefoot and pregnant and can't do the job" kind of way. More like a "your ankles look lovely in those stilettos" kind of way. Seriously, who notices people's ankles on the regular? A guy with a foot fetish that's who. I bet his eBay handle is *FeetAreLife,* and he's the guy who offered me sixty bucks for my used pink flats. Eighty, if I made sure they were extra stinky.

And yes, I sold them to *FeetAreLife* because, come on. Eighty bucks for my used shoes? What you do with them in private is none of my business while I spend that money.

While I'm not necessarily offended by the ankle comments in the office, I'm also not stupid enough to think it doesn't indicate a bigger problem. Namely, gender inequality. I'm positive the fact I was practically born wearing a bra is why I was passed up for the supervisor role. Nolan got it instead. That one stung. Fred said it was because of my experience level, but Nolan was hired months after me, and his sales numbers weren't as good. I was encouraged to apply again the next time a position opens up, which I plan to. But it's still frustrating that I know my gender is the reason I didn't get that job. I just can't prove it. The only evidence is that I've never once seen Fred compliment a man on his ankles or his suit or his new haircut. Well, except when Roger in IT went from having long, blond, rock star hair to a buzz cut. We didn't recognize him at first. It took the security office almost a week to stop checking his ID whenever he walked through the building.

So, while I'm frustrated with that sexist attitude, I focus on the fact that Fred is more like a grandpa type character to everyone here. He's always kind and considerate, and considering he's pushing ninety, I choose to focus on those qualities instead of his flaws. Fred leaving is going to be hard on everyone. He knows everything that happens in this office and makes sure everyone is treated with a certain amount of respect. If Nolan were to somehow step into his position, not only could I kiss any attempts at moving up in the company goodbye, the entire culture would change. "Slightly sexist" would be a thing of the past. "Obviously passive-aggressive" would be the new norm.

The only thing I can do in response to this information is gulp. Loudly. Francesca must understand my hesitation because she's finally the one who responds first.

"When's his last day?" She shoves a bite of soup in her mouth, seemingly unaffected by Nolan's news. I know her better than that, though. The soup is just a way to keep herself from saying something that could have repercussions.

He takes another sip, prolonging his answer, probably for fun. Making sure all eyes are on him, which means only the two of us, but that doesn't matter to him as long as he has a captive audience, he says, "Six weeks. Just enough time to move someone into his position and get them trained."

Gotta love Francesca. While I'm practically frozen in place, and this time it's not because my sore muscles are revolting, she's acting like nothing Nolan is telling us is a big deal. Like our work lives are not about to be turned upside down. I'm all about people getting promotions and all, but no one needs a passive-aggressive boss. It's just not good for morale or my ability to control my emotional eating habits.

Wiping her lips with her napkin, she finally adds, "I heard Fred talking about interviewing some outside candidates the other day. I guess that makes sense now. Wouldn't want to promote internally for a job like that."

Nolan's face freezes. "Why not? We have great internal candidates."

"Too many morale issues," she says without skipping a beat. "Can you imagine how people would turn on each other? It would be like the *Hunger Games* around here."

"The what?"

She looks at him quizzically. "The *Hunger Games*?"

He continues to give her a blank stare.

"Dystopian book series turned into movies?"

More blank stares.

"Jennifer Lawrence as Katniss?"

That's when it finally clicks. "Oh, yeah! I loved her in *The Jeff Foxworthy Show.*"

Francesca laughs through her nose quietly. "Of course, you did."

"What?"

"Just a tickle in my throat." Seriously. I don't know how this woman can run circles around Nolan and he never catches on. "Anyway, I hear the first candidate is coming in sometime this week to interview. I'm sure Fred could give you the schedule."

Nolan clears his throat. "Yeah. Yeah, I know." He shifts uncomfortably and tosses his now empty cup in the trash. "Anyway. I just thought you should know Fred's retirement is coming up soon."

"Okay, thanks." She takes another bite and goes back to ignoring him. After a few seconds, he either takes the hint or can't stand not being in the know and bolts out of the room.

I turn to look at my co-worker. I can feel my eyes are still wide. "This isn't good, Francesca."

She shakes her head. "Not at all."

Then something occurs to me. "Wait, is Fred really looking to hire from outside?"

She shrugs. "No idea. But it got Nolan all ruffled, so at least it buys us a few minutes to figure out what we need to do now."

She's brilliant when it comes to Nolan, but she's wrong when it comes to us. We already know what we need to do. We need to update our resumes and fast. The office environment is about to get tense.

Looks like my recipe search will have to wait until later. Damn that universe always thwarting my plans.

CHAPTER TEN

CARLOS

Nick didn't show up to work out today, so I'm left to do leg day on my own. Thankfully, the assisted squatting bar isn't being used by a class today, so I can safely get in my workout without a spotter.

I'm not upset at all. I'm kind of glad for the time to think. And to be honest, I'm not all that surprised either. Besides his inconsistency lately because of "work", or so he claims, there is a possibility he's avoiding me as well. That's typically what happens when someone is bitched out by text.

The day after my date with Marley, I made sure to let Nick know how unhappy I was that he set me up with someone who isn't my type at all. It was a total dick move, and the entire thing was a waste of both of our time.

Yes, Marley is beautiful. Yes, she has a banging body. But that's where my interest in her ends. She's smart and witty and goal oriented. Not at all the kind of woman I want.

More important, I'm not the kind of guy she wants. That's really what it boils down to—honesty. There is no reason to make her think I'm looking for a relationship. I'm not, and I don't want to disappoint anyone by pretending otherwise. My interests in women are three-fold:

1. Holidays and visits with my mother.
2. Acquaintanceship and fun conversation with co-workers.
3. One night of pleasure with anyone else who may catch my eye.

I draw a hard line at anyone who wanders outside those boundaries. And Marley, as charming as she was, is someone who needs a strong, self-assured man who thinks she's dynamic and wants to partner with her to help her succeed.

So, when the night ended, I thanked for her an interesting evening, explained why Nick won't be starting his own matchmaking business anytime soon, and shook her hand. Then traded business cards with her, of course.

She may not be my type, but if I know my boss well enough, at some point I'll need information that only a consulate officer can provide. By the same token, she may run into a former French military operative who needs an employment excuse to stay in the states. Neither of us was upset about the situation enough to miss the potential advantages to keeping each other's business numbers handy.

Wiping my face with a towel and resting before moving onto the sled machine, I look around the open space, assessing the other patrons. I ignore the men and the trainers. I'm sure they're all nice people, but not who I'm looking for.

I focus on the women. There's a very pregnant woman walking slowly on the treadmill. "Pregnant" either means married or looking for a baby daddy. Moving on...

An elderly woman is flipping through a magazine while peddling on the recumbent bikes. Maybe if I was fifty years older...

Rian is talking animatedly to a trainer. Abel is his name, I think. She's not who I was looking for, but I'm not turning away either. I've seen her around a couple of times since dinner and she's funny. She always looks like she wants to clock her trainer. It's entertaining. Thinking about it makes me smile...

Then the woman I was looking for walks by. There. The woman

Nick hit on a few weeks ago. Blonde, big boobs, wears nothing but a sports bra. She leaves it all hanging out for everyone to see. That's the kind of woman I go for. One who shares my appreciation for the human body and all the pleasure it can give and receive.

My eyes, though, they gravitate back to Rian who appears to be threatening Abel with a medicine ball. I chuckle quietly when he rolls his eyes, snatches it out of her hands, and slams it on the floor, startling her. She wasn't expecting her next exercise to require her to spike a medicine ball.

Wait... she's not who I'm supposed to be watching. I force my gaze back to the woman I was waiting for and watch for a few seconds as she climbs on the hyperextension bench to do some lower back work. As she bends over and flexes into the upright position, I can't help but admire her shoulders. A lot of women let those muscles go, but she doesn't. They're just as tight as the rest of her.

Which reminds me, I have a leg workout to finish. Sighing at my lack of focus, I put my hands on the sled, use all my strength and push. It takes a few seconds for it to get going, but soon, I'm using all my leg power to move it across the room and back. I hate this exercise, but it's fantastic for the glutes, hamstrings, and calves. I give the sled full credit for my not having chicken legs. It also gives me a chance to channel my irritation at Nick. If he hadn't set me up on that bad date, I wouldn't be so distracted by the one I shouldn't want.

Don't want. I don't want her. That's what I mean.

Lost in my thoughts about work, women, and life, the sled goes quickly and soon enough it's time for my post-exercise dinner—a chocolate protein shake with greens, flax seeds, and a banana to replenish my sugars. Low on calories and high in protein, it's my treat for a job well done.

Sliding up to the counter of the smoothie bar, Tabitha glances up from her blender and gives me a nod in greeting. She can't hear me while that thing blends, so there's not a reason to say anything.

Tabitha and I clicked immediately when I first started coming here. She's been working at Weight Expectations for longer than most of the trainers. She used to work as a bartender but got sick of the hours, and when this job opened up, it fit exactly what she needed. She gets to sleep at night, which she says helped tremendously while raising a teenage boy on her own. Plus, she was out of the bar scene. There is no mistake she can hold her own. She's not one to mince words, and I could see her pulling out a baseball bat if she needed to. But from what she says, she was tired of the nightlife. Tired of people drowning their sorrows in booze. Tired of keeping an eye out for predators. Tired of having to look over her shoulder when she locked up.

Here, she gets to do what she does best—chat with her customers and make them drinks to lift their spirits. In this case, though, the spirits are already partially lifted from endorphins. The rest is just because she enjoys her job.

"Your regular?" she asks me after checking out the last customer.

"You know it."

Tabitha begins doling out the ingredients and throwing them into the blender jar. It still blows my mind that she doesn't need recipes. She's done this for so long it's like second nature to her.

So is getting into my business. "I heard you had a hot date last night."

Like I said, always in my business. Clearly, word travels fast around here, and I'm not surprised she's already caught wind of it. I'm just a little stumped by who told her.

"How did you find out?"

She gives me a look like she'll never tell and quickly secures the jar into the base, turning it on instead of answering.

It's short lived, though. Thirty seconds later she's pouring my drink into a plastic cup and securing the lid for me. "One of my regulars saw you. I don't know if he was working there or dining. He's not one I go out of my way to remember."

Opening my straw, I shove it into my cup and take a long pull. I taste chocolate, banana, and a hint of cinnamon. Just the way I like it. "That's not very nice, Tabitha," I chide after swallowing. "He just wants to be your friend."

"Yeah, well, he's an annoying friend. He needs to work out more and take up space at my bar less."

I shake my head at her, pretending to be shocked by her behavior. "Tsk, tsk. I thought you loved all your customers."

"I love *most* of my customers. A few of them grate on my nerves. We'll just call it a personality conflict."

"Fair enough."

"So, anyway." And here we go. The inquisition is about to begin. "How was your date?"

Another sip. Another swallow. Another few seconds to avoid the topic. Tabitha won't let it go. I know that. I'm just tired of trying to justify why my dates never end up going anywhere.

"She was lovely." That's a good answer. Pretty perfect, actually, because it's true.

Tabitha looks genuinely pleased. "Glad to hear it. Does this mean you're going to see her again?"

And there it is. I should have known better. I prepare myself for the same conversation she and I have had numerous times before. "You know I'm not interested in a relationship."

"Not what I asked."

"I will probably see her in a professional setting."

"Not what I meant."

"Fine." I take another quick swig. "No, we won't be seeing each other again. She's not my type."

"Let me guess—she was smart, beautiful, and motivated," Tabitha says while ticking off her fingers.

"Exactly." I nod. "You know that's not the kind of woman I go for."

"Yeah, I know. What I don't understand is why? You're a nice guy. Easy on the eyes, not hurting for money. What's the problem?"

There are about a thousand answers to that. But to make things simple, I'll only give her my main one. I've been thinking about it more and more lately, so what the hell? Maybe saying it out loud will make something click in my own brain.

Leaning my arms on the counter, I push my drink to the side. "My mother always used to say the only purpose of a relationship is to hang out with someone until you gradually get bored enough that you want to find someone else to be with."

Without skipping a beat, she says, "Your mom sounds jaded."

"Maybe. Or maybe she was just wise."

"Or maybe she was just heartbroken and never let it go."

Pushing back, I grab my drink again. "Please. I never saw my mother cry. Not once."

Tabitha sighs. "Oh, Carlos, Carlos, Carlos. You may be the smartest businessman I know, but you are an idiot when it comes to emotions."

A lesser woman would offend me with these same words, but that's the great thing about Tabitha. We've been friends for years and she loves me just the way I am. "By all means," I say playfully with a wave of my hand in invitation, "enlighten me."

She leans her arms on the counter, settling in for this conversation. "Women who don't cry have trained themselves to hold back the hard emotions."

I smirk because she's wrong. "I know a whole group of women who knit for fun who would disagree with you. They almost never cry."

"I will ignore the knitting part because I have no idea how that is relevant. But you misunderstood me. I didn't say women who don't cry in front of *you*. I said women who don't cry *ever*. Let me ask you, this group of women that you know. Are any of them in relationships?"

My mouth slams shut because every single one of them is attached. They are some of the smartest, most successful, emotionally strong women I know. And yet, they are all in a relationship.

"That's what I thought. They just don't let you see that side of them, but their men probably do," Tabitha adds when I don't respond to her assessment. "I'm willing to bet your mother never cried about anything *at all* because she was burned so hard by a man, she shut it down. Her wisdom, as you call it, was a defense mechanism, Carlos. Not truth."

I keep the straw firmly in my mouth, so I don't end up saying anything. I honestly don't know how to respond anyway. I always assumed my mother was just a wise woman who prided herself on being able to do it all—career, motherhood, friends. It never occurred to me her lack of dating had anything to do with being hurt before I was old enough to remember. I thought she was just content with the way things were.

I feel like part of my world just shifted, and I'm not sure I like it.

"I'm sorry."

I look over at Tabitha who is now giving me a sympathetic look. I don't like that either.

"I may be all wrong. I don't know your mother. She might be that rare woman who loves the single life."

I nod, because she might be. But suddenly, I don't think so. I think —I think maybe she was and is lonelier than I ever realized. That the look in her eyes when my dad came over through the years wasn't just sadness for her boy who didn't have a live-in father. Maybe some of it was sadness for herself as well.

Taking a deep breath, I nod at Tabitha's apology. "Yeah, my mom is the strongest, happiest single person I know. Except for me of course."

She and I laugh at my quip, but it doesn't feel as funny as it might have twenty minutes ago. If I misunderstood my mother for all these years, did I also misunderstand myself?

Suddenly I wish I could take my mother's words back. Saying it out loud didn't help at all. In fact, I'm more confused than ever.

"And me," Tabitha adds. "You know I have no desire to ever get married again after the shit I went through with my ex-husband. Dating? Sure. Sex? Sure. Companionship? I'm game. But I'll be keeping my last name, thank you very much."

"Ah, Tabitha, you're proving my point. Single life is where it's at." I flash a panty-dropping smile at her, even though it would never work. We're too good of friends for her to fall for my fake flirting.

As I finish my smoothie and toss the cup away, another customer takes her attention away from me. Rapping my knuckles on the counter twice so she knows I'm leaving, she nods again as I walk away.

I like Tabitha. Our relationship is easy. There's no attraction beyond good conversation and the occasional dinner with friends. It works for me.

Or at least it did. This new philosophical side of her, I can't get it out of my head. And I don't like it at all.

CHAPTER ELEVEN

RIAN

I hate having to admit Francesca is right. Mostly because I don't like being wrong. But after several days of being tortured whenever I walk, stand, sit, roll over, lie down, breathe, basically just being alive, I've not been able to forget that my muscles are revolting against me. I need some relief and Bengay isn't cutting it anymore. Plus, I'm tired of smelling like peppermint. People keep asking me for gum, and I'm assuming it's because the odor reminds them they need fresh breath.

But I need for my body to stop hurting, and the only three options I could think of were springing for a massage, hot tubbing, and Francesca's suggestion of yoga.

Massage fell off that list in about one second flat simply because a stranger would be touching my naked body. Ew. No. Hot tubbing remained for a few seconds longer until I remembered this isn't a spa so there wouldn't be glasses of bubbly champagne to go with the bubbly water, plus I'd have to put on a bathing suit in the one building where pretty, skinny people congregate. So again—no. That leaves me with one viable option. I'm not happy about it, but walking like a ninety-eight-year-old woman is not a good alternative either. No tall, dark, and handsome do-gooder has offered to help me across the street yet, so there isn't even a silver lining to this pain.

I made the mistake of asking Abel for his thoughts on yoga. He, of course, got his bright, torture-loving smile and went on and on and *on* about the health benefits of making regular stretch a part of my workout regimen. I'm still not convinced. But I did pay for a six-month gym membership package and need to use it. Included is access to almost all their classes, and since I can barely move, Zumba is out of the question. But I also hate the idea of throwing away money by not doing something.

In hindsight, I should have remembered I'm not really a commitment girl, but signing up gave me a ten percent discount. That's how those sales agents get you. They get into the heads of people like me and find out what makes us tick. What makes us spend. Then, they flash a shiny discount at us, and once we've signed on the bottom line, they guilt us into coming four times a week to get our money's worth. I know because I do it all the time at my job. Every day I convince people to upgrade their cable package. Football lover? We have a fantastic NFL package. Love to DIY? There are channels you only dream about with the home improvement package. Music lover? We have not one, not two, but three music video channels in our premier package, and not those crappy former music video channels that only play teen reality shows now.

See? I'm the queen of the upsell. I've won the office award for it twice. Which is why I'm even more disappointed in myself for falling for the tactic.

Abel doesn't notice my irritation, though. He barely notices how much trouble I'm having walking up the stairs. Why isn't there an elevator in this place? Isn't that an ADA requirement or something? Damn these old buildings and their being grandfathered into old building codes.

Huffing, partially from exertion and partially because I just really like to complain while I'm at the gym, I keep a heavy grip on the stair railing, practically using it to pull myself up.

Abel, agile asshole that he is, trots to the top and turns around, staring down at me. "What's taking you so long?"

I glare at him, still slowly climbing. "Did you forget about that rope thing you made me do already?"

He barks a laugh, which is not funny to me at all. But the sound is fitting since I'm more than happy to refer to him as a dog until I get control of my body back.

"I told you to take it slow since it was your first time."

"You most certainly did not," I argue, almost to the top. I'm almost... there... just a few... more... steps... "You yelled 'Just ten more seconds!' and then your stopwatch conveniently broke for fifteen more."

He shrugs confirming that his watch accidentally broke on purpose, just like I thought. He denied it, but he doesn't fool me. My watch has accidentally broken on purpose before, too. Just usually on the "quitting early" side, not "keep going until you die" side.

Taking one last excruciating step, I'm finally on the second floor of the gym. I've only been up here once—when I was taking a tour of the facility before signing my life away for that damn discount. There is a track off to the left that overlooks one of the exercise areas, but to the right is where most of the exercise machines are. Not the treadmills. Those are all downstairs. No, these machines I could easily get tangled up in with as many wires and hangy-down things are attached to them. But there are also a couple additional rooms for classes. I guess the yoga room is up here. Makes sense. It is quieter than downstairs. Not that I'll ever know for sure. Unless this class does something miraculous to my body, there's no chance I'll be able to make it back downstairs to compare properly.

"Are you going to bitch this much during yoga?" Abel asks, as he leads me to the back where we approach a dark room. The door is open, and several older women are taking their shoes off and putting them in cubbie holes against the wall. "I might pretend I don't know you if you are."

"No guarantees, buddy," is all I can think to grumble when I realize I have to bend down to take my own shoes off. I groan when I reach down to my toes. I already hate yoga, and I'm not even bending for the health benefits yet.

Abel leaves me behind as he saunters into the room, all fluid movements and graceful steps. Must be nice to have muscles that recover quickly.

Okay, now I'm starting to annoy myself. I need to get over it and just get some relief already!

Finally freeing myself of footwear, I hobble into the room, not sure what to expect. The only thing I know about yoga is what I've heard— that hippies do it while sitting cross-legged and chanting "Oooooommmm." Oddly, I don't see any hippies in the room. Only people wearing normal workout clothes. I wonder briefly if I'm in the right spot until Abel calls my name.

"Rian!" He waves me over, which I find incredibly rude considering he's the one who can walk these days. But I obey because I don't find it rude at all. Just painful. "I want to introduce you to Helena. She's the instructor of this class."

This tiny blond woman teaches yoga? I expected long, unruly hair, and gauchos. Maybe the scent of patchouli mixed with body odor from the lack of deodorant. That's not what this woman is like at all. She's wearing short workout shorts and a tank top, fun socks pulled up to her knees. Her hair is pulled back into a tight bun at the nape of her neck. And when she shakes my hand, she has a firm grip. She looks like she's better suited to be running a marathon than helping me stretch. And she smells like lavender with a hint of lemon. Huh. I wonder what other surprises are in store for me.

"It's really nice to meet you, Rian," she says kindly with a big smile. What is it with all employees with perfect teeth? Is that a requirement to work here? "Abel was giving me the rundown on your new workout program."

I quirk an eye and look right at him. He gives me a condescending smile right back. "Yes, I did tell her how much you love to complain, but that it's all an act and means you just need to be pushed harder."

Looking back at Helena I ask, "Does he like to torture everyone, or is it something I said?"

Helena laughs and leads me over to a stack of purple yoga mats.

"Torturing you means he likes you. Just don't let him convince you to use the battle ropes. It's his favorite method."

My jaw drops. "That's exactly why I'm here. I haven't been able to move in days."

Helena sucks in a breath and shakes her head. "Oh, man. I feel for you. The first time he tricked me into that exercise, I thought all my limbs were going to fall off. Seriously, who thought it was a good idea to start me off with three sets of a hundred?"

I blink rapidly. Three sets of *a hundred?* I barely hit the floor ten times in thirty seconds. Clearly, I have a long way to go before I can claim to be fit.

"Anyway," Helena continues, "grab a mat and roll it out anywhere. Since this is your first time, I want you to really listen to your body. Push hard enough to feel it, but not enough for it to be painful. Sore is okay but sharp pain isn't good."

I nod, pretending I understand the difference. In my current state, sore and pain are basically synonymous.

Helena continues to greet people as they walk in the door while I get settled in the back. The way back. Since I've never done this before, I have no idea what to expect and no one needs my butt in their face while I figure it out. Nor do they need to see me fall over, which is a very good possibility.

Besides everyone having their shoes off, the one thing I like is that everyone seems quieter in here. I'm not sure if it's due to the nature of the class or because we're up here away from the music, but it's peaceful. Calming. I feel really mellow just being here and class hasn't even started yet.

My calm is short lived, however, when Helena announces it's time to begin. That's when my anxiety shoots up a notch.

"Stand on your mat, feet slightly apart and put your big toes together, like you're pigeon-toed. Arms together," Helena says calmly, the bounce she had her in step a few minutes ago gone, replaced by a very Zen teacher. "Breathe in through your nose and raise your arms to the ceiling, looking up at your hands." I, along with everyone else in the room, follow her instructions. "Now out slowly through your mouth and bring your arms back down. Again."

We go through a few more breathing movements with our arms going up and down. So far, I'm keeping up. If we do basic movements like this the whole time, I'll be just fine.

"Reach up to the sky, fingertips together." Helena looks up at her hands and breathes in. "Now fold your body over, reaching for the floor."

I can't help the groan that comes out of me as my back stretches forward for the first time in days. My toes are still so far away, and my stomach seems to be blocking my movement. Am I really supposed to reach my feet?

"Only go as far as your body can go."

Oh. I guess Helena can read minds, too.

"Touch the floor and look forward, stretching your neck and your back."

Um... I don't know that my head can go that way. But I try. Nothing happens, but I still give myself an A for effort.

"Now walk your hands out into the downward dog position."

The downward what? Breaking my less than perfect form, I look around the room to try and figure out what I'm supposed to do. Sure enough, everyone has their feet on the floor and are walking their hands forward, their butts still in the air. Hmm. I guess I can try...

It's not pretty. I have to bend my knees and spread my legs to get close enough to the floor for my hands to touch, but eventually I have walked my hands far enough out to look like everyone else. Sort of. I mean, their bodies are in sharp angles and mine like a deflated triangle, but that's close, right?

"And hold the position, feet flat on the floor, breathing in and out."

Suddenly there are hands on my hips. Why are there hands on my hips while I'm in a compromising position? The scent of lavender and lemon invades my nose, tipping me off.

"Relax, Rian," Helena says quietly to me, pulling my body backward and my feet flatter to the floor.

Do not fart, Rian. Do. Not. Fart. Squeeze those cheeks...

98

"Breathe slowly and let your body do the work for you," she continues. "Good. Is it sore or painful?"

"Uhhhh….." That's the only word that comes out. Partially because I don't know how to answer her and partially because the blood has been rushing to my head for about ten seconds too long. "Sore," I finally croak out.

"Good." Releasing my hips, she moves from behind me back through the class to adjust other people. I'm not sure if I'm more relieved to relax out of that stretch or because I didn't break wind with her behind me.

"Slowly, move one leg forward into a lunge position, arms out in a warrior's pose."

Again, I feel like a cheater looking around, because I have no idea what she's talking about. And again, when I see what everyone else is doing, I begin to wonder how my body is going to contort into that. Sure enough, everyone is lunging, right arm out straight, left arm straight behind them.

Welp, this is going to be interesting.

I try to move my foot gracefully forward like everyone else, only it sounds like a clap of thunder when it finally gets in position. My hands are still stuck on the floor and I can't breathe with my stomach pressed up into my ribs. I don't think this is what Helena was hoping for. Balancing on one hand, I put my other hand on my knee and push up.

I did it! I'm in a weird lunge position I'll never be able to get out of, but I did it!

Moving my arms out, I have a surge of pride run through my body. I'm balancing. In a warrior's pose. In yoga. Francesca would be so proud.

"Breathe in, bringing your arms up to the sky, looking at your fingertips—"

Wait, what? I just got balanced. Now I'm supposed to look up again?

"—and breathe out, lowering your hands to the floor, switching sides."

Oh, lord. It takes a few minutes and some serious concentration, but I make it to the other side. I'm breathing heavy and I'm sure there is sweat sliding down my back, but I did it, without falling into a heap on my mat. Maybe yoga is more my style than I thought. I feel like I'm getting both stretchy and strong at the same time.

"Breathe in, arms up to the sky, hold… now breathe out and lower yourself to the floor, pushing up into the cobra pose."

One more glance around the room to see people lying on their stomachs, pushing their upper body up like a snake. I, on the other hand, am still stuck in a lunge. How do they do this so quickly?

I refuse to give up, though. Lying down is right up my alley, so I get into position as quickly as possible and try to imitate the pose until Helena gives us the go ahead to release and drop our head to the floor.

I'm wiped. Contorting my body into different poses is more exhausting than I thought it would be. I'm glad to be taking a breather.

"Let's do that sequence three more times."

What?? I barely made it through doing it once. She wants me to do it three more times?

Groaning, I try my best to push myself back into the doggie style position, or whatever it was called. Forget keeping my legs straight. I need to use what little muscle I have to get upside-down-right.

Francesca better be right. Three more sequences and I'm going to need that "not really a nap" portion of the class. Badly.

CHAPTER TWELVE

CARLOS

"I'm serious, Carlos. I don't need to be on the phone fighting with the insurance company about why they keep denying coverage on my pregnant wife. Especially while she's on mandatory bedrest."

I pinch the bridge of my nose and take a deep breath in while I listen to Quinn rant through the line. Again. It's becoming a regular occurrence these days, and the worst part about it is, he's not wrong. Something is going on with everyone's coverage and we can't figure out what. Daily, I'm getting an email, call, or in-person visit from someone getting denied a dental visit or receiving a bill in the mail for medical services.

Karen, our benefits coordinator, has been on the phone constantly with the insurance company trying to sort it out, but it's not going fast enough for anyone's liking. Especially me. Not because I've been to the doctor lately, but because I'm the one who gets to take the brunt of it when Quinn is off his rocker.

And lately, he is always off his rocker. So much so that whenever security cameras catch him walking into the building, a "code pink" gets called out. Pink because Janie is pregnant and... well, I don't know why else. It just seemed to make sense, and we all figured out what it meant pretty quickly.

What I don't get alerts for, though, are the phone calls. Quinn is the only one who knows the direct number into my office without having to go through my assistant. It's convenient when we're working on securing a new client. It's not convenient at all when he's a raging lunatic like right now. I'm going to need to take advantage of our mental health coverage soon if this keeps up. Assuming it doesn't get denied.

"I don't know whose ass you need to ride, Carlos, but this needs to be fixed now. My child is not going to be born in some half-ass hospital with completely underpaid and inept staff because our benefits are fucked up, and I certainly don't have time to figure it out myself. I have knitting patterns to print out."

Again— no idea what he's talking about. I assume it has to do with Janie's love of knitting. Hell, she brought me some really amazing handmade gloves with a matching scarf and beanie once. Softest thing I've ever felt. But where Quinn's obsession is coming from eludes me. I'm also not sure how Janie hasn't stabbed him with her knitting needles yet. I have a hard time believing he's not this obnoxious at home.

"I know." I finally cut off his rant. "I'm calling another meeting with Karen as soon as we hang up so we can figure out what's going on. She said something about having a new account rep so I'm sure it's just a communication breakdown."

"Well, they better fix it." Sounding calmer, which is always a bad sign, he tacks on, "Also—"

Oh, boy. An "also" is never good. I grab my pen and note pad because I have a feeling Quinn has another idea on how to expand the company and I need to be prepared.

"—Janie and I have been talking."

"Okay," I say while wiggling my pen between my fingers. But inside I'm thinking, "Those words are never the start of anything good."

"Janie's going to take some time off."

I freeze. Janie is a brilliant account manager. As in, genius-level smart. Not only does she manage accounts, but because of her degree in architecture, she spends a lot of her time out in the field looking at the structural design of the buildings we secure to ensure the best locations of our equipment. Essentially, she does the job of two people. And she does it so efficiently, it could be argued she does the job of three.

"When you say taking time off, what exactly does that mean?"

"A year. Maybe longer."

My pen freezes in my hand. Good thing Quinn is on the phone. If he knew the death daggers that were coming out of my eyes, he'd fire me on the spot. Account managers themselves are a dime a dozen. But by the nature of this business, the background checks are extensive. Our checks rival those done by the FBI and CIA. According to Alex, our resident hacker-turned-straight, we're more thorough as well, but obviously I can't verify that. Nor would I want to try. I'll leave the hacking into national security systems to him. I don't look good in orange or jumpsuits. The combination of the two would be hideous.

Janie being gone for longer than just maternity leave puts a huge kink in the plan we've had for her absence, not to mention, our budget. It would have been nice to know this a couple months ago when we were planning the fiscal year.

"Don't look at me like that," Quinn growls through the phone. I glance around to the corners of my office looking to see if there is a hidden camera somewhere. It honestly wouldn't surprise me. "And stop looking around the office. There aren't any bugs you don't know about."

So, he just has ESP. Got it.

"I'll get with Nancy and start running the ads today," I continue. "How soon is she leaving?"

"As soon as her replacement is trained."

I don't bother expressing my frustration. It's just a waste of time, and obviously, I don't have any to spare now that I need to find someone, or someones, with particular skillsets. Not only that, any candidates can't ever have gotten so much as a speeding ticket. This is going to be an uphill battle.

"I'll do my best to get her position filled as quickly as possible, but you know there are federal hiring guidelines I'm required to follow."

"I'm sure you can find a work around."

I chuckle humorlessly. He knows as well as I do there is no "working around" federal requirements. The only way to speed up the process is to pray for a knitting needle in a haystack to drop right in my lap.

Looks like I won't be working banking hours for a while.

"Anything else I need to be ready for, since I have your undivided attention?"

A muffled sound comes through the phone and Quinn begins cussing under his breath. "Shit. Dammit. Fuck... okay, sorry. What was that, Carlos?"

So much for undivided attention. "Never mind. Not important."

A rap on my door has me looking up to see Karen in my doorway, looking as frustrated as I feel.

"You have a minute?" she mouths, hearing Quinn babbling on about an overlay or something. At this point, he's gone off the rails again, so I'm only half paying attention as I wave her in and gesture to the chair in front of me. I think everyone in the office is hoping he'll calm down once the baby is born. He's a phenomenal boss, and I can say with all honesty, this is the best job I've ever had. I don't see a future where I wouldn't want to work here or under Quinn Sullivan. Unless Janie keeps getting pregnant.

I swear if they turn into a "nineteen kids and counting" couple, I'm out of here.

Okay, fine. No, I'm not. We'll just add "Code Pink" to the official employee handbook.

"Hey, Quinn, I know you're still trying to figure out that hook stitch and all—" Karen's eyebrows furrow in question. *Yeah, I don't get it either, Karen.* "— but Karen is finally off her call, so I'm going to get with her on this insurance issue."

Her eyes widen and she sits forward, waving her hands back and forth. "I'm not here!" she mouths frantically. "Code pink! Code pink!"

I almost start laughing at her determination not to talk to our boss, until he yells, "I'm serious, Carlos! Someone's head is going to roll if this doesn't get fixed soon!"

"Understood. Thanksforcallingbye," I say quickly and hang up before he can get another word in. Probably not the best way to secure my job, but I'm betting he's already forgotten and moved onto another minor irritation he can torture me with later.

Collapsing back in her chair, Karen blows out a breath. "When is that woman due? Please tell me it's soon."

"I wish. August? September? Something like that."

She shakes her head. "Poor guy is going to have a coronary before then."

"He can't." I toss my pen back on my desk and pinch the bridge of my nose again. Suddenly, I have a headache. Not sure if it's from all these conversations or the caffeine detox I'm doing. My guess is the conversations. "We don't have the insurance to cover it."

Karen picks up the legal pad she carried in with her, presumably so we can get down to business. She's pretty no-nonsense that way, which is why she's incredible at her job. In her mid-fifties, Karen is a recent college grad. Married at twenty-five, she quit working and immediately started a family, raising several kids for years. But once they were all out of the house, she was bored and decided to go back to school and start a career. Her husband supported the idea completely and somehow, she fell in love with HR, benefits in particular.

Turns out, she has the perfect personality for it. Plus, she still makes us cookies sometimes. Not that I'll eat them unless it's a special occasion, and cardio day. But it keeps everyone else happy as well. It also helps soften the blow when she has bad news.

By the look on her face, I bet she wishes she brought cookies to my office.

Steepling my fingers together and leaning my elbows on my desk and level with her. "You have bad news, don't you?"

She sighs. "It's not good. It's also no different than it's been for the last week."

"They can't figure it out either."

She shakes her head regretfully. "I've tripled checked all our entries to make sure it's all set up in our system correctly. The account rep has checked their system, and it's all correct over there as well."

"Then why are all these claims getting rejected?"

"They're looking into it. But it seems to be somewhere in the claims division."

"Are you sure they aren't screwing with us? Trying to not cover things to save money?"

"They can't do that. That would be fraud."

She has a point.

"And we've paid the premiums on time? Quinn didn't accidentally change bank accounts or something, did he? I can't keep up with him these days."

Karen tries not to laugh at my outburst. She knows how frustrated I am right now.

"That was the first thing I checked. Everything is paid up."

Then what could this be? I rub the pad of my thumb over my lip as I think. If everything is entered correctly and we've paid up, then it wouldn't be an intentional issue. Maybe human error, but maybe not.

"Quinn didn't authorize a system update to the HRIS and forget to tell me, did he?"

This time she doesn't even try not to laugh. "Nope. We have the same systems as al—wait." She freezes to think, her eyes moving back and forth as her brain keeps up with whatever conclusion she's coming. "Son of a bitch!" she finally yells and jumps from her chair, storming out the door.

"Wait!" I call after her. "What happened?"

She turns around and takes the two steps back to lean on my door-jamb. "I think I know what happened. I'm calling right now so they can sort it out."

I turn my hand palm up, gesturing to her. "You gonna tell me what you think is going on?"

"Nope. I don't want to get your hopes up." She turns around to stomp off again.

"So, what am I going to tell Quinn next time he calls?" I yell.

"Tell him I want a raise for figuring this out!" she calls back over her shoulder, not stopping this time.

I chuckle under my breath. "I'm gonna need a raise, too, Karen. Or at least his first born named after me," I say under my breath. Unfortunately, I'm going to have to make do with a stiff drink instead now that Janie's shoes need to be filled on top of everything else. And then it hits me…

I may have found that needle already, in a woman I can't keep my mind off of. Well, that was easy. And yet… I suspect things are about to get very complicated.

CHAPTER THIRTEEN

RIAN

Sundays are my day off. Really, weekends are my days off, but Sundays are special. I refuse to get out of my jammies, and I lie on the couch watching TV all day. I work at Sendeke Telecom so, of course, I have the best package out there. It would be a shame to let it go to waste by not taking advantage of it at least once a week.

Right now, I'm obsessed with Marie Kondo. Yes, her show can teeter on the boring side with all the emotional back stories, many of which aren't even that emotional. But I find her technique endearing. There's something sweet about thanking her items for what they've done for her—no matter how small and insignificant the item seems.

So, I'm not sure how I found myself sitting at the smoothie bar on a Sunday afternoon when I should be taking mental notes on how to downsize while silently judging the hoarders on TV. But, ever since finding out Fred is retiring, I've had a restless energy. I can't describe it. It's like a constant hum all over my body. It's not that I hate my job. I just never realized I was using Fred as sort of a barrier to other inner office issues. Without him there, I may hate my job quickly.

Plus, Carlos has started invading my thoughts a lot lately, and I can't figure out why. Fine. I might know. It's probably guilt.

I didn't mean to act rudely after he told me he was God's gift to women… but come on. The man literally said his purpose in life was to give women sexual pleasure. That one statement confirmed what I had already assumed just from watching him here.

Carlos Davies is pompous and arrogant, and not in a good romance novel kind of way. He is selfish and smarmy. I'm kind of surprised I've never seen him kiss his own biceps while staring in a mirror longingly at himself.

And yet…

Yes, there is as "yet". That's the worst part in all my swirling emotions. I enjoyed talking to him, minus that one odd incident. He was funny and smart. He has an eclectic taste in friends and is obviously driven if he's the COO of a major security firm. It's a little weird that he is so strict on his diet, but I guess it's a little weird that I'm not very strict on mine.

It was easy to push the thoughts aside during the work week. Francesca provided a lot of good distraction. Especially when Nolan tried to lecture us on the health benefits of kale. I'm sure he's still trying to find information about the Great Kale Overdose of 1912. I will never understand how he believed an entire village of people died after eating too much of the leafy green.

My thoughts are much, much harder to keep control of on the weekend. I finally gave up and came here. I figured I'd have a healthy smoothie, do a little treadmill, and be fully prepared to tell Abel tomorrow that I've already worked out once this week and it's my easy day. He won't believe me, which is why I've already taken a picture of the inside of the building with the time a date stamp. Can't be too prepared with that one.

Now, if only I could motivate myself to get on that death machine…

"I wasn't expecting to have drinks with you again so soon."

I look over just as Frank takes a seat next to me.

"Frank!" I say with probably too much excitement, but how can I act subdued? This is the man who changed my perspective on tequila. "I didn't know you came here on Sundays."

"I'm here every day, gorgeous. It's practically my home away from home."

"I've heard that," I say with my lips wrapped around my straw. "You're like the gym mascot."

A hearty laugh rumbles through him and I fully understand why Tabitha likes him so much. He's just so easy to be with. It's as if he has no expectations of anyone. He just enjoys who they are, no matter what that means.

It hits me out of nowhere that maybe I could take a page out of Frank's book. Maybe the reason I'm feeling so consumed with thoughts of Carlos is because I'm at war within myself. Part of me wants to like him, but a really strong part wants to judge him as well.

That realization cements it for me. I need to give Carlos another shot. Not to fix anything he did wrong, but so I can fix my own preconceived notions. Maybe look beyond what he presents on the outside to see the flawed human being underneath.

"I know I'm considered a staple around here, but I had no idea some called me the mascot," Frank says with a smile, and Tabitha immediately places a drink he didn't order in front of him. "Thanks, Doll."

Tabitha winks over her shoulder at him and gets back to another customer. When he looks back at me, I just raise an eyebrow.

"What?" His tone indicates he's asking a question, but the smile on his face and playful glint in his eyes say he knows exactly what I'm thinking.

"Did you order that?" I gesture to his drink.

He picks up his straw and begins removing the paper. "No."

"And somehow Tabitha just knew you wanted it."

"It's my usual."

Turning to face front, I put my own straw in my mouth and mutter, "Mmm hmmm," while sucking. "Mascot," I whisper.

After taking his own long drink, Frank turns his head to me. "Can I at least be a really virile mascot, like a lion or a wolf? Something sexy."

His comment makes me choke on my drink in laughter. Tabitha

comes from out of nowhere, handing me napkins to cover my mouth so I don't spray liquid everywhere.

"What happened?"

Through my coughing, while Frank continues to pat my back, I laugh out, "Frank wants to be sexy like a wolf."

Tabitha cocks her head, and I expect her to ask what the hell we're even talking about. Instead she thinks for a second and says, "A wolf? How about a jaguar? I could see you as a jaguar."

Frank's eyes light up even more. "Oooh! A jaguar! Yes. If I'm the gym mascot, that's what I'll be."

Having sorted that out, Tabitha taps her hand on the counter once and heads to the cash register. I shake my head at the ridiculousness of it all, getting the last of the liquid out of my airway. I also note that the pineapple/mango smoothie doesn't taste nearly as good coming back up as it does going down.

Frank leans in to speak quietly to me. "So, now that you know I'm here every day, including Sundays, you must realize that means I know you *don't* come on Sundays. Which begs the question, why the change in routine?"

I can't tell him the truth—because Carlos is invading my thoughts and I had some restless energy I needed to get out. As great as Frank is, I haven't even figured my own self out this time. I don't want the complication of trying to explain it to someone else, too.

"I guess what they say is true. Those endorphins are addicting."

"Hmm." I can't look at him. I don't think he bought that explanation and looking at him will confirm it. "You sure it doesn't have anything to do with a certain dinner mate you got cozy with the other night?"

My head whips over so fast to look at him, it's a wonder I don't break my neck. "I beg your pardon. I didn't get cozy with anyone except Jose Jose and his amazing enchiladas, thank you very much. Besides, how would you even know? You were too busy making googly eyes at Tabitha to notice anyone around you."

Deflection. Works every time.

He waves me off with a noncommittal noise and crosses his arms.

"That was nothing. Tabitha and I flirt like that all the time. It keeps my skills fresh for my girlfriend."

"Wait." My brows furrow. I wasn't expecting that. "You have a girlfriend?"

"For the last seven years."

"Then why didn't you bring her with you to dinner?"

He shrugs like the answer is a no-brainer. "She has her life, and I have mine."

"But... she's your girlfriend."

"Right."

"Don't you enjoy spending time with her?"

"Of course, I do. That doesn't mean I don't have time for other things, too. Honey, I'm retired. I can spend my morning at the gym, have dinner with you, and still have six hours in the middle there with her. She gets more of my time than anyone else. You just don't see it."

Huh. I never thought of it that way. Suddenly, I'm looking forward to retiring if it means living life like Frank does.

"It also means I have more time than most to hone my powers of observation. So, tell me, has a certain muscled man caught your attention? Is that why you're here?"

Dammit. I was hoping Frank's mind was slipping a little with age. But, of course, he's sharp as a tack. Probably because he only drinks the good booze keeping his brain fully lubricated. That also means I'm doomed from all my poor people drinks. Never underestimate how excited a poor college student gets when Boone's Farm is on sale.

I sigh deeply, not wanting to open up to Frank, but not feeling like I can leave him hanging either.

"I think... I feel like maybe I misjudged him a bit. Like maybe first impressions aren't always accurate, and I need to rectify some things."

He nods in understanding, arms crossed over his surprisingly broad chest. Seriously. Is there magic in that tequila?

"Those are some very astute observations."

I shrug. Not because I disagree but because there's more to it than that. Much more to it. I'm just not willing to admit it to anyone yet. Not even to myself.

Frank sits silently while I get lost in my thoughts. I don't want to be attracted to a man like Carlos. That's just setting myself up for the inevitable pain of rejection. It's not a new thing for someone like me because it always follows the same pattern.

Boy accidentally meets girl he's never noticed before.

Boy is shocked to discover he likes girl more than he expected.

Boy and girl spend time together.

Girl gets her hopes up that boy might be different than the others.

Boy suddenly realizes girl likes him in a romantic way and tells girl, "I like you like a friend but not *that* way."

Boy starts dating skinny/pretty girl who he falls madly in love with.

Girl gets invitation to boy's wedding after he completely drops her friendship because he's busy with the skinny/pretty girl.

I have no interest in going through that again. It was bad enough when it happened in college. And a few years post college. And a shorter version in my early 30s. And before all that, a variation in high school that didn't end in a wedding invitation, but did end in my going to prom by myself. In hindsight, I was a way better date than he would have been anyway. Especially after he had too many shots in the limo on the way to the dance, only to be falling down drunk by the time they got to the hotel ballroom where he barfed all over his date's sparkly shoes.

He should have stuck to that top-shelf tequila instead of on-sale Boone's Farm.

"Somehow, I think there's more to your thoughts than you're admitting," Frank says, reminding me he's sitting there. Watching me. I hope I wasn't making some weird facial expression as I ran like a track star down memory lane. There's no strolling when that rabbit hole of past rejection begins.

"I'm just... processing." It's the truth, but only as much as I can give right now. I need to get myself together and compartmentalize my emotions. Put them in nice, neat little boxes that I can lock and store away until I need them. Which will be never.

As I wrap my brain around it all and come up with an emotional game plan, Carlos strolls up to the other side of the bar. He looks...

good. Even in an unremarkable sleeveless t-shirt and black gym shorts, he just stands out as a mecca of male beauty.

This is my chance at rectification. My chance to stop my preconceived notions in their tracks and give Carlos a chance to prove there's more to him than meets the eye.

Decision made, I place a smile on my face in greeting just as Carlos looks up at me—

And looks away.

No smile.

No reaction.

Not even recognition that he's ever spoken to me before.

It turns out, my pre-conceived notions were, in fact, correct.

I am invisible to Carlos unless there is no one else around.

Now, I just need to prepare myself for his pending engagement which is sure to come soon. If history repeats itself, that'll be in about six months.

Swiveling on my stool, I brace myself to climb down. I don't have any desire to sit here, waiting for Carlos to suddenly realize we've had a conversation. Before I can make the eighteen-inch jump, a hand gently rests on my forearm.

Frank.

"You need to know Carlos doesn't come here on Sundays either."

Looking in Frank's eyes, all I see is compassion and concern. Two things I'm not used to getting from a man. Not even my own father who isn't emotionally distant, per se, but doesn't understand "lady emotions". His words, not mine.

Twisting my lips into a weird half-smile, I nod once and pat Frank's hand. I appreciate his gesture, but the unsettled energy in my body is back. It's different this time, though. It's not a hum as much as a buzz of disappointment and anger.

If my workout mirrors how I'm feeling right now, I might end up having to take an easy day tomorrow after all.

CHAPTER FOURTEEN

CARLOS

Sitting down on the row machine, I adjust the settings for my height, my strength level, my workout type. Once everything is set, I pull.

And pull.

And pull.

But even racing against myself and my personal best doesn't seem to calm down my mind, or my body for that matter.

Normally, working out helps my brain compartmentalize itself. The stressors of work are pushed aside as I feel the burn of my muscles. So, it would make sense that the stressors of women would also be locked away, right?

In theory. But I've never really had any stress related to dating. Sure, there was the failure that was my weird crush on Olivia from the office. But it was short-lived and despite what other people in the office thought, didn't faze me as much as they assumed. I could have corrected them on that, but we were in the middle of rapidly hiring a bunch of people and moving half our offices to the Fairmont building. I had better things to do than tell a bunch of co-workers my interest lied strictly in the physical.

However, it was part of the catalyst to me bettering myself in a physical sense and that has only opened up more options, so I can't really complain about it.

Unfortunately, though, my brain can't seem to sort out this issue with Rian. And by issue, I mean, that she keeps ending up in the forefront of my thoughts. It's been that way since dinner a couple weeks ago and it's irritating me. Ever since that night, she keeps popping up in my thoughts when reading, watching TV, eating, suddenly I find myself wondering what her opinion would be about it.

I'm starting to think there was more in that meal than baked chicken and steamed broccoli. I have no other explanation to why she intrigues me so much. But she does. The entire time we sat around that table at Jose Jose I had two thoughts:

One... I need a copy of Rian's resume. I never know when I'll need to fill a position quickly. The more Rian talked about her job, the more of a match she seemed to be. I need someone who knows the ins and outs of what Cipher Security Systems can offer but can also anticipate a client's priorities before they even get that far. Rian is personable and quick-witted. And now that Janie is leaving, turns out I was right to have this thought process. Assuming Rian can pass the extensive background checks, I have no doubt Janie could have her up and running in a matter of weeks.

Second, and this is the big one... Rian intrigues me on a personal level. I don't know what to do with that. She's smart and funny. She's a strange mix of saying exactly what she thinks and being reserved in her opinions. Like she has a strong personality but isn't completely confident in her own voice. She's not a surface-level person and strikes me as the kind of woman who won't settle for anything less than deep when it comes to her relationships.

All of that has been rolling around in my head for over a week, which is how I ended up here on a Sunday, trying to exhaust my muscles enough for my brain to finally shut off.

That's also how I accidentally ended up looking right through her at the smoothie bar. It wasn't intentional. I just didn't expect her to be there and suddenly, I moved into my default mode—look, but don't really see anyone. I immediately recognized my mistake, but what could I do? Draw attention to myself and her and make a scene?

She hurried away and I almost went after her, but then I saw Frank. The smirk on his face stopped me from making a move. It's as if he could read me, read my attraction to her. But he's wrong. I couldn't be attracted to her. She's not my type. Not physically. Not emotionally. Not mentally. None of it.

So why do I feel so guilty?

Maybe because after she left, Frank approached me, shoved a finger in my face and growled, "You don't deserve a woman like Rian."

I was a little taken aback at the comment but tried to brush it off. It didn't work. Probably because he's right. A better man would have chased after her and apologized.

Grunting, I pull through my last ten seconds before relishing the sweet relief I feel as I place the "oar" back on the machine. I'm covered in sweat and breathing heavily, which feels good. My mind, however, is still a swirling mess of conflicting emotions and ideas.

I look around, trying to decide where my next attempt at emotional numbness should come from. Rowing is technically cardio, but I think I maxed out my upper body muscles today with the heavy weight I purposely added to the oars. Maybe I should jump on the treadmill and run a mile or two. Or maybe not. It's looking awfully steamy on that side of the gym, like someone left the wet sauna door open again. I hate trying to run in humidity, so I at least need to wait for it to clear out.

Stepping off my machine, I make quick work of wiping it down with sanitizing wipes and take a swig of my water. Hands on my hips, the steam seems to get worse. Something's not right.

I don't even have time to investigate before a shrieking sound fills the gym and lights begin flashing. Other faces look as confused as I feel. Is this for real? Is there really a fire in the gym?

Suddenly, one of the people at the front desk comes racing to the back. "Everyone out! Do not go back to the locker room for your stuff. We need to get out now!"

Panic begins to take over the room and people swarm to the exits. Most of us head to the back, but I have a sudden thought and take off toward the front of the building, past the smoothie bar where Tabitha is grabbing her purse, past the front desk where someone is already on the phone with I presume the fire department, and through the double doors of the on-site daycare.

"Dinah!" I call out to the woman in charge. I don't see her often because I have no need to come in this part, but when you've been an active member as long as I have, you tend to know everyone. "Dinah, do you need help?"

"Grab those bottles off the counter!" she yells back, pushing a crib that has at least three babies in it through the emergency exit.

Following her instructions, I grab as many of the cups and bottles as I can carry and follow her out the exit door. Part of me wishes I had my phone to take a picture. I'm not terribly sentimental, but even I have to admit watching the daycare kids walk out is pretty cute. One of the providers, an older woman with bright red hair has one toddler holding each of her hands, with a third holding his friend's hand. Another provider is carrying a baby and holding the hand of yet another toddler. And Dinah is towing the line with the crib of babies. In a weird way, it resembles a line of ducklings all following the mama duck.

I follow along as they calmly and gently guide the kids to the opposite side of the parking lot. It all runs smoothly until the fire truck pulls up with lights and sirens. The babies start wailing while the toddlers get all excited. I prepare myself to throw the liquid gold into the crib should it become necessary to take off after a rogue toddler determined to get a ride on said truck.

Fortunately, they all seem to have forgotten that they have the ability to let go of each other.

Situating everyone on the curb in an orderly fashion, the red-headed provider takes the cups off my hands and passes them out. Now the excitement really begins for the kids. It's like they have a front seat to dinner and a show! Or maybe I'm just having my post-workout sugar crash and really wishing I had my wallet so I could go grab a bite.

"Well, that was some exciting stuff, huh?" Dinah has a huge smile on her face, despite just helping half a dozen small people run out of a burning building. Or a possibly burning building. The fire department hasn't had a lot of time to find the source of the problem yet.

"You guys are quick, Dinah. I hadn't even gotten to your room before you guys were gone."

She laughs heartily. "That's why they pay me the big bucks. I'm not taking any chances when that fire alarm goes off."

We watch as more people filter out of the front doors, the only people heading inside are dressed in heavy coats and fireproof hats. I find myself looking around for people I know, making sure everyone is okay.

Tabitha has her purse slung over her shoulder and is letting someone borrow her phone. Frank is standing in a group of people, no doubt regaling stories of when he was a first responder or something. The lady who was on the elliptical is looking around frantically for something. Very quickly, I realize what she's looking for.

I begin waving my hands and yell, "Hey!" When I know she's seen me, I start pointing to the row of children. Relief crosses her face and she runs toward us. As she makes it to our side, Dinah hands her one of the babies, making her cry.

"I'm so glad you guys are okay." Her voice sounds muffled against her child's head. "I knew you had gotten everyone out but there was still that moment of panic, ya know?"

Dinah rubs the mother's back and talks quietly to her until more parents come to collect their children as they find us. I keep looking through the crowd making mental notes of all the people I saw when I got here, and who I see now.

It suddenly hits me that there's one person I haven't seen yet.

Rian.

CHAPTER FIFTEEN

RIAN

Standing under the spray of the hot water, I notice that for the first time, my muscles feel really good. Relaxed in a way they haven't felt before. And my lungs feel... I don't know even how to describe it. It's like they've been stretched in all the right ways. Is this what people mean when they talk about feeling the post-workout high? My entire body feels both rejuvenated and relaxed at the same time, and my thoughts are more centered.

It is the oddest feeling. I think... I think I could get used to feeling like this a few times a week. I might even be able to start pushing myself more. Of course, I'll never tell Abel that. He would be so disappointed if he had no one to verbally spar with.

Besides, I don't have *that* many endorphins running through me. Let's not get crazy.

Turning around, I lift my head up to get my hair wet and shampooed. The room is foggier than normal, but I suppose I have the water up hotter than normal. And someone is in the stall next to me. I guess we all had some emotional weight to work off today.

I can't believe I suddenly see the appeal of coming here. It's not the actual exercise people like. It's what comes after. It's a sense of calm I don't know I've ever had before.

Rinsing my hair, I squeeze some conditioner into my hand and work it through my locks. Oddly, I feel like I should get a facial or pedicure, too. It's kind of wigging me out that I have this sudden desire to put more effort into my self-care. I may need to eat some French fries to balance myself out.

The room is getting foggier, which is so odd. How much hot water are we using? And why is it thicker toward the ceiling?

Wait.

Something's not right.

"Ummm....." I say just as the woman in the stall next to me asks, "Is that steam? Or is it smoke?"

I don't get a chance to answer before the high-pitched screech of the fire alarms begin blaring.

Oh, shit.

"What do we do?" I ask no one in particular, although likely my shower mate is the only one listening. "Do we have time to finish up?"

"I don't know." I can hear the panic in her voice, just like I heard it in mind. "But we need to hurry."

I begin rinsing frantically, not even sure what part of me I'm washing in the rising panic I feel. A smart person would just jump out of the shower. But what if I do that and it turns out this is a false alarm? Then I'll be running around naked and will end up reshowering. Plus, what if someone steals my stuff while it's unattended? Then I'll be naked while going home.

And why does this happen to me while I'm in the shower here?!?! I have half a mind to go flash my boobs in the gym, so people won't interrupt my showers because obviously this is a conspiracy to see me naked! Wait... maybe I shouldn't think like that. If this is a real emergency, I'm likely to actually flash my boobs, and I wasn't really serious about that being an option.

Oh, boy.

This is the mishmash of thoughts running through my brain in times of emergency. I should never work in emergency services. I obviously don't think clearly enough in times of stress.

I lean back to rinse my hair out again, but before it does any good someone runs in yelling.

"Everyone out now!!! Don't finish up! Just grab your towels and run!"

I guess there's my answer. Doing as I'm told, I shut off the water, reach my hand out for a towel, and fling the curtain open.

As I wrap it around me, I slip on my shower shoes and follow everyone else.

Gosh darnit! I think as I keep struggling with my towel. Of course, they don't have giant fluffy towels that can cover someone up totally. Oh, no. This thing is practically the size of a washcloth and I'm … not. If I wasn't watching the smoke above us turning black, I might be more worried about it. But clearly, I am running for my life. As in, really and truly running without a sports bra on so I don't die in a fire.

Turning the corner to get out of the room, I catch a glimpse as a few ceiling tiles cave in and someone screams. I don't think it's me, but I can't be sure in the chaos I'm feeling.

Holy. Shit. This is really happening. The gym is really on fire while I'm in it.

This, THIS is why no one should work out. See how hazardous it is to my health?

Okay, focus, Rian. Just follow everyone to the exit. The only flames were back there. We have time to get outside. Calm down.

It really only takes a matter of seconds for us to get out the front door and to the parking lot, even if it feels like much longer. Or maybe it just feels surreal. Never in my wildest dreams did I think I would be involved in a building fire. And certainly not at the gym. And certainly not while I'm in the shower.

And it hits me in the middle of all the chaos and confusion…

I'm standing in the parking lot with nothing but practically a hand towel wrapped around me. No one is really paying attention, which is good news. And my shower mate is also naked as a jaybird, but of course she's skinny and perky. Her hair is up in a messy bun and she has that freshly showered glow.

I still have conditioner in my hair.

Yes, I'm alive and don't have a mark on me. For that, I'm grateful. But I'm also suddenly hyper-aware that not only do I look like a drowned rat, my towel won't close all the way, so I'm flashing everyone a glimpse of my hip, my thigh, my muffin top. There is probably some side boob on display, too. So yeah, I'm feeling both humiliated and grateful to be alive, as I watch flames…

Wait… are those real flames shooting out of the top of the building?

My brain is spinning with the reality of what's happening and honestly, it can't quite keep up. It feels like I'm stuck in a movie or bad sitcom. Actually, a bad comedic drama is probably the most accurate, and I'm stuck as the side character everyone is laughing "with" because of the unfortunate set of circumstances.

Side note: I'm not laughing.

But I am trying to figure what happened without drawing too much attention to myself. That means eavesdropping on all the chatter around me. So far, no one really knows for sure, but the speculation is it must have been an electrical fire and started in the wall.

I'm no fireman, but it makes sense considering how long we watched the smoke roll in before the alarms went off.

Adjusting my towel again, I situate myself a little more sideways to hide the exposed parts of me. If we can't get back in the building for a while, I'm not sure what I'm going to do. Surely the emergency crews have supplies for a situation like this, don't they? I can't be the only naked person who has ever run for her life. In order to find out, however, I would have to push through this crowd of people and walk to the other side of the parking lot. Not a stroll I'm willing to make at this point. I'd rather stand here until the crowd clears out and I'm alone.

Looking up, I see Carlos walking toward me. Oh, no. Of all the people to finally notice me, it has to be him? I look down, not wanting to see when the judgement crosses his face. Because I'm sure he doesn't have nice things to say about this situation. I'm not perky and cute and glowy. I'm obese and my hair is still full of conditioner. Flashbacks of the high school locker room after PE bombard me and it takes everything in me not to allow tears to well up in my eyes.

In a few quick steps, Carlos is standing in front of me. Instead of saying something mean, though, he shocks the shit out of me when he pulls his shirt off and pulls it over top of my head.

I squeak, not expecting that at all. "What are you doing?"

"Covering you up." Cover me up, he did. Even with as big as I am, he's so tall and broad that his shirt comes almost down to my knees. I leave the towel wrapped around me so there is a double layer of fabric which makes me feel so much less exposed. Oddly though, I'm also a bit offended now.

A humorless laugh makes it way out of me. "Yeah, I wouldn't want people to see the fat girl in all her glory either."

He looks taken aback. "That's not why I gave you my shirt."

"Are you sure? That girl over there is also in a towel, but I don't see you offering a shirt to her." I point over to my shower mate whose towel is neatly tucked in leaving her hands free to talk animatedly about our escape from death and hug her friends. I wonder what it's like to feel that comfortable in your own skin.

"I only had one," Carlos defends.

"So?" That's it. That's the only comeback I've got. So now I'm naked *and* awkward. Awesome.

A strange look crosses Carlos's face. Like he's just putting together that he impulsively dressed me and didn't realize it until now. Like the entire exchange happened on autopilot. His face begins to turn a slight crimson shade. "Do you want me to take it back? I didn't mean... I wasn't..." He reaches for the hem of the shirt, but I pull away.

"No!" I blurt out, slightly distracted and unable to look away from the very nice six pack of abs that are covered by a sheen of sweat and the pecs that have a light dusting of hair over them. Whoever said forty is over the hill has never seen Carlos Davies shirtless and glistening in the sun. His strong thighs are flexed as he stands with his hands on his tone hips...

Focus, Rian! This is not the time to be drooling over Carlos's body. There is time for that after you are not standing naked in public.

Oh, yeah. I'm naked in public.

Aaaaand my reprieve from embarrassment is over. Although I must admit I feel better knowing I'm not mooning the people behind me. Suddenly, I feel ashamed of the way I'm reacting to Carlos's kindness. "I'm sorry," I blurt out while I have the nerve. "I didn't mean to react that way. I'm just a little shaken up from running for my life, I guess."

"Yeah, I don't think any of us saw that coming. You're okay though, right, Rian?" His face goes back to its normal shade and the look on his face is so sincere, I'm not sure what to think.

"I didn't know you knew my name."

He looks at me quizzically. "Of course, I know your name. I had a lot of fun at dinner that night."

Okay, now I'm really confused. "You did?"

"Yeah. You're really funny."

I notice he doesn't say beautiful, but I suppose there are worse things than being recognized for your humor by the opposite sex. Plus, this whole drowned rat thing isn't my best look.

"You said you work in sales, right?"

Weird topic of conversation to have when I'm naked outside a burning building, but I suppose it's not the strangest part of my day. And it's a welcome distraction from the last thirty minutes of my life, so I'm more than happy to go with it. "Yeah. I'm called a customer care rep officially, but basically my day is spent selling the various packages."

"So potential clients call in and you give them the rundown, figure out what their needs are, and sell them the right option."

"You make it sound pretty basic, but yeah. That's pretty much it in a nutshell."

"Do you like where you work?"

I shrug. "It's okay. I've been there long enough that I get all the perks. It sucks that I've hit the salary cap for my position, but I'm sure a supervisor job will open up. Again. Eventually." And I'll probably be passed up for the job by some other person who has a penis since upper management seems to think the ability for one head to function is reliant on the addition of the second one.

"You don't sound so sure."

Another shrug. "I've been passed up a couple of times with no reasonable explanation, except nepotism and maybe a hint of sexism in there."

"That bad?"

"Just disappointing. But I don't let it get me down. It is what it is." That's what I tell myself anyway. Deep down, though, I'm probably settling. But really, what do I have to complain about? I work for a solid company and get a steady paycheck that's ample enough to provide for me in one of the most expensive cities in the country. That's more than most people can say. "Anyway, why the sudden interest in my job? Just shooting the shit since all our stuff is inside and we have nowhere to go?"

"Actually, I have a sales position open at my company I thought you might be interested in."

I open my mouth to respond, but close it when nothing comes out. In the last thirty seconds, the man who looked right past me an hour ago at the smoothie bar, is now helping me out and giving me a job opportunity while said smoothie bar is burning to the ground.

No, really. Am I being Punk'd? There's no other reasonable explanation for what's happening today.

"Umm…" I croak out. "Okay. I mean, the timing is really weird with this—" I gesture to the building, "—and all, but I guess we don't have anything else to do. What kind of job are we talking?"

He smiles softly but immediately his demeanor changes into a more business professional mode. I'm impressed. It's hard to be professional when you're shirtless and sweaty and standing in front of a woman who is dressed only in your shirt and a towel…

I wonder what would happen if this towel just accidentally fell off…

NO! Stop it, Rian. That sounds like the premise of my mother's romance novels. Who knew this stuff happened in real life?

"It's an account manager position. Our current account manager is stepping down to stay home with her new baby that's going to be born, hopefully sooner rather than later." He shakes his head and runs his hand down his face at that last statement. I suspect there's more to that story, but I don't ask. "Anyway, I'm needing to replace her and after talking to you at dinner, I looked you up a bit. You have an extensive background in account management."

My eyes widen a bit at his compliment. He really Googled me? "I… um… I guess." Feeling flustered, I stumble over my words. He doesn't seem to notice.

"Anyway, I'm trying to get this position filled soon so—"

"Back up! We need everyone to back up!" We're briefly interrupted by a couple of fire and police officials pushing the crowd backward toward the street. More sirens are blaring, and we watch as a third and fourth fire truck pull into the parking lot and more people dressed in fireproof gear hop out.

That's not good. That's not good at all. Especially when we hear what sounds like an explosion, and we watch as part of the roof collapses.

"Holy shit," Carlos says, mirroring the sentiments of basically everyone around us. I've seen house fires on TV or in the movies. But to see it in person is a whole different thing. I have a much bigger appreciation for what it's really like. It's fascinating and yet completely upending a couple hundred people's lives.

I realize at that moment, that this situation goes beyond me racing out here in a towel. Or Carlos giving me his shirt. Or all of us waiting to get our keys to go home. People like Abel? He could be out of a job. Same with Tabitha and all the other employees. And I assume everyone got out, but what if someone is still inside and we don't know?

Suddenly, I'm feeling hyper-aware of how much more goes on in the world beyond my self-imposed bubble. Because if I'm telling myself the truth, that's what it really is. Carlos basically just said it… Sandeke Telecom is fine to work for but will never be better than just *fine*. So why am I settling? Why am I holding back? I don't want my life to catch on fire and I have nothing to show for it.

Okay, that was the worst analogy ever but inside, I'm feeling kind of keyed up. Like it's time to take my life by the horns and go for the best it has to offer.

I think I must have inhaled too much smoke to be thinking like this. But it doesn't stop me from turning to Carlos.

"Where do I send that resume?"

CHAPTER SIXTEEN

CARLOS

D*ear Members,*
As many of you know, the south location of Weight Expecta-tions suffered a fire on Sunday. The fire inspector has done a complete investigation and determined it was caused by faulty electrical wiring in the wall.

We're happy to report there were no injuries despite almost two hundred people being in the building. I credit our amazing staff for following our emergency protocol quickly and efficiently, and I'm proud to work with them.

Unfortunately, there's not only good news. Weight Expectations will be closed until further notice as we determine the best course of action for the building and its members.

However, I'm happy to tell you that as a member of our wonderful gym, our corporate office is giving our south members the option to utilize any of the other facilities in this time of transition...

Sighing, I hate to admit it, but I'm disappointed. I shouldn't be. I ran out of that building like everyone else. I watched the roof collapse. And really, the corporate office isn't required to let us use the other locations. Per our membership, we can't use them all. We just use the one we pay for. Or at least that's the plan I pay for since it was the closest facility and really, why would I need to go anywhere else? It had everything I needed.

It turns out, I tend to be a relatively simple man. If I find a business I like, I visit frequently, and my gym is a place I like. I have friends there. I have a routine there. Rian is there.

"Knock, knock." Teresa pokes her head in. "Mr. Davies, your appointment is here."

Speaking of Rian. The day after the fire, she emailed me her resume as promised. When I read through it, I became more and more impressed. She has downplayed her abilities significantly. Not only has she won a ton of awards for up sales, she's managed an impressive number of accounts, has a satisfaction rate of damn near one hundred percent, and included recommendations from bosses and co-workers alike. I need to pick her brain more because telecom is vastly different from securities. But if my gut feeling is right, and it usually is, she'll pick up the ins and outs quickly. Her raw abilities can't be taught. She's the kind of person who can be successful in any industry.

On a personal level, I hate that she's been stuck in a low-end position with no growth and no one to mentor her. Although, knowing what I do about the Sandekes, it doesn't surprise me all that much. But I'm also not going to crap on my own good luck finding her. She's the kind of person employers dream about hiring.

Rising from my chair, I take a moment to center myself and make sure I'm in boss mode, not guy-who-is-oddly-attracted-to-the-woman-outside-the-door mode.

Buttoning my suit jacket, I stroll to the door, take a deep breath, and open it.

"Rian." I make an extra effort to not smile like a creeper as she stands and walks toward me. She's dressed in plain black dress pants and a plain white shirt. She looks professional and confident. Already, she fits right in.

She also surprises me when she puts her hand out to shake mine. "Carlos. Nice to see you this morning. Thanks for the interview."

Waving her in, I shut the door behind us and gesture toward the leather office chair in front of my desk. "I'll be honest, I've been stressing about how I'd be able to fill this position with the right person, so the timing of our dinner was impeccable."

She stops settling on her chair briefly and furrows her brow. "You were considering me for this job after dinner?"

"Of course. Although it took me way longer than normal to ask you for it, which was my fault." I don't admit to my own struggles to wrap my brain around my attraction to her. Instead, I make a show of unbuttoning my jacket, and lowering myself into my own chair. It makes me feel more in control. "Obviously, I had more questions for you, but your skill set is what I'm looking for."

"There are a lot of people out there with my skill set."

"True. But there's a difference between being able to do the job and being able to do it well. We hire the best of the best here. The nature of this business demands it."

I may be misreading her, but she seems to blush a little bit. Does that mean she's pleased or embarrassed? Nervous? I'm not sure but now is not the time to figure it out. I need to stay focused on the task at hand.

"I'm... flattered."

Ah. So that was a pleased blush.

"You should be." Leaning back, I do my best to go into interviewer mode but I'm failing. Really, I want to know more about her, and this is a convenient excuse to do it. Effective and serves a dual-purpose, but convenient, nonetheless. "What do you know about the position here?"

She clasps her hands together and takes a deep breath. "Not much, really. Just what we talked about."

"Wait. You applied for the job without knowing what all it entails?"

She looks at me incredulously. "I've been a customer service rep for a really long time, and I'm good at what I do. I applied because I'm interested in finding out more. That doesn't mean I'm going to take it."

I can't help the grin that crosses my face. Feisty. I like it. She'll fit in well here. "Touché. And my apologies. How about this—after so many years of working for Sandeke Telecom, why are you interested in coming here?"

Rian licks her lips, and I watch as she chooses her words. It doesn't take long, but it's long enough for me to be really curious about what she's thinking.

"The day of the fire." I nod, encouraging her to continue. "I was standing there in your shirt—" There's that blush again. Completely warranted this time, of course. "—and you started talking to me about my job. A weird conversation in even weirder circumstances, but it got me thinking about how safe it is there."

I quirk an eyebrow. *Safe* is hardly the word I would put in any sentence about the Sandekes.

"There's no challenge for me. It's routine. And there's not really any room for growth, or at least none that I'm being considered for, so there's no concern about failure either."

For just a split second, she stares at the floor, looking really angry about that. It's quickly covered up by resolve as she expands her answer.

"But I realized how I want to get out of that safe box. This could be a great opportunity for me. It might be exactly what I've been waiting for."

It takes a few seconds of staring at her to pull my own thoughts together. I'm not sure what happened in that parking lot, but it sounds like she's tired of putting up with a misogynistic workplace that likes herding their employees like sheep. It also makes me wonder how many people as smart and skilled as Rian got sucked into the hamster wheel over there.

"Here's the deal." I drop my foot from the opposite knee and grab a packet off my desk to hand to her. "I've seen what you've already accomplished, and that's just on your resume and what's posted online. That tells me there's way more to your skill set than you know and certainly way more than the Sandekes are giving you credit for."

"To be fair, the Sandekes don't usually come to my office. They own the business, but that's like saying the president of this company hangs out with the little people.

"He does.

Her eyes widen just slightly. "He does?

I respond with a nod. "He does. He's extremely hands on and it's part of the reason we have such a fantastic reputation. This isn't some securities firm started by a bunch of investors to make money. There is a vision to have the most secure product out there. Because there are two truths none of us can get away from:" I tick them off on my fingers. "One, most of us can't keep up with how fast technology is being developed; and two, that makes some people dangerously greedy. People need a company that cares about the product as much as the bottom line, if not more so. And we don't care if you are a man, woman, transgender, white, black, purple with pink polka dots, have all your limbs, or have no limbs at all. If you are the best at your job, we want you, and we'll take good care of you financially or otherwise. I believe you are one of those people."

Welp. Cat's out of the bag now. I wasn't planning on saying all that to her, especially not so early in the interview, but the idea of her going back to that hell hole makes me ragey. Labor laws and proper treatment of employees is something I take very, very seriously. Even in school, some of the stories in my labor law and EEOC classes pissed me off. I truly believe there is a special place in hell for people who want all the money and all the power, to hell with anyone else.

That's part of the reason I like working for Quinn so much. Well, when he's not being a raging lunatic. He makes a point to take care of his people. Hell, most of his security team has an apartment provided as part of their contract. It eliminates one stressor out of their lives. And a stress-free employee is a happy employee.

So maybe it's not a bad thing I'm showing Rian all my cards. She needs to know this isn't your typical Fortune 500 company. This is a family, of sorts. We don't hire just anyone.

"You think I'm the person you're looking for?"

"You wouldn't be sitting in this room if I didn't."

She doesn't say anything. Just keeps looking at me. I can practically hear the cogs turning in her brain as she goes over my words.

"Let me ask you another question." Her eyes snap up to mine. "In your current position, how do you know what the customer wants? How do you know what package will really meet their needs?"

She blinks a few times and shrugs slightly like it's not something she thinks about. It's just something she does. This is good. That's exactly the instincts that make the difference between a good employee and a great one.

"Well, I guess it's just the little things they say and do while we're on the phone."

"Give me an example."

She thinks for a moment. "Okay. The other day a woman called and while I was looking up her account, she apologized for the noise in the background and said she has four kids under the age of ten."

"So, what did you do?"

"We ended up finding her a package that included all the kids' channels she could ever want and On the Spot Viewing for every TV in her house."

Leaning back, I toss out another scenario. "Let's say you work here and a bank calls. They're needing security across the board. What would you say?"

Her eyes move back and forth as she thinks. "Well, first I'd find out what kind of security they're needing. Is most of their banking online and how secure is it? Do they have a vault on the premises that needs monitoring? What about in-house security? Are they located in a suburban area or more of a downtown? What's worked so far for them and where have they had breakdowns in the past?"

She looks up and sees me smiling at her. She's got a lot of our process wrong, but for an on the spot solution, it's a great start. Instincts can't be taught and hers are bang on.

Looks like mine are, too.

I open my mouth to tell her all that in different words, of course, but I'm thwarted when my door suddenly opens, and Quinn comes barreling in.

Oh, good. Now he's given up knocking, too.

"Sorry to barge in like this." His disheveled appearance says otherwise. He's got circles under his eyes and his hair looks like he's been running his fingers through it. Plus, his shirt is wrinkled. Yeah, he's definitely at his wit's end again. "Janie has a doctor's appointment, so I need to make sure that insurance glitch has been taken care of."

"Is everything okay?"

"Just the regular weekly checkup and subsequent stop for Funyuns and Chunky Monkey. The glitch?"

"Should be fixed and all denied claims being pushed through. Turns out they upgraded one of their systems and it wasn't talking to ours. Their IT department had to fix it, but I haven't had anymore complaints. Karen was going to follow up today."

He clutches the doorknob tightly like it's either holding him up or holding him back. These aren't abnormal stressors, but he's not been handling them well. I have a bad feeling the next step is helicopter parenting for at least eighteen years. God help us all.

"I swear the insurance companies do shit like this on purpose so they can deny coverage until we catch it. We need to look at a new company next year," he grumbles.

I nod in agreement, even though I don't agree at all. We sorted through dozens of policies and dozens of agencies. This is the best deal all the way around, with a company that has the best reputation, even with this nightmare. I don't say all that, though. Instead, I stick with avoidance. "Well, we've got a few months before we can even start pursuing anything because we're under contract. But I'll definitely take it into consideration." No, I really won't. But Janie won't be pregnant then, God willing, so I'm banking on him forgetting.

"Good. The last thing I need right now is this bullshit. I'm trying to track down some yarn from a rare goat in Russia and no one has it. What, does this goat only shed when he wants to? Does he think he's a rock star and will only let himself be sheered when there is a total lunar eclipse which means everyone wants his wool at the same time?"

Okay, so he's officially lost it. I make a mental note to double check Xanax is an approved medication since Quinn is about two balls of yarn away from needing a dose.

Before I can respond, Rian jumps in.

"Have you tried Preda Depot?"

Quinn startles, as if he just realized someone else is in the room. But that doesn't stop him from immediately focusing on the important part. "What's that?"

"It's an online yarn store. Deals specifically in very rare wools like qiviut."

"You knit?" I don't know her that well, but I didn't peg her as the crafty type.

She laughs. "Uh, no. I tried to make a potholder once and ended up with a triangle. No idea how that happened."

Sounds about right.

"No, my sister likes to knit and crochet. I try to get her something interesting for Christmas every year. That's my go-to place. Although if she doesn't get married soon, I'm going to go back to Plain Jane's Fabrics," she mumbles under her breath, and I know there's a story there. Unfortunately, now is not the time or place.

Quinn nods his head, and I know he's absorbing her every word. "I'm not sure who you are, and I apologize for that since I haven't been around lately. But, Carlos, you need to give this woman a raise."

"I don't work here. This is my interview."

"Huh." He gets that look on his face when he has an idea. Usually they're pretty good, but I don't trust his thought process these days. "You ever think of being a personal yarn shopper? Always searching for deals on rare and exotic wools?"

It's official. My boss has lost his mind.

"Sorry," Rian says with a smile. "That's not really in my career plan."

"Bummer." Quinn is still holding onto the doorknob, but at least his knuckles aren't white now. "I know a whole group of women, well, and a man, who would pay good money for your services."

Rian's smile brightens even more. Looks like Quinn has charmed his way into her good graces. "If I change my mind, you'll be the first person I call."

Quinn nods and, as if suddenly remembering he has something to do, he hightails it out of my office, slamming the door behind him. I'll be happy when Baby-Brain Quinn leaves, but I have a bad feeling this is his new normal.

Rian returns her attention to me, but as far as I'm concerned, this interview is over. She just took my most wound-up customer- and yes, in some ways my boss is a client I have to keep happy- calmed him down, gave him some options, and had him eating out of her hand. She's sharp and quick on her mental feet. All good qualities in this business. Her company is stupid not to recognize that. Good thing I'm smarter than them.

Leaning forward, I rest my arms on my desk. I have a feeling she's not going to make this easy on me, but I'm not about to let this one go.

"When can you start?"

Rian's lip quirks up and I know this interview isn't over yet. "Not so fast. I have some questions for you."

Looks like it's my turn to impress her.

CHAPTER SEVENTEEN

RIAN

Peeling open the Tupperware lid, I gasp with delight. That feeling is very quickly replaced with disappointment when I realize what I'm looking at.

"We're not supposed to be eating potatoes, Francesca."

"Then it's a good thing I didn't bring any," she shoots back, peeling her own Tupperware open. Whatever shredded beef she's dishing out onto both our plates looks amazing. Man, I'm hungry.

I roll my eyes, knowing she's always trying to find a loophole. "Mashed potatoes still count as potatoes."

"I know it's hard to believe, but I didn't try to find a work around this time. Unless you count mashing cauliflower as cheating."

Looking back into the bowl, I take a quick sniff. Sure enough, it smells like vegetables. "But are they any good? I'm leery."

She snorts a laugh while licking the spoon clean. "You think I'd be eating them again if they tasted bad? You know me better than that. Many a vegetable has seen the bottom of my garbage can." While she may not be opposed to throwing vegetables away, that doesn't mean she's not opposed to passing them off as edible in an attempt to discourage me from making her do her share of the cooking.

Noticing my expression, she rolls her eyes at my skepticism.

"Don't look at me like that. Think about it for a second. What do potatoes really taste like?"

"Not like cauliflower."

"No kidding," she deadpans. "But what *do* they taste like?"

"I don't know." My mouth waters at the thought of savory mashed potatoes. The kind you get at a fast food chicken joint. They're my favorite. Then I remember that delicious giant baked potato I had last month at the new BBQ joint around the corner from my place. "Like fluffy, creamy goodness made with butter and sour cream and bacon bits and chives. And now I'm really disappointed that this is smashed up trees instead of potatoes!" I rant and bang my hand down on the counter dramatically. She's not phased in the least.

"Okay, calm down there, Ketozilla." She snatches the bowl out of my hand and begins putting the fake potatoes on our plates. Fortunately, she uses a different spoon. Unfortunately, it's my spoon, and there's no way I'm licking it clean now that something healthy has touched it. Now I have to wash it before I can eat. This day keeps getting worse. Cue the dramatic sigh I'm visualizing in my brain. "You listed off four different ingredients but not one of them was actually a potato flavor. These taste exactly like all that because I made it with all that."

Cocking my head, I narrow my eyes. She has my attention. "Go on."

"Okay. The key to mashed potatoes is to get the right consistency and then season it to taste. I just matched the consistency making sure there are no lumps and did everything else the same." Throwing one of the plates in the microwave, she slams the door and turns to face me. "Trust me. This is not the same as the quinoa crisis of last week."

That was a bad day. I still practically get hives thinking about it. Francesca swore up and down it tasted just like rice pilaf. But, oh no. That's not what it tasted like because she's a liar, liar, pants on fire.

Quinoa, or at least the way Francesca made it, tastes like cardboard with a hint of pepper and has some weird consistency that makes it completely inedible. I was so hungry by the end of the day I almost ate a Post-it note because it had a more palatable flavor and I needed some fiber. When I finally left for the day, my starving legs carried me straight to the Dunkin' Donuts down the block for some nourishment. And then I almost threw up on the treadmill from the overdose of sugar. Francesca has since promised to never make that crap again, but apparently, I'm still the target of her culinary experiments.

"So..." She plops down on a chair while we wait for the next minute and fifteen seconds for lunch to begin. I may not be convinced yet, but I'm too hungry not to give her the benefit of the doubt. "How was the bachelorette party?"

I glare at her dubiously. This is not a topic I wish to discuss. Ever. But since she asked, I feel I have no choice but to tell her. "Horrible."

"Oh, come on. It couldn't have been that bad. What's terrible about a bunch of women in their thirties going out on the town?"

Leaning back, I settle in to blow her mind. "Let's see, at the last minute, *Bendy*, the maid of honor, couldn't come. She got sick or something."

"Back up." She holds up her hand to stop me. "Her name is *Bendy*?"

"Yep," I say, popping the 'p' for dramatic effect. "I have a theory that her parents are yogis, but have never met the woman so I haven't confirmed yet."

"Solid theory."

"I think so. So anyway," I continue, arms crossed over my chest as I try to relax on this short-lived break. "She cancelled at the last minute so my sister recruited me to take over, which I didn't want to, but hysteria goes a long way sometimes."

"Which is why I'm glad I don't have a sister."

I nod in understanding. She dodged a bullet with some of this crap. "Basically, that meant I was responsible to call Ubers all night and make sure they were paid as we bar hopped. Lucky me, I also got to cover the cost of a detailed car wash after Lara, or Tara... maybe it was Kara, who knows... regardless, she barfed in the back seat of the car after too many Fireball shots."

Francesca grimaces. "At least it was Fireball. Surely the cinnamon smell wasn't that bad."

I snort humorlessly. "Tell that to my credit card."

"You really aren't making a case for me to ever have women friends, you know that?"

"Believe me, I'm questioning that myself. If that was a normal night out, I'll keep to myself from now on."

"Maybe you'll have better luck meeting some responsible adults at your new job." And just like that, my mood does a complete one-eighty. "Tell me all about it. When are you leaving me, and why are you not taking me with you? And tell me about the men. Is anyone hot?"

I feel my eyes light up. I'm so excited to start my new job in a couple of weeks at Cipher Security Systems. I honestly never expected to get the job, especially not during the interview. Maybe a few days later, but immediately? Didn't even cross my mind.

And full disclosure—I never would have applied if Carlos hadn't approached me directly. Somewhere over the years, I resigned myself to a dead-end job in a dead-end company, just because of the stability it provides. But what kind of career is that? Not a good one, now that I've seen what it can be.

I was also proud of myself for quizzing Carlos on the ins and outs of the company before accepting. I wanted to make sure I was making a smart move. I don't want to make the same mistake twice, but after a good thirty minutes of hearing how the accounts work and what kinds of services are provided, I feel confident about the change. I also feel really good about taking my career by the cajones instead of just plodding along.

"I've only met a few of the guys, but they're huge. I mean, seriously gigantic. I've never felt small before." I gesture to my plus-sized body, not in self-deprecation, but to make a point. "But I swear to you, I feel petite around them. And seriously, every last one of them is hot."

"Oooh, tell me more. Do they have another job opening? I'm always open to new opportunities, ya know."

Yeah. I know exactly what she means, the perv. "I'll keep that in mind when I get there. The whole place is just amazing. The people are awesome. And the company itself is growing fast. And they don't even do much marketing. Most of the clients come to them and all because of word of mouth. It's going to be really demanding I'm sure, but the perks are amazing."

Francesca rests her chin on her hand, elbow on the table. "How amazing? Medical? Dental? 401K?"

I nod excitedly. "All of that and it starts immediately. No waiting ninety days to make sure I'm a good fit. They do so many background checks and security checks. They know anyone they hire will be there until they die."

"Hmm. Sounds kind of shady. You're not joining the mafia, are you?"

I laugh because she's not wrong. If I hadn't gotten the grand tour and seen the whole operation for myself, I'd probably be skeptical, too. "No, I'm not joining the mafia. And yes, it freaked me out a bit until I saw it with my own eyes, but then it all made sense. Look at what their business is. Everyone in that building has to be on the up and up for it to stay at the top of the game."

The microwave dings and Francesca jumps up from her chair. It's no secret that she is a huge foodie, so I'm suddenly encouraged. If she's excited about her new mashed concoction, maybe I'll be able to resist carbs this afternoon before my workout. I'm supposed to have a class with Abel today. He'd never let me live it down if I ralphed all over him. Then again, I don't know yet where he ended up post-fire, so it might be a moot point.

True to form, she whips the plate out and is shoveling the faux potatoes in her pie-hole faster than I can even get my plate into the microwave.

"That good, huh?"

Her eyes roll in the back of her head and she moans as she takes a bite. "If all our healthy food shit tasted this good, my cholesterol would be so low, the company would be paying *me* to use their dumb premiums."

I shake my head in amusement and finally get my food cooking. "Speaking of, how did your last checkup go?"

She sighs and sits down, doctoring her food a little more with salt and pepper. "It's going the right direction but not fast enough. I've been instructed to keep doing what I'm doing and add exercise." She shudders at the thought. I don't blame her. That's the exact same reaction I had.

"You gonna join a gym finally?"

Chewing another bite, her eyes widen. "No way! Not after that fire last week. That was your gym, right? Were you there?"

I cringe. The entire thing, for so many reasons, is not something I'd like to discuss with her. Or anyone for that matter. I'd rather it all go away. Still, she asked a question, and if I dodge it, she'll circle back around. She's like shark smelling blood when she's onto some good gossip, which is great when I'm bored but not so great when I'm the subject of it. "Um.. yeah, I heard about it."

"The pictures online made it look so bad," she says absentmindedly as she eats. "I'm shocked no one got hurt. There were people even standing in the parking lot in nothing but towels. That's how fast it spread."

What?!? There are pictures of me in a towel? Online??

Suddenly, I'm not so hungry as much as I am concerned. How much side boob was flashing? Did I have a towel wedgie? Please, God, say I didn't have a towel wedgie!

Francesca doesn't even notice my sudden panic.

"I can't even imagine having to run for your life like that and standing on the streets of Chicago in nothing but a towel. Good thing it's July. Can you imagine if that happened and they were like that in February weather?"

She has a point, but I'm much more focused on the fact that she didn't recognize me in one of those pictures. Either I look way worse when I'm freshly showered and running from a fire, or the pictures are from behind to protect the identities of the innocent. Again, with the towel wedgie concern. I make a mental note to google it when I get back to my desk. Then I'll have to figure out who I pissed off in a former life to always make this kind of thing happen to me. I wasn't serious when I said I'd flash my boobs if it meant not being interrupted in the shower anymore. Clearly, the universe doesn't understand sarcasm and wit.

"We got an email from them the other day." *Divert her attention, divert her attention...*

"Yeah?"

"Yeah." The microwave dings just as my stomach lets out a roar of protest. Okay, fine. Maybe my hunger didn't subside with my panic. And maybe I'll eat the cauliflower anyway. Knowing my picture may have gone viral suddenly has me motivated in this endeavor. "They don't know what's going to happen to the building yet, but we get to use the other facilities until they decide."

Taking a bite of the meat, I gesture at it with my fork and nod my approval. She waggles her eyebrows understanding what I mean without saying a word.

"That's nice of them, I guess."

I shrug and continue talking, trying to be mindful of the fact that I'm chewing. "I guess. I'm not thrilled about having to get comfortable around a whole new set of people. Plus, it took me this long to figure out how to use their machines. If they don't have the same models, I'm going to get stuck again."

"Stuck where?"

Francesca makes a face like she smells something bad and my shoulders sag. Nolan. The one person I was hoping to avoid for the next two weeks.

"Stuck like Chuck," Francesca replies. It makes no sense whatsoever, but I think that's probably her point.

Sure enough, Nolan looks confused. "Who's Chuck?"

"The groundhog."

"The what?" More confusion. But Nolan isn't the only one. I accidentally take a bite of the fake potatoes and...

Oh.

My.

Gosh.

What is this heaven on my plate???

"Never mind that," I interject. "What the hell, Francesca? Why did you not make these before?"

She smiles at me and waggles her eyebrows again. Because nothing is sexier than fake mashed potatoes. No, really. I could kiss her for this. "Told ya so."

"Hold on, are you eating the groundhog?" Nolan asks, and I swear I almost spray my newfound favorite food on my friend.

"Yes, Nolan." The sarcasm is dripping from her voice. "We're eating groundhog. It's part of our low-fat/ low-cholesterol diet the doctors put us on."

"Huh. I've never heard of it."

Stifling a giggle, I thank my lucky stars my back is to him. How this guy never gets her sarcasm and always takes her at face value is beyond me.

"Anyway, Rian when you're done... eating—" I can practically hear the look of revulsion on his face. If I was a different woman, I'd probably make a point of licking my fingers in response, just to gross him out. But alas, I'm just me and was raised with too many stupid manners. "—I need to meet with you about training a new employee."

I look up at Francesca, feeling resigned. I hate that I'm always the one assigned to this job. They make me do it because I'm the best account manager they have. But all it does it give me extra work. No extra perks. No comp time. No raise. Just a pat on the back for a job well done, and then that person will probably jump over me to take the next promotion when it's available. It's irritating at best.

"You might want to make someone else do it," Francesca jumps in just as I swivel in my chair to face him but before I can say anything. "This one's leaving us behind for greener pastures. And by greener, I do, in fact, mean she's going to be able to make it rain."

I'm positive he has no idea she's alluding to the massive raise I'll be getting, but I don't care. The fact that his face has gone pale and he looks like a fish out of water has made this conversation suddenly much more interesting.

"Wha...where are you going?" he finally asks quietly, fiddling with the now full coffee cup in his hands.

"Cipher Security Systems." That's all I say. I don't volunteer anymore information. I'm more than happy to answer questions, but I'm not going to gloat. At least not in front of the guy who has made jabs about my weight, my personality, my food choices, my cubicle decorations... the list could go on forever. No, I'd rather him see that none of it matters to me. Even if that's a complete and utter lie.

That's the thing about words... even if they're said as a joke, they can still hurt. We just don't always recognize it when it's said with humor.

His eyes widen and chin drops. "The account manager position?"

"How did you know about it?" Francesca interjects, probably as fascinated by his reaction as I am.

"I applied for that job."

Abruptly, it's as if he realizes he didn't mean to say that out loud. Pulling his body back up straight, he clears his throat. "Well, I'll still need you to help train the new person since they'll be your replacement now. So, when you're finished, please come to my office for the details."

He turns on his heel and storms out the door, his usual bravado hidden under what appears to be an inability to process his own disappointment.

Turning slowly, I look at my friend, trying very hard not to look too smug. She, on the other hand, seems to find nothing wrong with being pompous in this moment.

She points her finger at the door while she chews. "That, my friend, is Karma at her finest."

I can't help the smirk that crosses my face as I turn back to my cuisine. Maybe the pretty people don't always get ahead like I thought.

CHAPTER EIGHTEEN

CARLOS

Hiring Rian was the best work decision I've made in a while. She only started two days ago and already fits into the culture like she's been here from the beginning. Everyone seems to love her, and why wouldn't they? She's funny and energetic. Witty and kind. And I can already tell she's going to be fantastic at her job. She's picking up the lingo fast and asks all the right questions. Looks like my track record of hiring the right people remains at one hundred percent.

I pride myself on that. On the fact that I've never had to fire an employee. We vet them so well, we've never had a problem. Although, I admit I was leery about Alex at first. When Quinn said he wanted to bring on a world-famous hacker who had done prison time as a kid for breaking into all the national security systems, I thought he was nuts. How in the hell could we promote safety and security when we had the one guy in the world who could get around any system we implemented? We fought about that one. Hard.

As much as I hate to admit it, Quinn was right. Alex wasn't really a criminal at the ripe old age of fifteen. It's more like he was bored, and who could blame him? With a brain like his, I'm sure the monotony of high school was torturous. Hell, it was bad enough for those of us that don't process faster than the smartest computer out there. But now

Alex has focus and more projects than he could complete in a lifetime. Isn't that every hacker's dream?

A muffled giggle has me looking back over at Rian. This is not the same woman I met at the gym. She seems lighter here. Happier. I didn't notice it before, but I suppose there really is something to the belief that a toxic work environment can bring you down. Because this woman hasn't stopped smiling since she got here. She probably sleeps with a smile on her face. It's not a complete change from her normal personality, but it's amplified enough for me to notice.

Hardly able to stay away from her any longer, especially because I don't know what she's laughing about and for some unknown reason I have an overwhelming need to know, I do my best to saunter nonchalantly across the room and to her desk area.

Around here, we don't have high cubicles. The partitions are only about a foot taller than the desks so we can stay more of an open concept office and still give people the ability to spread out in their own space. Makes it easier to brainstorm and work as a team. Plus, I find that productivity goes down when people feel isolated behind drab gray walls. This way, people can socialize while they work. As long as the job is done right, everyone is happy.

"I know it seems redundant," Teresa, my assistant, says to Rian as I walk up, "but confidentiality is key around here. We have about a zillion forms to sign regarding what can and can't be disclosed outside the office. They are all iron-clad and come with heavy legal repercussions. So, I want to reiterate, make sure you're very aware of what you're signing."

Rian smiles kindly at her. "I promise I will. And I appreciate the precautions. I would never want to put anyone at risk because I accidentally shared information with the wrong person."

"How's it going?" Both ladies look up when I interrupt their conversation. "Getting the lay of the land?"

Lay of the land? What the hell, Carlos? This is an office, not an excursion.

Neither of them seems to notice my cringe, instead smiling like they're the best of friends.

"Just finishing up all her new employee paperwork and making sure she's up to speed on our protocols," Teresa says cheerily. "All that boring HR stuff we require. Oh! And we need to set up a meeting with our financial advisor to go over your 401K with you. There are quite a few stock options to choose from."

Rian puts her hand on Teresa's arm. "Thank you. I've never had a 401K before, so it feels very adult-like. And, Teresa, I don't find any of this boring at all. You're a lot of fun, and I'm enjoying everything I'm learning so far. I don't think I realized how complacent I was in my last job until a couple of days ago. There's so much to learn here. It's exciting."

Teresa laughs as she begins gathering her papers. "Oh, you haven't even seen exciting yet. The last few days have been dull in comparison to our usual normal."

She's got that right. Just by nature of the business, there's always something urgent happening. Whether it be bodily protection for a client in danger, or financial protection for an account at risk, every day is something new. Fortunately, we don't deal with most of it. That's not our function on the back end. But because we're in such close quarters, we still hear all about it. Add into the equation how quickly all the lieutenants have all dropped like flies because of a woman, and half the time I feel like I'm living in a romantic suspense novel.

"I'm looking forward to it." Rian quickly flips through her copies, grabs a file folder, and labels it "HR".

"If you need anything, you know where to find me," Teresa says as she stands. "I'll leave you in the capable hands of the boss man now."

They say their goodbyes quickly, and Rian swivels her chair to look at me as I lean against her desk.

"It looks like you're settling in okay, so far."

She bites her bottom lip, trying to stifle a smile, but she's not fooling me. She's practically vibrating with excitement for this job. Good. The more excited she is to be here, the more of a team player she'll be. Not that I was worried.

"It sounds ridiculous, but I'm so happy here already." She looks around the room, stars practically twinkling in her eyes. "You know how sometimes it hits you out of nowhere that you were just kind of trudging through life in a pallet of grays, and then you make one change, and suddenly everything is in technicolor?"

I raise one eyebrow. "No." I actually do, but I'm really curious about how her thought process works and what her opinions are. Internally, I'm trying to convince myself that it's all about knowing my employees, but I'm doing a terrible job at it. Reality is, I enjoy being around her. I like hearing her talk and her ideas. This is not something I anticipated when I offered her the job.

Okay, that last part might be a lie. I may have had an inkling of interest that night we all went to dinner. But Rian isn't my type and I don't do relationships, so I'm not about to throw gossip and drama into the office mix.

"Hmm," she responds. "I guess I sound a little off my rocker when I put it that way." She waves her hand like she's erasing her last statement from the air around her. "My point is that I really love it here already."

"I'm glad. It's not going to be all socializing and having fun though. We work hard around here," I say, because my boss persona is feeling the need to put up some boundaries seeing as I'm enjoying watching her way too much.

"Oh, I know. And I'll be ready, I promise." Her face goes from serious to confused. "The only thing I can't figure out is what Code Pink means. Whenever it happens, everyone gets this scared look on their faces and they all stop talking and pretend they need to use the bathroom, or they need coffee."

I can't help it. I throw my head back and laugh. I can imagine exactly how we all look when our secret code goes out over the intercom. For someone not privy to the information, I'm sure it's nothing less than entertaining.

Wiping a tear from my eye, I do my best to explain. "You met our boss Quinn during your interview. He came barreling in, probably talking about yarn or something."

She nods. "Yeah. Did he check the website I recommended?"

"No idea. He's not exactly in his right mind right now."

She cocks her head and furrows her brow but doesn't say anything.

"His wife, Janie, is pregnant with their first and has been put on bedrest. Let's just say, he's not handling it well. So, whenever we see him heading this way on the security cameras, a Code Pink goes out to give everyone a heads up to make themselves scarce."

"Aww. He's just excited to be a daddy."

"Oh, no." I shake my head vehemently. "It goes beyond normal new daddy excitement. I'm pretty sure the guys in security are trying to convince Janie to lace his dinner with Valium."

Rian laughs. "Sounds like my bridezilla sister."

"So, you have experience with this kind of thing. Great! I'll make sure all his calls are transferred to you from now on."

Her jaw drops open. "I don't think you can trust me with that kind of responsibility yet, Carlos. I mean, I've only been here two days."

"Considering his wife is who will be training you on our current clients, I feel like you can handle it."

"Well, look how that worked out." Rian purses her lips, clearly unamused. It makes me laugh again and soon she's joining me.

"Oh, yeah. You're going to fit in great around here."

She smiles brightly at my comment, and I can't help feeling good about making her feel good. Weird. I'm not opposed to giving compliments to people when they're deserved, but I find myself wanting to give her more, so she keeps looking like that.

"Hey, can I ask you a personal question?"

Aaaaaand, my defenses go up. I'm not opposed to knowing the people in my office, but I have no interest in them knowing much personal stuff about me. First, because I'm the boss. And second, because it makes me uncomfortable to get that close to most people. But, it's Rian. Somehow, her intensions feel trustworthy. I'm not sure why, but I might as well find out.

"Um." I clear my throat trying to dislodge my discomfort. "Sure, I suppose."

"Which gym are you going to until they rebuild ours?"

The pressure in my chest deflates as quickly as it came.

"That's not exactly a personal question."

She shrugs. "It's not office related."

She has a point. "I thought you were going to ask about my childhood or boxers or briefs or something."

What the hell was that? Why would I ask that? Apparently, I need to reevaluate my own meds because, clearly, I can't think when I'm around this woman. But in true Rian fashion, or so I'm learning, quick wit and sarcasm are her comfort zone so my inappropriate statement in the workplace is thankfully brushed off.

"Those aren't personal questions. Those are best left for when you're lying on your therapist's couch. Although, I recommend not getting too comfortable on that couch and keeping your pants on."

"Noted," I say and quickly move the conversation back to where it should have been all along. "There's another Weight Expectations location not too far from here."

"Really?"

"Yeah. You take the El to get there, but it's only one stop north."

She grimaces. And not just a small flash of expression. No. She is clearly revulsed by the idea of taking the El.

"I mean, you can probably drive there if you want."

"No, it's not that. Getting there is okay. But having to take the El on the way back? After working out? That's so gross."

"So what? You'll fit in with all the other people who smell on public transportation."

She laughs through her nose. "That makes it so much better."

"The other option is pretty ingenious." I lean in closer so I can lower my voice. "You could always shower there before you leave."

Rian mimics my position and leans in closer as well. "You're mocking me, aren't you?"

"Yes, I am."

Both feeling amused, we pull back and I go back to leaning against the desk.

"I think I'd rather contribute to the odor problem on the train. We both know what I look like not-so-freshly showered at the gym. Drowned rat isn't my best look."

Suddenly, I'm assaulted with images of her standing outside the gym—in just a towel, with the skin of her side on display as she tries to blend into the background; wearing my shirt, determined to stay strong and unashamed; talking with a fire official who helped her sort through the remnants of car and house keys they eventually found inside the building.

The images are clear as day, and I'm stumped as to why I'd have such a strong reaction. Is it because it was a traumatic event? Is it because I've had more than one person send me pictures asking about my involvement? Or is it just because it's Rian? In a towel. And nothing else.

Huh. I need to figure this out quick. Or maybe I just need to be an overly encouraging boss and invite her to come with me. You know... so she doesn't get stuck going alone. Because that's the polite thing to do.

"So, listen," I begin, but we both get sidetracked when Nancy, our HR director's office door swings open more forcefully than normal. Probably because a behemoth of a man just opened it.

He's easily over six feet and has a confident swagger as he buttons his well-tailored suit, canvas and leather photojournalist bag slung over his shoulder. Not to mention, he's got a jawline that looks like it's been chiseled straight out of the finest black marble. Personally, I hadn't noticed that part until Teresa mentioned it. Twice.

Right on cue, the office essentially stops, every single woman in the room staring at him, jaws agape. Rian included.

This shouldn't bother me as much as it does. Gabriel doesn't even work here yet, but he will if I want to keep my track record intact, and he's already become the next most eligible bachelor, with all his attention being vied for.

And yes, he's most definitely eligible. Nancy sent me over all his information before his interview that obviously just ended. Legally, we can't ask if our employees are in relationships, but in our line of work, particularly the security side, we don't frown on them volunteering the information. Our background checks would eventually pick up on it anyway, so it just expedites the process. Plus, it's always good to know there is next of kin in the very unlikely event something goes wrong on a job.

Pausing briefly, Gabriel looks around the room at all his admirers. I'm sure it's not the first time it's happened so he very smoothly, channels an Idris Elba smolder. "Ladies." He nods in greeting, his British accent ringing out for everyone to hear.

Teresa, who just happens to be in the vicinity when the door opens, should be grateful she's walking by a chair, because her legs literally give out and she collapses into said chair as she watches him walk away.

My mood continues to sour. I don't have a thing for Teresa, but I still don't appreciate her collapsing dramatically in the office. Quinn needs to stop recommending attractive employees. I have no room in the budget for smelling salts.

Glancing down at Rian again, I see that she's still staring and following Gabriel with her eyes. Since she's distracted, I don't bother with good-byes. I just walk away.

This is one of the many reasons why I don't date people in the office. It's not just because I'm the boss or because a bad breakup in the office place could end up being a volatile situation. It's because I work for a freaking GQ magazine. Every single man who works here is buff, beautiful, and practically a genius. I can hold my own, but I'll never measure up to what these guys are.

Looks like my mother was right. I don't have any desire to be someone's relationship placeholder. Not even for Rian.

CHAPTER NINETEEN

RIAN

Carlos disappeared in the middle of our conversation at work, which I found kind of odd. I chalked it up to him wasting too much time chatting with me when he had actual boss stuff to do. Still, I was a bit disappointed. I was enjoying talking to him. He's not nearly as smarmy as I originally pegged him to be. I think. At least he doesn't come across that way at the office. I'm still unclear if I'm on his list of people he talks to outside of the office, but I suppose it doesn't really matter. We never were friends, just friendly acquaintances, and even that description is pushing it.

Still, it was weird feeling disappointed about his absence. He wasn't really absent, just in his office, but I kind of—dare I say it—missed him. I know, I know. This is the same guy who has looked *through* me more than once at the smoothie bar. But it feels like something has changed. Shifted. He seems to go out of his way to talk to me now, which I like. My heart speeds up just a bit when he's near me and little butterflies seem to hatch in my stomach. I'm not sure if it's just the excitement that comes with having a new friend or something more, but it's a bit disconcerting, and I'm trying not to think about it too much. I'd rather not be disappointed later.

Once I settled down from my conflicting feelings, his disappearing act left me some time to contemplate my after-work plans and I finally caved. As soon as I clocked out, I took the El one stop to a different location of Weight Expectations just like Carlos had suggested. I really, *really* considered not coming at all, but now that I don't have a cooking buddy, I'm more afraid of falling off the wagon than trying out a new facility. I've made too much progress in creating new habits to backpedal now. Well, not on the scale. That hasn't moved much, the bastard. But I have noticed my skin looks smoother, I don't get winded as easily, and, shock of all shocks, I enjoy a good mashed cauliflower.

Francesca's recipe may have started my obsession, but I did a little veggie stalking of my own. Did you know you can mash it and make it into a pizza crust? I had no idea! Now I'm curious what I can do with other vegetables. I might even try cooking with kale next.

I know. Things are definitely getting crazy in my world.

Maybe I need to make a doctor's appointment to see if I have the flu. Craving healthy food clearly indicates some sort of medical emergency, doesn't it?

In lieu of those results, though, I ventured to the train station after work, took my five-minute ride, and ended up here. At the Mall of America's version of Weight Expectations.

I'm not kidding. The building alone is at least three times as big as the one I'm used to, and I'm almost positive there is some sort of pain-inducing exercise machine disguised as a roller coaster somewhere in this madness. Because that would be my luck. I'd be hanging out, enjoying the ride, when… SURPRISE! Time to do squats. I can practically hear Abel's maniacal laugh over it now.

Even the locker room here is bigger. I thought there were enough shower stalls at Firehouse Grill, which is how I lovingly refer to my original location. Man, was I wrong. There are dozens of individual showers. Each of them comes complete with their own door. A DOOR! There are no magnetic curtains to fight with, so it sticks to the wall instead of to itself at the bottom. Nope. Here, a tiny click of the latch behind you means you are safe and secure in your own little stall, which is gloriously bigger than the other ones, no contortionism needed. I bet no one had to flash their boobs around here to take a peaceful shower.

Wait! Forget I said that, Universe! I'm not complaining, I swear! Please don't throw me out on the street in a towel again...

Wandering through the room, even with my negativism, I must admit, the setup is impressive. Downstairs houses all offices, the child-care center which is practically the size of my former elementary school, basketball and racquetball courts, and even a huge café. Tabitha is either going to be excited to work in such a fancy place, or she's going to be pissed she lost control by not being in her own little smoothie bar. It remains to be determined.

The upstairs has everything else. All the weights. All the studio classrooms. All the equipment. And all the treadmills.

Holy cow, there are so many treadmills. There's probably double the number there were at the old place. And they're newer. Sleeker. Fancier. Almost all of them come complete with a tiny, pretty woman with perky boobs wearing a sports bra as a shirt. Well, except that one guy whose sparkly shirt is only slightly bigger than a sports bra. But at least it matches his sparkly headband.

Awesome. Not only am I never going to be able to figure these things out, but I'm going to look like a puffalump next to all these other people. I've got to try, though. Rian Thompson is no quitter! Well, except that time I joined the summer swim team. But it wasn't my fault! No one told me until after my registration was already paid that practice started at seven in the morning over summer break. So really, I didn't quit. I was tricked. Two totally different things.

Finding the lone, unused treadmill amidst the sea of bouncing boobs is a bit of a challenge, but I'm finally climbing up on the machine, ready to get my workout set to go. Except...

What the hell kind of treadmill is this? There are no buttons anywhere and no indication if the thing is on or not. Maybe it's not plugged in?

Climbing back off, I find the cord and follow it to verify the existence of electricity. Yep. It's there. So, I climb back on before anyone thinks the machine is available for use. Looking around, I hope someone notices and takes pity on me. But no. No one seems to notice my struggle. Or maybe they're ignoring me. Either way, no assistance is offered, and I still can't figure this damn thing out. Seriously, is it broken? Maybe there's a switch hiding on the back that needs to be flipped.

Climbing back off, I search every part of the machine for something that might lead me to success. And by success, I mean, the ability to even begin. Forget going fast. Let's just... go.

I climb back on, recognizing that if I keep this up, my entire workout is going to consist of stepping on and off this thing. Just my luck—stair-climbing is my least favorite workout ever.

Hands on my hips, I cock my head to the side and glare at it. "What is the matter with you?" I grumble.

"I feel like we've done this before."

I startle and throw my hand over my heart. "Ohmygod, Abel, you scared me." And kind of pisses me off. No one noticed when I was struggling, but suddenly, now that a hot trainer is standing over here, all eyes are on us.

"I'd say I was sorry, but the look on your face kind of made my day."

"Your life must be super boring if I'm that entertaining."

He shrugs. "Could be worse. Things could be so exciting I could live on the other side of bat-shit crazy."

"Point made. Are we going to have our regular weightlifting class here anytime soon?" I already got the email about it from him, but since I'm behind schedule, I might as well procrastinate more. Can't let Abel get too complacent.

"You already know the answer to that, so let's not start a bullshit conversation in the name of avoidance, okay?" He leans over and touches the screen in front of me, bringing my machine to life.

Drat. Foiled again. And also... made a fool of.

"How the hell did you do that?" I exclaim, looking all around the machine again. Seriously. I literally heard a motor start whirring as soon as his finger touched the screen.

He chuckles lightly. "It's a touchscreen. No buttons needed. You control it all up here."

Sure enough, as he emphasizes the word "here", it jerks beneath me and off I go.

"Intervals today, right?"

I nod and get my footing. As much as I enjoy Abel's company, though, part of me wishes he would go away so I didn't have an audience. I know there were a few gym bunnies at the old place, but they're everywhere here. Someone is liable to get hurt if they can't concentrate on what they're doing.

"Abel, I think you need to go somewhere else."

Oddly, his face falls and he looks like I kicked his puppy. "Why?"

I make a show of looking around. "You're fresh meat, man. The new guy on campus. These women are going to be on you like white on rice, ooohhhh.... Cauliflower rice!" I snap my fingers together, because that is the best idea I've had today! I wonder how long it takes to cook. I need to look that up. "Does this monitor have wifi? I need to look up a recipe," I ask absentmindedly.

"Wait, what? What does rice have to do with me leaving?"

I huff. "Keep up, man. I need a recipe for cauliflower rice. I have a craving now. Does Google work on this thing?"

He bats my hand away just as I reach for the touchscreen. "Unless you want to end up flying off this machine, I suggest you stop pressing buttons on a machine you don't know how to work."

"Excuse you," I announce indignantly. "How do *you* know I don't know how to work it?"

"Because I just watched you spend ten minutes making sure it was plugged in before I turned it on for you."

Rolling my eyes at his haughty assessment, I argue, "Maybe I watched you close enough that I learned."

"Doubtful. It took you three weeks to figure out the one that had a big bright "on" button flashing in your face. I've already wagered you'll never figure this one out."

My jaw drops and I crinkle my nose. "With who?"

He points behind me, and I glance over my shoulder to see Tabitha giving me a smug grin and waving her traitorous fingers at me. "Benedict Arnold!" I shout, but I doubt she hears me. The person next to me on their own treadmill does, however, and shoots me a dirty look. "Sorry. Not you."

"Now that we're on the same page," Abel continues as if he didn't just shatter my friendship with the smoothie lady. I'll show her. Today, I'm ordering from someone else. See how she likes it when her friends turn on her. "What are you talking about me leaving?"

"Abel. Look around you." He does. "All these women are running faster than they were five minutes ago, and it's all to make you notice their boobs."

"Hmm." He looks more amused than he should. Is that a flirty smirk I see? "That might not be a bad thing."

"Uh, not if you want to keep your marriage alive. It might be best to avoid the gym bunnies. And that cougar over there." I point her direction. She's definitely older than the rest of them, but the blonde hair, fit body, and Double D's remain the same.

"Oh, yeah. About that. I'm getting a divorce."

"What?!" Shock doesn't even begin to describe how I feel. I'm stunned. So much so that I immediately put my feet on the steel edges of the treadmill so I can stop walking and focus on this conversation. It has nothing to do with my lack of motivation. Nope. Not at all. "But, when? Why? I mean, none of that is my business. But you seemed so happy." And he did. Anytime his family came up in class, he always talked about how much he loves his little girl and how proud he is of his wife in her modeling endeavors.

His demeanor changes slightly. He doesn't look defeated, exactly. But now that he's told me, I definitely see a difference. There are circles under his eyes, and he doesn't carry himself as confidently as he did. I could also be making it up in my head, simply because I know what's going on, but I don't think so. I think I've been so wrapped up in my own drama I missed the subtle changes. Now I feel terrible.

"I was happy. We both were. Or so I thought." He leans in a little closer, so no one overhears but I don't miss Nosy Rosy behind him turning her head to get a better eavesdropping angle. "She got a really great job offer in New York and said she couldn't pass it up."

I gesture like I don't understand and step back onto the machine, careful not to fall. "Uh huh. So, she goes on a business trip like normal people. I don't get how this leads to divorce."

"Apparently, her agent said she would have more success if she lived there and could go on last minute auditions."

"I call bullshit."

"Yeah, well, considering her agent is already her new boyfriend, I would agree with you."

For the umpteenth time since I've gotten here, my jaw drops open. Under the circumstances, though, I close it quickly. "I'm so sorry, Abel. That's horrible. What a shock."

He shrugs and quirks his lips to the side in sort of a half-smile that doesn't quite reach his eyes. "At least she left Mabel with me. That's the only good part to the story. It's a lot harder being a single parent now, but millions of people make it work. I can, too, right?"

He has a good attitude, but I still feel bad for him. It must totally suck to be blindsided like that by the person you thought you were going to be with for the rest of your life. At least his classes are going to fill up once the grapevine starts spreading this tidbit around. Because you know all the single ladies are going to show up trying to turn Abel's eye.

Well, damn. I have a hard enough time doing his class without fresh eyes on me. She ruined everyone's life with her immature choice, didn't she? Now I'm pissed off at his ex, too.

Abel reaches over and suddenly the treadmill is going faster.

"Hey!" I grab the handles to help balance myself. "What are you doing?"

"No more distractions. Time to get your butt moving."

Narrowing my eyes, I purse my lips in response. "You could at least be a little nicer in your grief."

"HA! It's my excuse to make you work harder."

I sigh dramatically. "Is it too soon to say I hate your ex, too?"

A huge smile crosses his face. There's my Abel. He may have been knocked down, but he'll get up again.

Crap. Now I have Chumbawumba running through my head.

"It's never too soon to loathe her. But it's too soon to get off this machine so keep going."

I flash him a dubious look. "You think I can figure out how to turn this thing off?"

"I have faith in you. Come find me when you're done, Rian. We have work to do."

Abel turns and saunters out of the room, his swagger on full display. I'm sure he's making a show of it now that he realizes this new location is full of fresh meat, as proven by all the eyes following him as he leaves.

I have a sinking feeling as so many heads crane at once to watch and sure enough, my premonition is confirmed when sparkly headband loses his balance, falls, and flies backward off the machine.

At least I'm not the only clumsy one.

CHAPTER TWENTY

CARLOS

"Have you checked Funko Dunko? No? That's the one I told you about last week." Rian types as she's on the phone, not missing a beat. "I'm sending you an email with the link now. Don't disregard it this time! You could've been searching interesting baby patterns for days instead of stressing about it."

Yes, I'm eavesdropping. No, I don't understand half of the conversation Rian's having. But that doesn't stop me from listening in as she talks to Quinn. Somehow, she ended up answering his random call last week about some ridiculous issue. I'm pretty sure he was following up on some new hire information, but considering the conversation in front of me, I never really know anymore.

Anyway, when Rian accidentally intercepted his call, she was able to talk him off the ledge about making yarn fire retardant or something. Then they started talking wool. Then, they started talking patterns. And now he calls her line directly when he needs help figuring out what Janie's looking for and how he can make his wife and her knitting friends happy.

She is truly the greatest hire I've ever made. Even Nancy keeps saying what a godsend Rian is for answering his calls. Not that any of us mind.

Okay, fine. We all mind. Mostly because none of us ever know what the hell he's talking about if it's not related to the business, nor do we know how to help him. It makes me feel a little guilty for not trying harder as he spirals more and more into insanity, but Rian's got it completely under control. Well, mostly.

"Do I need to email Janie instead?" Rian threatens playfully, then throws her head back and laughs at his response. "Well, you didn't tell me it was a surprise! Listen, I know you'll probably miss the email and pretend it went to spam or something..." She pauses and smiles. "Yeah, you will. Don't lie to yourself. Anyway, when I have some down time, I'll do a quick search and see if I can find what you're looking for. I'm positive there are knitting patterns for baby beards. I might even find one that doubles as a binky holder."

What the...? You know what? I don't even care that much about what she's talking about as much as the fact that it's keeping Psycho Quinn off my back so Bossman Quinn and I can get some work done.

We've got "Gabriel the god" hired. Teresa's nickname, not mine. A few others are in the works. The insurance nightmare is fixed, thanks to Karen putting two and two together. Quarterly taxes are being processed. And Rian will be up and running by the time Janie pops. The only thing we haven't figured out yet is the architectural part of Rian's job.

Janie is an anomaly because she's always done double duty. She managed the accounts and made recommendations, yes. But with her architecture background and aptitude toward visualizing spatial design, she was also able to recommend very specialized packages for our clients. That's just not a strength Rian possesses, and to be honest, Janie isn't your average, everyday person. Basically, she's a genius in an awkward, clumsy package, which is why Quinn is so head-over-heels for her.

I wonder, briefly, what that must feel like—to be in love with someone like that. Does she take his breath away, in a very literally sense? Does she make him want to be a better person? Does he stare at her like a creeper from across the room like I'm looking at Rian?

No. Nope. Nu-uh. That's not what I'm doing here. I'm merely

paying attention as my employee talks to the president of the organization.

"Okay. Okay." I can tell she's starting to wind down the conversation. It's a good thing, too. I really do need to find out when she plans to get with Janie to go over the current accounts. "I promise it's no big deal. I'll find some great stuff that they'll love. Okay. Call me if you need me. Okay, bye."

She hangs up the phone, the smile still on her face. Either she's really good at faking her interest in this topic, or she genuinely enjoys talking to Quinn. I have the overwhelming need to find out which it is.

"Hey."

She looks up and smiles brightly at me. "Hey!"

Gesturing at the phone, I say, "Quinn?"

"Yeah. I don't know why you guys are so weird around him. He's so much fun to talk to."

That's the first time anyone has used those words in a sentence about Quinn in the last couple of months, so I assume she's either trying too hard to fit in or has a bat-shit crazy streak of her own.

"Oh, come on." She nudges me with her foot. "I'm serious."

I hold my hands up in a defense pose. "I don't doubt that at all."

She laughs lightly. "Give him a break. He's not mean or demanding. He's scared shitless."

I sigh because she's right. "You're right. When he doesn't have a screw loose, he's an amazing boss who really trusts his employees to get the job done."

Rian nods vigorously. "And?"

I look back and forth quickly, trying to figure out what she means. "And what?"

She waves her hand at me. "Give me more. What else do you like about Quinn?"

"Really?" I deadpan. "We're gonna play the I Love Quinn game?"

She smiles and it hits me straight in my gut. There's genuine happiness on her face, and I put that look there. It's an oddly satisfying feeling.

"Of course, we are. He's a big ole teddy bear, and you'd be good to remember that."

I roll my eyes and then drop my chin to my chest. "Fine. He's kind and generous, and his butt looks great in a suit. Are you happy?"

She barks out a laugh and that's another sound I like hearing a little too much. I need to get control of this and quick.

"Yes. Thank you." She reaches over and pulls up the calendar linked to her email. "By the way, since I know you're about to ask, again," she takes on with a playful smirk, "I emailed Janie and I'm going to meet with her on, um... Tuesday next week to make sure everything is squared away with the current accounts. Will that work for you?"

I furrow my brow. "Yeah, but you're going to their home? I thought Quinn didn't want anyone over there."

An amused sound comes from Rian. "Janie vetoed that real quick. She wants to go over everything in person to make sure I really know the accounts backward and forward. Plus, it helps that I'm the only one around here who will humor his baby craziness, so he has a fondness for me," she adds with a shrug.

"A fondness, huh?" I smile at her and realize...this feels an awful lot like I'm flirting with her. But I'm not, right?

Flirting is sultry smiles and licking my lips and small touches, isn't it? Laughing and smiling... not the same thing. Maybe? Either way, I'm liking Rian more and more. Almost too much. No, definitely too much. I don't need this kind of complication. And I don't need to lead her on.

She turns back to her computer, which is good timing because I know my face just fell with the realization that I'm playing with fire. I need to get out of here. Quick.

"It's hard not to have a soft spot for the person who knows how to get specialty yarns. If I show up with that binky pattern, he may just adopt me—" Rian begins but gets interrupted when Nancy opens her door. It seems like she's always interviewing someone these days.

Out she comes behind her interviewee—Rebecca from the gym.

When we went over her resume, I had no idea this was the same

Rebecca that likes to use the suspension bands at the gym. The same Rebecca that gives subtle glances and chest stretches to gain the attention of her fellow workout partners. The same Rebecca who is also subtle and timid in bed, as I found out not too long ago.

It was just one night. It wasn't earth-shattering. It was just mindless sex. A way to scratch the itch. A good lay. Scratch that. It wasn't even that good. She's a bit like a dead fish in the sack, but honestly, sex is never really *bad* for men. Not like it can be for women. As long as we finish, there's nothing really awful about it. In this case, it just wasn't something I had a desire to do again with her.

Needless to say, though, when Rebecca walked in for her interview, I was shocked to see her because I never, ever hire someone I've hooked up with. Maybe that's one of the reasons shallow relationships are best. I don't accidentally dip my, um, *toe* into my applicant pool.

Rebecca struts out of Nancy's office looking like she knows she nailed the interview and the job is hers. Nancy, on the other hand, is wild-eyed and making a slashing motion across her neck. Nancy always has a game face so the fact that she doesn't can only mean one thing—Nancy wants Rebecca out of this building immediately and banned from the premises. This is not good news for our receptionist search, nor for my vetting skills. I need to pay better attention. It feels like I'm losing my touch.

Unaware of the gestures being made behind her, Rebecca makes eye contact with me and approaches at a rapid pace. "Carlos," she says breathily once she's standing inside my personal space, completely ignoring the fact that we're at a place of business and her very obvious advances are inappropriate. But I'm so thrown off by my thoughts about Rian, I'm practically frozen in place. "I'm so happy to have run into you now that I'm done. Nancy was just lovely." She looks over her shoulder to give Nancy a saccharine sweet smile. Nancy's smile looks a lot more forced. Turning back, she puts her hands on my chest. "I'd love to—" A quick lick of her lips so her intentions aren't mistaken. "—catch up. How about some coffee?"

The vibe in the room completely changes. Or at least, in this area of desks. I can practically feel Rian's eyes watching my every move wondering how I'm going to respond. I shouldn't be considering how she feels about this situation, because it shouldn't matter at all, but I am and that pisses me off. Somehow, I've developed a crush on Rian and it's clouding my ability to do my job right. I was too busy staring at her across the room like a prepubescent teenage boy with no game than complete a thorough enough check on Rebecca to make sure she wasn't the loose woman from the gym, who may or may not have a screw loose. And I'm too keyed up to remove Rebecca's hands from my body, even knowing all eyes are on me.

So now, I'm in a predicament. I need to get Rebecca out of the office, and I need to get away from the woman I suddenly realize I may have feelings for. I can only see one way out of all these messes.

"Sure," I respond, hearing a small gasp come from Rian. Not exactly what I was hoping would happen, but what choice do I have at this point? "I've got a little bit of time before my next meeting. Care to join me now?"

Rebecca bites her bottom lip seductively, and I'm no longer sure how I ever found that attractive. Her lips look slick and wet and sticky. I can only imagine getting whatever that crap is all over my face if she tried to kiss me.

"Lead the way." Her voice takes on a sensual quality that also sounds fake, but there's no turning back now. Not that I want necessarily to. I'll play it off later and tell Nancy it was the fastest way to get Rebecca out of the office. I just won't mention it was also the fastest way to get away from Rian as well.

Reaching my hand out, I gesture for Rebecca to pass me. As she does, she stops and looks at Rian quizzically. "I'm sorry, but do I know you?"

Rian's face is devoid of any emotion as she says, "No."

"Hmm." Rebecca's head bobs once to the side. "I guess you just have one of those faces." Then turning back to me, she winks and heads toward the elevator.

I follow behind her, mechanically putting one foot in front of the other as I lead her to the elevators, out the front door, down the street…

I'm only half-listening to her yammering on about some random celebrity gossip and the latest plot line to her favorite firefighter show. I should be putting more effort in, just to be polite, but my thoughts are too busy swirling with confusion of my feelings for Rian.

I don't like her, do I? I mean, I like her. She's amazing. She's smart and witty and kind. Her smile lights up a room. She's the only person I know who could see past how annoying Quinn is these days to help find ways to make him less crazy. She's just... phenomenal. But...

But what?

The entire walk to the coffee shop, the only thing I can think is how I don't do relationships. I'm forty years old and have never had a girlfriend for a reason. I have no desire to spend time with someone until they decide they'd rather hang out with someone else. Quick, simple, in and out, is better for me.

Women like Rebecca are better for me.

Pulling open the door of the closest coffeehouse, Rebecca walks in first, her air of confidence bordering on arrogance. Not the gentle self-possession Rian has. She walks with purpose, but also kindness. Like she sees others around her and...

No! Stop it, Carlos! Stop thinking about Rian. You are here with Rebecca.

Clearing my throat, I try to focus on my, um.... date? Is that what she thinks this is? I hope not, or I've got even more problems to figure out.

"What would you like to drink?" I speak quietly, feeling like I'm walking through a bad dream. Here with a woman I don't like so I can avoid the one I do like, all while trying to save face at the office. I'm seriously losing my touch.

Rebecca twirls a hair around her finger. "I'll let you decide since it's your treat, but make sure it has mocha in it. I like a little mocha swirl in my coffee. And my men."

I'd be offended by her inappropriate comparison of skin color to food if it's wasn't for the fact that I'm half Puerto Rican and half Norwegian, so the description doesn't fit me anyway. Which makes me even more disappointed in myself for not vetting her properly. Especially if making assumptions about people without gathering information first is her norm.

"I'll go find us a place to sit." Rebecca walks off, and I'm left wondering how suddenly this became my treat.

I shake my head and place my order, pushing aside any discomfort I feel. No, I probably won't see Rebecca again, except at Weight Expectations, but she's a decent woman. Interesting, if a little dense. Easy on the eyes. Well, except for that lip gunk. But really, I could do worse than spending half an hour chatting over a cup of hot java.

"Carlos!" a barista calls and places two drinks on the counter for me to grab. Rebecca has made herself comfortable in an oversized chair, her purse on the one next to her. As I approach, she looks up from her phone, smiles at me, and moves the bag.

"I got you a white chocolate frappuccino," I say as I relax into my own chair. It's a little lumpy but not bad for as old as it probably is. "I hope that okay."

"Sounds perfect," she purrs and purses her lips, exaggerating the blowing motion. When she finally sips, her moan can practically be heard across the room. I watch, fascinated. The more she does these things that are clearly supposed to be seductive, the more I wonder how I ever found it attractive.

Is this what a midlife crisis feels like? It must be. There is no other explanation for it feeling like my perception of the world has turned completely upside down.

Rebecca lowers her cup and looks up at me, practically batting her eyelashes. "I was so excited when you called about the interview, especially since it had been a few weeks since we, well, you know." She smiles shyly at me, because yes, I know exactly what she's implying. "It was as if fate brought us back together, don't ya think?"

No, not really, is what I think.

"Uh huh," is what I say.

"We were just so good together. It's like we had this connection. Not just physically but like a spiritual connection. Whenever our eyes would meet across the room or in the mirror, it's like the stars would align —"

I try hard to keep engaged in the conversation, but the more she talks about how connected we are on a spiritual level, the more I zone out. And the more my thoughts return to the woman I'm trying hard to run from.

How is it possible for me to like Rian so much? She's not my type in any way. She's... not shallow. She has depth and wit and thinks outside the box instead of following the crowd. From what I can tell, she's not interested in being better than anyone else. She just wants to be the best at what she does, or at least, not the worst.

Maybe that's not what's bothering me. I like Rian. Fine. She's like-able. But why the sudden change in *me*? Why do I suddenly have feelings I've never had before? Feelings strong enough that I'm not as focused on my job as I should be, which is something I've always prided myself on. Man, it's almost like Quinn having a hard time paying attention because he's so in love with his baby.

Wait.

Waitwaitwaitwait. I'm not in love with Rian. Even if I'm attracted to her, it's way too early to be in love. Am I in like?

Holy shit. I'm in like with Rian.

And I'm back to acting like a prepubescent boy with no game. This isn't going to work for me. I'm better than this. So is she. So, the question is... what do I do with this now that I've figured it out?

My phone vibrates in my pocket, and I shift on my chair as I grab it, tuning back into Rebecca who doesn't seem to have noticed I was lost in my thoughts.

"- mercury was probably in retrograde last time we were together. That's why it didn't work out until now, don't you think?"

"Uh huh," I respond absentmindedly as I open my text. It's from Tabitha.

Tabitha: I need to let off some steam. Meet me at Luma after work?

Perfect. She'll know exactly what to do about my newfound feelings and since she doesn't do many of her own, won't judge me for it.

Me: Do I have time to workout first?

Tabitha: Yep. We're leaving from here.

Clicking my phone closed, I make a note of the time and realize if

I'm going to go out to drinks, I need to get some stuff done at the office. Now to figure out how to end the coffee date politely.

"It's just amazing how the universe works."

I pause momentarily, and I think Rebecca is finally done talking, I jump in, not wanting to miss the opportunity.

"Well, it was really good seeing you." I quickly stand, ignoring the look of shock on her face.

"Wait," she says, confused. "You're leaving?"

I slap a smile on my face, trying to diffuse the blow she is no doubt feeling. "Well, with all the expanding we're doing, I still have a lot of work to do." Buttoning my suit jacket, I stand up taller, hoping to look the part I'm presenting to her. Not that it's a lie. I *do* have a lot of work to do. "Nancy has a few more candidates to interview, but she'll let you know the results in a couple of weeks."

Rebecca closes her eyes and shakes her head just slightly. "Hold on. So, I don't have the job?"

"Today was just the interview. It's our process to meet with several people for each position. Just to make sure we have the right candidate."

"But…" she starts, and I find myself feeling a tiny bit sorry that she's going to be disappointed. But the look on Nancy's face after the interview is imprinted on my brain, so there's no way she's being hired. I hope this isn't the only job she applied for. "But you'll put a good word in for me, right?"

I smile kindly, hoping to soften the blow. "I'll be sure to give Nancy my thoughts."

Rebecca relaxes a little and smiles seductively again. "Wonderful. I'll see you soon."

Hopefully not, I think as I race out the door and back to the office. For the first time ever my lack-of-dating life is coming back to haunt me and a new emotion I haven't felt before comes flooding in…

It feels an awful lot like regret.

CHAPTER TWENTY-ONE

RIAN

I hate weight training. It's my least favorite exercise. Well, behind running, yoga, those band things that hang from the wall, and the rope. I'm sure that list will get longer the more Abel has his sadistic fun, but I can confidently say weights are my top five most hated exercises.

Today, however, I'm grateful for the outlet. Nothing works out your anger better than bench presses. Unless punching someone in the face counts as stress relief but somehow, that's frowned upon. It's unfortunate for me, because today I'm chock full of emotion that needs to get out.

Oh, who am I kidding? That's downplaying what I'm feeling. I'm pissed. Really pissed. Pissed that I was starting to like Carlos as more than a friend. Pissed that Carlos left for coffee with that woman. Pissed that I allowed my feelings enough leverage that I didn't see this coming and feel hurt.

The kicker is, I'm not even sure why I feel this way. Carlos is my boss, not my friend. We went to dinner one time accidentally, and he struck up a conversation by default. He barely even looks at me at the gym. The only reason he has any interest in me at all is because I'm good at my job. So why did it hurt so bad when he took off with that, that gym bunny?

Abel continues counting, and I can tell he's supporting the bar more than normal. It could be the fact that I'm pressing more weight than normal. What can I say? I was afraid it was too light, and my anger would have me accidentally throwing the bar over my head. Better be safe than sorry and all that crap.

"Fifteen. Awesome work—Sixteen? Seventeen? Eighteen? Whoa, whoa, whoa." Abel grabs the bar and pulls it away from me. "You're doing great, but slow down before you hurt yourself."

Too late. I'm already hurt. Not the kind he's talking about, but of course, I'll never tell him that.

"What's with you?" he asks, as I sit up and mop my brow. And my back. And down the front of my shirt. Boob sweat—it's a real thing. "I've never seen you so hyped up about working out before. Usually you're bitching about how your muscles ache from the walk up the stairs."

"Maybe I've turned over a new leaf."

"Not likely. Wanna talk about it?"

"No. I wanna talk about why your wife walked out on you and you're still happy-go-lucky." His face falls and I know I've crossed the line. Shame fills me, and I find myself staring at the floor, face flaming. "I'm sorry. That was uncalled for. I didn't mean to take this out on you."

"You're forgiven. But you also have a valid question." He sits down next to me on the weight bench, which is weird. Like we're having a moment. I'm not sure if I should crack a joke or cry on his shoulder, so I don't do either. I just listen. "I don't know. I guess our marriage wasn't all that great anyway. May is kind of self-absorbed and demanding. At first, I was stunned and a little sad that she left, but after about a week, I realized I was more relieved than anything."

"Really?"

"Yeah. I wasn't walking on eggshells, making sure she wasn't unhappy anymore. Even Mabel seems happier. I never realized how much tension was in the house until she was gone. I think, in the beginning, I wasn't really sad as much as I was shocked, and my pride was wounded."

Sounds about right. I don't have any reason at all to be jealous of Carlos taking other women to coffee. I don't even think I like the guy most of the time. But seeing him lose interest in our conversation when a beautiful woman walked in the room stung. It was just a reminder that I'm always the "interesting one", until someone more interesting comes along. Talk about a blow to the ego.

I nod in understanding and take a deep, calming breath. "How many more reps do you want us to do?"

"I have a better idea. Ladies, follow me."

Abel walks the four of us in his class downstairs. Our class has gotten smaller since we don't have our normal location to meet at. I suspect it's because all the "regulars" are scattered around at the various facilities, depending on what's convenient. I feel bad for Abel because it's like he has to start his entire business from scratch, but selfishly, I'm glad we get more one-on-one time.

Abel takes us into a room I've never seen before. It houses some of the larger weight racks and exercise machines, not just free weights. He pulls out some punching bags that look like they've been resting in a corner for a while. Then, he hands us each a set of gloves.

"I know what you ladies are thinking."

"That this could come back to haunt you?" Dee asks, and we all laugh. Even Abel.

"No, but now that you mention it, the first rule of boxing is that you only punch the bag. So always remember rule number one." We all groan, even though we're not serious while Abel continues explaining how to stand and how to twist to punch.

It takes a few minutes for us to get into it, but after a while, even I have to admit boxing is kind of fun. Jabbing the bag as hard as I can, I feel my tension starting to melt away. It helps that I'm envisioning my boss's face on the bag. And maybe his nuts. Some people call it psychotic. I call it motivation.

"Nicely done, Rian," Abel says supportively. "Make sure to tighten your core when you twist. Really concentrate on your form. This is about quality not quantity."

I jab right. I jab left. I make sure my feet are in the right position and I twist with purpose. My muscles feel tight yet relaxed at the same time. My mind begins to feel more Zen.

"Okay, Rocky, let's try a new one." Abel comes up behind me, probably to make sure he doesn't get in my line of fire. Smart man.

I drop my arms and put my hands on my hips, breathing deep. Abel's face lights up at my obvious enjoyment.

"You're enjoying this, aren't you?"

I nod and try to slow my breathing. "It's getting out all my pent-up aggression."

"Good. Let's try something else. Turn and face the bag." I do and Abel stands behind me and puts his arms around me. I don't think I ever realized how big he is until now. If only he was a few years older and not the bane of my existence most days.

Grabbing my arm, he helps me position it up in the air, elbow out. "This time, it's going to be like a sideways jab. Pretend the person you're visualizing—"

"That obvious, huh?" I interrupt.

"You never work out this hard without cracking jokes. Blatantly obvious. Anyway, pretend you're punching them on the side of their head. It's called a roundhouse hit, so make sure you have an arch in your movement." He moves my arm slowly to show exactly how to swing and exactly where he wants my punch to land.

"What do I do with my feet?" I ask, suddenly very, very into exercise. I know my muscles are going to hate me tomorrow, but right now I don't care.

"Just stand with your feet apart. Your whole body will twist into the movement, working your core in a different way."

It's slow going as my body gets used to the motion, but soon Abel is leaving me to help the others out as well. As I punch, slowly but methodically, I feel like I've found my exercise. The thing that not only helps my body, but my brain as well. I didn't realize how angry I was, but I also realize it's probably not just about Carlos.

It's about my sister's constant and subtle ridicule lately. It's about Nolan's sarcastic mockery. It's about the sexist environment I allowed myself to work in for so long without giving myself enough credit, despite all my awards.

It's about not loving myself enough because I've been too busy internalizing what people said around me.

I blink back the tears I feel welling up in my eyes. I don't understand why this is making me impassioned, but every punch feels like an emotional release of some sort. I make a point of wiping my sleeve over my face, pretending to be wiping away the sweat when really, I'm making sure the rogue tears don't have the chance to fall.

I keep jabbing.

Jabbing at my anger.

Jabbing at my disappointment.

Jabbing at my hurt.

Jabbing at this strange sense of sadness I didn't know I felt.

I jab and I jab and I jab until I'm drenched in sweat and emotion.

And then as if I'm conjuring him, the one I'm visualizing is suddenly in front of me.

"Go away, Carlos," I say in between punches, which are coming harder now. I resituate my body to do front jabs again since I have a sudden and overwhelming urge to get more power behind my punches.

"I just wanted to make sure you're okay."

I never look up, not trusting myself and those rogue tears from coming back. Nothing says "psycho" quite like crying over your boss in front of your boss. "Why wouldn't I be okay?"

"You just seemed to be giving me the cold shoulder since I got back from coffee."

"Oh?" I feign innocence and continue to take my aggression out on the bag. Out of the corner of my eye, I see Abel watching from a distance. Not that he has to worry. If Carlos bugs me much longer, I might just swivel my body and use him as the punching bag.

He leans in closer. "I didn't mean to hurt your feelings."

Stopping, I pant heavily and put my hands on my hips. "You didn't. You left for coffee with a blonde bimbo and when you got back, I was busy. You're my boss, Carlos, not my friend. I prefer to keep any of my personal emotions to myself."

He takes a step back and nods his head just as Abel approaches.

"Good work, Rian. Let's move onto some front push kicks. They're fantastic for your flexibility, but you aren't going to be able to chat while doing them. You're going to get winded quick." He's talking to me but never takes his eyes off Carlos. I wish I could say I'm mortified by his behavior and coming to my defense however subtle it is. But realistically, it feels good that a man thinks I'm important enough to stand up for. It doesn't matter that Abel is my trainer and would never go for someone like me. I'm important to him as a friend and that's more than I can say for most people.

Carlos takes Abel's hint that he's not welcome here. At least not now. Nodding his head once, he looks at the floor, defeat written all over his body language. "It's okay. I'm leaving anyway."

As he mopes off, Abel turns to check on me. "I take it that's who you've been visualizing?"

"I don't really wanna talk about it. I wanna kick something."

If anyone understands my feelings are too fresh right now, it's Abel. Partially because his were the same way a couple weeks ago. Partially because we both know how inflexible I am and trying to get my leg up high enough to kick the bag isn't something I would normally volunteer to learn. If I think too hard about how this is going to look, I'll chicken out and right now, I need the outlet.

"Okay," is the only thing Abel says. No judgement in his voice. No curiosity in his stare. Just a common understanding and desire to help. "Let's get to work."

CHAPTER TWENTY-TWO

CARLOS

I knew when I left the office I had made a mistake. Sure, it took me sitting on that lumpy coffee shop chair for ten minutes to finally come to that conclusion, but I knew.

When I got back, I found out exactly how big of a mistake it really was.

The normal vibe surrounding Rian's work area had completely disintegrated in the time it took me to consume one large black coffee. There wasn't laughter during her phone calls. There weren't smiles when I would walk by. Hell, there wasn't even eye contact. She didn't just ignore me; she went out of her way to avoid me.

If she saw me coming, she'd get up and book it to the restroom. Or she'd pick up the phone and dial a client's number. Or she'd suddenly have an important question to ask Nancy.

All the remaining focus I had for my job dried up as I tried to figure out how to fix it. I knew I needed more guidance, that's where Tabitha would come in. But the immediate need was to get rid of the black cloud that suddenly hovered over Rian. It was disconcerting and jarring. And humiliating to know I had caused it.

Determined to apologize in some way, I was so grateful to see her at the gym, but the entire exchange made me feel worse. She's right.

We aren't even friends. We can't be. This is the whole reason why I don't get close to people in the office. Why I don't get close to anyone, really. But it doesn't make me feel any less like a dick, and I still need to fix this. Somehow.

Grateful for Tabitha's invitation to drink tonight, I pull open the door to Luma. It's not a loud bar. More of a lounge with food options. It's nice for the over-thirty crowd that wants to be able to hear their conversations and enjoy some appetizers while they consume copious amounts of booze.

Maybe I'll meet someone interesting here tonight. Someone I can take home to help me fuck away my worries.

Sighing to myself, I know that it won't happen. Not anymore. No one I could ever meet will ever compare to Rian, and I just don't have the desire to put in the effort anyway. Maybe I can just get drunk and Uber home.

Looking around, I finally catch a glimpse of Tabitha's trademark curly dark hair and make a beeline straight to her. I could use a friendly face.

"What's he doing here?" I look over just as Rian plops down next to Tabitha on a red, vinyl couch. She's staring at me like I'm the most disgusting thing she's ever seen. So much for the friendly faces. I know it's a front, though. Rian doesn't find me disgusting, even though I wish she would. It would make this so much easier for both of us.

"How much have you had to drink so far?" It's an honest question. Not only does she look appalled at my presence, she looks completely sauced.

Waving a half-empty margarita glass at me, she slurs, "Not that it's any of your business, but this is my third margarita. Why do you care? I'm not a skinny blonde bimbo you can take home and have your way with, only to disregard later."

I try hard to ignore Tabitha, who is looking back and forth at us, eyebrows high enough to practically touch her hairline. I know I'm going to hear about this later.

I want so badly to say I care because I care about *her*. I care because she intrigues me. I care because she's like no one I've ever met and for the life of me, I can't figure out why. But I chicken out. Not in front of an audience. And certainly not when she's too drunk to remember in the morning. Instead, I give her my fall back answer.

"Because you're my employee."

She looks away and her face flames like I've slapped her. I'm sure that's how my words felt to her, and I hate myself for being such an asshole.

Tabitha pats her hand on Rian's thigh and gently says, "I'm going to get another drink. Do you want anything while I'm up?"

"Nope. But I might need to pee."

Tabitha laughs lightly. "Hold it as long as you can, babe. Once you break the seal, you'll be in there every ten minutes."

Rian takes another sip and goes back to ignoring me. Tabitha, on the other hand, is practically laser locked on her target and unfortunately, that's me. Grabbing my arm, she practically drags me across the room.

"What in the ever-loving hell is going on?" she practically hisses in my ear.

"I don't know what you're talking about," I say quietly, refusing to look her in the eye. Instead, I put all my focus on the bartender and placing my order. "Whiskey. Neat."

"Don't give me that." Tabitha ignores my attempts at ignoring her. Not that I expected anything less from her. "You know exactly what the hell I'm talking about."

"How many times are you going to say 'hell' in the course of this conversation?"

"As many times as I want. And you're terrible at distraction." Leaning up against the counter, she grabs my chin and forces me to look at her. "Seriously, Carlos. Rian's been here for less than an hour, and she's already three sheets to the wind. At first, I thought she was just letting loose but by the time she started her second margarita she was babbling on about how her boss is a dick and office romances are frowned upon for a reason. And then you walk in and she's practically shooting daggers out of her eyes. And now you're drinking?" She glances down just as my drink is placed in front of me.

"Thanks, man." I pass over my credit card with instructions to go ahead and start a tab. I have a feeling two fingers isn't going to cut it tonight.

Tabitha's eyes widen again. "Seriously? You never drink, Carlos. Your body is a temple and all that shit. What's going on?"

Her never ending observations and questions finally break me. Leaning in, I start rambling. "I don't know, okay? I hired her a couple weeks ago and she's the best employee I could have possibly found. She's smart and funny. The customers love her, not to mention the staff. She brings this wonderful air of professionalism without losing her personal touch. She's a fucking delight to be around and I find myself staring at her across the room, not getting my own work done. She's a distraction of the best kind, and I fucked it all up when I went to coffee with Rebecca."

Tabitha holds up her hand to stop me. "Hold up. We'll get back to Rian in a second, but first you need to tell me about Rebecca. Ridiculous Rebecca? From the gym?"

"You gave her a nickname?"

A *pffftt* sound comes from her lips, like I should know better. "Of course, I did. I name all the weirdos."

Now I'm concerned. "Do I have a nickname?"

"Sure. Complicated Carlos."

"How have I known you for this long and never knew you gave me a nickname? And why am I complicated?"

"Because I never told you. And this conversation should answer part two of your questions. Now answer mine," she demands. "Why the hell did you go to coffee with Ridiculous Rebecca?"

"Language, Tabitha."

"Focus, Carlos," she shoots back, clearly getting irritated with me.

Running my hand down my face, I finally give. This conversation will never end if I don't tell her everything and I need her help anyway. I might as well deal with the inevitable.

"I hooked up with her about a month ago."

Tabitha gasps and throws her hand over her mouth. "What the hell did you do that for?"

Rolling my eyes, I find myself getting sick of all the questions. I know I came here to pick Tabitha's brain, but suddenly it doesn't seem like such a good idea.

"Why wouldn't I?"

"Because she's not just ridiculous, she's got a screw loose. Seriously, how did you not see it a mile away? You're usually more discerning than that."

I chuckle humorlessly and take another sip of my drink. "Obviously not. She showed up in my office for an interview today and let's just say my HR manager was less than impressed."

"Sounds like your HR manager is paying more attention than you are." I wish she was wrong but these days I agree with her. "But that doesn't explain how you ended up at coffee with her."

Furrowing my brow, I tug on my ear. Suddenly, I'm feeling fidgety. Must be the drink because surely this isn't embarrassment. I have nothing to be ashamed of. I took a woman out to coffee.

A crazy, slightly delusional woman I never should've hooked up with in the first place, but that's nothing to feel guilty about.

Except that it ended up hurting Rian.

Okay, maybe a little humility isn't the worst thing I could be feeling right now.

"Carlos," Tabitha warns when I don't respond quick enough. "Spill."

I sigh and drop down onto the barstool. "I didn't vet her application well enough. If I had done my job right, I would never have let Nancy call her. The second Rebecca walked in the door, I knew there was no way we were going to hire her. But she was already there, so Nancy didn't have a choice but to do the interview."

"Who's Nancy?"

"My righthand man."

Tabitha takes a huge suck of her straw and gestures for me to continue, as if she wasn't the one who just interrupted me.

"Anyway, I was talking to Rian when they got done, and Nancy wanted Rebecca out of the building as soon as possible. Rebecca started coming onto me, and I was so confused by talking to Rian, and

Nancy was giving me signals to hurry and get her out, so I caved and took her out to coffee."

"Hold on. You were in the middle of a conversation with Rian when you ditched her for a psychotic one-night stand?"

I halfheartedly glare at her. "She's not psychotic."

"You forget I'm the ears of the gym. I know everything and trust me, hide your bunny with that one."

"I don't have any pets so no worries there. I don't know what to do, Tabitha. What do I do?"

She looks at me for a few seconds, considering what I'm asking. Finally, she smiles like a cat that ate a canary. "You like her."

Reeling back, I look at her like she's lost her mind. "What? What are you talking about?"

Leaning in, Tabitha pokes my chest. "You like Rian, romantically, and you don't know what to do with that."

"I don't know what you're talking about," I say, turning to shoot the rest of my whiskey. I'm going to need more liquid courage to get through the rest of this conversation. She's right, but I'm not sure I'm ready to admit it to her. Hell, I barely just admitted it to myself.

"You do. You were talking to her and you realized you liked her, and it freaked you out. So, you went out with Ridiculous Rebecca to get away from your feelings because you're a man and a stupid one at that."

Whipping my eyes back to hers, I can't help the initial feeling of offense. "What does that mean?"

"You know what it means. Am I wrong?"

I open my mouth to argue, but quickly realize she's right. My whole body deflates when I admit it. "No. You're not wrong."

"Mmmhmmmm." She nods her head, cocky arrogance written all over her face. It's probably well-deserved pride, but irritating nonetheless. "About which part?"

I glare at her, which of course makes her smile again. She's getting way too much enjoyment out of forcing me to face my problems. "All of it. And you can stop looking so damn happy about it."

She nudges my shoulder. "But I *am* happy. This is amazing, Carlos.

You've never had any interest in a relationship before because the right person hadn't come along yet. But Rian is great."

"She is, huh?"

"She is," Tabitha says with a nod. "So, what are you going to do about it?"

"That's what I'm asking you. I hurt her, Tabitha. And I don't know how to fix it. You're a woman. Tell me how to make this right."

Tabitha turns to look back at Rian who is still sitting on the couch, inspecting her glass like she's surprised there's nothing in it anymore. I want to go sit next to her so badly, but at this point, I'm sure it's the last thing she wants.

"First things first, maybe you should buy the lady a drink."

"You think?"

Inspecting Tabitha's face, I see nothing but kindness and compassion there. It's totally different than her normal sarcastic bravado. But she's my friend. I came to her for a reason and it's because I know she won't steer me wrong.

"Yeah," I say to myself, mustering all my courage. "Yeah, okay. I can do that." I flag down the bartender and place an order for a strawberry margarita and another whiskey to calm my own nerves.

It takes forever, and yet way too quickly, my drinks are set before me and the most nerve-wracking conversation I've ever had with a woman is about to begin.

"You can do this," Tabitha encourages. "She's one of the good ones."

I nod once and slide off my stool, heading directly toward this woman who enchants, intrigues, and scares the ever-loving shit out of me.

Sitting down, I reach the drink out in offering. In her inebriated state, Rian doesn't notice it for a solid ten seconds. When she does, her face breaks out into a delighted grin. "Oh! A margarita! Thanks!"

She clumsily grabs the beverage out of my hand and drinks a significant portion of it before leaning back, a satisfied look on her face. It's pretty impressive. But I'm prone to ice cream headaches so drinking any cold beverage quickly is likely to make me take notice.

"Carlos," she slurs, head bobbing back and forth on the back of the couch. "How come the pretty people get everything? They don't leave anything for the rest of us."

Her eyes are heavy, and I know she's close to passing out. But it feels like this is an important moment. Like she's sharing a part of herself that she normal doesn't share with anyone. Yet here she is, sharing it with me.

Granted, she's completely shit-faced, but I'll take what I can get right now.

"I think people do a good job of pretending they have it all. But no one ever has everything they ever wanted in life. Even if they put on a good front."

She doesn't respond and I assume she's pondering my words. For the first time, I feel like we're beginning to hash this whole mess out. Until I feel something sticky slide down my leg.

Is that… margarita?

"Rian," I say as I grab her drink from her hand and put it on the floor next to us. She doesn't respond, unless you count her soft snore. "Rian," I say again, gently nudging her. Still nothing.

"Way to go, Carlos." Tabitha shakes her head, amusement all over her face. "You bored the poor girl right to sleep."

I ignore the jab. I've got bigger problems. Mainly, how to get Rian home now that she's passed out.

"You don't happen to know where she lives, do you?"

Tabitha shakes her head. "Nope. But I'm not sure she needs to be left alone tonight. Looks like you're up, lover boy."

No. No way. "I can't take her home, Tabitha. She's passed out."

Tabitha snorts a laugh. "So? You afraid she's going to upchuck on your fancy duds?"

"No. It's just not safe for a woman to go home with a strange man."

"So, you're a strange man now?"

"Stop twisting my words. Isn't there some kind of a girl code or something?"

She nods vehemently. "Oh, yeah. For sure. But this situation is a little different. Are you planning on taking advantage of her in her inebriated state?"

"What? Of course not! Why would you even ask me that?" Frankly, I'm a little hurt she would think something like that about me. You can't be too careful these days, and the word "yes" better come out of a woman's mouth before I'll even considering going there.

"Good." Tabitha looks satisfied with my answer which makes me even more frustrated, only this time for different reasons. Mainly because she believed me so easily. What kind of a girlfriend is she?

Okay, now I'm even confusing myself. We need to figure this situation out quick.

"You screwed up. She needs a knight in shining armor. You're the closest thing we've got right now. Take the opportunity to fix this."

I look back down at Rian who looks so peaceful in her drunken stupor. "So just take her home with me?"

"Take her home. Take care of her. Make her breakfast in the morning and *talk it out*." Her emphasis on those last words aren't lost on me. "Tell her how you feel, and trust that her anger is because she probably feels the exact same way."

"What if it doesn't help?"

She shrugs. "Worst case scenario, you have a sexual harassment suit on your hands, and after a lengthy legal battle, she becomes your new boss."

Oh, well, that's reassuring. "You're really helpful," I deadpan, but all Tabitha does is smile.

"It's part of my charm. Now order an Uber and get her in bed. She's about to start drooling and I plan on sitting right there as soon as you're gone."

We spend the next several minutes ordering a car and getting Rian up and out the door. It takes a bit to maneuver her as she goes in and out of consciousness, never giving any hint of when her sleeping status will change. At any given moment, she could have her arms wrapped around my neck, smiling and giggle like a schoolgirl with a crush, only to pass out again and drop like deadweight forcing us to catch her.

But finally, we've made our way to the waiting car and settled her in.

"Don't worry," Tabitha says as she tries to pull Rian's seat belt out. Somehow, she's gotten both their arms tangled up in it. "I'll close out your tab for you."

"Oh, shit! I forgot about that!" Narrowing my eyes, I watch as she finally gets the belt untangled. "You're going to run it up first, aren't you?"

The seat belt clicks. "Consider it my payment for my stellar matchmaking skills."

"This isn't matchmaking, Tabitha. This is making sure she gets home safely."

Huffing with exertion, she stands up and grabs the car door. "Same thing. Don't screw this up. Let her sleep it off and *talk to her*, Carlos. This may be the only shot you get."

With those parting words, she slams the door and heads back into Luma with my limitless black Amex.

I'm so screwed.

CHAPTER TWENTY-THREE

RIAN

M y head is pounding. That's the first thought that crosses my mind, and even that is too many words to concentrate on at once. What was I thinking going out last night and drinking so heavily?

It wasn't even the number of drinks. It was how fast I had them, and on an empty stomach at that. Plus, I'd just finished my workout, so my metabolism was faster than normal.

Or it could just be that I have a low tolerance level and am a cheap date, but that doesn't sound nearly as bad ass as "my metabolism was fast", so I'm sticking with that explanation.

I was so pissed off, though, and just wanted to have some fun to get my mind off my hurt. Maybe meet some people. Make some friends. Have a good time. Instead, I babbled to Tabitha about how shitty my life is and how much my boss is a dick.

Oh, shit! I hope I didn't tell her Carlos is my boss! I'm humiliated enough as it is...

Snuggling back into the pillow, I try to calm my mind, relaxing my body as I enjoy my bed. Obviously, there's one benefit to drinking heavily—I don't remember my old mattress being this comfortable. It must be because my body hurts so bad.

Come to think of it, my pillows aren't normally this comfortable either. And they don't normally smell like a certain man's very sexy cologne.

Oh, shit. Why do my pillows smell like sexy cologne?

Wracking my brain, I try to put the very foggy memories of last night together.

Met Tabitha at the bar.

Drank three strawberry margaritas in succession.

Yelled at Carlos.

Drank another—

Wait.

Carlos.

CARLOS!

Sitting straight up in the bed, my eyes pop open. Despite the room spinning, I'm coherent enough to know a few things: This isn't my bed. This isn't my room. This isn't my apartment.

I look down. This isn't even my shirt!

Oh, nonononononononono.

Praying to the god of exercise or bad decisions or whoever will listen, I look around more. This is clearly Carlos's room. The bed is made with gray sheets that have a higher thread count than anything I own. A darker gray down comforter covers the lower half of my body. There is minimal furniture in here. Just the bed, a long black dresser, and a nightstand with a picture of Carlos and a beautiful older blonde woman. I would wonder who the Barbie was if it weren't for the fact that they look so much alike, there is no denying it's his mother. His skin and hair may be darker, but the blue eyes are the same. She's a knockout. No wonder he only goes for blonde pretty girls.

Focus, Rian! There are bigger issues at hand here. Like whether or not I came onto my boss.

Oh, please don't say I came onto Carlos. Please don't say I went home with him and slept with my boss. I don't want to do the walk of shame today. Or any day, but today in particular because today is right now, and I'm not emotionally prepared for this.

Breathing in through my nose and out through my mouth, I'm suddenly glad for my short-lived stint in yoga. At least the lone class I took taught me how to slow my breathing down, so I don't hyperventilate. The last thing I need is to pass out and bang my head on his nightstand. My luck, I'd end up with a black eye I'd have to explain away for weeks. Been there. Done that. No one believes you when you say, "No, I don't have a boyfriend. I really am that clumsy."

Just as I breathe in, the door opens and the man of the hour walks in. Suddenly, I forget how to exhale, as I watch him, trying to gauge his expression. He doesn't look like a man who got laid last night.

And it hits me. Of course, he doesn't look sated. Why would he have sex with *me*? He's got women like Rebecca knocking down his door. Beautiful women who look beautiful on the arm of a beautiful man. I'm just—me.

Taking a deep breath now that my diaphragm is finally cooperating again, I decide to confront the situation head on. Might as well get it over with.

"How did I get here?" The sound of my own voice makes my head pound. Grabbing my forehead, I squeeze my eyes tightly.

"You got too drunk to make it home on your own," he answers quietly. I have a strong appreciation for his consideration of my headache, but I'm still confused.

"Why didn't you take me to my place?"

"You passed out before you could give us your address."

"Oh." I think back on last night and don't remember anything beyond him handing me another drink. I'm not sure that's the important part in this situation, though. The fact that I'm in his shirt with no bra on is a much more pressing issue. Licking my lips, I ask the question that is giving me the most anxiety. "Did you undress me?"

"I did."

Pulling the sheet tighter around me, I can't help the overwhelming sense of embarrassment.

"I, um..." I clear my throat when it tightens. "I don't look like the women you usually undress."

"No, you don't."

Shame floods my body. All I want is for him to leave the room so I can get dressed and flee the scene.

"You're beautiful."

I blink.

And blink.

And blink again.

Of all the words I ever expected to come out of Carlos's mouth, those two were well below options like "the Avengers are real" and "I've decided to become a monk". There is always a possibility I'm hallucinating. Tequila does some weird things to my brain sometimes. But I think I heard him right and damn, if it doesn't make me feel good.

Pushing off the wall, he sits down next to me, staring at the curtains that are blocking out the sunlight, seemingly lost in his own head. "You aren't my normal type."

And now the good feels I had are gone, the shame filling me again.

"You're smart and funny and quick-witted."

Nothing I haven't heard before. They're nice words and all, but nothing deflates an ego like hearing that you at least have a good personality.

"I haven't wanted to be near someone so much since... I don't even know when the last time was." Looking over at me, he has a glazed look on his face. I've never seen this look on him before. Maybe he's the one who drank too much Jose Cuervo? I can't decipher it. "Why, Rian? What is it about you that makes me want to be a different person? To throw caution to the wind, even though I know it's a bad idea. Even though I know you deserve better than a schmuck like me?"

Wait. I'm confused now.

My heart rate speeds up. Am I hearing him correctly? Is he saying he likes me? Not just as a person or co-worker or friend, but as a love interest?

I blink a few more times, giving myself a few seconds to build up my courage before whispering, "But you left me to go get coffee with Rebecca."

"I did."

"Why are you saying all these things if you did that?"

"Because I never should've left. I don't know what's happening to me, but I don't want the shallow surface-level relationship with you. I want you to know me. And I want to know you. And I don't know what to do with those feelings."

My heart swells. I've never met anyone like Carlos before. He's egotistical, arrogant, and says some of the stupidest things I've ever heard. But he's kind and smart and struggles with his own issues like everyone else. And he's grown on me over the last few weeks, and not like a fungus. It's to the point where I look forward to seeing him every day. I just thought it was a one-sided crush, and even that might be a stretch, which is why I never put too much thought into it until now.

Blinking away more nerves, I finally whisper, "Then why don't you just get to know me?"

"Do you want that?"

I stop to think about it, really think about it. Do I want to get to know Carlos better, or am I just intrigued because someone like him could like someone like me?

It's a hard question to answer, but the longer I ponder it, the more I know a very pressing truth—if I don't get to know him, how will I be able to decide if I like him? I owe that to myself. To find out if this could be something great before settling on the idea that I don't deserve a man as physically beautiful as Carlos.

"I think..." I lick my dry lips, ignoring the cotton feel of my tongue. I really hope my post-binge drinking morning breath isn't as horrid as I suspect. "I think yes."

"Yes, you'd like to get to know me?"

One side of my mouth quirks up in a half-smile as I nod. Just once. Wouldn't want him to think I'm desperate or anything. But the strangest thing happens in reaction to my response.

Carlos smiles. A real, non-smarmy, full wattage, happy-go-lucky smile. Occasionally, I get to see a genuine response from him. It doesn't happen often, but when it does, it makes my heart stutter. Like I'm getting a peek under the mask he likes to wear for everyone else. It feels both thrilling and a bit on the intimate side.

And it makes me know I've made the right decision.

"Wanna go to a wedding with me?" I blurt out and immediately throw my hand over my mouth. I can't believe I just did that.

He smiles. "Who's getting married?"

"My sister. Next week. She's a bit of a bridezilla, and it might be a good idea to have someone there who is on my side."

"Someone who knows how to take care of you if you take the edge off with too much tequila?" he jokes, that megawatt smile still gracing his pretty face.

I crinkle my nose. "I hate to say that's why you would be there, but in all honesty, the bride does seem determined to drive me to drink."

He lets out a hearty laugh. I like this side of him already. The carefree, happy, relaxed man in sweats is a much better version than the suave, reserved man who keeps himself perfectly coifed. Even the fact that his hair is hanging in disheveled waves is endearing. "Well, then, yes. I think I would love to go to a wedding with you."

I bite back a smile and look down at my fingers fidgeting with the sheet. I'm not sure how to feel now. Of all the things I expected when I woke up in a strange bed a little bit ago, securing a date for my sister's wedding, in my boss that I don't even like half the time, was not even close to the top of that list. But it feels pretty damn nice, even if I don't trust where it will lead. I suppose I'll find out relatively quickly and enjoy it in the meantime.

"Come on," Carlos says, pushing up off the bed. "I made us breakfast."

"Oh, um, that's okay. I'm kind of on a diet." Crinkling my nose, I squeeze my eyes shut. I shouldn't have admitted that. Now he's going to think I'm a stereotype—the heavy girl on a diet. I bet he thinks I drink Diet Coke with my dozen tacos, too.

But instead of saying anything, he laughs. I'm not sure how a large woman subsisting on low-calorie, low-carb, high-protein food is funny, but he seems to think it's hilarious.

"I know we haven't really started getting to know each other quite yet." He ignores the glare I am unsuccessfully shooting his direction. "But I thought you'd know my eating habits by now."

Now I'm very confused. "Why would I know your eating habits?"

"Because you made fun of me at the restaurant the night we ate with Tabitha, remember?"

"Oooooooh." I do remember. I remember the naked chicken, bland vegetables, and basically colorless food. It wasn't appetizing at all. I also remember the amazing enchiladas I ate. Dammit. Now I do want those tacos. But with a full-calorie drink. See? No stereotypes here!

"I only eat clean, even when the woman next to me is moaning over her enchiladas," he tacks on as an apparent afterthought. "So, I made us vegetable omelets."

Now that I can do. I shift on the bed, waiting for him to leave so I can throw some clothes on, but he just stands there, looking confused again.

"Um… what are you doing?"

He blinks and snaps out of his thoughts. "What?"

"I know you said you want us to get to know each other, but I don't think we're comfortable with being barely clothed in front of each other quite yet." I gesture down to my body, reminding him that I am still pantless, thanks to him.

He just looks at me, like he's considering something. The longer he stares, the more my emotions get all tangled up. Is he regretting what he said already? Is he remembering someone else from his past in his bed? Is he wishing the egg omelets were actually enchiladas like I am? There are so many possibilities.

Taking two slow steps toward me, he ends up standing in front of me. My heart beats just a little bit harder as I look up at him, wondering what he's thinking. We stay like this for longer than should feel comfortable, but since I don't know what's going on, I don't mind. Something about this moment feels monumental.

Finally, slowly, he moves. His hands make their way to my cheeks and he tilts my head up. I feel my breath hitch at his touch and the feel of his rough, warm hands. Keeping my eyes trained on his, I watch as he leans down to me, closer, closer… until his firm lips press mine.

Carlos is kissing me.

Carlos is kissing me!

CARLOS IS KISSING ME!

It's unexpected and gentle and perfect. His lips are soft and warm, and he doesn't push for more than just a long, lingering press of his lips on mine. My stomach flutters and when he breathes in, I'm forced to hold myself back from grabbing him and tackling him on the bed.

Eventually, he pulls back, but not away. I hold my breath as he stares into my eyes, not wanting this moment to end, but also not wanting to blow my morning-after tequila breath all over him.

"What?" he asks, eyes searching mine.

I quickly put my hand over my mouth. "Morning breath."

That giant grin is back, along with my thundering heart. "Yep."

Covering my hands with my face, I groan in embarrassment.

"I am just kidding, Rian. You're too easy sometimes," he says with a chuckle. "Take your time. I'm going to finish up breakfast." As he turns away, he grabs a pair of his sweatpants and gently places them on the bed. "Here. You'll be more comfortable in these."

I grab my chest, trying hard not to hyperventilate or squeal with joy when he walks out the door. Both possibilities are very close to the surface, so I try to stick with regular swooning.

Carlos likes me. *Likes* me, likes me. And he left me his sweatpants, so I'll be comfortable.

I stand corrected. Maybe the walk of shame will be worth it.

CHAPTER TWENTY-FOUR

CARLOS

"I can't believe I'm going to say this, but that quinoa was pretty damn amazing." Rian shakes her head like she's truly stunned that seeds can be both healthy and full of flavor. "The last time I had it," she grimaces, "let's just say it didn't taste like that at all."

I smile and try my best not to just stare at her as we chat. She's been here since last night and she could stay for days without me trying to get rid of her. There's no clinginess about her. No expectations of forever. She's content to introduce me to the joys of reality TV while I introduce her to the joys of clean eating. It's easy and relaxing.

If this is what relationships are like, maybe I have been missing out. Although, I suspect it has less to do with the relationship part and more to do with Rian. She's not the first woman to spend the night with me, but she's the first who doesn't seem desperate to stay. She's just here because we're having a good time.

"I don't know why people hate quinoa so much," I remark as I sit down next to her on my couch and stretch my legs out, propping my feet up on the coffee table. "It's really good if you know how to cook it."

"Key phrase: know how to cook it. My food buddy, Francesca, tried it for the first time and made me her recipe guinea pig." She makes a gagging sound, complete with her tongue sticking out. "I still can't look at donuts the same."

"Sounds like she didn't do it right. Not sure what donuts have to do with anything, though."

"And you don't want to know. Trust me." She freezes, eyes glued to the competition show on the screen. And suddenly, she's yelling. "What?! How do you not know the capital of Idaho is Boise? Even I know that, and I haven't taken World Geography in twenty years!"

I continue to stare at her as she waves her hands around in indignation until she finally looks over at me. "What? You can't win on these competition shows if you don't know basic trivia. I don't even know how these people get on these shows."

"You have very strong opinions about this." And I'm highly amused witnessing it.

"I have strong opinions about a lot of things. Usually they aren't worth expressing though."

"That is the biggest lie I've ever heard you tell."

Turning to me, she gapes. "What are you talking about? I'm terribly mild-mannered and complacent."

I shake my head slowly. "Opinions stated with a thick coating of sarcasm are still opinions."

She turns back to the TV and shifts to settle in more. "I think you have me mistaken for someone else."

"Really." Shifting myself to face her more, I begin ticking off examples on my fingers. "Let's see, quinoa is almost always horrible…"

"That's not opinion. That's a fact."

"Only idiots end up on reality TV…"

"I never said that."

"Physicals are the devil's way of tricking us into exercising, so he can get a good laugh at us trying not to die at the gym…"

"Obviously, you've never done the rope. My back was just fine until that day."

"Stop interrupting me."

"Well, stop putting words in my mouth." She grabs my hand and pulls it down, so I can't count out all her opinions.

"Every single one of those is something you actually said," I press with a laugh. "Don't even deny it. You know you called Weight Expectations the devil's playground. And don't pretend that seeing flames shooting through the roof reminded you of a random picture you saw of Hell or something. You've been calling it that long before the fire. You just hate exercise. You'd rather sit here and watch TV."

"Uh… duh. Of course, I would."

This is one of the reasons I like her. As much as she tries to pretend, she's not chocked full of opinions, she has as many as the next guy. Her presentation of them is just different. It's full of humor, so even if they disagree, people don't ever hate her for them. It's very non-confrontational. No wonder she has such an easy time with clients.

"I do have one thing I need your opinion on, though."

"What's that?"

I take a jalapeño almond out of the can I'm hiding next to me and put it up to her lips. "Open."

She does, which both surprises and pleases me. Popping the almond in her mouth, I watch carefully as she chews.

Suddenly, her eyes widen. "Mmmmm." Looking a bit stunned at this new flavor combination, she sits up. "Mmmm… what is that?"

Holding up the can, I read the logo on the label. "Jalapeño almonds. Just one of many flavors in the Nutrageous family of nuts."

"I need some more of those."

Turning back to the TV, I settle the can in between us so we can share as we veg. Very quickly, I realize she's not wrong. These people truly are idiots. Frankly, they're kind of boring, too. Bring back that cooking competition. At least there was some talent there. Alas, Rian has a team she's rooting for, so I'm stuck waiting for them to lose before suggesting another show.

"Hey." I nudge her knee with mine not wanting to bring up this topic, but desperate to get out of my boredom. "I need one more opinion."

Digging for another nut, she doesn't even look at me. "What's that?"

"How do you want to handle this at the office?"

Her hand stills, but she doesn't turn to look at me. Instead, her neck begins to break out in red splotches. I hate to put her on the spot like this, but we need to be on the same page. At least, that's what I've heard from people who've done this dating thing before. "I don't really know. I mean, on the one hand, dating isn't a big deal."

"But it's an office romance."

"Exactly."

Knowing she's nervous, I decide to diffuse things a bit. "Do you know we have a code for this? For office romances?"

"Are you serious?" She looks at me wide-eyed. That's a good sign. "This has happened that many times?"

I nod and pop another almond in my mouth. "I'm not sure what's in the water there, but for a time, all the lieutenants were dropping like flies. Quinn was the worst about it, but there've been quite a few lately."

"All office romances?"

I have to think about how to answer that. "Sort of. You know how we have that branch in the Fairmont building?" She nods. "That's where almost everyone lives. So they get to know each other really well."

Rian grimaces. "That's a little too much office camaraderie if you ask me."

"Agreed. Why do you think I live here?"

We go back to watching TV, the elephant in the room lingering in the corner. I don't say anything, letting her absorb her own thoughts. I don't want to push her. I'm too afraid I'll accidentally push her away.

When the show breaks for commercial, though, she jumps right back into the topic at hand. "Anyway, what's the code?"

"What?"

"When there's an obnoxious office romance? What's the code?"

"Oh. Code Red."

"Hmm." She grabs another few almonds. "That sounds awfully ominous."

"It's the color of Cupid's arrows."

Rian breaks out in laughter, and I'm pleased to see she's already getting used to this. To hanging out and talking about uncomfortable topics so there's no misunderstanding. "I don't know who made that up, but it's a terrible code."

I shrug knowing full well it was probably me, not that I'll ever admit it. What I can admit, however, is part of why I don't want that code to be called out about me. Tossing another almond in my pie hole, I steady myself to tell her the whole story.

"A couple of years ago, I had an assistant named Olivia."

She nods but doesn't look at me. "I heard."

That causes me to pause. "Seriously? The grapevine already gave you their version?"

She shrugs. "I don't really know what version I got. Just that Olivia was your assistant, you had a huge crush on her, she had a crush on someone else, and eventually the turmoil got to be too much, so she left."

I rub my hand down my face and shake my head. This is what I get for letting the rumor mill do its thing and not try to correct anyone. "That is not exactly what happened."

"So, you didn't have a crush on Olivia?"

"I think the word crush is a bit of an exaggeration. Yes, I was interested in her, but only in the physical sense."

"You only wanted her for sex."

Looking at Rian, I consider sugarcoating my answer, but she deserves the truth. "Rian, I'm serious when I say that's the only kind of relationships I've had before. I know it doesn't make sense to most people, but until you, I had zero interest in a dating relationship."

She nods, but I can't read the look on her face. Is she upset with me for having sex with other women? Is she disgusted with me for not even bothering to get to know them first? I can't tell and it jars me. "So, then what happened?"

"Nothing happened. That's the thing. The rumor mill decided I had legitimate feelings for her because they don't understand how someone can be happy being single."

"Well, it is a bit unorthodox," she jokes, a small smile gracing her lips.

I smile back. "It is. And honestly, I didn't feel like I needed to set the record straight for anyone. I'm the boss. And it was no one's business. So, I just let them think what they want. I can see now that it's been biting me in the ass behind my back."

"Well, behind your back is where your ass is located."

I pretend to be shocked by her joke. "Are you making fun of my pain?"

"No. I'm making fun of the totally cliché predicament you're in. That's what happens when you work in an office full of women."

I snort a laugh. "You'd think so. But no. It's the lieutenants who give me the most shit about it still."

She clears her throat and her neck begins to splotch again.

"What?" I nudge her with my shoulder.

"Oh, nothing."

So, denial is going to be her game? She's got another thing coming if she thinks that'll work on me.

"Nope. Tell me."

She shoots me wide, phony innocent eyes. "There's nothing to tell."

"You are a horrible liar, and I made you delicious quinoa. Spill."

Rian laughs at my attempt. "You're going to try to convince me to throw someone under the bus because of quinoa? Oh, you have a lot to learn about women, don't you?"

Reacting before I can think, I squeeze her knee in the right spot to make her squeal and grab my hand.

"Don't do that! It tickles."

"Oh, it does, does it? Tell me." I squeeze again. She squeals again. "I'll keep doing it until you tell me who told you about Olivia. I know you're holding out on me."

"No, I'm not!" she shrieks and tries to bat my hand away. "I don't know anything! I know nothing!"

"You are the world's worst liar and have really strong fingers." I move my hand to her ribs and begin tickling her there.

She continues to shriek while I continue my assault on her body, until eventually we find ourselves lying down on the couch, me on top of her wedged between her thighs, kissing her with abandon. And boy, can she kiss. I swear she has magical lips as she sucks on my bottom lip and my tongue. She has no idea how wild she is driving me. Normally, I'd take this as my green light to get to the good stuff, but with Rian, this *is* the good stuff. Or at least the beginning of it. I don't want to risk driving her away by taking things too quickly.

Finally, after what seems like hours, and quite possibly is based on the fact that the television suddenly has an entirely different show on, I pull back.

"I don't want to mess this up," I whisper and give her a soft peck.

"Then don't." She kisses me back.

"I know it sounds stupid, but I don't want to give the office any reason to get in our business. And they will, ya know?" She nods, and I can tell she truly understands what I'm getting at and why. "Until you and I know where this is going, I'd prefer to keep it to ourselves. I don't want anyone to influence us on purpose. And you know they will."

Rian nods in agreement and smooths my shirt down my chest. Or at least she pretends to. Really, I think she's trying to feel me up. It would be rude of me to stop her. "Especially the lieutenants."

"Especially the lieutenants," I agree and lean down to kiss her again. Before our lips meet though, it hits me out of nowhere. "Wait. It was Steven who told you, wasn't it?"

She throws her head back, whooping up a storm. Finally, she nods again.

"Son of a bitch. They're worse than the Golden Girls in church the day after Mardi Gras."

"Shut up, Carlos." Rian grabs my shirt in her fists and pushes on me. "I wanna make out with my boss, and I've got limited time until I have no choice but to go back to work."

Smiling, I lean back in and go for the kill.

Day one of my newfound dating life, and I can already call it a success.

CHAPTER TWENTY-FIVE

RIAN

I am late. So, so late. I'm not worried about being fired, or even reprimanded for that matter. Call it perks of dating the boss, but I don't want to take advantage of the situation. I'm not that kind of girl.

Wouldn't it be nice to be that kind of girl? To put in half the effort because you've got the boss right where you want him? But alas, I'm full of integrity and care about my work ethic. And I'm not a total bitch.

Racing to my desk, I throw my purse into my drawer just as my phone rings.

"Why do you look like you just ran here?" Teresa asks.

"Because I basically did."

"You realize no one cares if you're a few minutes late, right? Next time, just bring food. That way you aren't late, you just brought breakfast."

"Isn't that the pitch for a burger joint?"

"Huh." She looks up to the ceiling in thought. "I knew it sounded too good to have come from my brain."

Picking up the phone, I try to get my breathing under control so I don't sound like a total spaz while talking to a client.

"Cipher Systems. This is Rian."

"Um, hi. Yes." The voice on the other line stammers. "I'm looking to get my home outfitted with security. I was given a referral."

Dropping into my seat, I grab a pen to make notes while I wait for my computer to boot up. "Well, great. I'm glad you called. Can I ask who referred you?"

"The Landon Michaels Agency."

"Wonderful. Can you give me just one second? I'm going to pull up a new screen to get all your information and get my hands-free set plugged in, okay?"

"Okay."

Placing her on hold, I finally turn my computer on and get everything set up and ready to go. Carlos surprises me when he reaches over my shoulder and places a large cup of coffee on my desk.

Smiling up at him, I don't bother hiding my surprise. "Well, that's unexpected, thank you."

"You're welcome," he says in between sips. "New client calling already?"

"Yep." I grab my headset and plug it into the phone, situating it on my head. Years in customer service has me unconcerned about how ugly these things look. They're effective. That's about it. "She said the Landon Michaels Agency referred her. Why does that sound familiar?"

His coffee cup freezes, midway to his mouth. "I did a presentation to them a few months ago."

"I wasn't working here a few months ago."

"I know. They're everywhere, but subtly. The Landon Michaels Agency works with victims of sexual abuse. More specifically, human trafficking and bringing offenders to justice. We monitor all their online activity to makes sure no one can get through the firewalls. And we do security in one of their safe houses pro bono."

"Whoa. I had no idea. But why would they give someone a referral?" Turning back to my screen, I open up the data system.

Carlos puts his cup down and settles in next to my desk. "They must have a really high-profile case that needs our help."

I pull my hands away from the keyboard like I've been burned. If it's a high-profile case, that means it's really, really important. I don't want to screw it up.

"Relax," Carlos says, reading me like a book. "Just do what you do best. I'm going to stay right here so I can help you if you get stuck. Just write anything down you need help with."

I take a beat to center myself and nod once. Then, reconnecting the line, I put everything out of my mind except the job at hand.

"Okay, sorry for the delay. Are you still there?"

"Yes, that's okay. I'm still here."

"Let's get started with some of the basics. Can I have your name?"

"Janet."

We take a few minutes to get some general information on what kind of service they'll need. It takes a bit to get through it because she's hesitant with every question. Whatever happened to her is making her extremely paranoid and harder to assess. But Carlos continues to oversee my conversation and never gives any indication that I'm going about things wrong, so I take my time.

"Okay, Janet, let's talk about your security needs. The Landon Michaels Foundation doesn't normally refer clients, so I'm assuming you're going to have some very specific needs. Can you give me some details so I can start figuring out what kind of package might work for you?"

She pauses long enough for Carlos to take more than one sip of his coffee, but I don't want to push her on this. Finally, it's as if she's found the words she's looking for and she goes for it. "Okay, listen. This is for my sister. You might know her. Jennifer Johnson is her name, but you probably know her under the name Jenny Juggs."

I try really hard, but I can't stop it when my jaw drops open. Everyone knows Jenny Juggs. Not because she's a porn star, but because she's an EX-porn star who just won millions of dollars from her former production company in a civil lawsuit. Turns out, while Jenny was the most popular online star at one time, she wasn't exactly a willing participant. According to the television magazine show I watched last weekend, Jenny was essentially manipulated into the life and given drugs daily to keep her complacent. That's not hard to believe. Clips of interviews over the years show her to be clearly on something, sometimes to the point of being almost incoherent.

After a botched suicide attempt a couple of years ago, she was put on an involuntary psychiatric hold where she refused to allow her "manager" to visit and called her estranged sister instead. It took about ten seconds for one of the hospital case managers to call the feds and list her as a victim in the situation.

The details that came out were almost unbelievable. Her having no memory of making her first movie, her having a sober moment during a porn award ceremony where she suddenly realized what she was being awarded for, her virtual disappearance from the public eye until it was time to testify against the man who claimed to be her employee for all those years. I remember being gripped to the program and so sad for this woman who slipped through the cracks. And yes, the porn industry is changing and there are organizations devoted to making it a respectable industry with good working conditions, but Jenny was sucked into the dark side. It was ugly, and it's a miracle she made it out alive.

Carlos immediately nudges me, a look of question on his face.

"I have." Concentrating on keeping my voice stable while I twist and turn, I look for my pen that has suddenly disappeared. Figuring out what I'm looking for, Carlos grabs it from under my keyboard and hands it to me. "The story was all over the news a couple months ago. Congratulations on your win. I was genuinely pleased to see a little bit of justice done."

Jotting down *Jenny Juggs* on the paper I flash it at Carlos whose own response mirrors my own.

Janet huffs in annoyance. "Yeah. Well, it's little consolation. My sister has been so traumatized she refuses to leave the house but is still terrified to be here. I'd give the money back in a second if it meant she could live a normal life again. Preferably before she ever met that immoral asshole."

"Hopefully we can help with that. Let's start with what you're hoping to get out of this."

Good, Carlos writes. *Don't get caught up in the drama. She's a real person who needs our help.*

I nod at him. I admit to being stunned that I'm talking to Jenny Juggs's sister, but mostly because my heart hurt so bad for her when I watched that story. To be able to genuinely help her gives this job a whole new spin.

"That's what makes this really hard. We don't really know. The death threats have died down since the trial ended, but we still want the home to be monitored. Maybe onsite security. And for sure, we want cameras in the house."

I hear some indistinct talking in the background. Assuming it's Jenny, I make sure to phrase my questions carefully.

"All of those are really easy for us to do."

"I know they're easy. We've used them before," Janet says sternly. I suspect she's not annoyed as much as she just doesn't trust what I'm telling her. And why would she? Her sister was manipulated by people for years to the point where it went to a massive public trial. She's right to be leery. "But the company we're using now leaked some pictures of Jennifer in her own house." I bite back a gasp. "We need someone who is trustworthy, and I've got an attorney on retainer anytime that trust is broken now."

Thinking quickly, I make a request that I hope doesn't backfire.

"Is she there with you? In the room, I mean?"

Janet goes quiet, and I assume she's trying to decide how to respond. Finally, we end up on the same page. "Yes."

"Would she be willing to be on speaker so the three of us can talk at the same time?"

The phone muffles and I assume Janet is relaying my request. Carlos gestures in question and I nod. I've got this. I want this account so badly, and not because I enjoy my job. I want this account because I know we can make a difference for this woman.

"Okay, you're on speakerphone."

I give Carlos a thumbs up. He nods his approval and grabs his coffee cup again. I guess he's confident I've got this covered.

"My name is Rian and I'm one of the account managers at Cipher

Systems. Jenny, I know this is really hard on you, so I want to make this as painless as possible."

"Please call me Jennifer. I don't ever want to be known by that other name again," a soft voice says back to me. She doesn't sound at all like the strung-out porn star I saw on television. She sounds meeker and much more frightened.

"Absolutely. Jennifer it is. Janet explained a little bit about what you're looking for, but I want to make sure we're really sensitive to what you need. Let me ask you a question, did you ever see the movie *Catch Me If You Can?*"

Carlos looks at me quizzically. I just smile back at him and hold up my finger to give me a minute.

"The one with Leonardo DiCaprio?"

"That's the one. His character is the best con artist in the country, probably world. Part of the reason he's so good at it is because the Feds are chasing him, so it's a game. That's the whole reason it's exciting for him. Every day he gets to prove he's better than the Feds."

"I'm sorry, what does this have to do with getting my sister security?" Janet demands, and I have no doubt she's rolling her eyes at me.

"Give me one second and you'll see my point. Jennifer, do you remember that at the end of the movie, the FBI hires him to work for them, taking down other con artists?"

"Yeah. I remember that."

"They didn't change what he's good at. They just changed the game. Now the goal is to be better than every other con artist out there. To beat them. In a way, we've done the same thing."

"How so?" Janet again. I knew she'd see the connection quickly. Now I just need to convince them of why this is a good thing.

"We have a man here named Alex. He is arguably the world's best hacker."

"No, no, no," Jennifer interrupts. "I don't want a hacker to have access to cameras in my house."

Janet immediately jumps into the conversation, and I listen quietly as she calms her sister down. When they're finally quiet, I continue.

"Jennifer, I know you don't trust anyone right now. You shouldn't.

But the reason Alex works here is because he changed the game. His goal now isn't to hack into things. It's to build firewalls so strong it keeps all the other hackers out. He gets to show them he's the best by showing they're not as good as he is."

I know by the silence on the other end of the line that they're thinking and probably communicating with eye contact alone.

"But how..." Jennifer's voice cracks. "How do you know I can trust him?"

It's a valid question. And I only have one answer for her.

"Because he's married to a psychiatrist who works with trauma victims every day. If anyone will put in his all to make sure no one can ever get to you like that again, it's Alex."

Carlos pushes off my desk and walks away. I assume that means he thinks I've got this under control, which is quite a compliment. Or he's typing up my pink slip right now. Either way, I'm happy to give this woman back a little bit of her stolen dignity.

"And, Jennifer, I need you to know something else," I continue. "All of your information is confidential. On a professional level, we strive to give you the kind of security you need to feel confident that you can let your guard down in your own home. That you have a safe space. But on a personal level, these are some of the best people I've ever worked with. You aren't a client. You're a person. And you will be treated with respect whether we're on the phone with you or just monitoring your account."

A soft sniffle comes through the speaker and I know I've hit my mark. Not as the account manager talking to a prospective client, but as a human being talking to another human being.

"Okay," Jennifer finally says. "I'm still learning about how to do my bills and stuff. I wasn't really old enough to have it mastered yet when... well, you know. So, my sister will be your point of contact."

"That's not going to work for me." The words blurt out before I can stop them. I don't know why this is important, but something just tugs at me. The gasp I hear, though, makes me realize that came out wrong. "That's not what I meant. Sorry." I chuckle lightly. "I got ahead of myself. I do that when I'm excited to help a client." They make sounds of relief on the other end. "What I meant to say is, I'd like to be the point of contact for both of you. This is about making you feel secure, Jennifer. So, let's just make it a point to have all three of us on these conversations."

"But it's just faster if she does it."

"Faster, sure. But you're working hard to learn all about this stuff. The least I can do is make sure you're in the loop, and I can answer any questions you have."

"Okay. Thank you."

"My pleasure."

And it really is. Jennifer Johnson has been through a lot. As a result, she has insecurities that will take years to overcome, if she ever does. But here she is, stepping out of her comfort zone to make a better life for herself.

And damn if that doesn't inspire me to do the same.

CHAPTER TWENTY-SIX

CARLOS

We've spent a couple nights this week on my couch. Well, not just the couch. Some of it has been spent eating at the breakfast bar. And there have been a few bathroom breaks here and there. But mostly, we've hung out and watched bad reality TV. It been the most fun I've had in a long time. Not because of the shows; they have been truly horrible. What's made it fun is the company.

Rian has made me watch some bridal show and told me more about her sister's wedding and how afraid she is that she's going to resemble a tomato in her bridesmaid dress.

I've made her watch a business investment show and told her more about how I got involved with Quinn and ended up running half of Cipher Security Systems.

But our favorite has been a cooking competition. It's led to her giving me recipes for cauliflower everything, which I'm still on the fence about.

We've laughed about stupid things and opened up about serious things. The conversation has never gotten too heavy, but we really are getting to know each other. It's been exactly what I was hoping for. And for the first time ever, when she leaves, I'm oddly sad. Sure, I get goodbye kisses that rival any makeout session I'd ever had. But once she's gone, I miss the conversation and the connection. I miss *her*.

I can't stop the questions that infiltrate my mind about how this is going to work in the office, but that doesn't stop me from texting her all day every day. It's just more of the same stuff...

What was your childhood like? Was it weird having your parents live in different houses?

Where did you go to college, and did you join a sorority?

What the hell is that bachelorette thinking wearing a tiara to the first meet-and-greet. Doesn't she know that screams high maintenance?

It is a running, pleasant conversation, that blurs my nights right into my mornings, where others join in on our design show discussions. I don't think I've ever talked to Nancy about shiplap before, but by the way her face lights up during the chats, I'd wager she has a nautical theme going on in her house.

The ease of the conversations and the ensuing laughter makes work pass by in a flash. The comradery is infectious, and everyone seems happier to be productive. Even Quinn stopping by doesn't faze me anymore. And when we finally leave every day, it just seems part of a new normal routine that we both end up at Weight Expectations, where I am currently staring at her like the creeper that I am.

My new favorite pasttime is watching Rian work out. It's hilarious. I don't mean that in a bad way. I'm not kinnearing her so a picture can go viral. No, I'm laughing because the relationship she and Abel have is so funny.

I personally don't use a trainer because I don't need it for motivation purposes or to learn what exercises to do that will benefit me. But I've observed them for long enough to know how the trainers work. How can you not notice them? They're hard to miss when they're wearing the same basic outfit—black pants, black t-shirts with the gym logo on it, sometimes a black gym hoodie. They all have a different teaching style, which obviously draws in a variety of clients. But one thing is true for all of them. They like keeping their clients on their toes.

Some days, they'll be using weights. Some days, they'll be outside in the small yard tossing giant tires. But today, today Abel has pulled out the bags and boxing gloves.

"Whatcha watching?" I didn't realize Nick was behind me, nor did I realize I'd been standing here watching for so long. But Rian is that entertaining.

Her class started out with just jabs, but Rian got bored and started dancing around the bag. Abel is clearly not pleased by her new fancy footwork, if his scowl is any indication.

"Rian."

"Who?"

I gesture my head toward the scene in front of us. "Rian. She's my new account manager. She's giving Abel a run for his money right now."

We continue to watch as she turns her jabs on Abel and his abs. At first, he backs away, but then she says something I can't decipher and he's back. She probably bet him some pushups or made a snark about not being a young pup anymore and his abs not holding up during a fight. Either way, he's taking it like a champ. Eventually, she tires out and stands in front of him, hands on her hips and challenge in her eyes.

"She doesn't seem like your type." I forgot Nick was still standing there. Or maybe I just assumed he got bored and left.

Suddenly feeling defensive, I look over my shoulder and sneer at him. "And why would you say that?"

His pause tells me he's taken aback, which he should be. My defenses are on heightened alert when it comes to Rian, and I don't even know why. All I know is that he'd better tread lightly when it comes to her or we're going to have a big problem.

"Slow your roll there, Hothead. I was gonna say because she's not wearing any makeup or fancy workout clothes. And she seems friendly. Your type is plastic, made up, and one spoon short of a set."

"Which didn't stop you from setting me up with Marley."

He waves me off. "Marley was an error in judgment. I was hoping you were becoming less vain. Obviously, my timing wasn't off, since it appears you've turned a new leaf. I just picked the wrong woman to set you up with."

Okay, fine. I'll accept his comment even if I shrug it off. Whether or not Rian's my type isn't his business. Not when *I* don't even know for sure if she's my type yet. I mean, I hope so. But I haven't done this before, so I have no idea how to gauge any of it. And part of me keeps wondering when someone else is going to catch her eye and she moves on.

Wait. The gym grapevine informed me Abel is now a single man. Maybe I need to be keeping a closer eye on this guy.

I watch with rapt attention, eyes narrowed now, as Abel points to the floor and she resists. Finally, after what appears to be an emotional charged spat, she gets down on her hands and knees.

I chuckle out loud when I realize she did, in fact, challenge him to pushups. And she lost.

"She's cute, man." Nick catches my attention again, and I realize I'm wasting workout time watching this very funny, very interesting woman. Not that anything to do with Rian is a waste of time, but Nick has flaked on me so many times lately, I better take advantage of him being here.

"I guess," I finally say, lying down on the weight bench and adjusting my body underneath the bar.

Nick stands over me, ready to spot, and snickers. "You don't guess anything. You like her. I can tell by the goofy grin on your face whenever you look at her."

"So, what if I do?" Grunting, I push up the bar and move my feet so I can balance better. This conversation will be much more comfortable if I'm not just sitting idly by for it. Plus, if he says something that pisses me off, it's safer for both of us if I have a hundred and fifty pounds of weights holding me back.

He gets in position behind the bar to spot me and shrugs. "So, go for it."

Fifteen reps later, Nick helps me guide the bar back in place so I can sit up and get some clarification. "Can I ask you a question?" I ask as I wipe the towel down my face.

He situates himself under the bar. "Sure."

"How come you're still single?"

Before pushing up even once, Nick is sitting upright on the bench again. Looks like I accidentally gave him an out. "I guess I just haven't found the right person yet."

"How do you know?" He looks at me like he's trying to figure out if I'm for real or if I'm yanking his chain. It's wigging me out. "You know what?" I wave my hand in dismissal. "Forget it. I don't wanna know. Lie down. You're getting soft in the chest. You need to work harder."

Nick doesn't move a muscle except for his jaw, unfortunately for me. "First of all, my pecs are harder than one of these flat weights." I roll my eyes at the exaggeration. "And second, I don't want to forget it. You never get deep, which means you're having some sort of existential crisis right now."

"Ok, Oprah." I pat the bench. "Talk show is over. Seriously. Lie down."

"Nope. Listen. Relationships are complicated. People are complicated. The only way to know if someone is right for you is to keep being with them. Either the connection will get stronger, or it'll fade away. Mine have always faded away."

"That's not actually helpful."

He shrugs. "There's no crystal ball with dating. Sometimes it works. Sometimes it doesn't. But the journey is worth it if you're putting in your all."

Is it though? Is it worth it if you only get hurt in the end? Or if you end up hurting someone else?

But what if no one were to get hurt? I look over at Rian who is still powering through her pushups. Well, until she collapses to the floor, Abel laughing next to her.

"You want my opinion?" Nick says behind me. "Never mind. I know you do. That kickboxing cutie that you are still staring at isn't your type. And that speaks volumes about how great she must be. You can't help who you're attracted to, but when it's there, you can't deny it either."

I tear my eyes away from her. "Sounds like you have some experience with this topic."

He grabs a drink, even though he hasn't done anything yet except exercise his mouth. "Of not being able to control who you're attracted to? Yeah, realizing you're bi means realizing the heart wants what the heart wants. And sometimes there's nothing you can do about it."

I freeze. "You're bi?"

Nick flashes me a grin. "You sound surprised."

I am. But I'm also an insensitive dick who likes to jack with his friends, so I school my features and say the first thing that pops into my head. "I am."

He freezes, and I can tell he's had this conversation before. I'm guessing it hasn't always gone well. "You got a problem with it?"

"Yeah, I do." We both stand up and take menacing steps toward each other. I'm not worried though. I've got the upper hand on this one. "You've known me for how long? We've been working out together, using the locker room together for how long, and you haven't hit on me yet. Am I not good enough for you?"

It takes a second for Nick to realize I'm fucking with him, but when he does, he throws his head back and barks out a laugh. When he finally pulls himself back together, he points at me and shakes his head. "You're a dick. You seriously had me going."

I shrug, still keeping up part of the act. "I'm hurt, man. I'm a vision of manhood, and you've never even looked at me as more than a friend."

He shorts a laugh and adds a ten-pound weight to the bar. I do the same on the other side. "You're a little too pompous for my taste."

"What?" I put my hand over my heart and fake hurt. "I thought you were my friend."

"It's not you, it's me." I give him a pointed look at the cliché line. "We're too much alike to make it work. I've got to be the prettiest one in a relationship, just like you. So lay your ass down on that bench and give me another fifteen."

Narrowing my eyes, I say, "Sounds like a proposition."

"You wish." He stands up, walking behind the bench again. "Actually, I'm on call so you never know when my phone is gonna ring."

I roll my eyes and follow his instructions. "You're a really shitty workout partner, you know that? Always putting your job first?"

"I know. How dare I leave you on chest day to save someone's life? There's a special place in Hell for me."

"Damn straight."

We go through three more sets, then switch positions. And yes, I make multiple jokes about him being on bottom, which irritates the shit out of him, so I feel really accomplished. But it also gives me time to think more.

"How did you know you were bi?"

Nick cocks an eyebrow at me like he's not the one who started this whole conversation. But now that we're "sharing", I have questions and no one else to ask anyway, so it might as well be him.

"It's not really that hard to figure out. The attraction feels the same."

"Oh, yeah. Right. I guess that's not really what I meant. I meant..." I mop my brow with my towel again. "Yeah, I don't know what I meant."

"Is this about that chick again?"

I feel my eyes widen but quickly get myself under control. Just because I have questions doesn't mean I feel like giving my own answers. So, I do what any man would do in my situation—I begin taking the weights off the bar and avoid all eye contact.

"What if it is?" I ask defensively.

He rolls his eyes. "Don't get your panties in a twist. I want to make sure I know what we're talking about so I can help you out, not so I can give you shit. I already said she's cute."

I observe his body language and facial expressions for as long as I can before he starts to think I'm flirting. Either he's really good at deception or he really isn't trying to give me grief. Might as well throw caution to the wind. At this point, I have no idea what I'm doing. "Yeah, it's about Rian."

"What's the problem? You're not new to dating."

"No, I'm not new to hookups. But liking the person I'm with enough to continue long-term isn't something I'm familiar with."

He looks amused as we finish re-racking the weights and wiping down the bench. "You're maturing, my friend."

"Or I'm losing my mind."

"Maybe. That's what happens when you've been hiding from relationships for a long time and someone finally comes along who makes you want different things."

"Is that what happened to you?"

He blushes and looks down. "I don't know what you're talking about."

"When you realized you were bi." Suddenly I notice his expression. "Wait. Did you... have you met someone?"

"What? Why would you think that?" He treks over to the other side of the room, me catching up quickly. There's something he's not telling me, and if I have to fess up, so does he.

"I was wondering if that's how it felt when you realized you were bi, but suddenly you've gone all shy and emotional." Grabbing his shoulder, I pull him to a halt and roughly turn him toward me. "You met someone, didn't you?"

"I don't know yet. Maybe?"

Well, now I'm really intrigued. If we're both going to try out this relationship thing, we might as well talk each other through it. Or coach each other. Isn't that something guys do? They don't talk about their feelings or anything, but give each other advice and slaps on the ass or something?

"What's she like? Wait. He? She? I don't know how to have these conversations with you now."

Nick laughs at my confusion and then points at me. "You don't need to know because we're not talking about this. I'm not even as into this person as you are to that person..." He points to Rian, who is doing her best side kick and failing miserably. Abel's standing behind her trying to help her with her form, but I wouldn't be surprised if she knocks them both off balance and they end up in a heap. "When I get there, we'll talk. Until then, it's just a thought stream. Nothing more."

"Okay. I give," I say, throwing my hands up in front of me. "But before I let this topic die, I'm just going to say one thing."

He groans and wipes his hand down his face. "Yeah? What's that?"

"Don't worry about me. Eventually, I'll get over the hurt of you picking him over me."

He snaps me with his sweaty towel and demands we get back to work. But not before I look Rian's direction right as my prediction comes true. Abel loses his balance just as Rian does and they tumble to the floor.

CHAPTER TWENTY-SEVEN

"**M**y wedding is in four days, Rian. You can't just change your RSVP at the last minute so a girlfriend can come with you."

I roll my eyes as I follow Laney around the table, putting plates on top of the placemats after she sets them down. I'm trying really hard not to slam the plates down, no matter how angry she makes me. My mother saves these particular red plates for special family get togethers (also known as regularly weekly dinners), and I really don't want to hear her bitching about how hard it is to find an individual matching plate because "Dillard's never has the same patterns twice." I'm not sure how hard it is to find a matching red plate on this little thing called *the internet*, but at this point, it's a moot point anyway.

I just need to make it through two more hours of family time without breaking anything. There is a reason I've been avoiding this scenario for the last several weeks unless absolutely necessary. The closer it gets to the wedding date, the more psychotic my sister becomes. And the cuter her fiancé thinks her attitude is.

Of course, he does. He's the one who has to take her home and not get shanked overnight. It wouldn't behoove him to tell her to shut the hell up. Sleeping with one eye open is practically impossible.

Not breaking things, though, doesn't mean I can't fight back. "It

229

never occurred to me that my sister wouldn't give me the option of a plus-one," I remark through gritted teeth. "If I had known my sister was trying to keep the wedding down to an intimate three hundred people, and not one person over, I wouldn't have asked anyone to come with me. Silly me for not assuming I was a singleton. Will I be sitting at the kids table, too?"

I want to add that if she's so worried about going over the maximum number of guests, I'm more than happy to skip it myself, but I don't have enough patience for a guilt trip from my mother.

Laney ignores my jab about the seating arrangements, which means I'm probably being relegated to the back somewhere. I'll address that issue later, if at all. At this point, it's not worth fighting about if it means not having to sit with all her snotty friends and put up with their judgmental glares. "You don't date, Rian. Why would it even occur to me that you would bring someone to *my wedding*?"

"I do, too, date. What, do you just think I'm some sort of recluse that sits at home and drowns her loneliness in a bowl of ice cream every night?"

Her eyes scan up and down my body like there's an obvious answer to my question.

I gape at her, not quite sure why I'm unable to believe she would even go there. She's been doing it a lot lately. Where did my sweet little sister go and why did she leave this horrible monster in her place? "Don't look at me like that. And certainly, don't forget that until you decided running was your life, you loved ice cream more than me, which is why *you* were the fat sister for ninety-five percent of our lives."

She slams the napkins down on the table. "How dare you bring that up in front of Bradley?" The fiancé who is currently ignoring us and rubbing his stomach while watching a football game. "I worked hard to get where I am, and you have no right to make a mockery of my ability to take control of my health. Maybe if you would put down the fork for once, you wouldn't feel compelled to resort to rude comments to make yourself feel better."

I take a menacing step forward. We haven't come to blows since we were in elementary school and she stole my pink bow on picture day. I got the bow back, but no one bothered to pull the grass out of my hair which has always given us a good laugh, but not today. Today, I'm remembering how angry her condescending tone can make me and that I can kick her ass if it comes down to it. No wonder I like kickboxing so much. Subconsciously, I knew it would come in handy before this damn wedding.

"And maybe if you didn't always belittle me and my body shape and how it's going to ruin your wedding, I wouldn't feel compelled to make rude comments," I throw back at her.

Laney throws her hands in the air. Apparently being called out for your own bad behavior is exasperating. Seriously, when did she become such a princess? She was never this high maintenance until she put on a pair of running shoes and did that Couch Potato to 5K challenge. "Do you even know how hard it is to make all the colors and shapes proportionate and visually pleasing if not everyone matches?"

"Well, maybe if you still hung out with all those friends you ditched when you became a skinny bitch, you would have a fat guy friend who could be my escort!"

She gets ready to shoot off another barb, but before she does, it seems she has a light bulb moment. Turning to Bradley who has already mastered the art of ignoring his new bride, she asks, "Hey, babe. Do you think we could switch around the order of your best men so Kyle can be Rian's escort? She's right. That would balance everything out."

I drop my chin to my chest in defeat as they begin chatting about who would look best escorting whom, because patterns or something. I don't even know. I should have known better than to waste my breath arguing with her. She's so far up in WeddingLand she can't see the destruction in her own wake.

"It's almost over," my dad says as he brings in a giant pan of lasagna for my mom who has conveniently been hiding out in the kitchen during this exchange. "Just keep your mouth shut and focus on how much booze I'm paying for at this thing."

This is the most my dad has ever spoken to me about my sister's wedding. Actually, it's the most he's spoken during a family dinner since she got engaged. It never occurred to me until now that my mother and sister are probably driving him as crazy about it as they are me. And I can go home to get away from it. He's stuck here in wedding hell. Poor man. I feel like we should hug it out or something.

My mother comes in, all smiles and oblivious to the smack down that almost was, with a salad that she strategically places right in front of my plate. I take a centering breath, resisting the temptation to roll my eyes about it again. I don't know how many times I can tell her I'm fine. I'm on a diet and go to the gym regularly. But since I haven't dropped a hundred pounds, she doesn't believe me. Why can't anyone believe that you can be heavy and healthy at the same time? My own doctor confirmed it the other day at my regular checkup.

"Okay, everyone. Let's eat!" Mom claps her hands together like she's a modern-day version of Carol Brady, and my sister and her plus-one make their way over to the table.

"You're right, Rian," my sister begins.

Wait. What did she just say? Is this… is this an apology?

Glancing over at my dad, I see an encouraging look on his face. Maybe he was right. Maybe this is just normal pre-wedding behavior and the sister who used to follow me around and tell me I was her hero is still in there somewhere.

"I am?" I ask cautiously, still not completely believing this is happening.

She nods at me and gives me a genuine smile. "You are. We can shift the bridal party to accommodate Kyle escorting you. Visually, it'll be so much more appealing."

I blink a few times but give no other response. I could start the fight back up again, but what will that accomplish? I genuinely don't care about any spatial awareness in her wedding pictures or what weird friend of Bradley's walks down the aisle with me. I'm only in this wedding because she's my sister and deep down I love her, even if I don't like her at all.

Instead, I choose to do what my dad has already advised—keep my mouth shut and focus on the booze. The wine he is currently pouring in my glass is proof enough that at least one person in the house recognizes that most of the women in this family are certifiably insane. The small nod of his head when I look at him for support is confirmation that we're in this together.

Four days to go. Just four days to go and she'll be on her honeymoon, my mother can throw away the fabric samples littering every spare surface of the house, and life can return to some sort of normal.

Settling into our seats, my mom immediately moves back into wedding planning mode. I guzzle more wine in reaction and my father doesn't miss a beat giving me a refill. He's a good man, that one. "So, what's left to do on our list, anyway?"

My sister whips out a small spiral notepad from underneath the table. I have no idea where it came from. Was she sitting on it? Is there a shelf under there? Who knows. Regardless, I'm both impressed and slightly irritated that she's basically a magician.

Flipping through the book, she begins to read down the list. "Let's see. We need to make sure my dress is steam ironed. The guys are picking up the tuxes on Friday. Don't forget to make sure the cummerbunds are slate gray, not metallic gray, Bradley. They aren't the same, and it'll totally clash if someone has the wrong color." She gives him a pointed stare. He just smiles and nods as he sprinkles parmesan cheese on his lasagna. "The rehearsal dinner needs to be confirmed. Are you positive we got the large back room, Mom? You know that front room will be too small and the staff at Omise is always trying to book that one first. I'm sure they like the visibility for customers to see they have the space, but I just don't think it's enough room."

"I'll have your father call and double check tomorrow, honey." My mother shakes her head in rejection as I pass the lasagna plate to her, opting for a larger than normal serving of salad instead. I shrug and dig into the noodles myself. Normally, I'd follow my mother's lead, but it's my cheat day. I refuse to feel guilty.

"Okay." Laney puts down the notepad and dishes out her own oversized portion of salad. "I think the last thing on our list is to finalize the seating chart. I was almost done but *Rian*," she practically spits my name in my face across the table, "decided at the last minute to bring a date."

"Oh!" My mother claps her hands together in delight. "I didn't know you were dating someone. Is this a new thing?"

I nod and take a deep breath, grateful for the conversation change. I'm not thrilled it's moved to my love life, but I'll take what I can get at this point. "It is. We've known each other for a while, but this will be our first official date."

"You really think bringing him to my wedding, especially when you have bridesmaid's duties, is the best idea when you're trying to impress a guy?"

My irritation returns, but I try to tamp it down. "I'm not trying to impress him, Laney. I've already done that. I'm bringing him because we enjoy each other's company. And because you're driving me to drink," I add, mumbling into my wine glass as I take a sip.

Unfortunately, she doesn't miss my snark. "What was that?"

"Oh, nothing," I feign indifference. "Just needing another drink."

My dad takes that as his cue to refill my glass for a second time. At this rate, I'm going to be rip-roaring drunk by the time the dishes are cleared. My sister, on the other hand, continues looking at me with critical eyes.

Finally, I can't take her stare anymore. "What?" I blurt out.

"Rian, are you sure you should be eating that?" Laney points at my plate.

I purposely place my fork on the table as gently as possible, knowing my arms are stronger than they look, and this plate doesn't have a chance if I lose my cool. Crossing said arms, I lean them on the table. "And why would you ask me that?"

I shouldn't go there right before her wedding. I know I shouldn't, but I am itching for a fight being in this house and am already feeling the effects of the alcohol. Plus, after being under fire for the last several months about everything in my life, about the digs on everything from my weight, to my date, to my job, I can't help myself.

My sister doesn't even notice how close I am to losing my shit. "Because we don't have anymore fittings for the dresses."

Aaaaaand that's it. I'm done. Wiping my mouth with my napkin, I turn to my mother. "Thank you for dinner. I need to go."

"What? But we just started eating." I barely register her protests as I stand and smooth down my shirt. It's unnecessary for the shirt, but idle hands and all that.

I ignore the protests of my sister, who is spouting off about how overly sensitive I am, and my mother's complaints about wasting food. Instead, I grab my bag off the floor to make my way out.

The last thing I say before walking away from them all is "See ya, Dad," as I kiss him on the cheek. I might be mistaken, but I swear he smiles in support and understanding as I leave.

I know today is a rest day and a cheat day, but this crap has me all wound up. Looks like I need to box out some frustrations. Good thing Weight Expectations has locations all over the greater Chicago area. And I've got a free pass to use the closest one to me.

Finally, a silver lining to that whole fire thing. Membership has its perks, after all.

CHAPTER TWENTY-EIGHT

CARLOS

This week has been a blur. We haven't been this busy at work in a long time. Really, it's my fault for not anticipating better. I've worked for Quinn long enough to know when he starts off a sentence with "We're expanding into…" or "We're upgrading our systems…", I should immediately clear my schedule. When he says both in the same conversation, I might as well cancel any and all vacation time and immediately contract a caterer to bring dinner every night.

Granted, we've made several new hires, added multiple client accounts including Rian's delicate project, updated our accounting system, and changed the provider in charge of our employee stock options, but all of that has led to some very late nights in the office. The long hours have also cut my time at the gym short, which I hate, but the bright side is I've had more time with Rian. A lot more time. I told her several times this week she didn't need to stay late. None of the expansions have anything to do with her specific job. Plus, she's still in training. But she insisted on taking advantage of the extra hours to get up to speed as quickly as possible and lend a hand where needed. Secretly, I think she was also using it as an excuse to stay far away from her family.

Hell, the random shit she's told me about her bridezilla sister has me running scared, and all I'm doing is attending the wedding. I can't imagine how stressed Rian must be having to participate. No wonder Quinn doesn't make her blink twice.

Knowing Rian needed me here to support her is what motivated me to jump in a cab and spend my Saturday afternoon in a church. When she mentioned the open bar at the reception, I knew my attendance was especially important. It's not pretty.

Well, actually, it kind of is. Even with raccoon eyes and bedhead, Rian always looks pretty. But I suspect the bride would be way less forgiving of her bridesmaid passing out than I would be. Not only is this the perfect excuse to see her outside the office, I'm genuinely worried about how this night will end. I'm not sure if Rian's family is always hypercritical of her. I hope not. But either way, I'm not taking any chances. She needs someone in her corner who doesn't care what anyone else thinks. That's me.

The white church sits on the corner of the block, grand and ornate in its architecture. The structure itself must be at least a hundred years old, but it's obviously been lovingly maintained by the congregation. Stepping through the oversized wooden doors, I realize my assessment is right. Stylistically, the interior is more open and airy than the original building would have been. Plus, there are some columns that are clearly not original and probably added for structural support. New carpet. New paint. And it looks like new pews in the sanctuary. I'm impressed by how whoever designed the space was able to update it while maintaining the character of the time period it was built.

The only thing I might change is the decorations. There is no doubt a wedding is about to happen because flowers and tulle and small twinkly lights are everywhere, in every shade of red. I didn't even realize there were so many variations, but apparently, whoever is in charge grabbed one of those color wheels, picked a point on the red side, and just kept moving their cursor back and forth from pale pink to vampire food red when deciding on the decorations. There is no other explanation for how nothing in here is the exact same color and yet everything matches correctly.

"Carlos."

That's my cue.

Turning, I can't stop my mouth from falling open. Rian isn't just gorgeous, she's practically a vision sent straight out of one of my fantasies.

Her dark hair is long and wavy, as if it's been styled for a television appearance. Her smoky makeup makes the blue flecks in her eyes sparkle. Her skin is so flawless, she's practically glowing. And that's just above her shoulders.

My eyes continue their path downward, taking in her outfit. The red dress cinches under her ample breasts, not only showing off her cleavage, but also accentuating her hourglass shape. The flowy fabric ends mid-knee and her strappy silver heels show off her sexy calves that flex whenever she walks. Kickboxing has definitely built up some of that muscle. I also notice that her toenails are colored a shade of pink which makes her skin look more tan than normal. Who knew I had a foot fetish? I'm not even sure I did until this moment right here, because damn, those are some sexy toes.

"You look... wow," I'm finally able to croak out, still unable to stop staring at her.

A slight blush covers her cheeks, and I can tell she's pleased with my assessment. "I look like an apple."

"Red delicious is my favorite."

It's her turn to look stunned, but then she bursts out laughing. "There ya go, turning on the charm for the ladies again."

I can't help my smile. I like making her laugh. I like making her happy. It feels like it comes naturally when I'm around her. "It worked, didn't it?"

She nods gratefully. "It did. Thank you. It's been," her eyes widen with emphasis, "a *looong* day."

Looking down at my watch, I realize how grievous that statement is. "It's not even two o'clock yet."

"So, you understand my point."

"Your crazy text messages helped clarify things for me."

She groans. "Seriously. She spends weeks bitching about how I don't do enough to help her, but the second I try to spread out the train of her dress so it doesn't wrinkle, I'm trying to take over for the wedding planner? How is helping her look nice in her dress taking over? And since when does she have a wedding planner?"

I pull Rian close and put my arms around her, hugging her to me. Rubbing her back, I quietly reassure her it's almost over. Just a few more minutes until the ceremony begins and Bridezilla pulls back her claws. I also make a mental note to have a strawberry margarita waiting for her as soon as the bridal party is introduced at the reception. She's going to need it.

It takes a few minutes, but eventually she takes a deep breath and pulls away feeling much less tense than she did a few minutes ago. "Thank you. For being here, I mean. Just knowing there's at least one person who couldn't care less about this shindig means a lot."

I open my mouth to tell her there isn't anywhere I'd rather be, which is the truth, but I'm cut off before I begin.

"Rian." Her attention diverts to someone behind me and immediately she pulls away further and some of her shoulders tense up again. It automatically puts me on high alert.

"Mom. What's wrong? Does Laney need something?"

Ah. And now I understand where the tension came from. I'm feeling a bit of it myself the longer her mother looks at me like she's assessing who I am, why I'm here, and what my intentions are.

Yeah. I'm understanding Rian more and more.

"No, nothing at all. I just wanted to know who your... friend... is." She continues looking at me like I'm surely a figment of her imagination. Or the Big Bad Wolf here to blow the church down.

Rian doesn't even seem to notice, just immediately snaps into action. "Oh! Of course. Sorry. Mom, this is Carlos. Carlos, this is my mom, Riann." Her hand moves back and forth between us as she speaks.

Rian's mom, who I'm now referring to as "The Creeper" since she hasn't yet blinked while she stares, holds her hand out to shake mine. "Are you sitting on the bride's side or the groom's side?"

The question confuses me. Did she not just see me hugging her older daughter? Rian never mentioned anything wrong with her mother, so I can only assume this is another one of the famous passive-aggressive comments that seem to be the norm in this family.

"I told you I was bringing a plus-one, Mother." Rian crosses her arms over her chest defensively. The movement distracts me momentarily when the tops of her breasts jiggle. That's not being a jack ass. She just has a really nice rack. However, I sense a showdown coming on, so I tear my focus away from my favorite part of her red dress and put it back where it belongs... on the simmering family drama.

"You told us you were bringing a friend, not a date. If we'd known you were bringing a man, it wouldn't have been such a nasty conversation."

Somehow, I doubt that, but I opt to stay silent. I might be here for Rian's sake, but this is something they need to work out. I'm not *that* important in her life yet.

"I did tell you it was a date. Laney opted not to believe me, and you took her side. That's not my problem." Rian drops her arms and waves her hand as if she's done with the conversation. "It'll be fine. I don't have to sit at the bridal table, and Aunt Helga is in the hospital, so it frees up one extra place setting at a regular table. I'm sure Laney won't mind when I tell her the visual balance issue has been fixed."

No idea what that comment means, so I avoid it while doing my best to help her out. "Well, I'm a picky eater, so I doubt I'll do more than just sit there anyway."

Rian's eyebrows shoot up. "Uh, no way, Mister. There is a huge dance floor, and I want to try that move we saw on that dancing show the other day."

I groan my response. "I told you I don't know how to salsa. My mother is Norwegian. We only dance slowly in a circle. With a pole in the middle."

For the second time in as many seconds, Rian's eyebrows shoot up again. "Did you just say you know how to pole dance? Does Nancy know about this extra skill set?"

She squeals as I grab her waist and pull her flush to me. "That is not what I said, and don't you dare go starting the rumor mill at the office. You're still in your probationary period, ya know, and the boss doesn't take kindly to rabble rousers."

She laughs, knowing full well that I'd be a fool to fire her for several very important reasons. Number one being how good she is at her job. "Oh, well, by all means, we'll keep it a secret."

"Yeah, you do that," I respond playfully, interrupted only when her mother clears her throat.

"Well, since that's all settled, Carlos, we're delighted to have you. Now I don't mean to be a buzzkill but the ceremony is set to begin in about five minutes, so, Rian, you need to head back to your sister."

"Okay. I'll be there in a second."

Having been dismissed, Rian's mother turns and walks away, back toward a man with a flower on his lapel. I assume he's the usher, which means I really do have a short amount of time before he escorts the mother of the bride down the aisle.

"I need to go sit down," I say, kissing Rian on the nose. "You'll be fine. At this point, it's so close to being a done deal, there's nothing else your sister can spring on you."

"You underestimate her ability to surprise me in the worst possible way."

I smile at her sarcasm. "Then just remember there is an open bar as a reward for playing nice."

"Dating for less than a week and you already know the way to my heart," Rian says with a laugh and gives me a quick peck on the lips. It's the first one we've had in a couple of days and my chest feels full just knowing she did it in front of her mother. "I'll see you at the reception?"

"Text me if you need a ride," I tack on as she walks away, her hips swaying back and forth accentuating those sexy ass calves. Seriously. She's a knockout.

Having no reason to hang out in the foyer anymore, I make my way into the sanctuary where there is more of the same... flowers, tulle, twinkly lights. It's not gaudy, but it's certainly not simplistic. The flowers alone must have cost a fortune.

I'm shocked by how many people are here as well. What are

there… a couple of hundred guests? It's the largest wedding I've been to since Marlene and Mart got married straight out of college almost twenty years ago. Back then, inviting everyone you'd ever met was the thing to do. It's not something I can see for myself, though. Seems like such a waste of money. I'd rather have something small and simple. None of this bigger is better crap. Only the closest of friends and family in attendance; people who would truly be happy for us and not here simply for some free food and drinks.

Wait. What's happening here?

I've never really thought that hard about getting married beyond "it'll never happen". But for some reason, being here with Rian is making me look at it from a different angle. Is it something I'm actively pursuing? No. But I guess if the right person came along, I wouldn't be terribly opposed. Maybe. Maybe? Hell, I don't know. I'm blaming my sudden interest in getting married on all the bridal shows Rian made me watch last weekend. I knew we should have stuck to cooking shows, but no. I had to shy away from the Food Network in the name of resisting temptation. I should have known better.

Putting my hand on my forehead, I make sure I'm not feverish. Surely, I'm getting sick. I'll take some Tylenol when I get home. But first, I have a ceremony to sit through, and it's going to take some extra focus to pretend I'm not bored out of my mind.

Right on cue, the music begins indicating the start of the ceremony.

Rian's mother is the first one escorted in. She clomps down the aisle, not at all graceful but beaming with pride, nonetheless. I finally see the family resemblance in the smile. Rian got more of her mother's features than I realized.

Once she's seated, the bridesmaids begin making their way toward the front. I'm not sure how many of them there are, mostly because they all look the same. Same hair style. Same physique. Same red dress. Same small bouquet of white roses. It's like watching a Barbie parade. Everyone is identical to the one before.

Until Rian appears. She outshines them all. And yet…

Something is wrong. Her smile looks forced, her nostrils just slightly flared, and she refuses to make eye contact with me when she walks by.

My eyes follow her, as if the back of her dress will give me some idea of what happened and how I can fix it. Well, that and it gives me a great view of those legs again.

Focus, Carlos.

When she left me standing in the lobby, everything was fine. Not fantastic, but not tense like this.

Stumped, I decide to make sure she has an extra strong margarita waiting at the reception. Whatever has happened in the last few minutes has obviously shaken her up.

Catching a glimpse of the next bridesmaid, I suddenly know what's got Rian so upset, and rightfully so.

Walking down the aisle wearing the same red dress, carrying the same white rose bouquet, sporting the same hairstyle is the last person I expected to see here—Ridiculous Rebecca.

What is she doing here?

CHAPTER TWENTY-NINE

RIAN

Five minutes earlier...

Hustling back to the bride room, I steel myself for whatever my sister throws at me now. I swear I can't win with her no matter what I do. I can't wait for this wedding to be over and for my sister to get laid. Lord help us all if Bradley is a terrible lover because she'll never be nice again.

I can hear her ranting before I even open the door, but the words become clear as I step inside.

"Oh, there you are." She rushes to me, relief on her face. I don't trust it. That means she needs me to do something. "I need you to do something for me."

Called it.

"Bendy's not here yet."

"What? How is she still not here?"

I've never met this woman, but I don't know how my sister calls her best friend and maid of honor. She didn't show up for the bridal shower because she was "working". She has never been to a dress fitting with us because "something came up". She was supposed to meet up with us at the bachelorette party, but she got "sick". Basically, she's done nothing for this wedding, shirking all the responsibilities to me and making me the target of most of my sister's wrath. And now she's going to miss the whole thing.

"It's okay." Laney is uncharacteristically calm amidst this latest crisis, which I admit frightens me just a bit. "She's caught in traffic, but she'll be here in time for the reception."

I bite my tongue from reminding her that I was three minutes early for my hair appointment this morning and she still told me I was inconsiderate for making her wonder if I would be on time. Nor do I tell her if I ever have the pleasure of meeting this Bendy woman, who has a stupid name, I may just punch her in her bendy parts for all the crap she's pulled.

"So anyway, listen." Laney grabs my chin and turns me toward her, possibly also rubbing some of my makeup off in the process. Good thing it's caked on. I have a few spare layers. "I need you to stand in as my maid of honor."

That's it? That's easy. I'm the last person to walk down the aisle before the maid of honor. It just means Laney goes a little early. Which means I'm missing something.

"Okay, no problem," I reply, hoping if I stay calm so will she. "I can hold your bouquet along with mine. No big deal."

The irritation flashes in her eyes and I know I've made some sort of mistake. "Except it *is* a big deal. This means we have an extra groomsman. I had it perfectly balanced, but now you have to escort two groomsmen and it's going to be all off balance because Kyle is on the larger side and Dirk is not."

Do not roll your eyes. Do not roll your eyes. Do not roll your eyes...

"Don't roll your eyes, Rian."

Oops. Apparently, just thinking it wasn't enough.

"This is my wedding," she hisses. "I want everything to be perfect. But it's falling apart. I'm missing my maid of honor. The bottom of my dress is wrinkly." I resist giving her a pointed look about that one. "The bouquets ended up being white instead of ecru."

Her breathing gets shaky as she rants, and for the first time in a while, I can see how much anxiety she has. Not for the first time, however, I wonder how all the other women in the room are capable of playing on their phones and chatting with each other while the bride, the woman whose important day it is, is beginning to have a panic attack. Is this what female friendships are supposed to be like? No one really cares about anyone else, but as long as their hair looks good, it's okay? And how did my sister fall into that crazy narrative?

I don't know and now is not the time to care. Even if she drives me crazy, even if she's passive-aggressive and rude, even if she's embarrassed of her fat sister standing up with her skinny friends, it's not about me. It's about my little sister having the wedding of her dreams.

Putting my own feelings aside, I immediately flip into protective big sister mode. Placing my hands on her shoulders, I do my best to calm her down. "Okay, okay, stop. Breathe. In through your nose, out through your mouth." We take a couple of deep breaths together, and she slowly pulls herself back together. "If it comes down to it, we can ditch a groomsman at the last second. Let's give it a few minutes to see if... Bendy," I stumble over her name, trying not to laugh at that part, "makes it on time. Okay?"

She nods rapidly and takes another deep breath. "Okay, yes. You're right. Just a few more minutes."

"I know you want this to be perfect," I continue slowly. "And it will be. No one is going to notice if we shift things around at the last second, as long as we play it off, right?" She nods again. "Okay, good. Now keep breathing and think about that handsome man at the end of the aisle who can't wait to be your husband for the rest of his life."

She takes one more deep breath, her body calm, and a smile finally peeks out. "Thank you, Rian," she says loud enough that only I can hear. It feels very much like one of those sisters-only moments we haven't had in way too long. "I'm so glad you're here. You always make everything better."

Clasping her hands between mine, I smile back at her, letting her words of love wash over me. This is the sister I grew up with. The one I love fiercely. I'm glad to see she's still in there somewhere. She's buried under a mountain of lace and tulle but she's there.

The door opens as we continue to breathe, and the wedding planner walks in, my father right behind her. "Places everyone."

"Oh, no," my sister groans. I look back at my sister and remind her again to breathe while the other bridesmaids, who continue to be oblivious to this crisis, filter out the door.

"We got this," I say encouragingly, refusing to let go of her hand. "Just a few more minutes."

She nods again.

"Honey, you look so beautiful." Good old dad diverts her attention and offers her the crook of his arm. "You ready to go get married?"

Laney takes one last deep breath, squares her shoulders, and pops her chin up. Looks like my job here is done. I don't know how she's going to hold that stiff of an upright position. The bridal walk doesn't start until we wander through the building and down to the sanctuary, but I suppose she's faking it until she makes it or something. As long as she's happy and doesn't pass out, I don't really care.

Walking behind the other bridesmaids, we follow the wedding planner down a few different hallways. I'm sure we look like a bunch of red ducklings. The visual image makes me giggle under my breath. My sister and I may have had a moment back there, but it doesn't change the fact that the ridiculousness of this whole thing makes me question if I ever want to have a wedding. I can't imagine how much money my parents shelled out, and for what? Laney has been so stressed about everything being perfect, I doubt she's even going to remember most of the day.

Forget that. Someday, I'll just run away and have a Vegas drive-thru wedding. No muss. No fuss. Just in and out, and maybe even pick up some tacos while we're there.

That is assuming I ever get married. Which is not an assumption I want to make yet considering I've been dating Carlos for all of ten seconds. Nothing dashes a girl's hopes and dreams like setting the expectations too high. Right now, I'm just happy with the idea of dancing with him tonight. Maybe taking him home with me. Maybe getting a little frisky...

Okay, Rian, that's enough. It's been a long time since you've been with a man, but this circus comes first. Fantasies later... But keep that Vegas Taco Bell idea in mind for retirement when I need a project. Driving through to get married and tacos at the same time is a great idea...

After more turns and hallways than I remember, we finally reach our destination. We all line up behind a giant closed door, small bouquets of white roses being handed to each of us. Laney is right. This is definitely not ecru and looks slightly out of place with the rest of the decor. Maybe she's not as crazy as I originally thought.

The wedding planner's hand sits on the knob, ready to open the doors, when suddenly a ruckus diverts all our attention.

"Wait!" a woman screeches and what I told Carlos about how he underestimates my sister's ability to make my life hell—it comes back to haunt me. I wasn't just right. I was so beyond correct, I should have seen this coming. But never in my wildest dreams did I imagine that this is who my sister refers to as Bendy.

"I'm so sorry," the woman gushes, throwing her purse onto a random chair and jumping on one foot as she tries to maneuver her spiky heel onto the other one. "My cab took a wrong turn and ended up stuck behind a massive accident."

My sister looks so delighted for this woman to be here, she forgets the panic attack she almost had mere seconds ago. Instead, she helps her balance. "It's okay. We never would've started without you."

Lies. We were absolutely about to start without her. In fact, I would love nothing more than to push her back out the front door and tell her she's uninvited. But of course, that's not going to happen.

"Rian, move forward." My sister waves at me so I can make room for the worst best friend ever, family comradery and sisterly love forgotten.

Bendy, also known as *Rebecca* to some of us, finally looks at me and pauses, contemplating. It's the exact same look she gave me last week after her interview, and I know she's trying to figure out if we've met before. "Hi, I'm Rebecca. Do I know you?"

I could tell her she practically taunts me at the gym on a regular basis when she struts around the man I'm dating in nothing but a sports bra. I could tell her she caused a massive fight between that same man and me after he chose her over me in a moment of nerves. I could tell her all of that, but I have a feeling not only would none of it ring a bell to her at all, except for Carlos's name of course, the information would only serve to inflate her ego. Call it self-preservation but no way in hell am I going to make her feel better about herself. Instead, I stick with denial.

"No."

"You can have this conversation later," the wedding planner hisses angrily. "The wedding is starting right now."

Nodding once and quirking an eyebrow at us to make sure we're all obeying, she takes a breath and pulls the doors open. I want to tell her there will be no conversation later, that there will be lots of drinking later but no conversation, but I bite my tongue and practice my internal dialogue, hoping this time I'll be able to talk myself down and into faking my emotions better.

Step, pause, step, pause. Step, pause.

So far, so good. Wait. I need to add breathing and blinking in there. And maybe a smile. Dammit. This isn't as easy as I thought. I need to work on a better poker face.

Step, pause, breathe. Step, pause, breathe, blink. Smile. Step, pause, breathe...

I stumble once before giving up the internal narrative. Obviously, I'm confusing myself with so many things to think about. Thinking about nothing is probably a better move. Except when it comes to Carlos. No matter what, I will avoid looking at him. I don't want to see his face. I don't want to see his expression when Rebecca walks down the aisle after me, with her stupid perfect hair and stupid perfect makeup and stupid perfect figure. She looks like Eve following the apple as it rolls down the aisle, and I just don't think I can take the disappointment I'll feel when he decides she's a better date than I am. Because that's bound to happen, right? It did last week. She was better at conversation, so he ditched me and left with her.

No, Rian. No.

Trying to talk myself off the ledge of panic, I remind myself that he already explained his actions. He already said he wants to date me. He doesn't want to date her. I have no reason to worry.

But I can't stop it. I can't stop the barrage of emotions and insecurities that comes crashing down on me as I step up the three stairs and move to my place. I can't stop the heat of embarrassment I feel looking like *this* while standing next to everyone else who looks like *that*. It's one thing for Carlos to just see me. But all my flaws are on display in a much bigger way.

My sister was right about that spatial awareness thing. I throw everything off balance, and I'm too afraid to look at Carlos and see his expression when he realizes it, too.

Also, does this panic thing run in the family? I never noticed it before, but now, I, along with my mother and my sister, have immediately jumped to the worst conclusions in a ten minute period of time. I may need to review my new mental health plan.

Situating myself at the front of the church, I turn to watch my sister walk down the aisle, making sure I don't accidentally look at my date. As much as I don't like her right now, even I have to admit Laney makes a stunning bride. The mermaid cut fits her like a voluptuous glove, the delicate train trailing behind her. Even her face is glowing, the fear and panic from just a few minutes ago forgotten as she keeps her eyes locked on her groom.

I focus on them. Focus on the looks they give each other. The words they say as they commit to each other for a lifetime. The rings they exchange, the tears they try not to shed, the love they obviously share. I focus on *them,* so I don't have to focus on me.

As the ceremony ends and the newlywed couple is announced, I cheer along with everyone else. I smile as brightly as I can, displaying excitement I don't necessarily feel.

And as I walk back down the aisle, escorted by an equally chunky groomsman, I clutch tightly to the white roses and make sure never to look in Carlos's direction.

CHAPTER THIRTY

CARLOS

The second I saw Ridiculous Rebecca, I knew things were shifting into really bad territory for me and Rian. And why wouldn't it? It's like the universe has it out for us and likes to throw our insecurities back in our faces.

Actually, that's not really true. I'm not insecure about anything. Well, maybe a few things. Things like people and relationships and commitments. But I'm pretty confident in who I am. And who I am is a guy that has decided to take a chance on a woman who suddenly can't look me in the eye. I'd bet my entire collection of Gucci ties that her avoidance doesn't have anything to do with me, though. It has everything to do with Ridiculous Rebecca bringing all her self-doubt to the forefront of her mind. Add onto that the stress level she's been under for weeks, and it was a recipe for disaster.

What Rian doesn't realize, though, is that for all my preaching about not wanting to ever be in a relationship, I also have enough arrogance that when I know what I want, I go for it with all the confidence of a man who can't lose. Because, come on. When do I ever lose?

With the exception of basketball with the lieutenants, I don't lose. Ever.

And what I want now is Rian. I want to know her and spend time with her. I want to laugh with her and make her smile. I want to keep her liquored up when she needs to get through a stressful night and keep her sobered up when she needs to be somewhere the next day. I even want to dance the salsa with her. Because for a guy who has always shied away from anything beyond a hookup, I have finally met someone who makes me think more might be nice.

The other thing Rian hasn't figured out yet is that I'm getting tired of her avoiding eye contact with me. It was one thing when she was standing in front of that church. It was painfully obvious to me that she had no idea Rebecca was in the wedding until just a few minutes beforehand. I'm sure my invitation would have been revoked if she had. Which means she was processing the situation during the ceremony. That I could live with.

I could even stomach her avoiding my texts after that. Pictures would mean she didn't have time to respond to look at her phone and see me reminding her that I was here for her and no one else. Being announced as part of the bridal party meant being escorted in by a groomsman. First dances and speeches and all that other crap meant hanging out with the happy couple in support.

That's all fine and good, but I'm done waiting. It's time to remind her of what I said last weekend and how serious I was.

Strawberry margarita in hand, I make a beeline to the bridal table where Rian is sitting, pretending to be engaged in the conversation around her while she waits for the beginning of what will probably be the most boring seven-course meal in history. Seriously. How is a buffet not good enough?

I keep my eyes glued to her and finally, finally she looks up. I refuse to move my gaze, wanting her to know that I'm solely focused on her. She's the reason I'm here. She's the reason I want to try something different. She's the reason I want to open up to someone and share who I am. She's the reason.

"Carlos."

I come to a quick stop before barreling over the person who just jumped in my path. That might be a slight exaggeration, but where the hell did she even come from?

As I try to look around her, Rebecca keeps moving into my line of sight so I can't see Rian to gauge her expression. What I can gauge is someone in my way and now refusing to let me by. Ever the professional, I try to remain polite but am quickly getting pissed off.

"I was so surprised to see you here." Putting her hands on my chest, Rebecca uses that breathy voice that's supposed to be sexy, but now it makes me wonder if she has some sort of lung disfunction. "I had no idea you knew Laney, but it makes me excited that the universe keeps putting us together like this."

I try to sidestep her, but she's too quick and blocks me again. "The universe didn't have anything to do with it. I came as Rian's date."

"Who?"

"Rian."

"I don't know who that is. But anyway," Rebecca coos annoyingly, "I haven't gotten my job offer yet, and I'm ready to start as soon as possible. Do I need to call Nancy back again? I left her four voice messages, but she hasn't returned my calls."

"We've been really busy," is what I say. What I think is "She will never return your calls because you're crazy." But I'm too much of a gentleman. And I'm too busy watching Rian get up from the table and turn toward the exit. If she makes it out that door, there's no telling if I will find her again tonight. "I gotta go, Rebecca."

Disregarding her personal space, I move around her, accidentally pushing her out of my way when she doesn't move.

"Hey!" Rebecca squeals. "That was rude."

There's no reason to respond, so I don't. I'm hoping she finally got the hint that I'm not interested. If I'm really lucky, she also got the hint that I'm not interested in her job capabilities either.

What I *am* interested in is getting to Rian before she pulls that door open...

Grabbing her arm, I stop her just before she reaches her destination. Putting my other arm around her shoulders, I hand her a peace offering.

"Before you leave, you need to try this," I whisper in her ear. Try as she might to avoid me, she can't hide her shiver when my breath hits her neck. "I had it specially made for you."

"Strawberry margarita?" she asks a beat later, tentatively taking it out of my hand.

"You looked like you needed it."

Rian doesn't turn around, but she does take the straw in her mouth and suck, hard. When she's finally done drinking, she shakes her head, probably to clear her brain of the freeze. "Wow, that's strong."

"They added extra tequila."

Another sip and she finally lowers her defenses enough to turn around. It's progress. I'll take it. "I definitely needed an extra shot of something."

I brush a stray hair out of her face, still stunned by how beautiful she looks. "I didn't think your sister had time to pull one more thing over on you, but I guess I was wrong."

She winces and drinks again. At this rate, we're going to have a repeat of the other weekend. She shifts on her feet and looks down at her drink, where she's stirring the straw nervously. "Did, um…" She licks her lips, and I can tell how nervous she is to put her feelings on display. And why wouldn't she? We've been dancing around each other for a few weeks, but the dating part has only just begun. We're not very far into this relationship, but we're both scared of getting hurt. "Did you know she was going to be here?"

I shake my head. "No. I had no idea until I saw her walking down the aisle. It's probably a good thing you didn't look at me during the ceremony. My surprise face isn't very attractive."

Her lips twist into a shy smile before she peeks up at me from under her lashes. "I was afraid of seeing you look at her. Instead of looking at me."

And there it is. All the vulnerability that comes with relationships. The "what if I'm not good enough" and "what happens when they get bored of me and move on." I understand that feeling more than she knows. But what Rian doesn't understand yet is that she's looking at this all wrong. She's never been not good enough. She's always been better than anyone else.

"Rian, I am always looking at you. Even when you don't think I am."

She crinkles her nose, clearly uncomfortable about showing so many of her feelings and yet needing the reassurance only I can give her.

"I'm serious. Do you know how much I watch you during work hours? One of the days I had to stay late last week was because of how far I've gotten behind on my regular work. It had nothing to do with the special projects."

"Really?"

"Really. And you know what else?" I gently take the glass out of her hands and place it on the table next to us when she shakes her head. "I really want to dance with you."

Grabbing her hand, I watch her face until I see she's ready. Ready to come with me to the dance floor, to dance in front of her family and friends, and show everyone she's not afraid. Not afraid of taking what she deserves and enjoying every minute of it.

When I finally get the subtle nod, I take her hand in mine and lead her back through the room, past Rebecca who is very obviously shooting daggers in our direction, past her mother who still looks skeptical, past her sister who doesn't even notice what's going on outside her little bubble of happiness. I lead her onto the dance floor where I turn, take her in my arms and pull her close, to hell what anyone thinks. We sway to the music, just enjoying the feel of each other's bodies next to each other.

"Why me?"

Furrowing my brow, I pull back a bit so I can see her face but keep dancing.

"I know I sound like a lunatic," she continues. "Not able to just accept this for what it is. But I'm still having a hard time wrapping my brain around why you could pick someone like... her... but instead you chose me. Is this like a bucket list thing or something? Wanna give the fat girl a go, see what it's like..."

I pull her back to me while she finishes her self-depreciating ramble. For the first time, it occurs to me why we match so much. For all my self-confidence, Rian has self-depreciation. For my can-do/will-do attitude, Rian settles. But the flip side is for all my arrogance, Rian has a care for other people's feelings. While nothing gets in the way of what I want, Rian doesn't forget to enjoy what she has.

If this is going to work, she's going to have to pull me off my high horse when I need it, and I'm going to have to put her on a pedestal when she's struggling.

The idea is so new, I'm still trying to process it, but I know she needs the truth. And that truth is simple. "Because I finally found my perfect match."

Pulling back one more time, I smile down at her and the look of disbelief on her face. It's going to take time to convince her, but I'm up for the challenge. First, though, I need to get her out of her own head and being here isn't helping.

"Do you need to stick around here, or can we leave?"

She looks over her shoulder at the bridal table. Her sister and groom are obviously in their element, laughing with their friends and taking shots. Rian snorts a humorless laugh. "She won't miss me if I'm gone. My obligatory role as the sister of the bride is over."

"Do you wanna come back to my place? Just hang out?"

Rian clears her throat. "I, um, I have a room upstairs."

I try to keep my eyebrows from shooting up in surprise but fail miserably. "You do?"

She nods. "My dad said something about not trusting that we wouldn't all get sloppy drunk, his words not mine, and he'd rather spend the money on a few hotel rooms because he can't afford a funeral after paying for this wedding."

"I think I might like your dad."

Finally, a small smile graces her lips. "He's pretty much the only one who hasn't gone clinically insane over this event."

"I don't think you're insane. I think you're trying really hard to put your sister first so she can have her moment."

She looks up at me, surprised by my assessment. Probably because she knows I nailed it.

"But the wedding is over. Her moment is done. It's time for you to take care of you now."

She looks back and forth at my eyes, and I know she's trying to decide if I'm for real or just another asshole playing games. She'll figure it out. It might take some time, but I'm determined to prove to her that this is real. Every part of it. From the first dinner we accidentally had, Rian has blown me away with her wit, her charm, her love for other people, her beauty that starts on the outside and runs all the way through every cell in her body. She isn't just the best person I know; she makes me a better person for knowing her.

Finally, she nods. "Let's go."

Without looking back, I guide her through the room and out the door, not bothering to look back and see if anyone even notices.

CHAPTER THIRTY-ONE

RIAN

I'm not sure what I'm thinking taking Carlos to my hotel room. Maybe it's the double shot margarita he gave me. Maybe I'm sick of my sister thinking I'm not good enough, and I want to prove her wrong. Or maybe I secretly hoped *Bendy* saw us leaving together. Actually, that last one isn't even a maybe. The petty side of me really hopes she still has her eyes trained on his backside and knows it's coming with me. Because I'm tired.

I'm tired of being treated like I'm a Plan B. If the maid of honor doesn't show up, Rian will do it. If the new person needs training, Rian will do it. If the hot guy needs someone to talk to over dinner, Rian will do it.

Pressing the elevator call button, I try to push some of those thoughts out of my head. Two out of three of those issues already resolved themselves, but old habits die hard and feeling taken advantage of seems to unleash past issues for me.

Gotta love Carlos, though. He is undeterred by my bad mood and oddly, he almost seems a little too determined to make me feel better. I want to think it's because he cares, but what if it's just because I'm a challenge? Even worse, what if it's because I'm his employee, and he's just trying to make sure I don't flub up an account?

I really need to get out of here. I've held myself together for a long time, but my thoughts are starting to spiral, and there's no telling what kinds of conclusions I'll come to if I can't re-center myself soon.

We're silent as we walk down the hall to my room. The quiet doesn't feel uncomfortable, but it does give me a chance to center myself a little and realize how ridiculous I'm being. This man has pulled out all the stops for me tonight, and I've spent the last two hours trying to run away from him. Francesca would be so disappointed.

Unlocking the door to my king-size room, we walk in and flip the lights on. Carlos slowly paces around the room, taking it all in. I, on the other hand, begin tidying up.

"What are you doing?" he asks when he notices what I'm up to.

"If I'd known I was going to have company tonight, I would made sure not to throw my towel on the floor."

He chuckles lightly. "You're supposed to do that in a hotel room. It's the only place you can ever get away with being a slob and no one will yell at you."

"Valid point," I respond, and yet still hang up the damp cloth. "But even the maid deserves some common courtesy."

He yanks at his tie, loosening it so he can slide the knot down and take it off. "That's one of the things I like about you. Other people would say, 'It's her job.' But you say, 'She still deserves respect.'"

He tosses the tie over the back of the chair and begins working on the buttons of his shirt. Why is he getting undressed?

"She does. Also, why are you taking your clothes off? Awfully presumptuous, don't you think?"

His movements still, and I know I've pegged him wrong when he gives me a bewildered expression. "I'm getting more comfortable and making sure not to unnecessarily wrinkle my shirt. I'm not trying to get frisky."

Embarrassed, I feel my cheeks blush. Hopefully, I have enough makeup on to cover the splotchy spots. "Oh. Sorry. I just… um… I…"

"You just wondered why I was getting naked."

"Yeah." Even more heat fills my face. Even oil-based primer can't keep the color from showing now.

Opening his shirt, he reveals what's underneath.

"I'm not naked, see?" Sure enough, he's got a short sleeved white t-shirt on. Carefully laying his button down on the back of the chair over his tie, Carlos moves to the drinking glasses on the counter.

Mortified by my behavior and now my assumptions, I drop down on the bed and throw myself backward. "Ugh. I'm such a girl tonight."

Flinging my arm over my face, I cover my eyes, so I don't see the look Carlos is no doubt sporting. Unfortunately, it doesn't stop me from hearing his laugh.

"Well, I sure hope you're a girl. Although you do have enough makeup on to be a drag queen, so if I'm missing something, you need to tell me now. It's only the right thing to do."

"Har, har," I respond half-heartedly. I feel a nudge and when I look up, he's handing me a glass of something that smells alcoholic.

"Where did you get this?"

"Mini bar. I'll take care of it at the front desk later."

Taking the glass from him, I push myself into a sitting position. "Thanks." I take a quick sip and enjoy the taste of Fireball, my favorite. "So, tell me, Carlos, what did you think of the wedding?"

Finishing up a sip of his own Fireball that makes his Adam's apple bob, which is a weird thing to notice at a time like this, but this entire night has been kind of weird, he sits in the same chair his clothes are on and rests his arms on the arms of the chair. "It was… colorful."

Not the answer I expected, but it makes me laugh anyway. "Yeah, she wanted every coordinating color on that color wheel."

"Really?"

"Oddly, yes. I don't get it, but hey, not my wedding, right?"

He cocks his head and considers his next question. The longer it takes, the more I wonder why he's still looking at me.

Touching my cheeks, I feel myself beginning to panic. "Is there something on my face, or…"

"What did you think of the wedding?"

"What?"

"You asked what I thought. Now I want to know what you thought."

Lowering my hand back down to my lap, I try to pull up the memories. Truly, I don't have that many. Everything from the time the maid of honor ran in until now is more of a blur of feelings and tulle. I don't want to tell him that, though. How crazy does that make me sound? *"I know we've been dating for all of a week and you've never even seen me naked, but I freaked out the second one of your hookups walked in and can't seem to let it go."*

Yeah. That seems like a solid plan on how to make this thing work. Good thing I already have a standard answer ready to go.

"It was a lovely ceremony, and my sister is really happy."

One of Carlos's eyebrows quirk, a new expression from one I've seen before. I'm pretty sure it means he thinks I'm full of shit. "Really," he deadpans. "That's the answer you're going with?"

Yep. He thinks I'm a fruit loop.

"What?" I argue. "It's true."

"It is. But that was a pre-fabricated answer if I've ever heard one."

Pursing my lips, feisty Rian rears her little head. "Fine. You wanna know how I really feel? I'm glad the damn thing is over, and I'm praying my sister stops being a royal bitch now. That Bendy chick is wildly self-absorbed, and I have no idea what you saw in her. And there were way too many versions of red for one church to handle." Taking a swig of my drink, it feels good to finally let my guard down. By the look on his face, Carlos approves. "Oh, and one more thing. I hope my dad tips the bartenders well because that strawberry margarita was amazing."

"We can always head back downstairs if you want another one."

"Nu-uh. I'm done with that madness. Plus," I gesture his direction with my glass, "I wouldn't want you to have to get dressed again."

It takes about thirty seconds for his smile of approval to turn into something different. Something serious. Something I can't quite decipher. I don't think it's exasperation or annoyance. Maybe he's been drinking more than I realize.

Pushing to his feet, Carlos walks over to the bed in a very straight line, so my drinking theory is debunked. Instead, he sits down next to me and takes my hand in his and kisses my knuckles. My breath hitches and my lady bits tingle at the contact. I was not expecting that.

"Weddings are hard on everyone." He watches as his fingers trace mine, giving me little goose pimples up and down my arm. Holy sexy. Pass me more Fireball. "Especially the family. You have more responsibility than the friends. Everyone is stressed and snarkier than normal. And because they're your family, you don't have the option of telling them to shove it."

I bobble my head back and forth. "Well, I mean, I do have that option, but…"

"You're right," he jokes. "You do have the option, but you don't run with it because you're *you*. You're not going to be passive-aggressive like your mother. You're not going to be completely unreliable like Ridiculous Rebecca…"

"Ridiculous Rebecca?" I interrupt. "Where did that come from?"

"Apparently, Tabitha gives nicknames."

Huh. That makes sense. "Yeah I can see that. Do I have one?"

"I don't know, but I'm Complicated Carlos, so probably."

I feel myself relaxing enough to laugh at the comment. It feels good and yet a little scary that he's able to talk me down like this. I've always relied on chocolate and reality TV to make me feel better, but this is much more effective. "I'll make sure to ask next time I'm there."

"You do that." Looking up into my eyes, he smooths a hair back behind my ear. "My point is, you're the person who is going to help your obnoxious sister's wedding go off without a hitch, because it's the kind of person you are."

"A pushover?"

"Maybe a little," he says with a smile. "But mostly, because you don't let a little conflict get in the way of your love for her. You choose to give people the benefit of the doubt when others would just write someone off. You see past the mask people put on to the real person underneath. That's why I'd rather be up here with you than downstairs with anyone else."

I stare at him in disbelief. Either my brain has just shorted out, or I'm stunned by his admission. Because here's what I know about

Carlos: he doesn't let people in. His circle is kept small on purpose. Whether it's a form of self-protection or natural introvert tendencies, I don't really know yet. But what I do know is he has a slew of acquaintances but very few friends. Tabitha is definitely one. Nick, his workout partner, is debatable. And Nancy might tip the scale onto the friendship side. Other than that, people are kept at a distance.

For him to get this deep with me, to want me to understand him and why he gravitates toward me, is not just reassuring, it's huge. And now I have a decision to make.

I can thank him for his kindness and see if he wants to watch a movie, or I can continue moving out of my comfort zone and take what I want.

Seems like a no-brainer to me.

Before I can chicken out, I kiss him. Hard. Without hesitation, his body reacts, and he moves closer, putting his arms around me and pulling me close. My hands on his face, my tongue in his mouth, I kiss him…

And kiss him…

And kiss him…

I kiss him until my body screams for more, and once again, I act without thinking.

Pulling away, I stand in front of him, terrified and excited all at once. Terrified that he'll reject me, but excited because I know he won't. What I haven't noticed until now is that we haven't been dancing around each other all the time. No, Carlos has been waiting for me to be confident enough to dance with him.

Giving me his shirt after the fire, the conversations at my desk, watching me from across the gym when he doesn't think I'll notice—he's been patiently sitting on the sidelines waiting for me to figure out what the play is.

I think I got it now.

Turning around, I look over my shoulder. "Unzip me?"

Slowly, not with hesitation but making sure I don't change my mind, Carlos reaches for the clasp. His fingers lightly brushing my back has to be one of the most sensual things I've ever experienced.

When my back is fully exposed, I turn back around, and keep my eyes trained on his. The nerves of getting naked in front of him are overwhelming, but the thought of not taking advantage of this moment is even worse. Pulling the spaghetti straps off my shoulders, I feel the fabric slide down my body and flutter to the floor.

Carlos groans. "Holy shit, you're wearing a garter belt."

Okay, fine. Maybe I was a *little* hopeful something like this would happen when I got dressed. But mostly, I wanted to feel pretty during the wedding and dressing like a tomato wasn't cutting it. That's what sexy lingerie is for.

He adjusts himself in his pants, and I feel my confidence soar.

"There, uh…" he stutters then clears his throat. "Right out of college there was a buddy of mine who had a poster of Mia Tyler in an outfit like this."

I bite my lip. Of all the people in the world, Carlos just compared me to a supermodel. Not compared. No. *Equated* me to a supermodel. My automatic instinct is to brush off his comments, but his face looks so serious—he looks so reverent as he stares at me—how can I not believe him? How can I not trust his perception?

"Are you saying I remind you of Mia Tyler?"

His eyes snap back up to mine. "No. I'm saying she reminds me of you."

Oh, he is so *getting laid tonight…*

Slowly, I move toward him until I'm standing between his legs, my hands on his shoulders and then in his hair. He reaches behind me to run his hands down my back and cup my ass. His touch is sensual and erotic, and nothing has even happened yet.

"I want to take this slow," I say, taking charge of the situation. I'm not sure what kind of magic this garter belt has, but I feel powerful. "I want us to take our time and explore each other. I want us to get to know each other in ways no one else does."

One of his hands moves to my neck and I can't help but enjoy the erotic feeling of his touch. "I think you already do."

We stare into each other's eyes for just a split second before our mouths are back on each other and his clothes are coming off. Piece by piece, we're bared to one another. It's erotic and sensual and thrilling. Not just because he's the hottest man I've ever been with, but because there is no question that this isn't just about sex.

Tonight, it doesn't matter that he's got the physique of a Greek god or that I still have insecurities to overcome.

Tonight, it doesn't matter that he's the boss and I'm still learning the ropes.

Tonight, there are no thoughts of weddings, or sisters, or crazy exes that can't seem to let go. Instead, we are determined to give and receive pleasure, to express our feelings in a way words fail. Tonight, our relationship is taken to a new level.

Tonight, we are lovers.

CHAPTER THIRTY-TWO

CARLOS

N ormally, my alarm goes off at five o'clock in the morning at the latest. I like being an early riser and getting a jump start on my day. There are a million and one things you can get done while everyone else is hitting their snooze button. Plus, the older I get, the more apt I am to wake up earlier. I've heard those patterns are normal for a midlife man. But we're just going to pretend that I didn't just admit to technically being middle-aged. Most men I know in their forties have a dad bod and this bod isn't that.

But this morning, I went against my patterns and slept in. To be honest, it's pretty freaking awesome. Instead of being jarred awake by an obnoxious, robotic beeping sound, I woke up gradually as light filtered into the room.

Even though I'm awake, I'm not jumping out of bed to kick start my day. Nope. I'm lying here lazily watching Rian sleep. It's pretty freaking amazing and makes me question why I've always been such a stickler for those early morning hours.

Her eyes flutter a little bit, still covered in the heavy makeup she wore yesterday. It's a bit more smudged, and not the purposeful kind of smudge that's popular these days. This is more of a drunk party-girl look. But that's what happens when you get so caught up in each other you don't stop to do your normal nighttime rituals. I don't mind, though. Even with two-day-old makeup, she's still amazingly beautiful.

Which reminds me, it's Sunday. That's facial care day. I know Rian is going to think I'm nuts, but maybe she'll join me for a face mask. If I don't charcoal mask at least twice a month, my age starts to show in a very real way. These pores don't clean themselves.

Rian's eyelids begin to flutter as the room continues to get brighter. I watch as awareness takes over her features.

It takes a few minutes for her to get her bearings straight, but I know the second she remembers where she is and everything that happened last night.

"Hi." Her voice sounds groggy with sleep.

"Hi," I say back, careful not to move too quickly. I don't want to frighten her away.

"You stayed."

"You thought I wouldn't?" I reply, playing with one of her stray hairs. Her hair is soft and smooth, not crunchy with too much hair spray. I like the feeling of it on my fingers.

She shifts, making herself more comfortable, if that's even possible since this hotel mattress is amazing. It's like lying on a cloud. I need to check the label before we leave.

"I honestly…" She pauses and bites her lip. "I guess I wasn't one hundred percent sure you would be here when I woke up."

I sigh, although I'm not upset. I expected some sort of doubt from her this morning. That's why I've always been very, very clear about my intensions when I spend the night with a woman—what I want out of the night, what I want the next morning, and most importantly, what I don't want. The lines of this situation, however, are a little more blurred.

There are a lot more layers here. We're dating. We're friends. We're gym buddies. We're colleagues. I'm her boss. All of that is wrapped up in a not-so-nice package. Like after a five-year-old wraps a Christmas present. The good intensions are there, and it's pretty in its own way, but it isn't quite smoothed out.

"I'm sorry," she adds quickly. "I should trust you more."

Furrowing my brow, I vehemently disagree with her. "No, you shouldn't."

She blinks rapidly a few times, trying to process what I just said. "Wait, you're saying I shouldn't trust you?"

"No. I mean, I am trustworthy. This is just a new relationship. You're going to have doubts. We're both going to have doubts. Part of the fun is sorting through all those new relationship feelings. Figuring things out as we go. Surprising each other with the unexpected."

She smiles and I know my playful Rian is back. "Did you see that on a soap opera or something? Because those are some really pretty words for someone who hasn't done this relationship thing before."

Bantering with her makes me laugh. Plus, she's not wrong. "I may have asked a friend some questions about what to expect when dating."

"Oh. So, you really are researching."

"I want to do this right."

Her face takes on a serious, yet sensual quality. "So far, so good."

Her reassurance boosts my ego in a way I've not felt before. What I'm quickly learning is that I can be happy with myself all I want. But there's a different kind of ego boost that goes with making someone else happy, too.

Leaning forward, I kiss her gently on the lips, intending only to give her a good morning peck. But I couldn't stop my body if I wanted to and very quickly, a chaste kiss is turning into a full-on makeout session. I grab the sheet wanting nothing in between us, but before it moves, she pulls it tighter to her body. Confused, I look into her eyes, trying to figure out if I misread the situation. "What?"

"Um, it's daytime."

Now, I'm even more confused. "So… what does that have to do with anything?"

"It's light outside."

"Again, what does that even mean?"

"The lighting was much more flattering last night. But with all this sunshine, things," she gestures down to her body, "don't look quite the same."

I huff out a partial laugh. "So, you're saying it doesn't matter that I had my lips on every square inch of that body last night. Because there is daylight outside, I don't have access to it anymore?"

She considers my question before answering. "It's not that you don't have access, as much as you probably don't want to look while you are accessing."

Now it's my turn to consider. "So, should I wait for you to put clothes on before we have sex? Maybe we could order you some pants with a hole in the crotch or cut out the nipples of a shirt."

"Shut up." She laughs and nudges my shoulder playfully before dropping back down on the pillow. "Look. I have a nice rack."

"Yes. We can agree on that," I say with a waggle of my eyebrows.

"You can quit that, you perv." I immediately steel my features, trying very hard to be serious, and failing. "But this nice rack is very large."

"Uh huh?"

"And large means gravity tends to work against me."

I give up. "I'm still not following, Rian. You've gotta spell it out for me. Because from where I lie, boobs are boobs. And I like boobs."

Clearly frustrated, she makes an impromptu decision and whips the sheet off the upper half of her body and gestures to her breasts. "You see what I'm saying now?"

My eyes are locked on their target. "I don't even remember what we were talking about. But I'm definitely seeing something now." I lick my lips in anticipation and begin to lean forward. She, on the other hand, huffs in frustration and holds me off.

"Carlos. They're not pretty like this."

"Oh, I beg to differ. Can I touch them?"

"You are such a man," she grumbles. "These are not perky boobs. They're saggy and practically laying down next to me."

Flipping my eyes up to hers, I think I finally have an understanding. "Are you embarrassed because your boobs sag when you're not wearing a bra?"

"Um, once again, not model perky."

Rolling my eyes, I whip the sheet off my body and gesture to my lower half. "Hey, look, when my penis isn't hard, it sags, too."

The laugh that comes out of Rian is full and makes me chuckle, too.

"I cannot believe you just pointed to your flaccid..." She takes another gander and pauses. "Well, not totally flaccid. It's making some movement there. But your flaccid penis to make a point about my boobs."

Mission accomplished.

"Listen." Moving closer, I pull her to me now that the sheet is finally out of the way and I can feel all of her next to all of me. "I know you feel self-conscious because of the women I've been with before. But, Rian, they are nothing compared to you. What I was doing before was holding people at a distance. I kept things shallow and surface level so I wouldn't have to share myself. I thought I was all I needed."

"And I grew up thinking I was never enough."

"I know. We have a weird yin and yang thing going, don't we?"

She giggles. "I guess we do." Getting serious again, she expands on her concerns. "It's gonna take me some time."

"I know."

"And I'm going to need a lot of reassurance."

"I know that, too."

"Do you really want this enough to be up for that kind of challenge?"

Rubbing my hand up and down her back, I nod. "I've never been up for anything more in my life. See?" I gesture back down to the lower half of my body only this time I'm not saggy anymore.

Rian laughs again, a sound I'll never get tired of hearing. "You are an arrogant mess."

"Again, yin and yang, right?"

She nods, and her smile reaches all the way up to her eyes. So, I kiss her and kiss her and kiss her as I roll on top of her, settling my body between her legs.

I feel her everywhere. She's on me and around me and in me. She inhabits parts of me I didn't realize were there. Her entire self is consuming me. I've never been more turned on in my life. And yet, I still want more. I want it all.

This is why I could never be in a relationship before. This is why nothing was good enough. This is why no one was ever worth it before. Because no one was ever Rian. Funny how you don't even realize what you need until she's right in front of you.

I kiss down her jawline, my hands roaming her soft curves. Hearing her soft mewls of excitement get me riled up, and my fingers decide to do some walking. Just as she spreads her legs and I get ready to enter her...

The most annoying sound in the entire free world begins blaring through the room making us both freeze.

"What. The hell. Is that?"

Wriggling underneath me, Rian thwarts my plans at a morning quickie with the words, "We have to get up."

Dropping my body weight on top of her I groan in her neck. "I disagree. We're in a hotel room, all alone, about to have sex. We have to stay lying down."

She laughs and pulls me tighter, which does nothing to convince my body we're going anywhere.

"I wish we could, believe me. But that alarm is a reminder that we have to check out in thirty minutes. And unless I want to look like I just left an all-night frat party, I need to at least rinse off."

Unfortunately, she's right. "Fine," I grumble, and roll off her. "But only because I'm about to do the walk of shame and don't need to embarrass myself further by checking out late."

Chuckling, she saunters her way to the bathroom, with more confidence than I've ever seen her have before. Her hips sway just a little bit more. Her chin is held just a little bit higher. If it wasn't for the goth look running down her face, she would have succeeded in that sultry look she tossed over her shoulder.

"Ah!"

I smile, hands clasped behind my head and closing my eyes, knowing full well she's just looked in the mirror.

"Why didn't you tell me I look like I just left a metal concert? You wanted to have sex with *this* a few minutes ago?"

Picking up the sheet, I look down and find confirmation. "That would be a yes," I say before addressing my junk directly. "Sorry about that fella. We'll pick this back up later." I toss the sheet all the way off and jump out of bed. Sleeping in has done wonders for my energy level, so much so that it's almost instinct to smack Rian on the ass when I join her in the bathroom to shower. She squeals and bitches about getting soap in her eyes.

Once she can see again and the water heats up, I climb in and start washing off. I may have to put on yesterday's clothes, but I'm a guy. If I don't soap up certain parts every morning, no cab driver in Chicago will take me home when he smells me.

Turning the water down a little cooler, I try to convince Little Carlos that being naked in a room with Rian doesn't mean we're getting any. So far, he doesn't believe me. Maybe the addition of pants will help. Otherwise, it's going to be an embarrassing walk through the lobby.

"Um, Carlos?" Rian's voice isn't as confident as it was. She sounds shy and nervous which immediately puts me on alarm. What could have changed in the last few minutes?

"Yeah?"

"I don't want you to hate my family."

"What?" Pulling the curtain open just enough to see her, I find her leaning against the counter wringing her hands.

"It's just, six months ago my sister was my best friend. And then she started planning a wedding." Giving up her fidgeting, she begins to pace. "My mom isn't always passive-aggressive, and my dad is always quiet, but he really understood how hard this wedding was for me." She stops pacing and turns to address me directly, hands on her hips. "It's just... you only hear me bitching about my family, and I don't want you to think that's all there is to them. Just in case we run into them in the lobby or something."

Nodding, I choose my next words carefully. "My dad is the worst at relationships. I've never seen him with someone for longer than a couple months. But he's also never missed a visit with me my whole life. He calls at least three times a week. Attended every single sporting event I had through high school. Never missed my birthday.

"My mom is terrified of dating. Basically, she says it's pointless and ingrained in me that I wouldn't be a man who would just pretend I want something deep with a woman and leave them in the end. She's also a fantastic cook, volunteers at the nursing home, and loves me fiercely.

"Rian, families aren't perfect. People aren't perfect. They're going to have flaws. Love them anyway."

She quirks her lips, trying not to smile, and I can tell she's trying to decide if I'm for real or not. "You really mean that?"

I nod and duck back into the shower, rinsing the remaining suds off my body. "I do. And I promise not to judge them off this one event. Especially since your dad probably had to take out a second mortgage for the flowers alone."

"Right? I feel like I'm still smelling petunias. Now get a move on, Davies!" she calls and then she's gone.

By the time I'm out of the shower and dressed, Rian is already packed and ready to go. It's a good thing, too. The maid is knocking on the door just as we open it.

"Wanna come to my place?" I ask on the elevator ride down. "I need to change, but we can grab some takeout and binge watch more reality TV?"

"Don't pretend like you're asking me on a real date, Carlos Davies." She doesn't even look my direction while we banter until I take her overnight bag out of her hands. "You just want to watch more cooking competitions and don't know which channel they're on."

"Maybe." She laughs next to me as the doors open and we step out into the lobby. "But that's not why I'm asking. I have a regular Sunday routine—"

"Good morning, Carlos."

Rian and I stop dead in our tracks, conversation interrupted when Rebecca cuts right in front of us and puts her hands on me. I'm getting really tired of seeing this woman.

276

"I was hoping I'd catch you here. But I didn't realize you'd have," she turns and glares at Rian, "a friend chasing you around. What's your name, sweetie? I don't think we've met."

"It's Rian." My girl's nostrils flare in anger. "You know, sister of the bride and account manager at Cipher Systems."

Rebecca reels back like she's been slapped, and yet her hands don't move from my chest. "You mean you hired her before me? Carlos, why would you do that? We have something special."

Out of my peripheral vision, I see Rian's facial expression completely change. She's thinking the same thing I am—is this woman for real? I'm also wondering how Tabitha pegged her so quickly. She must do some sort of voodoo magic because I knew Rebecca was a little dense, but off her rocker never entered my mind.

But I've always been painfully honest in my relationships, even the short-lived ones and I think I might need to make myself clear again so there is no more question. No more beating around the bush or avoiding.

"Ridic—uh, Rebecca, Rian doesn't just work at Cipher Systems, she's also my girlfriend."

"What?" both Rian and Rebecca say at the same time. I figured I'd get that reaction from Rian, but we need to get through this conversation first before I can explain that yes, she is in fact the only one I'll be dating.

Rebecca immediately sees Rian in a new way, and I don't like the way she's sizing her up. "You're dating—*her*?"

"Yes," I seethe. I should have known this was going to take an ugly turn, but I was hoping it didn't go there.

"But she's—" Rebecca continues to look Rian up and down but stops as soon as she realizes Rian is bucking up to her.

"She's what?" Rian's anger is radiating through her. The security guard at the front door seems to notice and begins to rise in case he's needed. Not that his five-foot-six frame could stand up to Rian. I've seen her kickboxing skills. "What is *she*, Rebecca?"

Rebecca's eyes widen as she finally grasps the severity of her words. "She's—very lucky to have a man like you."

Rian shifts backward just slightly, satisfied that she's won this round. A jolt of pride runs through me as well. Just a few months ago, Rian would have let those comments get to her. But now, she's standing up for herself. And not just with passive-aggressive barbs.

Rebecca finally moves her hands off me and smooths her jeans. Clearing her throat, she removes the shell-shocked look from her face. "Well. You know how to find me."

"I do, but rest assured, Rian will be around for a very long time, so it's best if you move on. Oh, and I'm sorry to inform you, we filled the receptionist position already. We'll keep your resume on file for the next six months in case another position opens up."

I grab Rian's hand and walk around Rebecca, hopefully for the last time. I'm tired of playing games. And frankly, I need a nap.

"Uh, you aren't really going to call her if another position opens up, are you?"

I look over my shoulder at Rian like she's lost her mind. "Hell no. I'm pretty sure Nancy shredded her resume and then set the pieces on fire already."

Stepping out in the street, I flag down a cab while Rian laughs. "Oh, well, good. And by the way, you're doing a bang-up job on that reassurance thing, because that was pretty damn sexy."

"You think that's good, just wait until I get you back to my place."

Her eyes light up with excitement. "Yeah?"

"Yeah. I've got a charcoal mask you are going to die for."

She scratches the top of her head in confusion. "I… um … yeah, I didn't ever expect those words to come out of your mouth."

"Life. Changing," I mouth, just as the cab drives up. We climb in and head back to my place for a day of mindless television while we pamper our skin. Maybe if I get lucky, we can pamper each other as well.

CHAPTER THIRTY-THREE

RIAN

"Jennifer, this is Steven. He's one of my colleagues and is the guy in charge of determining how to best place the cameras in your home."

"Hey, Jennifer." Steven flashes a grin that would melt the panties off any normal woman. But Jennifer Johnson isn't a normal woman. She's terrified of just about everyone and has needed more hands-on attention than a normal client. While her sister is wearing shorts and a tank top because it's summertime, Jennifer is fully covered including a hoodie zipped all the way up.

We've made a lot of headway toward what she needs, but part of that is because I quickly discovered video messaging is a better way to do business with her. It lets Jennifer see who she's talking to, which goes a long way toward her feeling comfortable. When I pitched the idea to Carlos, he offered to let me use his office during our calls to ensure more privacy as well.

Plus, it gives me a chance to show her what our guys look like before they knock on her door. With the amount of fear she has, I felt like it was an important step.

"I know you're nervous about us coming to take a look around," Steven continues, and I appreciate him not pussyfooting around the situation. "That's why I want you to think of a safe word. Since it's just the four of us here, we'll be the only ones to know it."

Jennifer looks at her sister who nods, and then back at us. "Um, what kind—um, I mean, why do I need a safe word?" Her hand claps the top of her hoodie at the neck. I've learned that this is her tell that she's feeling panicky. Sure enough, Janet immediately begins rubbing her back.

"Two reasons. One, I want you to be able to verify that it's really me. When I knock on your door, all you have to do is ask me to say it, and once you hear it, you'll know it's all clear outside."

"Oh. Yeah, that makes sense." Her hand unclenches just a bit. This is good. Getting her to trust Steven will be the biggest hurdle to overcome.

"Also, if at any time when we're inside your home, if you want us out for any reason, you just say that word, and we'll book it outside, no questions asked until you give us the all clear to come in again."

I bite back my smile. When I explained the sensitivity of the account to Steven, I knew he'd be a professional. What I didn't expect is for him to get with Alex's wife to come up with ways he could do his job while making sure Jennifer always feels like she's in control. To me, that goes above and beyond his job description. I suppose it shouldn't surprise me, though. If Cipher Systems has nothing else, they have a code of conduct that would rival the Secret Service.

I'm pretty sure a few of our guys may have worked for a president before. I'll need to ask because now I'm curious how many of those Joe Biden memes were stages. They make me laugh every time I see them.

Jennifer's sniffle causes me to refocus on the task at hand and look up at her again. "I... um, I need to think." She puts one of her hands over her eyes, trying to control her emotions. Janet continues to comfort her, and my heart breaks watching this broken woman try to be brave. "I'm sorry. I just get really weird talking to people because I just always wonder if they've seen me... I mean..." She takes a deep breath and wipes her tears away. "I'm sorry. I'm working on it."

We sit silently, giving her a minute to pull herself back together.

What I want to tell her is how I admire her for taking on the people who hurt her so badly. What I want to do is give her a hug and comfort her. But the only thing I can do is work my hardest to make this set-up as easy as possible.

"Jennifer, I've been doing this for a long time and there are professional boundaries in place for a reason." I look at Steven, startled by his statement because I have a feeling he's just beginning. "But I'm going to cross them for just a second, in the interest of making this relationship work."

As he talks, I happen to glance up and see Carlos walking off the elevator. He's carrying two coffees. I can't help wondering if one is for me. But then he heads straight into Nancy's office. Drat. I'll have to make a coffee run later.

"I've never seen one of your movies."

Well, that's not at all where I thought Steven was going with this.

"Really?" I've talked to Jennifer almost every day for the last week. This is the first time I've picked up a hint of relief in her voice.

"Nope." He shakes his head and crosses his toned arms over his chest. "And I never will. I won't go into all the reasons why, but you don't have to wonder about that again. I've also talked to the colleague that's coming with me and he said the same thing. I made sure before adding him onto your account. No one you interact with in this organization has or will see you in one of those… movies." He stalls out at the end of his sentence, and I know he's trying to control his own anger. Apparently, Steven is passionate about human rights. Yet another reason he's perfect to work on this account with me.

Jennifer's entire body sags against the counter she's leaning against, as does Janet's.

"Thank you for that," Janet says. "Those thoughts torture her pretty much all the time. You should hear some of the disgusting things people think they have a right to say to her in public. She just wants to put this behind her, and they make it practically impossible."

"I can only imagine." Steven takes on a very seriously scary tone. "People can be vicious. I experienced my fair share when I came out of the closet."

Pretty sure the three women in this conversation all come to a full stop with this bomb.

"You're gay?" Jennifer finally asks. Thank goodness, because I certainly don't have the guts to clarify myself.

He nods once, completely unaffected by our reactions. "One hundred and ten percent into men. Not even bisexual over here. Again, that information is usually not important, professional boundaries and all. But if it'll give you just a tiny bit more comfort, so be it."

For the first time, I see Jennifer flash a tiny bit of a smile. "You know, there are plenty of gay porn stars who still do it with women on camera, no problem."

Her joke elicits a smile from me and a chuckle from Steven. I'm thrilled she is letting her guard down a bit. "I'm sure that's true. Fortunately, I'm not a porn star. I'm just a security guy who is dating someone."

Ugh. Why are we on a professional call? I have so many questions for him now!

"So, about that safe word…"

"Dignity," Jennifer replies quickly, no hesitation on her part. "My safe word is dignity."

"Perfect."

We go over a few additional details of what will happen when Steven flies out. By the time the conversation is over, Jennifer seems really comfortable with the idea of this man being in her home. I know it's all about her, but I'm also pretty proud of myself for this account. From what Steven says, this is arguably the trickiest situation the company has worked with, but it's smoothing out just fine.

When we hang up, I swivel Carlos's chair so I can nudge Steven with my foot. "I'm so impressed. You won her over faster than I thought you would."

He shrugs like it's no big deal. "I have found over the years that working with a client doesn't just mean finding the best way to keep them safe. If they don't *feel* safe, it doesn't matter what systems are in place."

"That's awfully astute of you."

"I'm an astute guy."

Carlos exits Nancy's office with two coffees still in his hand. My heart jumps as he heads this direction. I called him this morning to make sure it was okay to use his office first thing, so he knows we're in here. That means the java may be for me after all. I hope so. We had another marathon love-making session last night. After two days of not sleeping, I need the pick me up.

Steven grumbles, "Sometimes I wish I wasn't as observant as I am," but I don't really comprehend what he's saying. I'm too busy trying to push thoughts of Carlos flinging my leg over his shoulder out of my mind.

Gesturing for Carlos to come in when he waves, Steven crosses the room and opens the door. "I take it that's not for me?" He gestures to the coffee, but Carlos ignores him and hands it over to me instead.

"You know how to use the coffee maker in the break room," Carlos jabs.

Steven rolls his eyes and stalks off, mumbling something like, "Here we go again," as he leaves.

"How was your meeting?" Carlos gives me a quick peck on the lips. The gesture surprises me, seeing that last week we were keeping this whole thing on the down-low.

"It was good. Thank you for letting us use your office."

He waves me off and takes another drink. "I think you're right to treat this one with extra sensitivity. Whatever we can do to make sure she trusts we have her best interests at heart, right?"

"Yeah." I continue to swivel back and forth, and I think about how much goes into covering all areas of people's security. I'm amazed at the kinds of checks and balances put in place. "Did you know Alex is designing an entire system where she can check who has been monitoring her cameras?"

"He's been talking about doing that for a while."

"That's just so much effort to make sure someone inside the company isn't logging in when they shouldn't be."

Carlos shrugs like it doesn't take hundreds of hours to design a program like that. "She's paying us a lot of money to do it."

"I guess." Someday, I'll get used to it. For now, it's just really exciting to see things in action. "Anyway," I push myself to standing, "I need to go check on some other accounts and give them a heads up about Janie leaving. And I need to call the woman herself and see if she wants to meet again this week. What are you doi—" My question is cut off when he pulls me against his body. I don't mind getting a little PDA, but we're in the office. This is not our normal.

"I'm just giving you a hug. You raced out this morning, and I didn't get to snuggle with you."

Laughing, I relax into his embrace a bit. "But we're in the office. Anyone can see."

"So?"

"So, I thought we weren't doing that."

He sighs and allows me to put some distance between us. Not that I want it. I'm just not sure what changed.

Pressing the intercom button on his phone, he calls out, "Hey, Nancy."

"Yeah?" she answers through the speaker.

"Can you come in here for a second? I have a question."

"Yeah. Give me two minutes."

I narrow my eyes at him and cross my arms. "What are you doing?"

"Look," he says, reaching for me again, but now that Nancy is on her way, I take another step back. "I know this is new, but do you plan on getting tired of me anytime soon?"

"That depends. How often are you going to make me do a charcoal mask?"

"Oh, come on. It wasn't that bad," he argues.

I disagree. "You wanted to take a video of me as I tried to rip it off my face."

"I told you not to leave it on that long."

Rolling my eyes, I know we're never going to agree on this topic. "Regardless, it felt like my face was literally being scalped."

"You can't be scalped if it's on your face."

"I disagree."

"At least your skin is baby soft now."

I open my mouth to argue, but he's got me on that one. As painful as it was, my cheeks do feel soft as a baby's bum after being doused with powder.

"Ahhhh…" He points at me, smiling in victory. "I told you it would be worth it in the end."

Grabbing his finger, I push it away. "Still debatable. But how is this related to us canoodling in the office?"

"Did you say canoodling?"

I don't know why he's so ornery today, but the back and forth is making me laugh. "Stop distracting me, you weirdo."

A knock at the door has me moving even further away from him.

"Knock, knock."

"Come on in, Nancy." Carlos doesn't even look up. He's too busy staring at me, humor filling his eyes.

"Welp, that's my cue to leave." I pick up my coffee cup and start my way around his desk. "Thanks for the joe, Bossman."

"Not so fast." He stands up and crosses the room to close the door, leaving all three of us in the room.

Nancy and I look each other, confused, and then back at Carlos. Glad I'm not the only one who doesn't know what he's doing.

"Tell me, Nancy, do we have a company policy on fraternization?"

Oh, shit. This is happening. This is really happening…

My heart starts pounding and I swear my boobs begin to sweat. Is that a thing? Boobs sweating when I get nervous? I've never noticed before.

"Carlos—" I warn. I can't believe he's putting me in this position.

Nancy's eyes widen, and she looks back and forth between Carlos and me for a few seconds before realizing that she's not being as couth as she could be.

Clearing her throat, she finally answers him. "We don't have an official one beyond our policies on sexual harassment."

Stalking slowly toward me, Carlos keeps his eyes trained on mine. I'm not sure how I feel about this turn of events, but I think I might be flattered and excited. I told Carlos I would need reassurance that he was serious about me. There's no more confirmation that he wants to be with only me than setting the office rumor mill in motion.

"So, if I told you Rian and I were dating, that wouldn't violate any company policies, right?"

"Um, well, that depends." Taking her focus off Carlos and putting it onto me, she asks, "Rian, do you feel threatened or bullied into dating Carlos, or as if your job depends on whether or not you have sex with him?"

I look back at the man stalking toward me, a playful smile on his lips.

I shake my head. "Not at all."

"Do you plan on having sex in the office, in particular, on my desk?"

Carlos and I both turn and look at her quizzically for that one.

She shrugs like it's not the weirdest question ever. "Look, you want my blessing? I'm covering my bases before I give it. You can't be too sure in this office."

I burst out laughing at the ridiculousness of the whole situation.

"Of course not, Nancy," Carlos huffs. "Geez, what kind of a guy do you take me for? Is this legal or not?"

Nancy cracks the tiniest of smiles and winks at me. That, right there is approval enough. "You're fine. Just keep it professional, and if things get weird, I'm going over your head to shift the chain of command. She can always have a new boss to answer to."

Carlos's focus is back on me, a sensual smile playing on his lips. "That's not gonna happen." Before she can get to the door, Carlos is on me, kissing me like his life depends on it.

"Oh, come on!" Nancy complains loudly. "You couldn't even let me leave first?" As she whips the door open, she yells, "Code Red! Cupid struck again!"

I barely register Steven yelling back, "I knew it!" while someone else complains about whatever is in the water.

I'm too wrapped up in this perfect moment. With the perfect man. At my perfect job.

I guess this pretty girl really can have it all.

CHAPTER THIRTY-FOUR

RIAN

Six months later

"I can't believe I'm doing this," I grumble while signing my name. I make it extra hard to read just to be obnoxious. Somehow, my scribbly signature doesn't faze Abel.

"Come on, Rian," Abel says with a huge grin that I just wanna slap off his beautifully chiseled little face. "You love my class. And what a better time to join than now, when you get a discount thanks to our fantastic new facility?"

I look around at the new building and grudgingly admit that he's right. The old building was deemed a total loss, so the gym had to be rebuilt from the ground up. Everything in it is new. Even the floor plan had some modifications made, although the biggest changes are in the locker room. The gym gods apparently heard my bitching for long enough and convinced the plan makers to give us bigger showers complete with actual doors.

I almost threw my hands in the air and yelled "Hallelujah!" when I saw them. Okay, fine. So, I actually did do that. Tabitha thought it was funny, even if everyone else gave me dirty looks.

"I'm only signing this because of that discount," I say, handing my paperwork over to my trainer.

"I don't care why you're doing it." He takes it out of my hands and shoves it in a folder. "All I know is your ass is mine three days a week now. This is gonna be fun."

"Give me my paper back." I grab for the folder, but he holds it over his head so I can't reach it. I've never been good at climbing, so it is well and truly out of my reach. "I change my mind."

"Too late. You've already signed your life away." He bellows out a maniacal laugh, and I'm this close to using my kickboxing skills to punch him in the gut when another male voice stops me.

"Uh, care to tell me why you're trying to climb your trainer like a tree?"

I pause and look over my shoulder to see my boyfriend, with his arms crossed. He's not serious. He knows how Abel and I are, but it's still fun when he goes all alpha male.

I snap to attention, pulling my leg down from where it's wrapped around Abel's thigh. Huh. I'm better at climbing than I thought.

Pushing a rogue hair out of my face, I take a deep breath. "Just trying to get Abel to give me my paperwork back."

"Rian," Carlos says slowly. "We talked about this. Once you sign your name, it's over."

"But I thought you loved me," I whine, hoping to get him on my side.

Instead, he shakes his head. Traitor. "I do love you. More than anything. But a legal document is still binding and you are still required to pay him no matter what."

I drop my head back and sigh. "Fine. I'll go to his stupid class. But no sleds."

My pointing finger and mean face apparently do nothing to penetrate Abel's walls of indifference. "Extra sleds. Got it." He trots off with me shooting daggers into his back.

"One of these days, I'm going to sled right over his toe," I threaten, but we both know I'll never gain enough speed for that. More likely, I'd run into his foot, make a jarring stop, and throw my back out.

Getting older sucks.

Carlos puts his arm around my neck and kisses me on the top of my head. "You did a good thing there."

"Yeah. Just don't tell him that."

I didn't really sign the contract because of the discount. I signed it to help Abel out. We were all shuffled to different locations after the fire and Abel lost a lot of customers. For someone whose income is significantly affected by his ability to make commissions, it hurt his budget. A lot. Add onto it, he became a single dad during the same time period, so I know he's feeling the pinch. Hopefully, bumping up from two days to three days a week will help him give his daughter at least a little bit of a Christmas.

It's not like spending the money is going to kill my budget. I'm paid generously, and Quinn made good on that raise after the baby was born. I told him it wasn't necessary, but he insisted that I had proven my willingness to go above and beyond, and he didn't want to risk losing me by not recognizing it. I still think it was his secret way of paying me to keep helping him find rare yarns. What he doesn't know is I would be finding them for my sister's presents anyway, so it's not really extra work for me.

What has been extra work is training my new teammate... Francesca. She happened to find the second job opening at Cipher Systems, and when Carlos saw her resume, he immediately asked about her. I was shocked she met the qualifications for the job. I thought she had been working for Sandeke Telecom because she liked it. Turns out, she was just biding her time until the right job came along that used her architecture degree. Who knew?

So, she and I went right back to being cooking buddies, only this time we included Carlos in the mix. Since then, Teresa and a couple other people have joined in. I only have to cook one night a week now. It's glorious.

Carlos and I continue to meander around the gym, just looking at the new equipment and where everything is set up. The cafe is in the same spot, but it's all brand new. Tabitha couldn't be happier. All her blenders are state of the art, which she tells everyone who sits down at her counter. She even has real menus now.

"Everyone seems so excited to be back in 'our' space again," Carlos remarks, just as happy as everyone else. "It's no fun to work out when you aren't with your friends."

"That, and everyone is excited not to ride the El while stinky anymore."

He rolls his eyes, still not understanding my disdain for that form of public transportation. "It was a five-minute train ride, Rian. It wasn't that big of a deal."

"You weren't the one who was almost kicked off for leaving butt sweat on the seat," I argue, making him laugh. Yes, the asshole is laughing at my trauma. "Do you know how embarrassing that was? He thought I'd peed on the seat!"

Carlos is full on laughing now. "That was so funny."

I punch him in the shoulder. "Exactly how funny was it? Funny enough for you to sleep alone tonight?"

His face immediately straightens up. "Nope. Not that funny. Not funny at all. It was terrible. Please don't make me sleep on your lumpy couch."

"It's not lumpy. It's like sleeping on a cloud."

"A cloud filled with marbles."

"Well, my birthday is coming up. If you hate it that much, you can get me a new one."

"Done."

My jaw drops, and I squeal in protest. "Carlos, no! I was kidding!"

"Too late. I'm getting you a couch for your birthday. I'm sure I'll eventually be forced to sleep there for real, so I wanna make sure it's comfortable."

Rolling my eyes, I can't help but smile. "Always the planner."

He kisses the top of my head. "You know you love me for it."

"I do. More than anything."

He smiles that grin that's reserved for only me. "I love you, too."

Yes, we love each other. Ever since the first time Carlos told me after a quick weekend trip to Vegas where I had such bad luck, I had to switch to nickel slots so my money would last longer, we say it a lot. Not at the office, unless Nancy is standing there because it makes her gag which makes us laugh. Otherwise, we stay professional on the job.

But it's glorious being in love with your best friend, and now that we both realize our connection keeps getting stronger, we make sure to remind each other often. We're more secure in our relationship every day, and those three words are part of why we no longer say things like, "But why me?"

That conversation got really obnoxious really fast. We'd rather watch cooking shows on my not-lumpy couch.

Coming to the entrance of one of the weight rooms, I turn and put my hands on my hips. "Well, we're here. What do you want to do?"

Shortly after we started dating, Carlos and I stopped just ending up at the gym at the same time and starting purposely going together. Weight Expectations was already part of both of our lives. It just made sense to keep doing it together. I still go to Abel's class a couple days a week and he still works out with Nick. But some days we actually lift together. It's fun... ish. It's fun-ish.

Okay, fine. Showering together afterward is fun, which makes the pain of lifting actual weights worth it.

"I was thinking," Carlos starts with an ornery grin on his face. I know that look. He either wants to do leg day or he's horny. Glancing down at his crotch I realize he must be thinking about leg day. Dammit. "Stop looking at my junk." Busted. He knows me so well. Pulling me to him, I put my arms around his neck. "I *was* thinking about lunges, but you've distracted me. What do you say we blow this joint and go work on some calisthenics instead?"

"Really?" I giggle as he leans his forehead on mine.

"Really. I know I should want to stay, but I'm just in the mood to sit on your lumpy couch..." A small laugh bursts out of me. "Order some really bland takeout from that gluten-free fast-food place..." I stick out my tongue in disgust. "And spend the night making a meal out of my girlfriend."

"Oh, that's what you're in the mood for?" I ask playfully, as he rubs his hands up my back.

"Yep."

"I like that idea," I rasp, moving just a hair closer until our lips are just about to touch.

"Get a room!" Abel yells as he walks by, making me laugh so hard I pull back just enough to see the smile on Carlos's face as well. Happy is his regular mood now, and I love it.

Wrapping my arms around his neck, I hug him close, not wanting to miss this small moment of joy.

Over his shoulder, a construction crane is being used to lift the new sign on the wall.

"Weight Expectations: Where Great Things Happen" is what it reads.

It's not wrong.

It's not wrong at all.

The End.

ACKNOWLEDGMENTS

I can't start saying thank you to everyone involved in this process until I first thank Penny, Fiona, and the entire crew at SmartyPants Romance for this amazing journey. It was the most fun experience, albeit stressful at times, and I feel like I've grown as a writer and as a colleague because of it! And to the SPRU authors... you ladies are the best. What a fun experience to share with all of you!! Here's to more wildly accurate and inappropriate gifs in response to Fiona cracking the whip on us. Lol.

A huge shout out goes to Stella Weaver for her tremendous knowledge of the Knitting in the City books and always being willing to remind me of people, places, and details that my tiny little brain always seems to forget. I'm so glad we got to work on this new spin-off together.

Karla Sorensen, thank you for the daily chats as we challenge and stretch ourselves to do things differently than before. You are a true gem of an author and a person, and I'm so honored to call you friend.

Brenda Rothert and Andrea Johnston, your insight into these characters was tremendous. Once I got over my own whiny attitude, your rearranging suggestions worked like a charm. Of course they did. That's why you're the best.

Erin Sowell, thank you, thank you, thank you for putting yourself out there to make sure nothing I wrote would be construed as anything other than my wild imagination bringing these wonderful characters to life. Trusting you with my intensions and goals was hard, but you are an amazing human. I'm so glad I accidentally wrote your own journey! Fingers crossed your Carlos shows up at dinner. ;)

Marisol Scott and Sue Maturo, who knew there was so many details to Carlos's job? I mean, we knew, but I'm so grateful you guys helped me get it right. It's details like these that are so important and I'm forever thankful for your help!

And I can't forget Erin Noelle who jumped in at the last second to make sure this story flowed nicely. You are the best, my friend.

And now, the Sharks of Awesomeness and Carter's Cheerleaders, you guys are the best, most supportive readers in the world. Thank you for taking a chance on me and for continuing to love my work. I will never be able to make it up to you.

Thank you, Lord, for this tremendous opportunity and giving me the words to write during such a trying personal time. Your glory, not mine.

ABOUT THE AUTHOR

My name is ME Carter and I have no idea how I ended writing books. I'm more of a story teller (the more exaggerated the better) and I happen to know people who helped me get those stories on paper.

I love reading (read almost 200 books last year), hate working out (but I do it anyway because my trainer makes me), love food (but hate what it does to my butt) and love traveling to non-touristy places most people never see.

I live in Houston with my four kids, Mary, Elizabeth, Carter and Bug, who was just a twinkle in my eye when I came up with my pen name. Yeah, I'll probably have to pay for his therapy someday for being left out.

* * *

Website: http://www.authormecarter.com
Facebook: https://www.facebook.com/authorMECarter/
Goodreads: https://www.goodreads.com/author/show/9899961.M_E_Carter
Twitter: @authormecarter
Instagram: @authormecarter

Find Smartypants Romance online:

Website: www.smartypantsromance.com

Facebook: www.facebook.com/smartypantsromance/

Goodreads: www.goodreads.com/smartypantsromance

Twitter: @smartypantsrom

Instagram: @smartypantsromance

Made in the
USA
Monee, IL